LEGERDEMAIN

First published in Great Britain in 2016 by
The Book Guild Ltd
9 Priory Business Park
Wistow Road, Kibworth
Leicestershire, LE8 0RX
Freephone: 0800 999 2982
www.bookguild.co.uk
Email: info@bookguild.co.uk
Twitter: @bookguild

Typeset in Centaur MT

Printed and bound in the UK by TJ International, Padstow, Cornwall

ISBN 978 1 910508 88 6

British Library Cataloguing in Publication Data.
A catalogue record for this book is available from the British Library.

About the Author

Anne Wodehouse, a distant cousin of P.G. Wodehouse, grew up
in suburban New York but has lived in England since 1970. She
works as an English language examiner, mainly in Europe, but
also in Asia and South America. Her novel *Thin Hopes, Fat Chance*
was published by Citron Press in 1999.

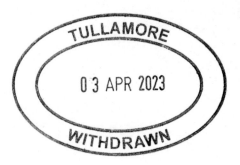

LEGERDEMAIN

Anne Wodehouse

Book Guild Publishing

To families, mine and others.

I. LEGERDEMAIN

On the new motorway, a few miles north of the big Midlands city, the handsome man and his pretty wife are locked in late evening traffic. They have barely moved in the last half hour. She can see that he has had a drink and she's remembering what he said to the magistrate the last time, how he told her he wasn't driving under the influence of drink, but of deep despair. He said he wasn't physically incapable of driving, but emotionally. The magistrate took away his licence for six months but you could see she didn't want to do it. She was far too young and attractive for the job. If only he wasn't so good at lying to women. If only they didn't believe him quite so often.

Suddenly, without warning, he presses his foot down hard on the accelerator. The big, powerful car shoots past the car in front on the nearside. He swerves sharply between the next two cars and exits onto the slip road into the service area, picking up speed all the while.

She gives a little scream. 'You're always breaking the law on the roads,' she tells him.

'I never break the law,' he snaps back at her. 'Never.'

They are moving to a new house, or rather she and the children are moving to a new house. He is staying in the city in a tiny rented flat. The flat is miserable, empty and cramped.

The lights of the buildings and the spread of yellow and red petrol pumps flash by in a blur. Still he is accelerating, now weaving in and out of the parked lorries. He is driving like a madman and, though she expected it of him, she is still caught off guard. The hairs on the backs of her arms rise up and shout danger. She feels she is in the room next door to death, just waiting. And, being a mother, in her last remaining moments, she thinks – thank God Ben is not here in the car with us. She glances over her shoulder at her daughter, deeply asleep in the back seat. Now why did she think that? What kind of a mother is she anyway?

But instead James allows the big car to slow. She watches the needle drop and when it gets to below thirty, she exhales.

'That's a stupid thing to say,' he says.

Sarah remains silent. She does not want to make him angrier. He takes enough chances out of bravado and impatience, even when he's not been drinking. She will not be drawn into an argument.

She breathes deeply and exhales again but he cuts her off before she can speak. 'What do you say such stupid things for?' he asks. He can see she's frightened but already he has forgotten why this should be so. Instead, in a random alcoholic distraction, he finds he too is thinking about the boy, at this moment maybe somewhere on the same motorway in the van with the movers. Should he have trusted them with his son? Just because he liked the way they good-naturedly heaved the furniture around this morning, just because they were young and enthusiastic, that doesn't mean they can be trusted behind the wheel of a 10-ton lorry. They probably drive like mad men.

'Just don't say it,' he repeats. He knows what else she is going to tell him. The movers will be at the new house before them. They won't have got lost.

'I wasn't going to say anything,' she answers.

'I know they won't have got lost. You don't have to say it,' he repeats.

It takes her a few moments to understand what he is talking about. Then she thinks, of course, the movers will have been at the new house hours ago. They'll be waiting to get in and unload. They'll be angry. And they're too young for the job, boisterous and irresponsible. She didn't like them.

They have made six mistakes. Six mistakes is a lot to make on one journey. And now they have missed their exit going south exactly as they missed their exit going north the first time. The straightforward journey has elongated beyond recognition, including a kind of post-pub amnesia after they stopped for directions. She doesn't know why any of this should surprise her. It is, after all, long past five o'clock. They are well into permitted drinking territory.

He knows that sigh and instantly it maddens him. He is thinking, if only she didn't have ice in her veins, maybe he wouldn't need to drink so much. He knows he drinks too much. She's destroying him. There's a new pain in his gut that was not there yesterday, buried deep and serious feeling.

'One beer,' he says, 'one lousy beer.' In fact he has had three double whiskeys, tiny pub measures. 'One beer,' he repeats, massaging the place where the pain is at its worst, though it seems to be spreading fast. It could be a blocked artery, or an aneurysm. His vision is already affected.

He attempts to accelerate again but now there is a car in front, only a few feet ahead, and no room for manoeuvre. He looks around him, trying to find a way out of the lorry parking area, and spots an opening up ahead. He guns the engine towards the opening only to find it leads back to the car park. He brakes sharply and again looks from left to right. There are acres of cars.

What are all these people doing here anyway?

Sarah glances at his taut profile. 'Yea?' she says. 'I'm the one that's stupid? So how many times have I lost my licence then?' She knows she's done it now.

James lets out an exasperated sigh. 'What are all these people doing here?' he asks.

She doesn't answer. The last few minutes have been too frightening. Anyone would think he'd had the American childhood he always wanted, mile-stoning his teenage years with the cars he'd written off, the little wrecked Corvairs and Corvettes, replaced immediately by means of great insurance policies. Well, who does he think he's kidding? His childhood was nothing like that. It was boring.

'You talk like an American,' she tells him, 'one lousy beer.'

'What?' he snaps around to look at her.

But he has again spotted something across the empty area behind the fast food concession. He turns the wheel sharply and accelerates past the huge plastic rubbish bins in their flimsy garden trellis corrals. He is heading towards a tiny, unlit exit where a car is stopped. The driver reaches out, inserts a card and the barrier lifts. James continues to accelerate. That arm is nothing, cardboard.

Again Sarah gives a little scream. It is at once obvious that he intends to crash through after the other car. In a flash of speeded-up seconds she thinks how lonely she has been all her married life and how unhappy. And now, if she's all smashed up, she's not going to get the chance to make a new life like she planned. She covers her face with her forearm and braces herself.

But miraculously the exit barrier fails to drop. In another second they speed through untouched. James laughs, triumphantly.

'Ha!' he says. 'Told you so.'

In fact the conversation has not happened, neither his telling her nor her not believing him.

In a few more seconds they overtake the car in front and instantly they are again lost, this time in the pitch-dark, empty countryside. Sarah looks behind her and already the lights of the motorway are gone. Ahead there is nothing, only a black void. She is astonished at the speed of this change.

James slows the big city car which is suddenly out of place on the narrow twisting lanes. For a while he concentrates on decelerating into each turn and accelerating out, but the road is made up of nothing but turns and he quickly loses patience.

'Well then,' he says but can think of nothing to add. His right hand twitches on the edge of the steering wheel, clearly wanting to raise up the pint glass to his lips.

Sarah notices. It is because of him that Ben is in the trouble he's in, shoplifting, the dope and lying. One vice is the same as another to her way of thinking. And he's only fifteen. How can it be his fault? It's not his fault.

'It's not my fault, you know,' James says.

'Oh yes it is,' she snaps back.

'If you'd packed the maps,' he says.

She is again taken by surprise. 'I packed the maps,' she answers.

They fall silent. They are both bored with this. Their arguments are as predictable as they are inevitable. In secret he would like to be back in the days before feminist outrage, when couples lived in peace and harmony. Wives knew their places. Husbands knew their rights. Women didn't make themselves inaccessible. That's exactly what she's done. She's made herself inaccessible to him. Absent-mindedly, he massages the pain in his gut.

Equally, in secret she knows she is a difficult woman. He has told her so often enough. Well then, he's better off without her. And without him she can start a new life, get things right second time around, though she hasn't said this to him. They've agreed, nothing's definite, see how it goes. She knows neither of them believes this.

'You know Ben says everyone does it,' Sarah says after a while.

James does not answer. He is bored with this conversation too.

'They all do it more than him,' she adds. She is thinking he's probably right. Stealing, drugs, police, these are after all now a normal part of growing up, aren't they? The rules have definitely changed, and about time too. It used to be you could hardly breathe for rules about what you were allowed to wear, what you said to your elders and betters. But she knows enough not to say this to James. 'What he needs are nice friends,' she says. She is repeating to herself yet again how this move will get him away from all that, a long way, but for some reason the repetition has grown hollow and unconvincing. 'What he needs are nice friends, like he used to have,' she adds. And there's Amy, not old enough yet, but she will be looking next year or the year after.

Still James is silent. He hates it when she brings up the reasons for the separation and the move. Ha! Who does she think she is kidding? Vegetables, chickens, getting the children away from the corrupting influence of the city. Ha! What she means is she wants a boyfriend with long hair and no job. Some jerk with beads. He knows she is bored with him. He can see it in her eyes. Why should he have to apologise for getting out the manila folders in the evening? It's where the money comes from. The money that she says is not what she wants out of life. Who does she think she's kidding anyway? Not him, that's for sure.

The pain in his gut ratchets up a notch. To distract himself, he sprays the windscreen and turns the wipers on. Bugs are hitting the glass like hail. 'Jesus,' he finally says and sprays the windscreen again. A chemical smell fills the car and they are both suddenly aware of the earthy, rank, odour of the surrounding fields, only then thrown into relief by contrast with the pungent cleaner.

Sarah looks out the open side window into the darkness. She knows he finds these turfy woody things deeply sensual and it makes him want to have instant sex. Already he's slowing the car.

'Let's stop somewhere for a drink,' he says.

'We can't,' she says. 'There's Amy.' Again she looks in the back seat at her sleeping daughter. 'And we're late. They'll be waiting for us.'

Turfy woody things, it's funny the way she doesn't even have the right words. She's making it sound like Barbie land. Well, all that will change when she settles into real country life. She's going to grow vegetables and keep chickens. The children can help her. They'll love it. And they'll make new friends right away. That's what children do, don't they?

He glances at her pretty, frowning face. So, for once she's not going to make some big deal out of it. That makes a change. She doesn't like him having a drink on a long journey.

But you have to do something to pass the time, don't you? He loses precarious concentration and accelerates into the next bend. Two wheels hit the gravel verge at speed and the big car slides slowly, gracefully, sideways. They are not at all alarmed. James turns the wheel out of the skid. But the car continues to slide until the same two wheels tip into the deep drainage ditch. Suddenly they are pulled off the road and the car comes to rest nose-down in the soft mud. The engine cuts out.

For the third time, Sarah screams. She is thrown forward until the seat belt stops her. Interestingly, it hurts more than she expected. Quickly she looks into the back seat but Amy is still sleeping peacefully. She appears not to have moved, though her blanket is now on the floor.

At the same time James becomes aware of the sharp smell of petrol inside the car. His senses are oddly heightened. Calmly he too looks around at the sleeping child and then finds he can't take his eyes off her. She is so beautiful. Why has he not noticed this before? She looks exactly like her mother, as if that sweetness can be learned.

He sees Sarah is watching him, equally calm. There doesn't seem to be anything wrong with either of them.

'Are you OK?' he asks her.

'I'm fine,' she answers. 'Are you?'

'My stomach hurts,' he tells her. But he does not know why he has said this. He has no pain anywhere.

'It's the seat belt,' she says, unbuckling her own. But she sees that he is not wearing his. Of course he isn't. She doesn't know any man who does.

At that moment, a white van stops on the bank above them. They see that it is new and clean, purposeful looking.

The doors open on either side of the van and two people jump out, a young man and a young woman. He slides quickly down the embankment to them. But she is heavily pregnant and slower.

'I'm a nurse. I'm a nurse,' she calls out. She drops to her bottom and eases her way down, careless of the mud and brambles.

At the car, the young man leans in Sarah's side. 'Are you all right?' he asks.

She sees, even in the dark, that he is handsome, and charming with it. He has that look about him of a handsome and charming man.

'I think so,' she answers. Her gold earrings flash. The gold bracelets slip prettily down each wrist as she tosses her long hair back and smiles at him. Suddenly everything about her is clink and sparkle.

A few moments later the young woman leans in James' side. 'Is anyone hurt?' she asks. With professional briskness she has spotted the child still sleeping in the back seat. 'Is she all right?' she asks.

'We're fine,' James answers, pushing the door open and heaving himself out of the car. 'See?' he says. He treats her to one of his most boyish and endearing grins. He is relieved that she has not smelled the drink and blurted something out. He's had that happen before. With luck they'll get a lift to the nearest garage and nothing more said.

She watches him carefully, registering the fact that he is a small man, tightly built and boyishly good looking. None of that, however, cuts any ice with her. In her work she sees a lot of these drinkers who smash up their cars. This one is far enough gone to be unsteady on his feet. And he's grinning away at her like a complete idiot. A broken neck would soon wipe that ridiculous look off his face. Yet, she has a second glance, just to make sure no ice is being cut.

'Are you sure she's all right?' Again she looks over at the sleeping child.

'She's OK,' Sarah answers. 'I gave her a pill.'

The young woman frowns.

'You did what?' James asks.

7

'A pill,' Sarah repeats, 'for the trip. She was upset.' The woman is staring at her. 'Only half of one,' Sarah adds. In truth, she has given Amy a whole sleeping pill, unable to face the tears and unhappiness this move has brought on, and then a second pill when the asthma started, of all days, she just couldn't cope with that on top of everything else. For some reason they are all three staring at her. Well, it was the best thing wasn't it? Amy has slept peacefully all day.

The young woman reaches into the back seat. She can feel the child is warm and breathing peacefully.

But James is swaying in an odd way. 'Sit down,' she tells him. 'At least let me check you over.'

At once, James drops to the ground. To tell the truth, he is a bit dizzy. He leans forward into a sudden heave of nausea.

'Are you sure you're all right?' she asks again. She attempts to squat by his side but finds it impossible and sits heavily instead, her huge bulge balanced in her lap. She takes his wrist in her hand and silently counts his pulse. 'It's much too fast, she says. 'You could be in shock.'

James withdraws his wrist. 'Really, we're fine,' he repeats. He tries hard not to sound impatient and ungrateful and, watching her serious concerned face, sees he has succeeded. He's usually pretty good with these plain ones. He knows he can make them feel good about themselves.

'What about your wife?' she asks, turning away from the impatient and ungrateful way he is treating her. If she weren't a nurse, she would be sorry they'd bothered to stop.

They both look over to where he, the young husband, is helping Sarah to climb out of the car. Because the car is wedged at an awkward angle, he has both his arms tightly around her waist to help lift her up. She leans heavily into him. For some reason it comes to her, the pregnant wife, that she is witnessing a playing out of something inevitable. And the raw perception cuts straight to her heart. Instantly she dismisses this as the hormonal nonsense of late pregnancy. What rubbish will she think of next?

'Listen,' James is saying. 'Do you think you could maybe pull us out?' He has spotted the trailer hitch on the back of the van. 'I have a rope,' he adds.

She looks doubtful, unwilling. But he, the husband, comes across to stand beside James.

'Happy to,' he says. 'No problem.' The two of them study the expensive city car in respectful silence. The women see at once how much they are enjoying this and exchange glances.

In the big car boot there is a jumble of boxes, clothes, food from the fridge, plants, and eventually the rope.

'Looks like you two are moving house,' the young husband jokes.

'That's exactly what we are doing,' Sarah answers. 'We've bought an old farmhouse near here.' She pauses. 'At least I think it's near here. We're a little bit lost.'

'Near here?' he repeats. 'Not the Casey place?'

'That's it,' Sarah grins at him. 'Mr O'Casey, you know him? You know the house?'

'You're moving in today?' he asks. 'Jesus.' Then he holds out his hand to Sarah. 'Clive,' he says. 'And this is Di.' He looks over at his wife. He takes out his wallet and hands a card to Sarah.

Sarah leans into the beam of the car headlights. On the card there is a picture of an impossibly ornate armoire and written over it, 'Clive Bavro, Posterity Antiques, furniture bought and sold.' Sarah looks at it and then at him. 'We have furniture,' she says.

'Ha!' Clive laughs and takes out another card. This one she reads out loud. 'Clive Bavro, architectural redesign and renovations, period properties a speciality.' Again she smiles at him. Her earrings flash, her bracelets sparkle. She too laughs. 'Are we going to need you then?'

'Depends,' he answers, unable to take his eyes off her.

James watches in silence. He has seen it all before. He has seen those gold chains flash and that bright hair swing. Someone is going to suffer. Well, it's not going to be him anymore, when he gets round to telling her, when the time is right. If only she didn't put it out for every man around. Even if she only pretended not to put it out, at least in front of him. And there is an odd taste in his mouth. In fact, he feels a little light-headed. Still, nothing a drink wouldn't put right, a drink and a nice quiet talk while you think about maybe having something different next round or maybe just sticking to the same thing you're drinking.

He is glad to hang back while the younger man hooks up the rope and checks the car for damage. He sees that she, the wife, Di, has climbed back into the van and is just sitting there. He has a sudden conviction, out of nowhere, that this move will cost him everything, despite Vanessa waiting for him and all that pretty certain to work out just fine, when the time is right.

But he brushes the thought aside as the big car is pulled back onto the road. Apart from a few scratches, it appears undamaged. The ditch too is barely disturbed. They would not have been so lucky in the city, ploughing into a brick wall or a row of parked cars. Perhaps he's wrong. Perhaps the move will work out for all of them after all. Perhaps it's an omen.

★★★

At the farmhouse there is a dim light coming from somewhere deep inside but no moving van out front. Someone has removed the Sold sign from the gate and propped it against the front door. James, driving with exemplary care, allows himself to put on a little speed.

'Where are they?' Sarah asks. 'Where's the stuff?'

The car headlights scan the matted nettles and ugly tangled brambles that is now their new front garden. She has expected to find their things unloaded by the front door and Ben huddled in an armchair, scared and cold, the movers impatiently waiting for them to arrive with the keys. Instead, if it weren't for the light, you'd think the place was deserted.

But inside, Ben rushes to greet them, pushing between the packing cases and haphazard furniture.

'The hippies let us in,' he says.

Sarah stares at him in disbelief. 'What hippies?' she asks.

He is surprisingly glad to see them. The place stinks. There's no food, no television. He doesn't know which room is his and, even if he did, there's nothing to sleep on. 'The two hippies that were living here,' he says.

'You're kidding,' his mother answers.

'It's OK. They were moving out,' Ben explains.

Sarah looks around at the ill-lit and ugly mess. She is surrounded by vague shapes that might be chairs, or might be packing cases, or might be more hippies. Who knows anything anymore? 'You're kidding,' she says again. Apart from all of them being all right, she is finding it hard to be glad about much of anything. A cold bleakness starts to creep up from the dirty bare floorboards through her pretty city shoes, upwards until it reaches her face and she grimaces involuntarily. She is too tired to do anything to stop it. Everything has been dumped in the wrong place. There is no food, nowhere to sleep. The whole thing is impossible.

'Hippies,' she repeats and laughs.

At the sound, both father and son turn quickly away. James returns to the car to unload, and Ben goes back into the deep cluttered room where he has plugged in one light and unrolled his sleeping bag. This is all he intends to do here, bringing to the wrecked country farmhouse his lolling, city attention span.

'They were actually living here?' Sarah calls after him. 'I don't believe it.' But she believes it absolutely. 'Why?' she asks, as if anyone sane would want to live in this godforsaken place. She stands for a long time alone in the middle of all the desolation that her determination has made happen. It comes to her that this is the first time in her married life that she has made something big happen, little things, sure. But this is a big thing. She finds that she is shaking. Quickly she picks up a box at random and carries it out to the cold stone room that might one day be a kitchen. James is there before her, holding the sleeping child.

'So,' he says forlornly, the alcohol in his bloodstream sadly depleted. 'We're here.' The encounter with the young couple and their white van has reluctantly made him remember himself as a young man, something he does not like to be reminded of. It is only in weak moments, like this one, that he thinks about their time together as a young couple, before the children, and how it all mysteriously disappeared overnight. What a joke. He hasn't stopped laughing about that one yet.

He looks over at her pretty, angry face. 'You'll never make this work,' he says.

'Don't be absurd,' she answers, her voice cold. 'Of course I will.'

He has caught her also thinking about the past. She guesses it is what people do when they move house.

The conversation dies between them.

James eases the weight of the child onto the other shoulder and shines the torch around the strange ugly room. They both stare in miserable silence. There does not appear to be a light switch or power point of any kind. In the dark, it is not how she remembers it. The walls are made of stone, covered with damp, flaking, white paint. She is sure they were neatly plastered and only needed a pretty flowered paper. The floor too is stone, great river-flattened boulders that must have taken half a dozen men to drag here and place them just so. She remembered pine floorboards that would have stripped and polished nicely. The ceiling is too low, the one window tiny and warped. Below it there is a grey enamel sink supported on breeze blocks. Apart from the fireplace, there is nothing else in the room, no cupboard, shelf or hook. In the house they have just left there were floor standing and wall mounted cupboards along the length of each wall, with handsome European chestnut doors.

The two step closer to each other but do not touch.

'Let's go to a hotel,' he says. A hotel will have a late night bar. They always do.

'It's too late,' she says. 'This is the country. Everything will be closed.'

Again he looks at her pretty angry face. Can this be true? He knows nothing about the country. 'Of course everything isn't closed,' he tells her. She is so pretty. He is a man with a pretty wife. In truth, he has liked being a man with a pretty wife.

She shrugs her shoulders indifferently. 'I'm too tired to go out again,' she says. But in truth she has liked having him to take care of her, to make the decisions.

Again they step closer but do not touch. They stand there, both obdurate and passive, saying nothing. Already they are looking back on this part of their life as finished.

2. THE GREEN COURTS OF THE EARLY MORNING

On the second day in the new house Ben sits on his bicycle in front of the window in the high attic bedroom. He is watching a lone articulated lorry manoeuvre around the sharp right-angle curves in the lane at the bottom of their drive, that is if you could call something that takes five minutes to walk, a drive. The lorry undulates around the field boundaries like some extravagant segmented worm. Even at this distance he can hear the satisfying swell of the driver downshifting and accelerating through the gears. His mother comes into the room. Ben looks back over his shoulder, then away again quickly. He knows the place is a mess, but somehow he has managed only to unpack and put to rights his magazines and comics. It seems the fact of being here and being unhappy has entered into his favourite objects and subverted them. It is hiding in his gunmetal money box. It has slithered into his maroon and sky blue football shirt and infused itself into his childhood Matchbox car collection, draining pleasure as it goes. He sees, however, that his mother is not going to say anything.

'What's that doing here?' She stares at the bicycle.

'We don't have a garage,' Ben answers, 'in case you haven't noticed.'

'I noticed,' she says. 'No one's going to steal it. This is the country.'

She goes over to the window and bends double to look out at the empty fields. 'My God,' she says. 'Isn't it beautiful?'

The sight of her in her bathrobe reinforces the unsettled, holiday feel of the morning. Absent-mindedly, she picks at the window frame, dropping bits of feather-light, ancient wood to the floor. Then she looks over at Ben. 'Your father is going to kill me,' she adds.

The words are a small note of warning. They seem to float in the air, looking for a way out. 'I could tell him you were tired, or that it

13

was a half day,' she adds, then changes her mind. He is not here. She does not have to tell anyone anything. Again absent-mindedly, she lifts his blanket off the floor and returns it to its proper place on the bed. Straightaway it slips to the floor on the other side. 'I could tell him you had a temperature,' she says, changing her mind again. 'You both had temperatures.' Amy is wrapped in her blanket on the floor in front of the now working television in the big sitting room, refusing to speak.

Ben turns back to the window. He is finding this conversation hopeless and pointless in equal measure. To his father, school is school and you go unless you have a temperature. A temperature is the only symptom he respects. But, they have explained, he is in the city and will be here at the weekends. Of course he doesn't believe them. He half expects to never see his father again.

A few minutes later, his mother is back with a pile of clothes, which she drops haphazardly into the empty drawers. When she is finished, she stands with her hands on her hips and turns full circle.

'This is going to be some great room, you know,' she says, not looking at the boy. Without thinking, she bunches his neatly-piled magazines and comics together in a careless jumble and pushes them up next to the wall with the side of her foot. 'Have I got plans for this room,' she goes on. 'Have I got plans for the whole place.'

Ben is still staring out the window, only half listening. In her voice he can hear that she wants to tell him something and, whatever it is, he doesn't want to hear it.

She comes over, puts her hand on his shoulder and looks out with him. She sees the fields are as they should be, glossy green and well proportioned. The hedges are trim and the trees stately. Picturesque white sheep dot the far hillside. She is satisfied at the wholesomeness of it all. There is not another house in sight.

Then some small animal movement catches her eye and she brings her gaze back to the overgrown ditch directly below them. In amongst the brambles, there is an old gas cooker on its side, and, judging from the irregularities, other things as well.

She is watching a large, grey rat disappear into the doorless oven. 'I put some food out,' she tells him, 'for the wild creatures, like the hippies did.'

He too has seen the rat but he does not bother to explain. She wouldn't know a wild creature if it had a sign on it. And as for the hippies, all they did was throw their rubbish out the back door. He's already looked for plants and stash and found nothing worthwhile.

★★★

The next day it is almost dark when Ben gets home. He stands his bicycle beside the collapsed corrugated shed where she has planned there will be a brick and tile double garage with up-and-over doors and security lights shaped like carriage lamps. He sees Amy and his mother are sitting in the kitchen, which is lit by candles set in saucers about the room. The light is very beautiful. Everything else is ugly almost beyond his experience, ugly like under the huge railway bridges where the city tramps sleep at night.

He sees they are watching him and he lashes out at the nettles that grow densely here as everywhere. He takes his time, kicking over each plant and trampling it into the ground. His face is tense and determined. He knows she is going to ask where he has been and for some reason he has lost his confidence in lying to her. This is a serious loss which he hopes will soon correct itself.

Sarah looks at her daughter and raises her eyebrows. The remains of a take-away burger meal are scattered in front of them. Sullenly, Amy refuses to look back. She has not spoken to anyone for two days and, though it seemed a good idea at first, she is now tired of it but unable to figure out a way to end the silence without her mother being grateful. For some reason she can't bear the thought of her mother's happy smiling gratitude. She breathes in a deep, wheezy breath and coughs as she exhales. Her mother is watching her brother and doesn't notice.

Ben steps into the room through the broken door and looks at the candles . 'What happened to the lights?' he asks.

Amy jumps up and throws herself at him, clutching him around the waist tightly with both arms. Roughly, he pushes her away.

'It's only this part of the house,' their mother explains. 'The rest is all right.'

Again Amy throws herself at her brother. She is ten and small for her age but still too old for such childish displays.

'Someone knocked the gate down,' he says.

'The gate?' Sarah repeats.

'Come and look,' he tells them, again pushing Amy away, but a little less roughly this time.

'Shall we?' Sarah holds out her hand for her daughter. 'Let's walk down and look.' Amy turns away from her mother and goes back to her chair. She breathes in another deep, wheezy breath and again coughs as she exhales.

But after they've gone, she does not want to be left alone in the darkening house with the whiff of little dead animals blowing through the derelict rooms. Silently, she follows them, some distance behind. She sees her mother has noticed.

Outside, the air is warmer and fresher than in the stone kitchen. It is a beautiful evening and absolutely quiet. Five minutes later, the three of them are standing looking down at the wooden field gate.

'It was the only thing in the whole place that didn't need fixing,' Ben says. 'The only thing.'

'Yes,' she agrees. She kicks the gate with her pretty white sandal.

He bends to lift the gate, then suddenly jumps back as if struck. His mother and sister hear his astonished intake of breath. He is staring at the ground, at two large brown toads. They are lying, side by side, with their insides splayed out around them in perfect, concentric circles, like some ancient and profane invocation. Coincidentally, high up in the top branches of the black trees, the regular night breeze picks up speed.

'It's the lorries.' Sarah says, looking away from the toads and up at the sudden sound, unnerved.

'What lorries?' Ben asks.

'The lorries today,' his mother answers. 'There were a lot of them while you were out.'

Quickly Ben looks away. He attempts to lift the broken gate but it is too heavy.

'Out at school,' she continues. And, when he doesn't answer, she laughs uneasily. 'Aren't frogs rare? Shouldn't we report this?'

Ben does not tell her that these are common brown toads and they are nocturnal. It is almost certain that it was their wheels two nights ago that caught them crossing the road and then the gate covered them over so they didn't get eaten by something else. And they are not rare.

After a while Sarah turns again to Ben. 'So, how was it?' she asks.

Ben looks at his mother and then looks away. 'It was OK,' he says. She knows he didn't go. 'So what did you do?' she asks.

He shrugs his shoulders. 'Nothing,' he says.

'Nothing,' she repeats.

James is going to kill her. She has let him get away with it again. She can hear his voice exactly as if he were standing there with them — *You didn't say anything? You let him get away with it?* It is, she knows, only an interim response, though the interim might last for many months, years even. Then one day he will say — *You let him off school the first day. You corrupted him right then. That was the start of it. And you lied.* She has no answer to any of this.

★★★

Later, in bed, Ben wakes up. He is hearing a funny noise. He gets out and stretches himself full-length on the bare floorboards in order to peer through the squat window. In the moonlight, he can see his father working in the garden. What is he doing here in the middle of the night? The broken gate is now leaning against the corrugated shed and his father is digging up the rotting posts that once led from the gate to the house along one side of the drive. Already, he has removed the wire and coiled it by the shed. He pulls out each post, carries it up and leans it against the wire. Then he goes back and fills in the hole before doggedly moving on to the next.

His mother comes outside and stands directly below his window. As his father moves within earshot, she says, 'You haven't eaten.' She waits for him to answer. When he doesn't, she shifts her weight from one hip to the other. She is holding a plate, with what looks like a sandwich, in one hand.

This time, he turns and looks at her. 'Can you hear that?' he asks.

She listens. 'What?'

'You can't hear it?' he says. 'Music?'

'It's not music,' she says. 'There's nothing around here.'

'It's music,' he says.

'It can't be,' she repeats. She looks forlornly out across the empty fields. There are no lights, nothing moves. There is only the constant sound of the night breeze in the treetops, every night always the same. Though she knows as soon as they are in bed the screech owls will start, worse than any traffic, because it is a living sound that's meant to cut right through you. Like a tiny baby crying, that's meant to do the same thing. Who would have thought it? This is the country.

'There's nothing for miles,' she says.

But he is not there to hear her. Already he is lifting another rotted post from its hole halfway down the drive.

★★★

In the morning, Ben is awake at half-past four. Without curtains, his east-facing attic is full of light. Besides, with no friends and nothing to do he went to bed much too early. He picks up his binoculars and goes straight to the window. Two large crows are pecking at the ground by the broken gate, where his father squashed the toads, but that is not what interests him. Across the fields, on the other side of the main road, he can just pick out a tall, black-and-white house. If he gets the focus right, he can locate the dormer windows above tree level. He has never seen anyone there, but there have been lights.

He moves the binoculars along the horizon. In their old house he saw something most days, old guys scratching their balls, young guys letting it all hang out, once in a while a girl. But girls are shy.

Then he hears his father say quite clearly, 'That's not the point.'

He listens for his mother's answer, and after a long wait, she finally says, 'They all do it.' Though they are in their bedroom below, their words are as clear as if they were standing right in front of him.

'They don't all do it,' his father snaps straight back. 'You're wrong. You always think everything is just a phase.'

'I didn't say that,' his mother argues.

'You didn't have to say it,' he answers. 'You and your washed-up opinions.'

The words washed-up cut through him like a knife through soft flesh. It is a long time before he hears his mother's reply. He hopes she isn't crying again.

'Look at those crows,' she says. Her voice is flat, almost disinterested. 'Look at the size of them.'

'You think he'll just come out of it,' his father says scornfully. 'In his own good time. Christ, you want to stand around and wait for his life to be ruined?'

'I don't want to stand around,' she says. 'And his life is not going to be ruined. Why do you think we're here?'

'I know exactly why we're here,' his father snaps back. They are silent. Then his father adds, 'I can't keep coming up here every time.' His voice trails off and again they are silent.

After a while Ben hears his father's footsteps on the stairs. Then, shortly after that, he appears directly below the attic window. His father picks up the rusted spade and the bent fork he has found in the corrugated shed and walks back to the place where he stopped the night before. It is as if the hours of sleep never happened, which, for all Ben knows, they haven't. Ben drops the binoculars carelessly on the floor and returns to bed. He stares miserably at the ceiling. He wishes he had some weed. He loves weed. His friends like weed and boast about it all the time, wankers. But he loves it. Of course he understands why this is so. It is because his parents argue all the time. He has read about this in one of his mother's magazines. Of course he knows these magazines are stupid and what they say is even stupider. Yet he has gone over and over the argument in his mind, looking for flaws in the reasoning, and he has been able to find none.

Then he hears his mother call from below. 'Are you awake?'

Today he has to go. He doesn't need to be told.

'Go back to sleep,' she says. 'You have to go today.'

***

At school, he refuses to let his mother come in with him. 'They're

19

expecting me,' he tells her. He watches Amy walk purposefully off towards her annex, where the little children are, the rucksack on her back too big and too heavy for her. He is suddenly sad beyond belief, as if something terrible that can never be changed has already happened to her.

'You'll be OK?' she asks. 'You're sure?'

'Go away,' he tells her.

Reluctantly, she leaves him at the small office, just inside the front door.

One of the three secretaries opens the glass partition and calls to the first uniformed girl to pass within her reach. She holds the phone with one hand, and the girl with the other. There is a sheaf of papers tucked up under her armpit. 'Take him with you,' she orders. 'Go.' Her pink cardigan is so piercingly bright, it seems to have appropriated all the available light from the small, shabby room.

But the girl is annoyed and she abandons Ben as soon as they are out of sight of the office. 'Go down there,' she says and walks off.

Ben wanders up and down the long, yellowing corridors that both look and smell exactly like his old school, walls that have been painted and re-painted with the nastiest by-products of the chemical industry. On his third trip past the main hall, from where he can hear a steady rumble of noise, a heavy, stooped man saunters slowly out from a closet and deliberately blocks his way. He stands and stares intently at the boy for several seconds.

Eventually, he asks, 'Do you know what they call me?' Ben looks up at the man's serious face. '*De vasto prato.*' He pronounces the words in some sort of foreign accent. Silently, he takes hold of the boy's arm and leads him back to the glass office.

All the secretaries are now on the phones. The one with the pink cardigan looks up at Ben and says, 'You again.'

'You know this scruffy young lout?' the man says.

The secretary looks at the man, a sideways, fluttering look. 'I saw you in the park,' she says.

The man laughs. 'My morning walk in the park. That's another excretive experience all right.' He laughs again, giving Ben an outrageous wink and walks away.

20

Ben waits. The minutes pass. Finally, the secretary comes to the open panel and hands him a piece of paper. She points down the corridor. 'You want to go through that door and keep going.' He guesses she is not being funny. 'It's the last door on the right.'

Again, Ben finds himself wandering up and down the empty corridors, past the high-windowed, closed doors behind which he can now hear the same low rumble. No one pays him any attention.

Some time later, a bell rings. The doors open and instantly the corridors are packed with moving bodies. The change is immediate and absolute. Sadly, Ben watches the small still life that has fitted snugly around no one but him over the past few days disappear in the haze of over-breathed air that has emerged with the bodies. He knows he cannot remain unseen much longer.

Sure enough, a hand grabs him from behind. 'What is this?' a voice asks. The same heavy, stooped man is standing in the doorway of one of the classrooms, again deliberately blocking the exit.

Ben hands him the piece of paper.

The man reads it and turns to the class straining behind him. 'Do we want this young layabout?'

The class groans.

'Pay them no heed,' he says, drawing Ben into the room. 'You stick with me.'

He keeps his arm across the boy's shoulder while he addresses the class. 'Any of you in Sports Day?'

Again, the class groans and pushes forward another few inches.

'If you're sneaking off,' he goes on, 'just remember that most of the bad things in life happen as a result of sneaking off.' He moves aside to let them through. 'Get caught,' he adds. 'I'm going to take it as a personal affront.'

Again, there are scattered groans. Two girls walk past, a little too close. 'We know that, Mr Raftiche,' one of them says, giving him a look.

'Yea, we want to affront you,' the other one adds, giving him the same look. 'We've been practising.' She laughs.

Her friend turns and hits her hard on the upper arm.

'We've been practising in Italian,' she says, still giving him the look.

21

Mr Raftiche watches the girls, unsmiling and solemn. 'A dangerous idea,' he says, giving Ben a pantomime wink. 'The best kind.'

Within minutes, Ben is again alone. He wanders outside, as others are doing, but then he does not know what to do next. The school is vast, vastly set in the middle of nowhere. There are empty fields on three sides and a fast road on the fourth. He wanders out to the road and looks in both directions. There is no sign of a town anywhere. Slowly, he drifts back to the sports field where rows of chairs have been set up. Even more slowly, he takes his place among the weirdoes and melon heads sitting there. Everyone else is on the opposite side of the track in tight groups, getting ready. In his old school he would have been one of them, winning the hundred metres, maybe bringing in the last leg of the relay.

Reluctantly he sits down to watch, nurturing the ready flickerings of misery and loneliness, encouraging them to grow into fully-fledged flames of rebellion. What does he want with this bunch of hicks anyway? Nothing, that's what.

★★★

Afterwards, his mother is waiting in the big city car. This is her new plan, to collect him every day. She and his father have thought this one up. That shows what they know. 'How was it?' she asks before he even gets the door open.

'OK,' he answers. He looks back at Amy, silent in the back seat. She still has not spoken. It's getting boring. 'Hi stupid,' he says to her.

'So what happened?' his mother asks.

'Nothing,' he answers.

'Nothing?' she repeats. 'All day?'

The boy looks sullenly out the side window as they drive along. 'I did Italian,' he tells her.

'Italian?' She looks over at him. 'Italian? You're kidding.'

★★★

At home, the electricity has given up in the stone part of the house. His mother has moved the kettle and toaster onto the hearth in the sitting room. Other than that, nothing is any different. The television is hooked up but without a proper aerial, it only works occasionally. The packing cases are where the movers left them. It is quiet, like the end of the world.

'Listen to that,' his mother says. Ben listens and can hear nothing. 'Don't you hear it?' she asks him.

Again he listens but still can hear nothing, except the clamour of things decaying, paint, plaster, floorboards, windows. Isn't anyone going to do anything? He steps over a length of splintered skirting board lying diagonally across the kitchen floor and throws his bag in the corner. He can see she hasn't bought any food today either.

'It's music,' she calls after his disappearing back.

***

That evening, Ben again squats at his open window with the binoculars. His mother was right. He can clearly hear music, too resonant to be a tape or radio. When he looks to the left, it seems to come from the left. When he looks to the right, it comes from the right. He adjusts the focus onto the black and white house in the distance but there is no sign of movement, no lights. The road stretches off in both directions, a forbidding exile.

He looks at the ground below his window. His father has dragged the old cooker from the ditch and put it with the wire and posts. His mother will have to find someplace else to feed the rats.

***

Later, in bed, he again wakes from a sound sleep and hears his father say, as clearly as if he were in the same room, 'No, you're wrong.'

Again, his mother waits before answering. 'But it just doesn't seem right.'

His father answers straightaway. 'When you're doing it, you only see other people who are doing it. You have no conversation for people who are outside of that.'

'Conversation?' his mother asks. 'What do you mean, conversation?

He's only fifteen.' His father doesn't answer. 'How do you know that?' his mother asks.

★★★

It's hot in the attic and Ben wakes again a short while later. He pushes open the window with his foot and sees his father below in the moonlight. The ditch is now clear of nettles and scrub. It stretches in a graceful crescent around two sides of the house. It's an odd thing to have around a house. No one else he knows has such a thing. But he has given up being surprised by the strangeness of this place, which is both boring and terrible. His father is standing at one end with the hose in his hand, watching the water slowly accumulate in the place he has cleared. What do they mean, he thinks, 'you have no conversation for people who are outside of that'? He answers his own question. They are wrong in what they think. Wrong and stupid. Weed, all that, he does it for one reason only. He does it because it makes him feel good. Why else does anyone do anything they're not forced to do?

★★★

The next day, Ben does not go into school. When his mother drops them off, he chooses a direction and starts to walk. Amy watches him go. 'You shouldn't do that,' she says. It's the first time she has spoken to any of them since the move.

'It's OK,' he says. 'Don't worry.'

'Where are you going?' she asks.

He continues to walk but again looks back at his sister. 'Don't worry,' he repeats. And then he grins at her, a gift freely given, lovingly even.

He walks for what seems like miles, past empty fields and thorn hedges. There are no road signs, no indication that he might be approaching a town. Soon, he is worn down by the hot, gritty stream of cars. He turns forlornly and goes back to the school.

A lone boy is picking up litter in the now empty playing field. Ben skirts the edge, keeping his distance, but at the same time following him. In a few minutes, the boy comes up to Ben and hurls his carrier bag of rubbish to the ground. 'Ratface is a wanker,' he says.

'Who?' Ben asks.

'Ratface,' the boy repeats, instantly exasperated. 'You're in his form.' Then he picks up the carrier bag and thrusts it at Ben. The two move off together, loose limbed and languid, the walk of young lions. 'They're all wankers,' the boy repeats, drawing a rollie from his pocket. He sighs and passes it to Ben.

★★★

When his mother arrives to collect him, he tells her without being asked. 'My form teacher is OK.'

'Oh?' his mother answers, giving the word a pleasing lilt. 'What's his name?'

'That's him.' Ben tilts his chin to indicate the tall, stooped man, standing at the bus bay, surrounded by girls.

★★★

For the rest of the week, Ben moves haphazardly around the school with his new friend, encouraged by Mr Raftiche and his advice. 'The urge to perform is not a sign of talent,' he tells the troublemakers. 'You know what I found out,' he tells the girls, 'I found out I'm too short for my weight and I have to add on nine inches.' Always his voice is solemn, his face serious, never laughing at his own jokes.

When he finds Ben alone, he puts his arm around the boy's shoulders. 'You'll be OK,' he jokes. 'You got to remember. Like History, any point of entry is possible.' Again he does not laugh.

★★★

That night, Ben wakes to hear his mother pleading. 'But we did it for him,' she cries out.

His father waits a long time before answering. 'No,' he pauses. 'We didn't.'

25

'All he does is wander around the place all the time,' his mother says. 'He's so miserable.' She waits. 'And Amy still hasn't said anything. What's that all about?'

'You deal with it,' his father answers. 'You're here all day. I thought that was supposed to be the idea.'

★★★

The next day, a Saturday, Ben does not come out of his room until the evening. Through the window he sees that in the night his father has carried wheelbarrow loads of rocks from what looks like the site of an old barn up to the ditch. He has placed them along the sides and filled in the gaps with cement, which he has mixed in a second wheelbarrow, now lying on its side by the back door. His father is gone but he has left the car for his mother.

Without being noticed, Ben slips out the front door and, keeping behind the scraggy hedge, makes his way down the drive. At the lane, he picks up the drumbeat straightaway. Instead of turning left or right, he climbs the stile into the field opposite. The field rises steeply, then drops down the other side to the main road. He vaults the low barbed wire and, almost as soon as his feet touch the pavement, a car stops. The door springs open. There is a blast of music.

'Hey kid,' someone calls to him. 'Want a lift?' The car is packed with boys. He recognises his friend from the sports field.

Ben climbs into the space where the back seat would be if it had not been ripped out to make room for two large, black speakers. There are two younger boys there already, wedged in sideways with their knees touching.

'Got any money?' the driver asks Ben. He has one elbow out the window, with the sleeves of his denim jacket rolled up like a shirt.

Ben pulls a pound note from his pocket.

At the same time, there is a crackling noise and a small shower of sparks from the tangle of wires that connects the tape deck to the dashboard. The music judders, but then picks up again straightaway. The driver cheers.

'Is that for me?' The other boy reaches back and takes the pound note from Ben's hand, treating him to a good-natured grin. He too has the sleeves of his denim jacket rolled up to reveal handsome, manly forearms.

Suddenly, there is a series of tiny explosions from the tape deck and more sparks. Again, the music judders, but keeps going. Both boys in front whoop with delight. The driver reaches out to turn up the volume, at the same time picking up speed. Fields and hedges flash by. Pulsations from the speakers pass directly into the three boys in the back, charging them with excitement.

'I got another one,' Ben shouts to be heard, again reaching into his pocket.

At that moment, the car lurches sideways with a squeal of tyres, and Ben is thrown face down, but not before he sees the black and white side of the pub closing in fast. There is a gut-churning moment of silence. The car stops dead, no more than a few inches from the wall. There is a second, briefer, moment of silence, before the cheers and whoops of the boys in the back. The driver turns to grin at them.

'Yea,' he says to Ben. 'No kidding. You got anything else in there? In your saddle bags?' He takes the second note, lets go a laugh and throws open the car door.

Ben scrambles from the back, last one out, and follows the others. He looks up at the high dormer windows and recognises them from his early morning reconnoitres with the binoculars. This time there is a girl in the middle window, dancing alone to the music coming from the pub below.

Ben stops in the doorway of the badly-lit room, poised, expectant, as if something he urgently needs is in there waiting. The room is filled with the music of a garage band, playing in the corner. The band is not bad. He does not blame the girl. He searches out his friends and can't at first find them. He stands, quivering with excitement, on the threshold of this dark, noisy room that promises the world of the lowest common denominator, where all the losers, the druggies and most sexually aggressive girls are to be found.

There is a burst of laughter from the bar and he sees the four of them pressed tightly together. The driver of the car is passing the pints around.

'Hey scumbag.' He calls Ben over and hands him the last of the filled glasses. 'Drink it up, puke it up,' he says, raising his own glass. The others adjust their positions to make room for the boy.

Ben lifts the glass and drinks. Time stands still.

3. WHAT CAN BE FAKED WILL BE FAKED

Clive, the builder, is looking at her and not at the job. These daily inspections of the work in progress are less to do with thoroughness and more with a referendum for his status in her eyes. They are talking about rabbits.

'It's the only hobby I know where can eat your mistakes,' he tells her.

Sarah laughs, modestly lowering her eyes, like a young girl. He is disappointed not to have progressed to – call me Sarah. Usually, his lady clients, the ones he takes a personal interest in, have made their move before now, some of them long before now. And if there is one rule around, it is always to let the lady make the first move, always.

This one, this Sarah, he wouldn't fast-lane her, even if he didn't have rules. It's funny that, the way each of them runs a different course. Sometimes you can let it rip. Sometimes you can't. You don't pay attention, you get it wrong.

'Shall I show you what I mean?' she is saying now.

He follows her up the two flights of stairs to the boy's room in the high attic, knowing exactly what it is she is going to show him. It is, after all, why he has put the hippie up there to work. She takes the stairs with a little skipping motion, faster than is comfortable for him. Her feet are bare. It is a good sign. He believes, even in the face of experience, if you put a man and a woman together in a room with a bed, anything can happen, instant fornication, anything. She is out of breath and brings one hand up to her throat. The sleeve of her man's denim shirt falls back. There is a brief flash of gold, of hidden treasure.

'Wow,' she says, knowing he is watching her. She leans against the door-frame, taking longer to recover than is strictly necessary. Here in the bedroom with him, Clive, the builder, one step behind in his tight jeans and sleeveless T-shirt, she is wary. She goes over to Ben's bed and pulls the blankets straight, hiding the slept-in sheets. Nervously, she looks back at him. It was always her mother's belief that if you put a man and a woman together in a room with a bed, anything could happen, spontaneous combustion, anything.

Clive walks over to the window and bends easily down on his haunches. 'Goddamn,' he says, running his fingers around the loose frame. His bare arms are sun-burned and muscular. She is openly staring.

He looks up at her and grins. 'The bugger,' he says, easing himself sideways. Not only has the hippie put the window in upside-down, but he's left a half-smoked roach on the floor. Clive covers it with his foot, still looking up at her.

She sees that the fabric of his faded black jeans is stretched to bursting point. In fact, one or two seams are already starting to split. Then she sees the half-smoked joint on the floor. She is not surprised at Ben, only concerned that no one but her should know about it. Luckily, in moving aside to get a better view, Clive's foot has covered it over and he hasn't noticed.

'Some view,' he says, looking out the window. He is waiting for one thing to lead to another and hopes it won't take too much longer. He is not really happy about the messed-up window, even though it is what he wanted to happen. It's going to cost him money to put right. Call it an investment, he tells himself.

The phone rings in the distance and she turns away. 'I'll leave you to it, then,' she says.

The next thing, she's gone, it seems to him unnecessarily fast. She could have pretended not to hear it, ringing way off in the distance like that.

Clive picks up the roach and puts it in his pocket. He looks back at the window. The last thing he wants is to be stuck up here putting right the hippie's fuck-ups. This is not what he had in mind. Angrily, he hits the frame with the flat of his hand. The entire window skews sideways, then slips slowly down until it is resting on the toe of his boot, bringing with it a section of moulded beam with the lath and plaster still attached. He moves his foot a fraction of an inch and the whole thing crashes to the floor. There is now, in front of him, a gaping hole nearly twice the size of the original tiny window. As he watches, another section of ancient plaster detaches itself and falls gently to the floor. He shakes the white dust from his boot. Fuck these fucking people and their fucking listed shit-heaps.

Downstairs, he finds that she is still on the phone in the front hall. She puts her hand over the mouthpiece and gives him a bright, expert smile. 'That was quick,' she says. She holds the smile and he sees that he is in her good books.

He shifts his weight uneasily and gives her a jaunty nod, holding her eyes.

★★★

As he turns out of the lane onto the main road, Clive sees the boy, Ben, getting off the country bus. The kid is big for his age and slouchy with it, wearing those shit-kicking boots they all wear, even with the school uniform. His sister follows behind, keeping well back, a pretty kid, like her mother, but mute. That's some disadvantage for a kid to have.

He slows the van and calls to the boy through the open window. 'You sleep up there in the roof?'

The boy stops some distance away and stares at him in surprise. He has seen his mother taking to this man, Clive. More than that, he doesn't know, or want to know.

'Yea, well,' Clive says. When the boy doesn't answer, 'Take it easy.'

★★★

In his room, Ben is dismayed to find half the wall suddenly missing and a broken window in the middle of his bed. He picks up a lump of plaster and drops it through the gap onto the ground below. He picks up two more pieces and hurls them into his father's moat where, yet again, the water has seeped away. He props the window frame beside the wardrobe and moves his bed to the other side of the room. Then he sits on the floor and scours the horizon with his binoculars. Even with half the wall missing, he can still find only the one house to look at and, of that, only one window and a small portion of roof. The dancing girl is not there today.

★★★

Late the following morning, Ben is standing alone in the middle of the dark, stone kitchen. He hears his mother cry out in the distance. The next thing, she is running down the two flights of stairs, moving fast.

She stops in the doorway. 'My God,' she says to him. He stares back at her, wanting to swallow the unchewed cereal in his mouth and unable to do so.

'My God,' she repeats and again gets no further. She is shaking her head in disbelief because, having seen it, she believes absolutely what Ben has done to the attic bedroom. 'Why?' she says and gets no further.

He tries again to swallow the cereal and fails.

At the same time, a van pulls up onto the grass by the back door and stops. The builder, Clive, gets out and turns to lift down a young boy. The boy is maybe four years old, fair-haired, and small for his age. Together, they walk towards the house. Clive takes in the lumps of plaster on the ground and the mother and boy watching him approach. He has not been looking forward to this morning, having to explain. He'll blame it on the hippie of course, but even so. And then to get stuck with the kid as well.

'Why did you do it?' she asks Ben in the last seconds they are alone. 'Do you hate it here that much?'

Clive picks up the child and steps through the open door, talking as he enters. He is talking to her, but not looking at her. He laughs and drops two large grey rabbits side by side on the table. They are freshly killed and smell of blood.

'You're not vegetarians?' he asks.

'Oh,' she says, looking at the rabbits.

Ben swallows.

The child, dressed only in a pair of red shorts, no shirt, shivers in his father's arms. The stone room is cold, as always.

'Vegetations, as my old gran used to say,' Clive adds. No one laughs. Both she and the boy are staring at the red, cut throats.

'Yea, well,' he says. 'I go for the prawn biryani myself.' This is not turning out to be a good idea.

Still no one laughs, but at least she is now looking at him. He rubs his hands together.

Suddenly, she looks away. 'You'll never guess what's happened upstairs,' she says.

'Ah,' he answers. Carefully, he lowers the little boy onto one of the chairs and pushes it in close to the table, so that the child's face is no more than a few inches from the dead rabbits. He takes his time with these things.

'Stay here Davey,' he says to the child. 'Don't move.'

The boy looks up at him with startled eyes. He is clearly afraid. At the same time, Ben eases his way towards the door, but his mother catches his arm and pulls him with her.

The little boy listens to their footsteps in the distance. He wants to run after them but is too terrified to do so. There is blood oozing from the nose of one of the rabbits. Their eyes are open and staring at him.

A few minutes later, Ben is back. He grabs his denim jacket from the chair where the little boy is sitting.

'Jesus, she's in a mood,' he says. He picks up three slices of bread from the messed up loaf on the table and folds them each in quarters, before stuffing them into his mouth. The little boy follows his movements with the same wide, startled eyes.

'Watch out,' Ben tells him. 'She'll eat you alive.' Then he's gone.

The little boy sits absolutely still and waits. The smell from the dead rabbits is making him feel sick. After a few minutes, when no one comes, he leans forward and throws up on the table, just a small pile. He looks at it for a few more minutes, then scoops it up delicately with both hands and puts it in his pocket.

★★★

Clive is using his up-front voice. He can see that she is upset. 'Don't worry about it,' he tells her. 'These things happen. It's not really his fault.'

'But he lied about it.' Her look is uncomprehending. It is not like Ben to lie about things he can't get away with. She herself would not have lied about this.

He peers out through the missing window and sees the boy loping off down the drive towards the road. He notices also that the big car is not by the shed. He listens. The house is dead quiet.

'So,' he says, turning back to her. She has just washed her hair and it is still wet, darker and curlier than usual. Those jeans, the bare feet, the kid's T-shirt, she looks like she knows exactly what she looks like.

She frowns at the broken frame. 'I don't understand why he did it.' She looks imploringly at him. 'Why did he do it?'

He waves his hand deprecatingly and takes a step closer to her, as if he had any answers. In the hot room, he can smell her shampoo. He breathes it in. She sighs unhappily and leans slightly back, bringing herself closer to him. If it wasn't that he knew better, he'd put his arm around her now. That was some sigh. That is some look. But if you want one thing to lead to another, you got to let these little opportunities pass by. You got to wait for the big one.

Suddenly, she looks up at him, a smile of understanding spreading across her pretty face. 'Is it the babies?' she asks.

'The babies?' he says, trying to think what she means. Then he laughs and scratches the back of his head. 'No, not the babies,' he tells her. 'I mean, yes, that's why I've got Davey. But she hasn't had them yet.' She has caught him off guard. It's funny that, since they took Di into hospital, he's hardly given her a thought, whereas when she was at home, he couldn't think of anything else. What with one baby not moving and getting everyone in a panic and the other one kicking the hell all over the place and giving her backache. What with the sample bottles every day and the midwife there at all hours, it was a relief when they took her in.

He follows Sarah across the room. 'Davey's a good kid,' he says. 'He won't cause any trouble.'

She turns and gives him a perfect smile. 'I'd better go down, anyway,' she says. It's funny that, the way you can tell when a smile is about something else or when it's meant for you. That was some smile.

In the kitchen, the little boy has not moved. She comes up behind him and rests her hand on the back of his chair.

'So, two baby brothers,' she says brightly. 'Or maybe sisters. And soon too.'

The little boy does not respond. He is holding himself absolutely rigid. From behind, she can see his neck is painfully thin, and exposed in a way that seems unfair and too vulnerable. His little shoulder blades stick out like wings. She notices also there is a new, unpleasant smell coming from the rabbits and a wet patch on the table beside them.

'It was nice of your dad,' she sighs.

On the other side of the room, there are two old fashioned wooden tea chests, both with the word kitchen scrawled in black felt tip across the front. Sarah lifts a layer of newspaper from the first and sees it is filled with car wash and oil cans. She puts the paper back and moves to the second. From this, she lifts a black iron skillet, large enough to cook a meal for a dozen. It takes both hands and all her strength to carry it to the table. She drops it with a thud in front of the boy, looking to see if she has made him laugh. It was an impressive thud. It is an impressive cooking pot.

But the boy's eyes are wider and more startled than ever. She leans forward and lightly brushes the fringe off his forehead. His hair is delicate, tender, as she knew it would be, and it falls back into place immediately.

'A baby brother for you to play with,' she repeats. Gently, she tucks the delicate wisps behind his ears. 'That will be nice.'

Then, to amuse him, she goes back to the packing chest and lifts out two more objects. One is an ancient, perforated spoon, black like the pot. The handle is almost as tall as the boy. The other is an old-fashioned, two-wheel grinding mill, the cogged teeth clearly visible inside the funnel. The boy eases himself sideways half off the chair so that one foot is touching the ground. She is arranging the spoon and mill on the stone mantelpiece and does not notice.

'These things belonged to my grandmother,' she tells the boy, keeping her back to him. 'Antiques.'

The boy is now visibly trembling.

She goes again to the tea chest and searches with both hands in the crumpled newspaper, though she knows there is nothing useful to be found. These old chests sat in the garage in the other house for years.

35

The label is from the last move. This time, she lifts out a large, curved cleaver. The blade is dull and mottled, the wooden handle worm-eaten. She gives it an experimental swing and again looks over to see if she has made the little boy laugh. She is about to ask if he would like to try it out. But as she turns to face him, the boy slips the rest of the way off the chair and runs from the room. He is gone so fast, she is left momentarily at a loss. She can hear him scurrying up the wooden stairs on all fours, like a frightened little animal. Bemused, she puts the cleaver on the mantelpiece beside the other objects.

The next thing, Clive is coming into the room carrying the boy. He is laughing. He sits the child in the same chair and arranges the little matchstick legs just so, but all the time he is watching her.

She too laughs, looking at the child and not at him. 'Maybe he needs something to play with,' she says.

Clive picks up the iron skillet. The muscles in his arms tense with the weight. He sees her watching and hefts it about a bit.

'Amy's got toys,' she says, 'if we could find them.' She tries hard to look at the boy instead of at his father. 'How about some drawing paper?' she asks him. 'Would you like that?'

Clive returns the iron skillet to the table. 'You don't see many of these around,' he says. Again, the muscles in his sleek arms ripple. He can't help but look at them himself. Then he glances briefly at the boy. 'You stay here Davey,' he adds. 'Don't move.' At the door, he turns back and holds up one finger in warning. But he is looking at her and not at the boy. 'You could cook a whole hog in one of those,' he says, jokingly.

When he is gone, she finds some writing paper and two pens. These she places in front of the boy. He picks up one of the pens then puts it down again without making a mark.

'Your mummy,' she says, 'she's very young.' She thinks for a minute, looking out the window. 'Two babies,' she says, experiencing a rush of jealousy, so intense and so perfectly without warning, that she has found herself momentarily defenceless.

There is a new, solitary, white cooker on the other side of the room, leaning sideways on the uneven stone floor. Moving fast, Sarah carries the skillet over and drops it on top. It covers all four burners.

She pours in water from the kettle, then adds salt and the remains of the butter from the table. She does not know exactly how to cook the rabbits, only that they will be tough and stringy like all meat not bought from the supermarket. But this is the country. This is what you do. The boy watches her every move.

She comes back and stands by the table, looking down at the carcasses. Reluctantly, she lifts first one, then the other, and lets them fall back onto the table. Already, they are stiff and rock hard, as if made of stone.

Then she has an idea. She goes over to the hearth and takes down the old-fashioned cleaver. The little boy watches her. Again, he has started trembling. Again, he is half out of his chair, one foot on the ground. She feels the blade with her thumb. It is hopelessly blunt, of course, but the weight of the thing will probably do the job. She tries an experimental chopping blow in the air. Suddenly, she hears a tiny, frightened squeak and turns in time to see the child again running from the room. Again, she hears him scurrying up the wooden stairs on all fours. This time, she is less surprised but more confused.

When Clive returns, he is pulling the boy by the hand and his expression is sheepish. 'Kids,' he says. Again, he pushes the boy into the chair, but this time he does not arrange the little legs. 'Sometimes, I think his only purpose in life is to make me look stupid,' he laughs and shoves the chair in hard so that the child is tightly up against the table, his frightened face again only inches from the rabbits.

'I have an idea,' she says, disappearing into the lean-to larder. A few seconds later, she is back with an ice-lolly on a stick.

Clive takes it from her and puts it in the boy's hand, opening the tiny fingers and closing them one by one around the stick. The boy is too frightened to eat. He looks as if eating has always been a heavy weight that troubles his life. Next to him, his father looks like he lives on nothing but meat.

As if reading her mind, Clive picks up one of the rabbits. 'Want me to skin these for you?' he asks.

She smiles with relief. He sees it is again meant for him and no one else.

'Where's your knives?' he asks.

She shrugs her shoulders prettily. It is a little girl's gesture. 'Who knows where anything is,' she answers.

'No knives?' he questions, looking around the room at the unpacked packing cases. The cleaver is on the table in front of him. He picks it up and, immediately, delivers four crashing whacks. The rabbits are neatly beheaded, feet off, oozing dark blood, all in a matter of seconds.

She laughs, taking a step backwards. Her bracelets jingle. Her earrings swing. There is suddenly a pretty flush to her cheeks. The little boy is deathly pale.

Clive picks up one of the rabbits and lifts it high in front of him. He grabs hold of the skin at the neck and with two great pulls the rabbit is stripped bare. He drops the skin nonchalantly on the table.

'You sexy devil,' he laughs, picking up the second rabbit.

She looks at him, not sure if he means the rabbits or himself. She is poised to disappear into the devouring gravitational pull that seems to surround him. Her expression is not reluctant.

He whips the skin from the second rabbit and drops it on the table beside the first.

'Your face,' he says, grinning at her. Oh yes, this is one investment that's going to pay off big time, and soon too. Who would of thought it, a couple of rabbits, a bit of blood. Just goes to show, with women you can't plan these things. Plan them, you get it wrong. Who would of thought, a couple of rabbits?

The little boy wriggles unnoticed from his chair and crawls under the table. The stone floor is deeply cold and slimy. He recoils in surprise and draws his knees up to his chin so only the base of his skinny spine and the tips of his heels are in contact with the cold. Still he can't stop shivering.

The flesh of the naked rabbits is a healthy pink. Sarah turns them over and examines them, forcing herself to let her hands linger on the viscous surface.

He decides to take a bit of a chance. 'Nice,' he says, looking sideways at her. 'I always think there shouldn't be any clothes between you and your clothes.'

She laughs straightaway, a good sign. But then she doesn't say anything else. Instead, she goes over and turns the heat down under the boiling skillet. He watches her move, his eyes taking in those tight jeans, that skimpy T-shirt, the beads, a bandana around her hair today.

He brings his attention back to the rabbits. 'Well, I guess I can do something here,' he says. 'If the kids can do it on Friday nights with a broken bottle.' He picks up the cleaver and, with the point, delicately opens a small incision. Again, he looks sideways at her and sees she is confused. 'The kids,' he says, 'amateur surgery, Friday night.' Of course, what would someone like her know about that?

She is watching his arms and hands rooting around inside the first rabbit. He withdraws his right hand and brings it up to his forehead to brush away the imaginary sweat, leaving a red smear. She stares, as he knew she would.

Holding her stare, he says, 'Like a lot of things, you'll appreciate this more if you have to wait for it.'

He sees her drop her eyes again, and give him her little girl's look, demure. He is pleased with himself for remembering the word demure and wonders how he can work it into the conversation. Suddenly, the look is gone and she is searching the room, uneasily.

'Where is he?' she asks.

At once, Clive turns his eyes to the empty chair where the child should be and realises he has been looking at it, empty, for some time now. 'Oh Lord,' he says.

★★★

It is Sarah who finds the boy, but not for a quarter of an hour. Relieved, she reaches under the table and tries to lift him out. He pulls away.

'Hey,' she says, then realises she does not remember his name. Keeping her voice gentle, she says again, 'It's OK, you can come out.' Still the boy cringes away from her.

She goes to the open door and calls. Clive is working his way along the inside of the hedge, moving fast with his shoulders hunched forward. He looks up at the sound of her voice, visibly startled, as if he had forgotten her existence. At once, he turns and runs towards the house, using reserves of power that are kept for such moments.

'It's all right,' she tells him quickly. 'He's all right.'

Clive keeps coming at the same speed, but the power has gone out of his run. He twists his hips easily, to avoid the piles of rocks by the moat and the two wheelbarrows side by side.

She leads the way to the table and bends to show him. But now there is no one there. She looks up in surprise.

'He was under the table?' Clive asks.

At the same time, they both hear the familiar scurrying noise on the stairs. But, when they get there, he is again gone. They can hear his footsteps pattering along the length of the vaulted landing towards the big bedroom at the far end. There is a sudden silence when his feet reach the carpeted room.

Clive stands with one foot on the bottom step. He does not go up. He has been in the big bedroom, alone, and knows the boy will come to no harm in there. Instead, he turns to her.

'Kids,' he says, shaking his head, giving her the little sideways look. He would like to see her in some of those smart clothes up there, maybe the black suit cut tight like a uniform.

She too shakes her head. 'It must be tough for him,' she says. 'He must miss his mum.'

It takes Clive a few seconds to understand what she is saying. 'Oh that,' he answers. He has not given Di a thought. Instead, he is thinking about the black dress with the row of tiny looped buttons down the back and about how she likes tight black clothes and what that means.

'Well, let's hope it's soon,' she says. Again, her voice is wistful.

'Yea, sure,' he agrees.

★★★

In the kitchen, he is cutting the rabbits into pieces for her. She reaches around him to spread newspaper over the table where he is working, brushing his arm with her left breast as she does so. At the same time, there is a crash of something breaking upstairs. The noise does not come from the big bedroom, but from the opposite end of the house. He exhales in exasperation, looking at her breasts.

'What now?' he says.

He takes the stairs two at a time, but before he reaches the top, the little boy is standing before him.

'What now?' he repeats. The boy is sobbing, with four fingers in his mouth, like a much younger child.

'What's that on your shorts?' Clive picks him up and carries him under one arm, feet dangling behind. There is an unpleasant smell coming from the wet patch on the boy's shorts. He has not brought a clean pair. Di never goes anywhere without a clean pair of everything. And she would have thought of toys. This whole thing wouldn't have happened if he'd thought of toys.

'Your mum is going to have something to say,' he tells the child.

For the third time, he sits the boy in the chair at the table and pushes it in tight. 'Don't move,' he says. 'Don't you dare.' He gives the back of the chair a final sharp thrust so that the boy is wedged tightly into place, his chest and his face pressed up against the rough wooden table.

The boy is looking at the blood on the newspaper. There is a smear on his father's forearm as well as on his face. He tries not to look at what is going on over at the cooker where she is, but his eyes are drawn to the steaming pot. A bit of pink, scummy liquid has spilled over and is running down the side of the new white cooker.

His father finishes washing his hands at the stone sink and turns back to the little boy. 'Don't you dare,' he repeats. 'Don't even think about it.'

She comes over and puts a blue saucer in front of the boy with two chocolate biscuits. Next, she pours a small amount of milk into a plastic cup. 'I wish we had something else,' she says, kindly.

But the boy is too scared to pick up either the biscuits or the milk. His stomach is tightened in a hard spasm and his throat is blocked with something also hard. He cannot answer.

'You must be hungry,' she says. 'I know I am. I'm starving.'

He looks at her with terrified eyes. He has almost stopped breathing. She catches the expression.

'Go on,' she says, laughing. 'Everyone likes chocolate biscuits.'

His father comes up to stand beside her. He waves his arm towards the boiling pot. 'There's plenty of room,' he says. 'Got anything else you want to put in there?'

He is standing close, hoping she will brush up against him, the same as before. She looks over at the pot, then turns back to watching the boy, a serious frown on her face.

'I'm starving,' she repeats. 'When will they be ready? What do you think?'

'What do I think?' he says, thinking this one, this Sarah, one minute, it's all looks and brushes with the old left tit, the next, who knows? And time is running out. The kid, for example, something's wrong there. Di would know straightaway. *It's a tooth*, she'd say, without even having to look, or *he needs a sleep*.

The next thing, out of the blue, she's leaning across him, both breasts pressing into his arm. As she moves further forward, he gets a good feel of her nipples beneath the flimsy T-shirt. This time, there is absolutely no doubt what is going on, no doubt at all. He is about to put his arms around her and press her towards him, when she speaks.

'You don't feel too good, do you?' She has leaned over in order to again brush the boy's fringe off his forehead and she lets her hand linger on his forehead, feeling how cold he is.

As she removes her hand, the boy gives a high-pitched yelp and falls sideways off his chair. Terrified beyond reason, he picks himself up and runs straight towards the open door. Mid-flight, he changes his mind, and turns towards his father. Clive, not sure what is happening, reaches out and grabs the boy by the back of his shorts. The boy falls face forward, hitting his head, hard. Sarah screams and brings both hands up to cover her mouth.

The boy wriggles free from his father's grasp and crawls fast on his knees towards the open door. There is blood on his face. Again, his father grabs him by the back of the shorts, this time with both hands. He swings him high up into the air, over the cooker, with its boiling pot. To the boy, it is obvious what is about to happen – *She'll eat you alive! I'm starving!* He arches his back, in a spasm of pure terror, again catching his father off guard. For one brief moment, he is free, but his father recovers quickly and breaks the fall. In doing so, his own arm catches the handle of iron skillet and sends it crashing down. Steaming, greasy liquid spreads across the stone floor. Bits of half-cooked flesh skew outwards. Sarah screams a second time and jumps back.

'Jesus!' Clive cries out. The boy is still struggling in his arms, attempting to free himself. 'What the fuck's going on?'

He now wraps both arms tightly around the boy's middle and carries him, face-forward, towards the table where the giant cleaver lies on top of the bloodied newspapers. The boy leans over and sinks his teeth into his father's arm, just above the elbow – *They'll eat you alive!* Clive cries out in surprise and pain. 'You little fucker!' he shouts, and sits the boy down hard in the chair.

At exactly that moment, a figure appears in the open doorway. It is the hippie arriving for work. He takes in the macabre debris on the table, the slimy floor with its lumps of parboiled flesh in odd places, the terrified child, blood all over his face, the incensed father and her, the cold-hearted Sarah, standing there, appalled.

'Man,' he says, looking from one to the other. He shakes his long matted hair and something about his person rattles along with his movement. 'Some bust up,' he says.

'Shut up, Tord,' Clive says. He is breathing deeply, to calm himself while holding the boy down with both hands. 'You're full of shit.'

'Man,' the hippie repeats. 'Someone's been nailing it to the wall.'

'Just shut up.' Clive speaks impatiently. 'Go up there and get on with it.' With his handkerchief, he is gently wiping the blood from the boy's face. It appears to have come from his nose and has now stopped.

The hippie raises both hands and backs from the room, without speaking again.

Tenderly Clive picks up the boy and carries him out to the van, whispering softly to him all the while, reassuring little things that come from somewhere deep in his own memory of childhood. He sits the boy carefully on the front seat and locks the doors. Again, he takes a deep breath before turning back to the house.

Sarah steps into the larder out of sight until he has passed. When she hears his feet start up the second flight of stairs, she goes out to the van. The child is now curled on the floor, sobbing. She watches him for several minutes, trying both doors repeatedly. He does not look up at her. After a few more minutes, she goes back to the house and climbs to the first floor. In the small bedroom, Amy's room, she finds a picture frame on the floor, with the glass broken. It is nothing, of no consequence. She stands at the bottom of the second staircase and listens to the two men. Clive is steadily angry.

'It's a fuck-up,' he is saying.

'You got it wrong,' the hippie, Tord, answers.

'It's a fucking fuck-up,' Clive repeats. 'Fuck-ups cost me.'

'I know, man.' The hippie's voice is pleading.

'I'm not paying for any more of your fuck-ups,' Clive interrupts. 'It's coming out of your fucking wages.'

'Man, you're way off track,' the hippie tells him.

'Me? Off track?' Clive laughs. 'You're a piss-head. I don't know why I keep you on. There's always something.'

'Man,' the hippie repeats. 'You got it all wrong.'

'Get out of my sight.' Clive slams the door and immediately his feet are pounding down the stairs. Sarah slips back into the small room until he has passed. Through the window, she sees him unlock the van and lift the little boy out. He holds him in his arms and rocks him back and forth for a long time. The child is limp in the embrace, his face buried in his father's neck, his matchstick legs dangling, his little hands holding on tight. In repose, he is a beautiful child. Quite undeserving of being entirely surrounded by them.

4. SAVE MY LOST BLACK SOUL

Towards the end of the afternoon Mr Raftiche leans his classroom chair back so that it is balanced on two legs. He is talking as she, the pretty one with the bright, curly hair, slides into the seat before him. He spotted her straightaway when she first joined his queue of parents almost half an hour ago.

'These kids,' he is in the middle of saying, 'they think it's some big deal to speak a couple of foreign languages. They think it's so hard. But you know, I'm impressed by them. I'm impressed at the languages they know.'

She gives him a polite, quizzical smile, not yet making any judgement.

'They can speak street, TV, sitcom, retro. I've even heard Queen's.' He laughs and watches her face.

She is still smiling, but it is subtly less polite. Quickly, he rocks forward on the chair and leans towards her, with both arms on the table. 'So,' he says, knowing he's got it wrong yet again.

'I'm Ben Sacheveral's mother,' she answers. 'Sarah.'

His face is blank for a brief moment, then all at once it lights up.

'Saddlebag's mother,' he says, grinning at her.

She smiles back at him, but now, not only has her smile lost its politeness, it has lost its steadiness as well. He has taken her by surprise.

'Don't worry about it,' he laughs. 'They have to call him something.' Now he is openly staring at her. 'I've heard worse, believe me,' he says.

His pleasure is so obviously genuine that at last she finds herself grinning back.

'Saddlebag's mother,' he repeats. 'Let me tell you something.' His voice is now serious. 'He's a good kid. I like him.' He pauses, but not long enough for her to add anything. 'Not feeling too good?' he questions. The boy has been absent from school for several days, come to think of it longer than that.

She tilts her head to the side with the same quizzical look that makes him want to put his arm around her and bury that pretty little worried face in his big burly shoulder.

Mr Raftiche understands at once. 'Ah,' he says. 'It's like that, is it?'

She frowns, also understanding at once that Ben has not been at school. So it's all started again.

Again, he leans back in his chair, but this time keeping all four legs on the ground. There is nothing jaunty in this situation. It is familiar, predictable, unimaginative.

'Listen,' he says. 'Maybe I'm wrong. Maybe he just missed a couple of lessons.'

At the same time, a hand reaches from behind him and places a teacup, no more than half full, on the table beside his exam papers and mark books.

He looks up at the face that belongs to the hand. 'Ruby,' he says, again with the same spontaneous pleasure. It seems to be his way with women, to love them all instantly, unquestioningly.

She is holding a tray with other cups. There is a slight tremble amongst the crockery.

'I know you're off duty,' he adds.

She gives him a sideways look and brings her free hand up to the collar of her bright pink blouse, where it flutters momentarily.

He turns to the boy's mother. 'This is one of our secretaries.' He looks back at Ruby. 'One of our hopelessly overworked, wonderful secretaries.'

There is another brief quiver about the cups. As if she could ever be off duty where he is concerned. Anything he can ask, anything he wants, the more difficult the better.

'I know you're off duty,' he repeats. 'But can you check a register in the office for me?' He hands her the boy's name, at the same time noticing that two buttons of her pink blouse have come undone, revealing absolutely nothing at all. Poor little flat-chested mouse. He is momentarily aggrieved on her behalf.

When she is gone, Mr Raftiche turns back to the boy's mother. 'Is it London you come from?'

She looks off into the distance, disconcerted by this unexpected man. 'More or less,' she answers.

He nods and looks off into the same distance, as if there is some undiscovered truth out there, something about her. 'I moved here from London myself,' he says. 'It's a whole lot cheaper and I always think it's easier to be miserable in a small place.'

He brings his eyes back to her face to see if he has made her laugh. She is studying him seriously. Well, he thinks, not everyone derives their inspiration from dark inner thoughts. Some people just like shopping and cutting the grass.

'Me too,' she suddenly says. 'I find it helps to read the papers. I like to read about all those people worse off than myself.'

He grins hugely at her. 'Yes, that too. It cheers me up no end.'

Instantly, in his fantasy, he is a magnificent creature, half man, half phallus. And she, Sarah, the new boy's mother, she is a goddess. He finds he is unable to take his eyes off her. His glance drops downwards to her lovely breasts and it takes an exhausting effort of will to force himself to look away. But, when he looks away, the curious gnawing pain starts up in the centre of his chest. It is a pain he has experienced many times before in just these situations. He forces himself to be stalwart and not cry out. He can endure anything for her. A goddess has that right.

★★★

In the office, Ruby finds that the boy, as Robert thought, has not been in school. She remembers him sitting in the deputy's office for most of yesterday afternoon, and wonders if there will be something about him in the book.

Sure enough, he is in trouble. She reads the brief entry. He has been caught leaving school premises, several times, always on his own. Then she glances quickly through the list, looking for her own son's name. Fortunately, it is not there. Wandering off, of course, that goes on all the time, but alone, it's odd, unusual.

★★★

Back in the hall, Ruby comes up as he is saying, 'So you see, it's not what you think. They all do it.' He breaks off, watching her approach and raises his eyebrows.

She nods her head and holds his look. She is sure he understands everything there is to be understood, always, without having to say a word. He turns back to the mother and Ruby bends to collect the cup.

Before she has even picked it up, she hears him say, 'It's not that I worry about. What I worry about is the way some of them can suck the guts out of a cigarette in three drags. You should see them do it. Now nicotine, that really is a problem.' Out of sight, he strokes the pack of cigarettes in his own pocket. Again he tips his chair back on two legs, way back, dangerously far.

The mother, the pretty one, laughs appreciatively. But she is watching Ruby, taking in the limp brown hair, the lurid pink blouse and the tiny fleshless frame bent in obvious homage.

Oh Ruby, Robert thinks, don't look at me that way, not now, not in front of her, the beautiful Sarah.

Oh Robert, Ruby thinks as she moves away, these tearaways in your class, they go out and get in trouble deliberately to be punished by you. I know they do. It is what I would do if I were in your class.

★★★

At the same time this exchange is taking place, 90 miles away, Ben sits huddled in an empty wooden shed. The shed is empty because he is the only one who has a key to the padlock. There are three expensive-looking bicycles leaning against the wall outside and leaning against them, an assortment of garden tools. Suddenly, a car starts up close by. Ben raises himself just far enough to peer through the small side window. It is, as he hoped, their car. They are leaving.

He watches them back out of the drive and disappear down the road. The car is expensive, a Rover, with unusual black-tinted windows so that he cannot see who is driving. He eases himself up higher and notices there is one small light on in the house, in the hall, though it is not yet dark. Slowly, he pushes open the shed door and creeps towards the back porch, keeping low behind his mother's raspberry canes. The unpicked, overripe fruit litters the ground. Crushed beneath his feet, the smell is intense.

He tries the back door but it is locked. He circles round the house, still keeping low, and tries the front door. It too is locked. He listens. There is nothing, no sound from inside. Boldly, he rings the bell. Again it is, as he hoped, silent and empty.

This time, he knows exactly what to do. He walks round to the back, not bothering to crouch. He puts one foot onto the stone urn, a second onto the lattice that supports the wisteria and, with one easy pull, he is up onto the porch roof. The grainy tarpaper scrapes his knees. He sees the cigarette holes are still there, the bigger ones satisfyingly filled with rainwater.

Next, he eases himself through the top half of the unlatched bathroom window and prepares to drop down onto the toilet seat. Then, without warning, it all goes wrong. He hits the bare floor hard and his legs crumple beneath him. Taken by surprise, he lets go a little scream as he lands. There is no toilet where there should be one. There is no sink, no bathtub, no shower. The room is totally empty. He is shocked beyond reason. He stares at the raw plaster and blank space. In his experience, there is no precedent for what he has found, no quick way to recompose the room as it was.

After a long minute, he picks himself up, opens the bathroom door and listens. He can hear only the sound of his own heart thumping. Carefully, he eases his way along the hall towards his old bedroom, pressing himself against the bare walls. The paper here too has been stripped and the blue carpet is gone. Then he remembers that it is lying rolled, tied with string, in the front hall of the new house. He is preparing himself to meet another desolation. At least this time, he will not be so taken by surprise.

He pushes open the door of his bedroom and again stops abruptly. A shiver of fear runs through him. Again he has found no way to prepare himself. The entire room is crammed full to the ceiling. There are suitcases, cardboard boxes, wooden tea chests, furniture, all heaped together. The room is so tightly packed that he can do no more than put one foot across the threshold. His window, the one that looks out onto the back garden and flat garage roof, is totally blocked. There is a tantalising glimpse of light, but it is beyond reaching. He puts his shoulder to one of the wardrobes. If he could move it, even a few inches, he could slip in. But it does not budge. He tries a packing case, but it is filled with books and beyond his strength. For a long time, he studies the room in the hope of finding a way through to the window so at least he could look out one more time at the garden where he played as a baby, and at the streets where he played as a child. There is no way through.

Finally, he turns away. It is now getting too dark to see anything anyway. By the light from the hall, he makes his way down the front stairs, not bothering to look in any of the other rooms. He goes through the kitchen towards the back door. There is an unfamiliar spicy smell here, some sort of food he can't identify, something exotic and of the street. Carefully, he slips out and the lock clicks shut behind him. He goes back to the shed and lowers himself onto his school bag in the corner, bringing his knees up to his chin and holding them with both hands. He shivers with cold.

★★★

At home, his mother puts down the phone and says, 'Nothing, no one has seen him.' James has only just walked in through the door. He still holds his leather case in one hand and his change from the taxi in the other.

'I can't keep doing this,' he says. It is too sudden, this getting out of the car and walking straight into her problems. He has his own problems to be getting on with now. 'We agreed,' he says.

She gives him a helpless look. 'I've been ringing round,' she tells him. 'He hardly knows anyone. He's just gone.'

'What do you mean, gone?' his father repeats.

'Gone,' she says. 'I don't know where.'

He drops his case and keys onto the table and pulls his tie loose. They are angry gestures. 'Listen,' he says. 'He's old enough to be out. He's stupid enough to be out.'

'It's not that,' she interrupts. 'He wasn't in school today.'

He is heading for the stairs but stops and turns back to face her. 'It's not my fault,' she says. 'I didn't know.'

'How could you not know?' he asks. 'You took him, didn't you?'

'Of course I took him,' she answers. She is not going to tell him about the other days he has not been in school.

He is watching her face. It occurs to him that he would like to be able to hurt her. Not to hurt her, but to be able to, just in case. But how can you hurt someone who has ice in their veins? Absent-mindedly he kneads the spot in his stomach where the pain has started up again.

'I went to the parents' afternoon and they asked me if he was off sick, so I came home and he wasn't here,' she explains.

He looks at her impersonally. 'And he wasn't here all day?'

The look cuts right through her. 'I don't know,' she answers. In truth, she has not thought about him, about where he might be or what he might be doing, for many weeks now. She has not kept her part of the bargain. 'I've been busy,' she says. 'I thought he was at school. I took him and he went in with Amy. I watched them.'

'You watched them,' he repeats, not believing her.

'Of course I did,' she says. 'And besides, Amy would have said.' Her voice trails off at the ridiculousness of this. Amy still has not spoken, at least not to her.

He turns away from her and climbs the stairs. Moments later, he is back, dressed now in jeans and a denim shirt. She has not moved. He picks up his keys from the table and, without saying anything, he goes out to his car. In another minute, he is gone.

'Ha!' she says to the empty house.

She stands at the open door for a long time, looking down the empty drive to the empty lane. It is not yet fully dark, and she is telling herself that, of course, Ben will be back any minute. There is really nothing to worry about, even if he is doing what she thinks he is with those new friends of his. But her stomach tightens, her fists clench. 'Ha!' she says again to the watery ditch in front of the house, the moat

James has put such huge reserves of time and effort into restoring. Then suddenly, standing there, it comes to her, an understanding of this need of James' to cling to things that are beside the point. It is because the point is too frightening. The next thing she knows she is thinking about that funny Italian teacher. *You have a daughter too, I hear,* he is saying. And when she told him about Amy's problems, the way she's not speaking, at least not at home. *Ah,* he has said. *Inevitably one child is the theme, the other the variation. A mistake you want to avoid.* Funny, serious man. *There's unlimited mistakes to choose from. I ought to know. Choose something else.* Strange man, with that odd serious way of looking at you, and the things he comes out with.

★★★

Meanwhile, back at the shed, Ben is searching through his school bag. He knows he has been asleep, but only for a few seconds, and now he is hungry. He does not at first notice there is a face peering at him through the window. When he does, he stops dead. A jolt of fear runs down his spine and along his arms to his hands. He drops the sandwich box he has just picked up.

The face in the window is black. It is a boy, probably no older but quite a lot bigger than himself. He is absolutely, undeniably black. Slowly, the boy moves around to the open door and stands there, staring at Ben. He is holding on to one of the expensive bicycles.

Ben stares back. He is looking at the black boy's hands, looking for a knife or maybe a gun. The boy has one hand on the bicycle, the other in his jeans pocket, a relaxed pose that does not fool Ben.

The black boy is the first to speak. 'How'd you get it open?' he asks.

Ben does not answer.

'You broke in?' the boy asks again. 'But why?' There's something about the way he speaks, about what he's asking, it's not right. But also, it's not frightening.

'What's it to you?' Ben answers.

The black boy takes his hand out of his pocket and Ben instantly recoils. It is a reflex gesture, unplanned and stunning. It is not lost on the boy.

'This is private property,' he answers.

'Yea?' Ben says. 'Tell me about it.' His voice is defiant. To the boy, there is something about what he's saying, and the way he's saying it, that's not right. 'Anyway,' Ben adds, looking at the bicycle, 'where do you think you are going with that?'

The boy is obviously taken aback, and straightaway Ben regrets his words. He knows he hasn't a hope of stopping him stealing the bike. He is both taller and heavier. And, in any case, why should he care about some stranger's bicycle?

'Take it,' Ben says. 'What do I care?'

Now the boy laughs outright. But his look is not amused, not like Ben thought it would be, amused at his expense.

The boy does not move away from the door. He just stands there and stares. 'Mind telling me something?' he asks after a few moments.

Ben hunches his shoulders further into his school jacket and looks down at the sandwich box. 'What?' he says.

'Where'd you get that key?' The boy is looking at the door and Ben sees that he has left the key in the lock.

'It's mine,' he answers.

There is another long silence. Finally, the boy says, 'I get it.' He nods his head slowly and looks away as if embarrassed. 'Did you used to live here?'

At the same time, Ben too understands. He understands, but it doesn't make sense. He looks at the totally black blackness of the boy. 'You're not the people who bought the house,' he says.

Again, it is not lost on the boy. 'The agent bought the house,' he answers, shifting his weight from one foot to the other. He waits a long time before going on. 'So what are you doing here?' he asks.

Ben shrugs his shoulders and looks out the window. There are still no lights on in the house. The boy must have come home on his own. It is absolutely quiet in the garden. All at once, Ben is overcome with sadness. It rises up out of his chest, and he is afraid that the boy will see it hovering in the cobwebbed eaves of the shed. Quickly, he reaches into his bag and pulls out a new pack of cigarettes and holds it out.

The black boy rests his bicycle on the open door, then he steps inside and squats down, accepting the cigarette. Ben lights up for both of them.

'How come you didn't buy the house yourself?' Ben asks.

'Because we were in Saudi,' the boy answers. 'That's why.'

Ben does not know what to say to this. The two boys finish their cigarettes in silence, then stub them out casually on the wooden floor.

'Want to come in?' the black boy asks Ben.

Again, Ben looks towards the dark house. 'I got to go,' he says.

The boy stands up and waits for Ben to do the same. Slowly, Ben replaces the exercise books, the remains of his lunch, his striped tie, into the shabby school bag. There's nothing else for it. He takes his time doing up the zip and buckles. All the while, the boy is watching him.

'I'm meeting my dad,' he tells the boy, guessing he is not fooling anyone.

The boy again picks up the bicycle and starts wheeling it towards the drive. 'My dad's in the army,' he tells Ben.

'He's a soldier?' Ben asks, interested.

'He's a jerk,' the boy answers.

'Oh,' Ben says, disappointed.

'He advises people, governments mostly,' the boy adds as an afterthought.

At the end of the drive, the boy stops. 'Are you sure you don't want to come in?' he asks again. 'You could you know.'

Ben shakes his head.

The boy shrugs his shoulders and swings one leg up over the bicycle. He pushes off, turning back for one last look. Then he's gone.

Ben lifts his bag and walks off in the opposite direction, but the weight of sadness in his chest is now so great he can barely keep himself upright. He follows the line of next door's privet hedge, Vanessa's hedge, to the corner where it turns. He turns too. The road in front of him is long and straight, bordered on one side by houses, on the other by the dark and deserted park. His eye catches a movement way over on the far side of the empty space. He at once recognises the black boy on his expensive bicycle. Without thinking, Ben turns onto the grass and follows. The boy seems to be heading for a small group of lighted shops in the distance, the newsagents, the fish and chips, the chemist, as familiar to Ben as his own skin. He picks up his pace until he is actually running. As he gets closer, he sees that he is right. The boy has propped his bicycle outside the chippy and is now inside waiting in the queue.

Ben comes to the edge of the grass and stops in the shadow of the hedge. He squats down and watches. Two other boys appear from nowhere and go into the bright shop. He recognises them at once. They too are as familiar to him as his own parents. Yet they are at the same time curiously unfamiliar. It has only been a few months and already they are gone from him. He wants to turn away but, cruelly, the weight of sadness prevents him from moving. In anguish he watches the three of them deep in conversation, his two best friends and the black boy. One of them is holding out a handful of coins and the other two are studying it. Suddenly, they all three laugh and pull away only to come together again as quickly as they separated, their shoulders and arms searching out points of accidental contact.

Ben watches them reach the front of the queue, place their order, wait, then accept their wrapped packages and come out together. In the bright shop lights, it is as if he is watching a performance on stage. He sees them loll against the shop front and begin to eat, their concentration unbroken. Suddenly, without warning, the black boy looks over in his direction. Quickly Ben steps back into the shadows. The boy continues to look. Ben steps back further behind the hedge. With each step he takes, he feels himself becoming more invisible, like the sad homeless people he used to see on the city streets, invisible as if they had somehow worn thin over the desolate months of homelessness. It is exactly how he feels.

It seems to take hours to re-cross the open space and return along the straight road. There is a phone box on the corner, diagonally opposite his old house. Ben dials the new number. His mother answers on the first ring.

'It's me,' he tells her.

He hears her draw in her breath. 'Where are you?' she asks. Her voice is shaky with emotion.

'I'm at home,' he answers. 'I don't have any money.'

At the same time, miraculously, he sees his father's car pulling slowly up to the kerb in front of the house next door, Vanessa's house. He is so surprised, he at first closes his eyes, thinking it is a kind of hallucination. It is something he knows can happen if you smoke a lot of stuff and has happened to his mates, but never to him.

He hears his mother's voice. 'At home?' she is asking.

His father is getting out of the car. 'Dad's here,' he tells her.

There is a long pause. 'What?' she says.

'Dad's here,' he repeats.

★★★

In the car, when they have been on the motorway for some time, Ben's father turns to him. 'Vanessa rang me. She was worried about you.' In fact she was affronted. He had to stop her calling the police. *But I saw him breaking in*, she has said. *If you don't stop him, he'll go on to worse things.*

Don't be ridiculous, he has answered her. *Of course he won't.*

'Anything wrong at school?' he asks.

Ben shakes his head.

'Are you sure?' his father repeats.

They drive in silence for a few more minutes. Then Ben says, 'Why didn't you tell me those people were black?'

His father looks over at him, surprised. 'Didn't I?' he says, carelessly.

Ben is silent for a long time. The big car is comfortably burning up the miles and he is almost asleep. Then, without warning, he says, 'You would have said if they were Germans.' He thinks for a minute. 'Or Americans.'

'Who?' his father says.

'You would have told me,' Ben insists.

'Are you still talking about the new people?' his father asks. He keeps his eyes steady on the road ahead. 'Maybe I would have. Maybe I wouldn't. What do you care anyway?'

James reaches over and switches on the radio. He flips through the stations, listening to each for a few moments before moving on. Eventually, he sighs and switches off. He has not had a drink all day. The pain in his gut is definitely getting worse, always at times like these when he's with her or the children, and sometimes when he's only thinking about them.

'You would have said.' Ben is right there, ready. 'You would have said, "Hey there's someone your own age from America".'

'Would I?' his father questions. 'Would I really?'

'You would of,' Ben repeats. 'I know you would of.'

His father looks down and sees that his speed is creeping up. He eases off a bit on the pedal. 'Shut the fuck up Ben,' he says.

Ben looks over at his father's profile. He hates him. He hates him most of all like this in the car. He is a confident and relaxed driver, using the big car to reinforce his idea of himself as a confident and relaxed person. Who does he think he's kidding?

'Besides, I thought your mother told you,' his father says, casually pulling out into the fast lane to overtake.

'She didn't,' Ben answers.

When he has finished his manoeuvre, James briefly opens his window. The night air floods in, bringing with it the smell of diesel fumes and hot faraway places where, Ben knows, black people eat spicy, exotic food while walking down the street in crowds.

'You could of told me,' he says again. 'It's interesting.'

'Jesus,' his father comes straight back at him. 'Just shut the fuck up about it, will you?' He slams his hand down hard on the steering wheel. 'Shut the fuck up. It's got nothing to do with you. You're just a dumb kid who runs away from school and smokes dope all the time. Think I don't know about that? Well, think again.'

Ben hunches away from his father as if struck. It is a gesture he has seen his mother do often, though he has no actual memory of it.

'Listen,' his father says straightaway, ashamed at his outburst. But then he can't think of anything else to say. A drink would put all this right. Maybe he could then apologise to his son. He knows that what he's said is wrong and the way he's said it is wrong too.

'Listen,' he tries again. 'I'm going to stop for a bit.' He looks over at his son's sullen face. 'You hungry?'

The boy does not answer.

'Guess I'd better quit while I'm behind, yea?' he jokes. But he is not, he knows, by temperament suited to jest and banter.

Still Ben does not answer. He is pressing himself as far into the corner as he will go, staring out the window into the dark, desolate countryside.

At the first lighted pub, James pulls into the almost empty car park. He opens the door and gets out, leaning back in to look at Ben. He looks so like his mother, sitting there all icy and hostile, refusing to meet him halfway, exactly like she does. Who does he think he is anyway?

'Just don't think you're some big somebody,' he says and shuts the door.

But before the words settle onto the hunched shoulders of the hungry, unhappy boy, his father has forgotten that he ever said them. Eyeing the deserted outdoor tables and dimly lit pub windows, he has other things on his mind. He pushes open the door and enters the silent room, already tasting the drink as it slips down his throat.

5. SMALL, DANGEROUS, FAMILIAR

After the accident with the boiling rabbits, there is a curious, lingering smell in the kitchen. Sarah is convinced something is rotting somewhere. She is down on her hands and knees, struggling to prize up one of the ancient flagstones when he, Clive, comes in through the open back door. She neither sees nor hears him. The stone is heavier than she expected and she is slightly out of breath with the effort.

He stands and lets his eyes wander over her from behind. Tail like that, he is thinking, could set a man up for twenty-four hours.

Suddenly, she cries out, half-raising herself and twisting around. Framed in the open doorway, with the bright outdoor light behind him, he appears to her as a faceless silhouette. For a brief moment, she is frightened. He is so big, so suddenly there, in his tight jeans and tight black shirt. Caught off guard, she struggles to regain her balance.

'Jesus. Take it easy,' he says.

She gives a nervous little laugh. 'You scared me.' She looks quickly back at the stone.

He comes over and squats down close beside her, also looking at the stone.

'It's loose,' she says.

'Yea?' he says, taking the screwdriver from her hand. He is thinking, down here on the floor, in those tight jeans and with the messed-up curls falling all over the place, longer now than they used to be, she is very close to what happens when no one is pretending anything.

He looks at her and not at the floor. 'People in the Congo live better than this,' he says. 'I've seen it on TV.'

She stands and wipes both hands down both thighs. 'I saw that programme,' she answers, knowing that he is right. The house is getting worse, not better.

He flicks his eyes over her pretty, bare feet, at the same time taking a blunt chisel from the toolbox he has brought in with him.

'I wouldn't walk around with nothing on,' he tells her. 'Floors like these.'

She gives him a funny, sideways look like she's not sure she's heard what she thinks she has, then again turns away before he can notice. 'What a mess.' She laughs ruefully. 'I think the whole thing's hopeless.'

He eases the chisel under the stone. 'No way,' he says. 'Nothing that can't be put right.' But personally, he agrees with her. These city types with their houses rich in history, they don't know shit. History, who the fuck needs it? The next thing, he is heaving the stone out. It rolls over twice with a satisfying thud. Underneath, there is only compacted earth, surprisingly dry.

She is clearly disappointed. 'Oh,' she says.

He leans imperceptibly closer to her. 'So, what are you looking for?' he asks.

She shrugs her shoulders prettily. He watches her hair, thinking of the catalogue of adult pleasure products out in the van, with their promise to excite and delight. If they could sell you those curls on those shoulders, you wouldn't need all that other stuff.

'I don't know,' she answers. She looks up at him. 'Can't you smell it?'

He leans closer still and breathes in. There is no trace of her shampoo today. He shakes his head, giving her his considered, probing look.

'You thought there was something under there?' he asks.

He goes back to his toolbox and pulls out a heavy iron jemmy. This he rams into the earth, putting all his weight behind it. On the third strike, there is the sound of metal hitting metal.

She leans in closer, allowing her arm to brush his arm.

He pulls the jemmy out, as surprised as she is. He kneels and begins to scoop the loose soil away with his hands. Almost immediately, he uncovers a small area of leaden metal.

'Oh my God,' she laughs prettily, 'treasure.' She brings both hands up to her pretty mouth. 'My God,' she repeats.

He lifts out the object. It is not, as they hoped, a locked box, but a small lustreless plate, tarnished with age.

He turns the object over in his hands, testing its weight.

'What is it?' she asks, excited. 'Is it valuable?'

He hands it to her. 'Could be,' he answers. He has worked on these old houses, on and off, all his life and his father before him, as well as most of his friends. And no one has ever found anything worth anything, not once.

'These old houses,' he says provocatively. 'You never know what you're going to find.'

'Really?' she answers, pleased.

As he bends to recover the scattered tools, his eye catches something else in the earth, something bleached white like a bone.

She senses the change in his movements, and turns to look as well. Already, he is squatting down, scooping aside the earth. She drops to her knees close beside him. He can hear her breath, a little quickened. Without warning, he feels a stirring of excitement.

'It's bones,' she says, also looking at the white object. 'I knew it. I knew there was something in there.'

He brushes the earth away, in a wide circle around it, whatever it is, not answering her.

Suddenly, he stops. His hand has come up against something else, something soft, maybe like skin, something some distance away from the bones. 'Jesus,' he says. He grabs hold and gently pulls.

She is watching him, ready to recoil.

Slowly, he draws out a leather shoe, small as if made for a young child, and built up high on the sides, the mud slips away. She lets go another high-pitched laugh.

He too laughs and takes the chance to move closer, now leaning the full weight of his shoulder against hers. Delicately, she lifts the shoe from his hand, not moving away, and turns it over in her own hands. 'My God,' she says again.

He looks back at the disturbed earth, at the white object, still protruding from the ground. For a long time he stares in silence, letting the shiver of dread grow. Then he turns to look at her, giving her his concerned, sensitive look. 'Are you thinking what I'm thinking?' he asks.

Put into words like that, it comes to her what it is they have found, and her expression changes to fear. 'It can't be,' she says again. 'Can it?'

Quickly, he puts his arm around her, giving her a stalwart, fatherly hug. He waits, not taking his arm away.

Finally, he asks, 'Are you ready?'

She nods her head.

'Sure?' he asks, giving her another hug, a little less fatherly this time.

She nods again.

Reluctantly, he removes his arm and bends to take hold of the protruding object. He twists it first one way, then the other, as he eases it out. He can sense the frailty of it. One false move, and it will snap. He again turns to look at her face and she holds his gaze.

All of a sudden, the object is free. She stares at it, and then lets go a third high-pitched laugh. In his hand, he is holding a clay pipe with a curved stem a good 12 inches long. He too laughs and reaches out to put his arm around her again but already she has pushed herself to her feet and is on her way to the sink where there is a scattering of unwashed cutlery. She returns with a large serving spoon. Her movements are bubbly, eager. 'Let me have a go,' she says. Again she kneels beside him and starts to dig.

He watches her slender, curved back, disappointed they have not found something more frightening. Now his embrace is no longer necessary. And just when one thing was leading nicely to another.

He is thinking, this one, this Sarah, she puts out, then the next thing she acts like she has no idea what's going on. This is not something he likes in a woman but he's prepared to let it go, this time. After all, he has enough ideas for the both of them.

Almost at once, she gasps in surprise and lifts out yet another object.

He bends closer. 'Well what do you know?' he says. 'Look at that.'

She brushes the dirt away to reveal a pair of tiny, iron spectacle frames, bent but unbroken.

'What do you know?' he repeats.

She turns the frames over in her hands and puts her fingers through the empty spaces where once there were lenses. He watches her excited little movements and it comes to him that he is wrong. It is not these strange finds that are making her move and laugh like that. It's something a whole lot simpler. Something he knows plenty about.

She hands the frames to him. 'Let's take up another one.'

Already, she has picked up the jemmy and is poking at the edges of the adjacent stone.

He rests his hand on hers. 'Listen,' he says. 'Maybe it's not such a good idea.'

'But why not?' she says. 'Who knows what's in there?'

Again, he gives her his thoughtful, assessing look. 'These old houses,' he says. 'You got to go slow, treat them with respect.'

She looks at the room full of river-flattened stones, not understanding. 'But we can put them back,' she says.

'Sure,' he says, doubtfully. 'You can.' But his expression says otherwise. She lets him take the iron bar from her. Their hands linger before separating. He sees how slender her fingers are, how delicate her wrists with their flash of fine gold chain.

'Besides,' he says, 'it's heavy work.' He looks at her lovely shoulders, her little girl's breasts, her tiny waist. Suddenly, he is thinking of Di, looking eight months pregnant before she even started the twins. And now, well, he hasn't the words to describe her gross quantities of slack flesh. True, he's noticed other men taking a lewd interest. But as for him, he likes them slender and small, so he can pick them up and lay them on the bed, so they can curl up in his lap afterwards while he watches TV, so they can pretend to boss him around in life.

'These old houses,' he says again. 'You never know what you're going to find, but you got to go carefully, one step at a time.'

He sees she is watching him, hanging onto his every word. Momentarily, he forgets his train of thought, the way her lips are parted like that, believing him.

'A long time ago,' he starts again, then stops. It sounds like he's talking to Davey, telling him a bedtime story. He picks up the shoe and studies it. 'You know they put these things in on purpose,' he tells her. He picks up the plate and turns it over, looking for a mark. He laughs, deprecatingly. 'To keep the evil spirits off.' Then he regrets saying it. She'll think he's a bullshitter. But she is still looking at him, giving him credit for knowing.

'So there could be other things?' she says.

'There could be,' he agrees again, making it sound like there couldn't. The last thing he wants is to spend the morning heaving up flagstones and then having to put them all back again.

'Oh,' she says, disappointed, turning away from him.

'Besides,' he lightens up, 'you don't want a whole lot of bad luck, do you?'

As he hoped, she turns back and grins. 'That's rubbish,' she says. 'You know it is.' She leans across to pick up the clay pipe, delicately brushing her breast across his bare forearm. Her gesture is careless, sexy in the way he likes best.

There's no doubt about it now, he thinks. All these weeks he's been coming to the house, he's given her more than enough time. He eases his left hand towards her right breast. The phone rings off in the distance, in the other part of the house.

She jumps up and starts for the door then changes her mind. She glances back and catches him looking at her buttocks. His look is rapacious, single-minded, and he makes no attempt to hide it.

Ignoring the phone, she waits in the doorway. 'Everything's falling apart,' she tells him, speaking quickly. The look has made her a little nervous. She fingers the beads at her neck. Her fingers appraise them, as if surprised to find them there. It's true, everything is falling apart, paint, plaster, gutters, wires. 'Guess you've got enough to do without adding to the list.' She looks again at the messed-up floor.

'List?' he says.

'Well, you know,' she answers.

'Sure,' he agrees, 'whatever you want.' Pretending not to hear like that, it's a good sign, very good. Most women, a phone is not something to be ignored, even in the bedroom, even when you're about to do it, something a man would never do. Take Di, for instance, *It might be serious*, she'd say. *Someone might be hurt and then how would you feel?* Well, he'd feel fine, just fine, thank you.

'Want to answer that?' he says, magnanimously.

But the phone suddenly stops. Clive waits and when she doesn't move, he again squats down. With his bare hands, he manoeuvres a second stone loose. The muscles in his arms strain handsomely and he spreads his legs further apart to strengthen his effort. She gives him a smile that can mean only one thing and steps back into the room. The next thing he is lifting the huge stone onto his knees and rising to a standing position at the same time. His movements are slow and calm, like he knows what he's doing, and, even if he didn't, it wouldn't matter because everything in life is a foregone conclusion in his favour anyway. He laughs. But the stone is too heavy for him and he drops it. All the time he is watching her.

One step, she knows, one step forward and that will be it. But Sarah has, without warning, found herself thinking about the Italian teacher, Raftiche, and his wisecracks. Funny man, the things he said have stayed in her mind, about being miserable in a small place, about the kids sucking the guts out of a cigarette. If only he dressed a bit better. If only he wasn't quite so, well, odd. And if only he didn't have a thing going on with that weird little secretary, that more than anything.

Clive laughs and wipes his hands on his thighs. 'Now we've done it,' he says. 'Upset the ghosts.'

He sees it was the right thing to say. Her worried look deepens, but it's no longer for real. It's for something else. And he knows exactly what that something else is.

At that moment, the phone starts up again in the other part of the house. Again she ignores it. She is frowning prettily at the messed-up floor. 'Let me try.' She bends down but he takes her upper arm.

'Steady on,' he says.

She sees how large his hands are, large enough to span her arm with some left over.

'This is man's work,' he says, not releasing her. Instead, he bends into her hair and breaths in her scent, making no attempt to hide what he's doing. He wants her to mention the phone so that he can be good about it, generous. He wants to be good to her.

But she doesn't move away. Instead she looks around at the floor. 'I'm really sorry about all this,' she says. 'I thought there would be something else.'

He leans in closer to her and slides his hand up her arm to where it is warm and slightly moist. He gives her his generous, capable look. 'A couple of hours' work. Don't worry about it.'

'I was sure there'd be something else,' she repeats.

He is ready with his concerned, regretful look.

She holds his eyes. Then she steps closer, touching his arm lightly with her fingers. 'Thanks for being so nice about it.'

To be fair, she never plans the course of events with these men. She merely slips her feet into love's waiting sandals. She read that in a magazine. Some joke, she thinks contemptuously. But the contempt, strangely, is for herself and not for the writer.

'Ah,' he answers, slipping his arms around her, a little surprised. He has still expected her to turn away from him. He is thinking, it just goes to show you can't plan these things. Like a good piss-up, the really good piss-ups are always unplanned. And then he lifts her high off the messed-up floor in an embrace. 'Ah,' he sighs, feeling how light she is, how lithe, how willing. But the phone is again ringing. He senses the flicker of concern in her, an imperceptible drawing away. 'Answer it,' he says, knowing he could not come back from her missing something serious, maybe something with one of the children. 'Go,' he says, pushing her gently away. There's time.

★★★

Vanessa is standing at her kitchen window, which overlooks the back garden next door. Since seeing the boy climb in the window, she finds herself looking a little too often. Of course she understands she is just keeping an eye out, as any good neighbour would, especially since James refused to let her call the police. He was actually angry at her. How was she to know? It was dark and the boy could have been anyone. What right has he to be angry at her?

She loves him of course, that goes without saying. But here she can't finish the thought except to say that the girl, Amy, has done it on purpose. The phone ringing and ringing the one time they can find to be together, what with her, the pathetic Sarah, needing him at all hours because of the house and the car and the boy running away like that. That's what kids do, don't they? They know somehow and then they figure out a way to spoil your happiness, unless you figure out first how to stop them, which is exactly what she intends to do. And, even if he didn't answer the phone that one time, she could tell he wanted to. Besides, everyone knows that asthma is mostly emotional. She, Amy, brings it on herself just to get attention. That's what kids do. Everyone knows that.

The garden is empty and still. He's late. Well, she's not waiting around for him to call and cancel again. Of course she understands he loves his children. That's to be expected. But that doesn't mean he can treat her like second best. She understands it is why she has never married. She is not willing to be second best to anything or anyone, like her friends who come way down the list in comparison to children and mothers-in-law and cars, even to dogs. Well, not her. She understands it is hard work keeping up her standards the way she does and also that the harder you work, the luckier you get, which has now proved to be true. James is her luck.

★★★

The following day, when Clive comes back to work at the wrecked farmhouse, she is not there. He stands in the kitchen. 'Fuck it,' he says. After their embrace yesterday, he has expected to find her here waiting, preferably in bed, preferably naked. Maybe he shouldn't have let that chance slip by just because of a ringing phone. He moves the stones back into position and knocks them down. It takes him less than ten minutes to replace everything as it was, though the floor now has a careless look it didn't have before. Then he wipes the plate, the pipe, the spectacle frames and the shoe with a new white tea towel he finds by the sink. Without their coating of mud, they are tatty and ugly. Without her here in the room with him, they are suddenly less interesting. He places them in the centre of her antique farmhouse table. It too is dirty and uneven, like the floor. The floor's a mess. The number of times he's told her you want to put as much concrete between you and those stones as fast as you can. But she won't have it. She thinks he's being funny. Unlike Di, Di appreciates a nice bit of vinyl. You used to be able to eat Sunday dinner off Di's vinyl, when they were first married. Now, well, let's just say there's not as much he can take for granted as he thought he could.

He turns his back on all the mess of it and goes through to the front of the house. He sees that the hippie has done a good job on the windows in the big room. That makes a change. But the ceiling plaster's falling out. Half the floor joists are rotten. The place is a shit-heap. He shoulders the warped morning room door open, springing the hinges loose from the frame. 'Fuck it,' he says. Then he goes back to the kitchen and stares restlessly at the coarse, misshapen floor. 'Fuck her,' he says.

He picks up a letter from the table next to him and reads the name, James Sacheveral. Carelessly, he tosses it back. Funny the way she never talks about him. Some women it's my husband this and my husband that, but she has never mentioned him, not once. That's a good sign. And he's never around, except maybe sometimes at the weekends. James, a nice name, smart, professional, unlike his name, Clive, which is corruptible, spivvish. He looks at the broken door, the fallen plaster, the unpacked boxes. Again he picks up the letter and this time he puts it in his pocket. 'Fuck it,' he says again.

★★★

On Saturday morning, as arranged, Mr Raftiche is driving Ruby to the hospital in the big Midlands city to see her sister, that is the one that's expecting the twins. The other sister, the hippie, he pushes from his mind, knowing he has no chance of resisting her should she decide, as he has seen her do with other men, to make herself available to him. 'You could, you know,' he is telling Ruby. 'There's nothing to it.' They are talking about driving and about her maybe learning.

Suddenly he slows and twists sideways to stare at a young woman sitting on a low wall by the side of the road. 'My God,' he says. She is wearing a full-length black velvet skirt and a tiny tight top with a number of scarves wound round her neck and shoulders. Her hair is longer than he remembered but the curls are the same. As the car slows, she jumps to her feet. 'My God,' he says again. It is her, Sarah, the goddess.

She bends and looks into the car, momentarily at a loss. It is not what she has expected. Unnerved, she throws her hair over her shoulders causing her beads to clatter, a tinny, atonal sound. She arranges her layers of bright scarves, which oddly produce the same little series of off-pitch musical noises. In movement there is a twinkle about her. 'I thought no one would ever come,' she says. 'But it's you.'

'Mrs Sacheveral,' he looks at her, unable to say more.

Up close, she is startlingly pretty, as he remembered. But now, the diva's velvet skirt, the slender, bright features. She is a star, but the star of something backstreet, a bordello or maybe a coven. He too is unnerved.

'Sarah,' she says. 'Call me Sarah.'

Ruby leans over him. 'Are you lost?' She too remembers the pretty mother from the parents' evening. But she doesn't remember that she was a hippie. Mostly she remembers Robert's look and she sees it is the same today. He's the one that's lost, not her. She also sees that, absent-mindedly, he is kneading the place in his chest over his heart. 'We thought you were a hippie,' Ruby adds.

She, Sarah, gives Ruby an odd look. 'I'm waiting for the bus,' she tells them.

'The bus,' Ruby repeats. 'Here? There aren't any buses here.'

Mr Raftiche is unable to speak. Reluctantly, he is remembering how much time it took out of his own life, being a hippie, until he put a stop to it. All that hanging around doing nothing, and how they could barely perform basic tasks such as washing and eating, without being stoned. And how they, the girlfriends, jumped into bed with anyone playing bad guitar. How he hated that, more than anything. He can't take his eyes off her. She is now more beautiful than ever, a little frightening. He does not want to think about her jumping into bed with any man like he used to be.

'There aren't any, are there?' Ruby is saying to him. He sees that she is clutching her pink straw handbag, pressing it into her skinny lap like someone is about to grab it from her.

'What?' he says, a little too sharply. Visibly, she flinches.

'Ruby's right,' he adds. 'Ruby is always right about these things, in fact about most things.' It comes to him that they are talking about rural buses about which he knows nothing. But it means he can offer her, the hippie goddess, a lift.

'Jump in,' he says. 'We'll take you.' The pain starts up in his chest, or has it been there for some while? Small, dangerous, familiar.

'But wait,' Ruby says. They are on the way to see Dianne in hospital. 'It's important. She might be having the babies right now.' She turns to Sarah. 'Where's your car?'

The pain in his chest cranks up a notch. He looks from one to the other. She is right. It is important.

'You're not going to the hospital?' Sarah grins. 'That's where I'm going.' She treats them both to a smile that stops the sun in the sky, that stops the heart in his chest.

Then she turns to Ruby. 'I don't have it,' she says, 'as usual.' It is a sore point, the way he leaves her without a car, without warning, when he could afford to do something about it, but she can't. He is punishing her and she will never forgive him for it.

On the wall behind her there is a small suitcase and a large box wrapped in girlish ribbons, clearly a present. 'Let me help you,' he says, getting out of the car. At once, Ruby follows, getting out of the other side. But in seconds, Robert has picked up the case and the package and put them in the back seat. Sarah slips in the open front door and Ruby sees that it is left to her to make her own place in the back, in fact to make her own place in the whole world, something she is well used to. Watching them, clutching her pink straw bag to her chest, she sees also that no matter how unconventional your life, like her with her gypsy clothes and beaded hair, there's nothing so conventional as when a man appears on the scene. 'Why are you wearing those clothes?' Ruby asks. 'You weren't wearing them last time we saw you.'

'Am I glad to see you,' Sarah says, ignoring Ruby's question. 'I thought no one would ever come. Is it safe, out here in the middle of nowhere?' She guesses it is a stupid question and takes off one of her scarves, revealing the pretty line of her breasts in the tiny tight top. She twists the scarf in her hands. He is staring at her, grinning like an idiot and she, Ruby, is all hunched up in the back corner like she's about to be attacked. It seems she must be his girlfriend, the way she looks at him and the way he cares about her, his kindness. If only they weren't both so strange and well, off beam somehow. Yet she takes off another scarf. Her neck is slender and girlish. She treats them both to another one of her twinkling smiles, first one then the other, twisting gracefully to do so.

★★★

Ten minutes later they are on the new motorway driving fast. Through the open window, Sarah gratefully breathes in the polluted air from the cars that speed past them. Casually, she lets her left elbow rest out the window. Casually, she turns towards the back and says, 'So, Dianne's your sister?' She doesn't know how much Dianne knows about her and Clive but guesses she is pretty smart about these things and knows a lot already. As for Ruby, she guesses she is equally stupid about the same things and probably knows nothing. And Robert, there's no telling anything about what he knows about anything. Take now, for instance, he's talking away and laughing all the time like a man possessed. If only he was a little quieter, a little less, well, weird and extravagant.

'One of them,' Ruby answers, as if defeated by the fact of having two sisters.

'You're lucky.' Sarah treats her to her warmest smile. 'I always wanted a sister.'

Robert again looks at her, the goddess, miraculously here beside him. He has no idea what she's talking about. He knows he is driving too fast, as if in the grip of some erotically charged good mood. Tentatively he presses his foot down harder on the accelerator and immediately the car responds. He lets out a whoop of laughter. He presses harder. The high-speed traffic roars past them, creating the unmistakable sense of something life-threatening.

'No,' Ruby says in the back seat. 'Don't.' But with the window open and him lost to reason, she sees there is no point in trying to get him to slow the car. She expects to die at any moment and this would be all right, to die here with him, if only she didn't have responsibilities. A mother can't die, no matter what. It isn't right. 'Please, Robert,' she whispers, 'please slow down.' But he doesn't hear.

A short while later, the green fields have given way to suburbs and Robert comes off the motorway. Stopped at the traffic lights, Sarah watches a woman walk around to the back of her house. She is carrying two bags of shopping, one in each hand. Sarah is suddenly inconsolably homesick. Without warning, she is sick for the sound of heels tapping on the pavement, and for the sound of a bus pulling away under the early evening streetlights.

The suburbs give way to city streets and they pass the acres of new cars from the factory, rows of them lined up, magnificent in their natural habitat.

Looking at them, Robert laughs. 'If I had it, I'd spend it, all at once.' He is finding it hard to think of the right words, sensible ones, to fit the situation. He knows he is talking too much nonsense, and laughing too loud. But she is so beautiful and suddenly looking so tormented. Why does he always feel like the one who comes in at the tail end of things? It is not how he wants to feel. In the mirror he sees Ruby huddled forlornly in the back. He sees how unhappy she too is, always trying to hide, always saying the wrong things. If he is coming in at the tail end of things, then where is she? Poor little sad sack, he is overcome with dismay on her behalf, on Sarah's behalf, on his behalf. It shoots through him, straight to the heart, dismay injected under the skin like a vaccine against the sickness of living. But injected how? And by whom? It is a question unwillingly called up. Absent-mindedly he massages his chest where the pain pulses with each heartbeat. Two unhappy women. He is finally silent.

★★★

At the hospital, Sarah is directed to the ward, but when she gets there she finds that Amy has gone. James has been summoned and collected her.

'We tried to call you,' the nurse speaks a little impatiently. 'She was ready to go. She's fine. Just make sure she uses her inhaler.'

Sarah lets out a sharp laugh, a little too loud. The nurse gives her a shrewd look.

It is, she thinks, exactly what James would do. Get there first, cut her out, make her feel even worse than she already does, having missed the call from the school when she had the attack, and now to miss the call from the hospital as well. She does not say any of this to the nurse, nor does she trust herself to laugh again.

She turns to leave, but once out in the corridor, someone suddenly calls her name. Sarah wheels around, and is startled to find Dianne waddling towards her. Ruby is not with her.

'I thought it was you,' Dianne says. She is pulling with her a portable drip and looks over at it rakishly. 'I'm being induced,' she tells Sarah, 'again.'

'Dianne,' Sarah exclaims, looking at the bag, the tube and finally, warily, at the unbelievable bulge of the twin babies. Whatever is in the bag, it seems to be running into Dianne's arm extraordinarily fast, as if the point is to cause her to swell to bursting point and therefore eliminate the need for a birth at all.

'What are you doing here?' Dianne says, then gets no further. She puts both hands across her bulge, with the fingers spread wide. There is a visible heaving under the flowered nightdress. She gives Sarah a wry look.

'I knew you were in.' Sarah continues to stare at the writhing lump. 'Clive told me. I came in with your sister and her friend. He gave me a lift.' Then she too gets no further. All this, the huge, distended stomach, the serious hospital paraphernalia, what is about to happen to Dianne, she too is dismayed into silence.

'Bet you thought I was having a nice rest. That's what Clive tells everyone,' Dianne says. 'I know that's what he says.'

Sarah nods her head. It is exactly what Clive has told her.

Dianne gives the drip stand a peevish shove and again follows after it with her exaggerated, lurching walk. 'What does he know?'

Sarah falls into step beside her. She has never seen anyone so heavily pregnant. It is a pregnancy with a lost woman attached as an afterthought.

'I have to walk,' Dianne says. 'It's supposed to help. Believe me, it doesn't.'

Sarah puts a hand on the dripstand to steady it. The bag is swinging wildly from side to side, causing the liquid to drip faster than ever. She has never seen a drip running in so fast.

'Are you sure this is right?' she asks.

Dianne looks at the bag. 'Nobody tells you anything,' she says. 'And if they do tell you, they get it wrong.'

She pulls open the next set of double doors and peers into the ward, as if looking for someone. 'This time yesterday, I was up in the delivery room, two centimetres dilated. Half an hour later, nothing. I undilated.'

Sarah stares at her, appalled. 'I didn't know you could do that. I mean, once you started.'

'You can't,' Dianne answers. 'That's the whole point.' She lets the door swing shut. 'There was half the doctors in the place looking up my legs,' she laughs, 'and all the medical students.' She lurches forward another couple of steps, then adds, 'Wankers. What if it was my right arm? Bet they wouldn't be so interested then.'

Again, Sarah stares at the lump, remembering herself at this time. 'I was out of it with Ben,' she tells Dianne.

'It's like football to them.' Dianne seems not to have heard. 'A long, boring wait in an uncomfortable place and maybe a goal if you're lucky.' She laughs. 'Two goals, in my case.'

Now Sarah looks at her face. She is truly surprised. This waspish humour is not what Clive has led her to believe. The things he's told her are not like this.

'Me too,' Dianne goes on. 'Last time with Davey, I was so doped up, one minute I was screaming the place down, the next thing he was there in my arms.' Her voice takes on the faraway sound of the memory of pain which, once past, has become sweet pleasure.

'Still,' Sarah says sympathetically, 'you'll be glad when it's over.'

'Glad,' Dianne answers, 'I've forgotten the meaning of the word.' Again she laughs. 'Twins.' Her laugh is both defeated and covetous at the same time.

Again Sarah puts both hands out to steady the drip. She is suddenly, unaccountably jealous. It is as sudden and as unaccountable as the homesickness that overtook her in the car. Two babies.

Having reached the end of the corridor, Dianne peers into the last of the open wards. 'You haven't seen my sister, have you?' she asks Sarah.

'Ruby?' Sarah repeats.

'She was here a minute ago,' Dianne explains. Slowly, laboriously, she turns herself and the stand around and starts the return journey. 'She's mad about him, you know, that Italian teacher.'

Sarah turns with her. Mad about him, for the third time today, something is cutting right through her, this time as if she is the helpless one and not Ruby.

'Clive says she's a messed-up schizo, but he's wrong,' Dianne says. 'She has a good heart and her life isn't easy, single mum and all that.'

'Single mum,' Sarah repeats. 'Ruby has a baby?'

Dianne laughs. 'If you could call it that. He's fifteen. Ruby was only fifteen herself.' Her voice trails off. She takes a few more steps. 'She's not my real sister. Well, half sister, same with the other one. That's real enough. If only she could figure things out a bit better, like how to lie, for example, how to live your life.'

Suddenly, Dianne stops and faces Sarah. 'You know the other day?' she asks. 'At your house?'

Sarah too stops and looks down the long dismal corridor. She knows at once what is coming. She has dreaded this since she first saw Dianne walking towards her. 'The other day?' she repeats, stalling for time.

'At your house,' Dianne tells her. 'You know, when Davey was there.'

'At my house?' Sarah again repeats.

'You'll never guess,' Dianne goes on, 'what he told me.'

Sarah is embarrassed into silence. She does not need to guess. She knows exactly what Davey will have said, about his dad, about her, about the way the two of them were together.

But surprisingly, Dianne is grinning away. 'Davey told me you were going to eat him.' She laughs. 'He thought you were, a what do you call it, a cannibal.' She laughs again.

Sarah looks at her, momentarily lost for words. 'A cannibal?' she finally says. She is thinking back to the little boy sitting there at the table with the cut-up rabbits, and then the way he kept running off and disappearing.

Dianne's lump heaves with her laughter. 'He watches too much television,' she says. 'He's always scared. Every week, there's something new to be scared about.' Again, she gives Sarah the rueful look.

'A cannibal,' Sarah repeats. 'He thought I was a cannibal?'

'Isn't that something?' Dianne shakes her head in amused disbelief. 'The things he's scared of,' she repeats.

★★★

The house is empty when Sarah gets back. She sees that someone has washed the pipe, the shoe and the spectacles and left them on the grey metal plate in the centre of the kitchen table. She picks them up one by one and examines them. The pipe is cracked and bits flake off in her hands. The spectacle frames are rusted and ugly. The leather shoe has a wet, slimy feel. Altogether, they are nothing but junk. She sees that Clive has put the stones back in place, but there's something different about them. They have a clean, shiny look they didn't have before. She is surprised that he should have washed her floor as well.

In the sink, amongst the cutlery and the new tea towel, which is now covered with mud, Sarah finds the large, bent screwdriver. But when she kneels to insert it under the loose stone, she sees what it is that Clive has done. The stones are coated with a clear varnish, dry on top but still sticky in the ridges. The screwdriver barely scratches the surface. She tries four or five stones, with no success.

She picks up the plate, the pipe, the shoe, the spectacle frames and carries them through to the front of the house. She wanders from room to room until she comes to the morning room door that is hanging sideways, half off its hinges. She is sure it wasn't broken yesterday, but nothing about the house surprises her any more. This random collapse is now a part of her daily life. She is only surprised at how easily it has become commonplace.

Behind the door-frame, the lathe and plaster is pulpy. Sarah pulls the frame loose and presses the four objects into the wall until they are buried deep inside. As she works, she is not thinking about the things that have happened today, about getting a lift with Robert, and his strange laughing talk, about Ruby being mad about him and having a son of her own. No, all that was just coincidence. She straightens the door-frame and hammers it back into place with the brass fire trivet. Repairing the hinges is beyond her. No, what she is thinking about is Dianne. It is for her that she has returned these objects to something like their rightful place, to assist her in her struggle which may very well be going on at exactly this moment. What she is also thinking about is flirting, which is a trivial thing, silly even, and how it's funny the way people only flirt with things that are dead serious, things like disaster, madness, and other people's husbands.

6. DEAR DISGUSTED

In terms of tears shed per square inch, Dianne's bedroom outdoes both hospitals and funeral parlours put together. She is in bed, writing and crying.

Dear Diary. A salty drop hits the page. *I have been sent home again to wait. Everything has settled down. That shows how much they know.* A second drop lands beside the first. *I have my clothes on,* she writes. She flips through the earlier pages and reads. *Tuesday — trace of albumen, fudge slice for lunch. Wednesday — BP 160/90, bought hair spray, Clive didn't turn up, what a surprise.*

She reaches across for her outsized bottle of economy cola on the bedside table and, in doing so, knocks the lamp onto the bare pine floorboards. It smashes with an exaggerated sound like an up-close explosion. It is not what she has intended and she groans out loud. With the despairing regard for material possessions of someone who has always known want, she is sorry to have broken the lamp. The fat on the underside of her raised arm quivers with a kind of fleshy resonance, and the babies both lurch, one to the left, one to the right.

'Jesus,' she says, again groaning, but this time in pain.

The little boy, Davey, comes into the room and stares at his mother with her eyes closed and her neck held way back at an odd angle. There is an even odder heaving in her huge bulge. He understands that there are some wild animals inside her. Of course, she has told him about the babies, but he doesn't believe her. She has sat him down and told him carefully, which is what grown-ups do when they're pretending. When she talks to his father about it, she shouts and cries. He looks at the broken lamp and wonders if one of the wild animals has come out, smashed a few things, then gone back inside her again.

Dianne winces. There is a sudden sharp pain in her kidneys.

'You little buggers,' she says, turning awkwardly onto her side, without seeing the boy. She lets out a great sigh that seems to come up out of nowhere and go on forever. She reaches out and picks up the plate from the table by the bed. On the plate, there are six cream eclairs. She is thinking about the evening meal in the hospital yesterday, one half of a small pork pie, one lettuce leaf and one tomato, not even sliced. The cream from the first eclair slides down her throat and is gone, but the taste of the chocolate lingers. Then, this morning, the nurse brought her a wisp of cornflakes and sugarless tea. She eats the second eclair in two bites, not bothering to chew.

The next spasm of pain takes up position higher than usual and starts to gather momentum. She eases her back over to the other side and sees the little boy watching her. Quickly, she brushes the tears and chocolate from around her mouth.

'Davey,' she exclaims. 'Where did you come from?'

The child runs across the room and solemnly picks up the diary from the floor, where it has fallen amongst the debris, and hands it to her.

'Thank you,' she says, studying his serious face. A couple of months ago, you couldn't shut him up. He was chattering away before his feet hit the ground in the morning, rabbiting on all day, even gabbing in his sleep. It was like having a happy little bird in the house. Now, he just creeps up and stares.

'Cat got your tongue?' she says to him.

Davey shakes his head, but does not answer.

'Take that out,' she says, pulling his fingers from his mouth. She reaches over and draws him up into the bed with her. It almost seems he is resisting her embrace, but then straightaway he burrows out of sight, under the covers.

Again, Dianne sighs. She eats the third eclair and the fourth with no loss of momentum. Absent-mindedly, she brushes at a crease of cream caught in the folds of fat under her chin.

She opens the notebook to a clean page. This time, she writes, *Dear Giselle.* Then she crosses out the name and writes in *Honoria. Giselle* is hopelessly wrong, but *Honoria* isn't much better. She is looking for a reassuring name, and it is surprisingly hard to find one. Finally, she crosses out *Honoria* and writes in *Inga.*

On the page, it is a small name, but immediately it carries weight. *Dear Inga*, she writes. *I have a problem. I am slim, five foot six, and eight stone. I can eat anything I want, but lately I have noticed a small amount of cellulite on the backs of my thighs and I am worried that this is just the beginning of serious trouble. What should I do? P.S. My sister is very heavy.* She goes back, underlines *very* and *heavy*, then adds a last sentence. *One of her thighs would feed Bob Cratchit's family for a year. Ha! Ha!*

She flips over to a clean page and writes, *Dear worried. It is good you have retained your sense of humour. Humour helps us to deal with life's problems. It sounds like you may be facing the beginnings of anorexia or bulimia. I urge you to seek help. As for the cellulite you mention, my advice is not to worry about it. Enjoy life, develop your sporting interests, get in touch with old friends. I want you to try repeating every day, problem? what problem?*

Dianne smiles derisively as she writes. She knows she does not like this Inga, a self-assured woman who knows how to tie a scarf, mints in the handbag, a thin woman.

'Yea, sure,' she says, looking down at her own thighs splayed out on the bed. One would feed Bob Cratchit's family and both his next-door neighbours for a year. 'Problem?' she says. 'What problem?' But the way she says it is nothing like the way Inga said it.

Davey shivers at the sound of his mother's voice, and pokes his head out from under the covers.

She draws him closer. 'Well, if it wasn't the cat, who was it then?' He does not answer but stares at her with solemn, frightened eyes.

She again reaches over for the 2-litre bottle of cola on the table. When she leans back to drink, it is as if the whole earth moves and Davey has to hold on tight to her sleeve to keep from being pitched off the bed.

From the same table, she picks up a small, flat packet and absent-mindedly reads the label. Again, she reaches for the notebook. *Dear Inga*, she writes. *What do you think of these new slimming patches? My sister is really trying to do something about her weight. But her husband says the only way slimming patches are going to help is if she sticks them over her eyes so she can't find the fridge. Ha! Ha!*

Underneath, Inga writes back to her, in large, humourless script, *Dear Doubtful. Excess weight can lead directly to a number of serious medical*

problems, diabetes, high blood pressure, even cancer. So, of course you must encourage
your sister in her efforts. She might find it helpful to join a local Weight Watchers group.

'Yea, sure,' Dianne interrupts. She opens the box and peels a patch
from the strip. She lifts her shabby maternity dress and slaps the patch
onto her upper thigh with the flat of her hand. The tiny, white square
is lost in the expanse of quivering, blue-veined flesh. She peels off
another patch and slaps it on beside the first. The two white squares are
still totally insignificant. She peels off a third and a fourth, arranging
them in a neat pattern. When she has finished, all eight patches are
firmly in place, spread across both thighs.

Davey looks at his mother's legs. He is not at all surprised at what
she has done, though it is more bandages than he has ever been allowed
to have at one time. The animals in her suddenly heave themselves
awake and again she cries out.

'You little buggers,' half laughing, half in pain. She rests both
hands on her bulge. 'They're kicking the stuffing out of me,' she says to
him.

Davey slides towards the edge of the bed, but she reaches out and
pulls him back. She puts both his hands on her stomach and holds
them in place.

'Feel that?' she asks.

Instantly, the little boy recoils in horror. He slips from her hold
and scrambles frantically backwards.

She draws in her breath to call him back, to reassure him, but
before she can find the right words, he is running down the stairs. She
frowns at the empty doorway. The health visitor has told her to put
the child's hands on to feel the babies when they move. She has said it
will make him less jealous later. But, every time, this is what happens.
She can hardly believe his terrified face. He was scared out of his
mind.

A wave of nausea sweeps through her, meeting up with the pain in
her kidneys. There is also a familiar burning, just below her left breast.
She groans, and again eases herself into a less miserable position, at the
same time reaching under the pillow for the pack of ginger creams. The
remaining two eclairs have lost their appeal. Propped uncomfortably
on one elbow, she eats six biscuits, fast, one after the other, washing

them down with alternate swigs of cola from the bottle. Slowly, the nausea recedes and the burning fades to a comfortable warmth.

Then, reluctantly, she rolls herself to the edge of the bed and lowers her swollen feet to the floor. She is worried about Davey. The house is too quiet. No sooner has she thought this, than the doorbell rings. She transfers her weight forward but sways back again in a punishing rush of blood pressure.

The doorbell rings a second time.

'Davey!' she shouts, lurching towards the stairs. 'Open the door.' She turns quickly away from the sight of herself in the dressing table mirror.

The bell rings a third time, little impatient bursts. At the top of the stairs Dianne's bad knee gives way and she slips sideways, jabbing her lump into the iron pipe banister that Clive has brought back from one of his jobs. The babies kick out angrily, aiming at the sore spot on the underside of her kidneys. She groans, waits for the pain to recede, then slowly makes her way down the stairs, one step at a time. Through the opaque glass in the front door she can see the silhouette of a small woman or a young girl.

'Davey!' she calls out again, but there is no sign of him.

'Are you all right?' the woman calls back through the closed door.

Briefly Dianne stops. It is a familiar voice though she can't at first place it, maybe someone she knows but doesn't like. She unlocks the door and opens it no more than an inch.

'Are you sure you're all right?' Sarah asks again.

Dianne stares in surprise. Here is the last person she expected to see, someone she hardly knows at all, someone she is hardly likely to get to know at all, and twice in two days.

'Clive said you were sent home,' Sarah says, smiling prettily.

Dianne pulls the door open. She knows Clive talks to this pretty woman while he's working. Without moving her eyes, Dianne takes in the tight jeans, the tiny white silk top, the pretty curly hair, swept up and tied with a scarf like a Russian peasant or one of those women who worked in the fields during the war. What exactly can she know about working in the fields? Nothing, that's what.

'I picked these for you,' Sarah says, handing Dianne a large basket.

'I don't know what they are,' she laughs. A delicate gold chain slides forward on each slender wrist. Rings flash.

Dianne takes the basket from her, barely glancing at the decaying berries. She has noticed how hard this other woman is having to struggle to keep her eyes off the again convulsing bulge. Well, let her suffer. 'I'm OK,' she says. 'Fed up.'

Sarah again laughs prettily. 'I know,' she says. 'Believe me.'

Dianne does not believe her.

'It seems like it's never going to end.' Sarah shifts her weight from one dainty foot to the other. Her toenails are painted silver. 'At the end.'

'Yea,' Dianne agrees.

Sarah lifts the strap of her pretty handbag higher onto her graceful shoulder and waits before speaking. 'You know your sister?' she says. 'You know yesterday when you were looking for her at the hospital?'

Dianne watches her sullenly. In her experience if people have to lead up to things it's not something you want to hear.

Sarah looks past Dianne into the dark messy room. As usual all the curtains are closed. 'I hope you don't mind my asking,' she asks. 'But what is her son called?'

Dianne shifts her bulk so that Sarah can't see in. The place is a dump. This is turning out to be an odd conversation, odder even than their encounter in the hospital yesterday. 'Nick,' she answers. 'His name is Nicholas.' But in fact she hasn't heard anyone call him that for years. The kids call him Carling, after the beer. She's not going to tell her this. Ruby says it's because he always wears black but she knows this isn't true. It's because he gets the stuff they all drink and smoke from the Paki shop where they ask no questions. She isn't going to tell Ruby this either.

'Does he wear black a lot?' Sarah asks.

'Sometimes,' Dianne shrugs.

'I think I know him,' Sarah says, frowning. 'He's friends with Ben.'

Friends with Ben, that's bad news. But again she's not going to say anything. She has enough problems of her own to be getting on with. Apart from feeling sorry for Ruby, it's nothing to do with her.

The conversation falters. Sarah twists the dark gold band on her wedding finger. Dianne looks back over her shoulder. Where is Davey?

'Well,' Sarah says. 'I guess I'd better go. If you're sure you're OK?'

But she doesn't move away. Instead she rests one hand lightly on Dianne's arm. 'Good luck,' she says. 'With everything.'

Dianne watches her turn aside. Strangely, the feel of her touch lingers. It was so quick, so unexpected, that it's already taken on the value of something rare and unusual. Dianne watches her skim down the path. From behind she is just as pretty. The expensive label jeans are tight but not too tight. They show off what's there but not so as to flaunt it. It's obvious that all the men in this neighbourhood will be thinking about her at night, in bed.

Dianne stares down at her own protruding front. And as for Clive, he's always been good at giving women what they want and persuading them that what they want is what he has to give. If only he wasn't quite so good at it. Then she looks down at the basket in her hands. There are two large green insects stuck together on top of the messed-up berries. They appear to be mating. Dianne groans.

In the dark room Davey is watching cartoons on television. Dianne lowers herself onto the swaybacked couch and again sighs deeply. After a few moments she takes the diary out of the pocket of her dress.

Dear Inga, she writes. *I think my husband is having an affair.* Unasked for, the tears well up in her eyes and slide caressingly over her bloated cheeks. It's the only caress that has been on offer for some time.

I'm sure he's having an affair, she writes. *What I want to know is, should I divorce him?*

And Inga writes back. *Dear Heartbroken. Don't be too quick to reach for the divorce papers. Marriage is a sacred and valuable institution, worth working at. Have you tried a marriage guidance counsellor?*

Painfully Dianne readjusts her position. Now one of the babies is lying on her bladder. Again she groans and remembers her mother's advice to always marry a man who loves you more than you love him. It seems that's a sort of marriage guidance. But she knows without doubt what her mother's advice would be if she knew about Clive and Sarah.

'Divorce the bastard,' she says out loud.

The next thing she knows, the back door has slammed and her mother is standing in the centre of the room.

'Who's getting divorced?' she asks, deliberately not looking at

Dianne. She bends down to hug Davey and her over-permed, scouring-pad hair brushes his delicate skin. He makes no response. 'Anyone I know?' she asks, casually.

'It's no one,' Dianne answers.

'Oh yes?' her mother says, instinctively recognising a lie. She has, after all, had years of practice herself.

'It's no one,' Dianne repeats.

'Well, that's all right then.' Her mother is moving around the room collecting the scattered little boy's clothes and shabby crockery. Like her daughter, she is a big woman, carrying too much weight and uncomfortable with it.

'Clive all right?' she asks, even more casually.

Dianne ignores the question. Her mother goes into the kitchen and there is the sound of water running into the sink. She comes back into the living room talking.

'Only he's never here.'

'Of course he's here.' Dianne interrupts. Already her voice is sullen. 'He's here all the time.' Her mother has been in the house two minutes. But that's what she does. She asks questions until Dianne is fourteen again. Then she goes all hurt and huffy and says, 'Well, I don't know.'

'Well, I don't know,' Dianne's mother says, turning away. She pulls together an armful of magazines. 'I only asked.'

But then she doesn't say anything else. She is staring at the magazine on top of the pile and Dianne sees her shoulders stiffen. Too quickly her mother drops the magazines and leaves the room. Again Dianne sighs. So Clive has left them lying around as usual, what he calls his tit mags, or worse, the catalogues. And now it has gone all quiet out in the kitchen and she'll have to go out and explain.

Instead Dianne picks up the notebook. *Dear Inga,* she writes. *My husband has a disgusting habit. Really it's a perversion. I can hardly tell you.* She imagines Inga reading the letter — yes, yes, go on, a perversion?

It's this, Dianne writes. *He reads porn magazines, all the time. Should I divorce him?*

And Inga writes back. *Dear Disgusted. I don't think you need to make too much of a few magazines. After all, it's harmless enough. My advice is to turn a blind eye to your husband's little habit.*

But before Dianne finishes the sentence, her mother is again in the room. She is carrying Sarah's basket, examining it in the dim light.

'What are these?' she asks. Then, without pausing, she says, 'He's lost weight, you know.'

Dianne looks over at Davey. He hasn't touched the chips she made him at lunch. As usual, he has all four fingers stuffed in his mouth.

'It's the smoking,' her mother adds.

Dianne lets go a sharp laugh.

'He shouldn't smoke,' her mother says. 'And he works too hard.'

Dianne raises herself up and reaches for one of her own cigarettes. If only her mother hadn't mentioned them. Upright, the pain in her back is worse and now the babies are pressing on her lungs as well as on her bladder. She is curiously out of breath.

'Funny currants.' Her mother brings the basket over and puts it in Dianne's lap for her to look. 'These are never redcurrants.'

Dianne sees the bugs have finished copulating and moved on. The pain too has moved, around to the front as if someone is tightening a belt across her middle. Now that she thinks about it, the belt has been there all day slowly getting tighter and tighter. She reaches down to ease it and the pretty basket flips over in a neat arc, landing upside down across her knees.

'What did you do that for?' her mother exclaims.

'What do you mean what did I do that for?' Dianne snaps back at her. At the same time she starts to shiver, as if suddenly exposed naked to a freezing wind.

Her mother sees her daughter's teeth are chattering.

'You can't be cold,' she accuses.

Dianne is shaking too hard to answer. And the tightness around her middle has increased.

Her mother bends to scoop the berries back into the basket. They are overripe and there is a surprising amount of bright juice on her hands, on Dianne's dress and on the carpet.

'These are never redcurrants,' she repeats. Then suddenly she stops and stares at her shivering daughter.

'Oh Lord,' she says.

Again Dianne lets go the same sharp little laugh. And now her mother too has started to shake, or at least the flesh on her top half, which has taken on a life of its own.

Dianne looks down at her feet. She is concentrating on trying to stop the wet coming out but, whatever muscles she tightens, it makes no difference. It just keeps seeping out. Amazingly there is nothing visible on the floor.

'Your waters broke,' her mother says, also looking at nothing.

Dianne jerks her head up, surprised. 'How did you know that?'

Her mother looks back, equally surprised. She has no idea how she knew. The two women stare at each other and shake. Slowly Dianne begins to grin. Her mother frowns in disbelief. The grin widens until it bursts out as another sharply bitter laugh.

'Go and call Clive,' Dianne gasps.

Obediently her mother leaves the room but returns almost at once with the phone, on its long stretched cord, in her hands. Her look of confusion has deepened. 'Where?' she asks. 'Where is he?'

Laughing and holding her breath at the same time, Dianne is unable to answer. She knows she should be panting through this first real contraction. She has practised it often enough. But right now, it is pretty much the stupidest thing she has ever heard of.

'Where is he?' her mother asks again.

At last Dianne exhales. She grabs the phone and dials the yard number. Someone will get him for her.

Her mother steps back, wary. All this laughing, it's a bit off. 'Maybe you should call the ambulance,' she suggests. 'Twins is not a laughing matter.'

A recorded voice informs Dianne the number she has dialled is not available.

'You should call the ambulance,' her mother repeats. Uneasily, she takes another step backwards. She is now standing in the middle of the spilled berries and hasn't noticed.

But already Dianne is dialling another number. 'I'm going to tell Clive,' she grins. 'I want to.'

This time Sarah answers straightaway. 'Dianne,' she exclaims. Caught off guard, there is the unmistakable sound of guilt in her voice. 'Well, hello,' she says brightly. 'This is a nice surprise.'

'Put Clive on,' Dianne demands. She has now managed to heave herself to her feet and she is holding the floor lamp with one hand for balance.

Davey stares hard at the television. His little shoulders are again stiff with fear. He sees that his mother has wet herself and the couch. It is not something she has ever done before. And his grandmother is making a mess on the carpet, standing in some berries, which is something she has never done before. They will soon be shouting at him, when they notice.

'He's not here,' Sarah tells Dianne. 'I mean he's here today, but he's gone out.'

'Gone out?' Dianne repeats.

'To get some supplies,' Sarah tells her. Then she asks, 'Is it the babies?'

Dianne doesn't answer. She is thinking Clive gets his supplies from anywhere and everywhere. He could be miles away.

She turns to her mother, but in between deciding she is right about the ambulance and getting the words out, everything inside her suddenly stops. Astonished, she rests both hands on her lump. The tightness is gone. The pressure on her bladder, the ache in her lungs, all gone. Again she laughs. She feels wonderful.

Her mother watches. This is like no other labour she has ever seen before. But then again, you never know. Labour, it's like entering a wilderness, a time before anyone knew anything about anything.

Sarah's voice on the phone is asking, 'I'll come, shall I? Do you want me to come?'

'No,' Dianne tells her. 'It's nothing.' She hands the phone to her mother at the same time letting go of the lamp, which crashes to the floor. Davey draws his little shoulders up as if about to be struck and stares hard at the television.

'It's nothing,' Dianne repeats. She walks fast towards the kitchen. 'A false alarm.' She smiles ruefully over her shoulder.

Her mother follows, still holding onto the phone. 'I'm calling the ambulance,' she says, stopping when Dianne stops. 'Your waters broke. I'm calling them.'

'Don't you dare,' Dianne orders her. She pulls things fast from the fridge, seemingly at random. 'I ought to know a false alarm when I meet one. I've been in and out of that place so many times I'm sick of the sight of it.' She slaps the bacon in the frying pan.

'Davey!' she calls in the new commanding voice. 'You want bacon?' The little boy doesn't answer.

'Why should I go in there just to sit around with them looking up my legs every five minutes?' Dianne asks. 'I can sit around here and look up my own legs.' Her words are now coming faster, her movements getting more urgent. 'I hate that place,' she adds. 'Besides, it's not time yet.'

Her mother takes the phone back into the other room and dials the ambulance.

Davey hears her say, 'Of course it's an emergency. It's twins.' He puts both hands in his mouth and stares at the wet footprints all over the carpet. The next thing, his mother is screaming in the kitchen, a long drawn-out scream like nothing he has ever heard before, except maybe the foxes under his window at night, and other night-time wild animals, which he knows are killing each other.

At the same moment there is a light tapping at the back door. Without waiting, Sarah lets herself in. She sees the mother and daughter clinging together in the middle of the kitchen. 'I knew it,' she says. 'I knew it was the babies.'

Dianne is moaning through the downward spiral of a dying contraction and her mother is pressing a dripping tea towel to her daughter's forehead.

'I knew it,' Sarah says again. 'I've got the car.'

When she can finally begin to breathe, Dianne allows herself to be led out to the waiting car. Though she can walk perfectly well, the two women are supporting her on either side. A moment later Sarah reappears running. She grabs the little boy by the hand and lifts him to his feet. He does not resist.

'Isn't it exciting?' she says, laughing with excitement. 'Two babies.' But he is terrified far beyond speech and doesn't answer.

★★★

A short while later, an ambulance pulls up in front of the house. Getting no answer at the door, the driver and paramedic go around to the back and into the now smoke-filled kitchen.

'Jesus,' the older of the two says, snatching the frying pan off the heat. There is a scattering of small yellow flames spread across the greasy cooker.

'I got it,' the younger man says. He picks the sodden tea towel from the floor and drops it onto the flames.

At the same time Clive's van pulls up behind the ambulance. Without turning off the engine, he jumps out, runs into the deserted kitchen and stops dead. The ambulance men are now standing in the smokey doorway of the equally deserted living room. Unsurprised, they register his presence. They are well used to the histrionics of expectant fathers, or the indifference.

'You the one that called us?' the older man asks.

The younger man goes across and turns off the blaring television. His partner follows, picking his way through the scattered chips and crushed berries, stepping across the up-ended floor lamp. He pulls open one set of curtains and lifts the window. In the harsh afternoon light, the little room is cruelly exposed.

'Your wife the one having the baby?' The older man again turns to Clive.

The younger man stares at the wet patch in the swaybacked couch. There's something been going on here all right. Still Clive doesn't speak. He too is staring at the mess in front of him. Lately things have been a bit slack, sure, but this, you used to be able to eat Sunday lunch off Di's floor.

The older man picks up Sarah's basket and studies the broken berries. He brings it over to his partner. 'These deadly nightshade?' he asks.

The two men examine the fruit. Clive stares at the strangely vacant room. Despite their presence, the three of them, the room is uninhabited. 'Jesus,' he finally says. 'What the fuck?'

★★★

At the hospital, the two midwives are undressing Dianne, who is now floppy with gas and air. They are staring at the white patches on her thighs.

'Maybe an allergy?' one of them says.

The other drops Dianne's stained dress with distaste onto the chair. She too stares at the patches. 'So many of them,' she adds.

Dianne clutches the mask to her face. She will not let them take it away from her and they have given up trying. Two more nurses enter the room and come straight across to the raised bed, followed almost immediately by two young doctors.

'This the twins?' one of the doctors asks. He is brightly curious, never having been in on the birth of twins before, that is never vaginally. He gives this one ten minutes before she abandons the attempt. Two more young men, students, enter and come across to the bed. There are now nine people in the room and Dianne is holding her breath in agony at the peak of another contraction.

★★★

Down the long corridor from the labour room, Sarah is standing at the window with Dianne's mother. Davey is sitting motionless on a grey plastic chair some distance away. The two women are watching a small group of mothers outside in the courtyard, in the shade, with their new babies in their arms.

'I didn't know until I went back for my check-up,' Sarah is in the middle of explaining. 'Not really.'

Dianne's mother turns to her. 'But it all worked out,' she says. 'Your boy's a strapping big lad.'

'Oh no, not Ben,' Sarah says fast. 'My second, my little girl.'

Dianne's mother looks quickly away. She is not sure she understands what this woman who employs her son-in-law is doing here or what she is trying to tell her.

'I breast fed,' Sarah says.

'That's right,' Dianne's mother agrees. 'Breast is best.'

The two women watch the new mothers in the shady courtyard. After a long while, Sarah says, 'I went to the inquest, you know. They said it was no one's fault.' Then she adds, 'I wanted to go.'

Dianne's mother glances sideways at the pretty, slender woman beside her. She thought that might be it, but hoped it wasn't. Why is it always the thin, pretty ones it happens to? How do you explain that? As if they've been singled out for punishment.

'They said it was just one of those things,' Sarah again adds. How harmless the words sounded at the time, failure to thrive. Even now, more than ten years later, it doesn't sound like something you die of. Why didn't anyone say? Maybe they'd seen it all before, all those babies. What's another one, more or less?

'I'm sure you did your best,' Dianne's mother says. She knows the words are less than nothing. Not many days go by when she doesn't think about her own tiny baby boy, born too soon and with them for less than a week.

'What I want to know,' Sarah says, 'is why no one told me. If I'd known, I'd have done something.'

Dianne's mother stares rigidly out the window. 'There was probably nothing you could do,' she answers. Nervously, she looks back at her grandson, sitting there so good and so quiet.

'I really didn't know,' Sarah insists. 'When I went back for my check-up and there were all the other babies that were born the same time as mine.' She stops. She is remembering sitting in the clinic waiting room with the other mothers. That was the first moment she did know. Their babies were pink and bonny. They had doubled their birth weight and were now wearing proper clothes, little trews and dresses. They screamed like there was no tomorrow. And she sat there with her dark-haired little girl whose head was still grossly misshapen from the birth, and whose face was wizened and bright yellow. She held one tiny, clawed, yellow hand and listened to that limp cry like a lost kitten – mew, mew, mew. She sat there and was *embarrassed*. Remembering that, she has not forgiven herself, even after all this time.

'Then I knew,' Sarah says. She waits. 'Then we adopted Amy,' she finally adds.

Dianne's mother does not know what else to say. Sometimes it's best to just let them talk it all out. She doesn't mind listening. And she can see that, while the baby herself has become a memory, the loss of the baby has grown strong and robust. Nervously she glances at the pretty, slender woman.

But Sarah has nothing more to say. In silence the two women watch the new mothers and babies outside in the shady courtyard, while at the opposite end of the corridor, the anaesthetised Dianne is being prepped for her Caesar and two perspex cots are waiting ready on the other side of the room.

7. ROBERT IN THE TRAFFIC, RUBY IN THE RAIN

At the sound of her voice, Mr Raftiche twists around and stares in surprise.

'Ruby,' he exclaims, registering an instinctive disdain for the way she is forever tiptoeing after him. But the trouble is, his contempt always ends up rebounding on himself instead. 'So,' he says more kindly, 'nice morning for a walk.'

She, for her part, is staring at the stick in his hand, a look of dismay on her face. Then she giggles girlishly.

'Oh that,' he sighs, bending forward to prize the compacted dog shit from the deep, fancy treads of his trainer. 'You see I was not exaggerating,' he says. He is sure she remembers, though it was not one of his more memorable jokes. She's a funny soul, always noticing things and storing them up. It wouldn't surprise him if she had a little notebook somewhere, 'Mr Raftiche's jokes', probably in pink ink, probably by her bed. No, more likely 'Robert's jokes', in her fat, juvenile handwriting.

Thinking of fat, he pats his fat stomach and looks at her. She is wearing a high-tension pink tracksuit that hangs forlornly on her slack frame. She is, what he remembers his ex-wife explaining, one of those women who fights a losing battle with self-loathing every time she buys a new outfit. Maybe if they'd had children, his ex wouldn't have cracked those wise guy jokes all the time. Maybe the same could be said of him.

'Or in your case, a jog.' He finishes the sentence they first started out with. But she looks up at him suddenly distraught. 'A hike?' He searches for the word, after all these years living in England, still uncertain about what is forbidden and what is allowed in this strange, vigilant language that he has come to respect more than his own. 'No, a constitutional.' He draws the syllables out to make her smile which she, at last, does. 'A constitutional,' he beams. It's funny the way he can make her quiver.

'Oh no,' she quivers. 'I just like to get out in the mornings.'

He turns away from her blush and lifts his other foot. 'Oh Jesus,' he says. The excrement on this shoe is deep green as if the dog had been fed on salad. 'Would you look at that?'

She bends forward to look, which was not what he has intended, at the same time making a nervous little grab for the stick in his hand. 'I'll do that,' she says.

'Oh no, no, no.' He draws back and lowers his foot decisively. 'It's nothing,' he adds and runs a few steps on the spot to demonstrate the truth of his words. Again he pats the bouncing fat on his stomach. 'My ex always said I was selfish, greedy and lazy.' He laughs and continues to jog in place. Now Ruby starts to jog as well, lifting each foot a little too high in that funny stiff-kneed, spinsterish way of hers though she is not really a spinster and has a huge hulking son to prove it. It's just unfortunate the boy was born without brains, sitting in the back of his bottom set French class fiddling with his privates.

'In other words, I'm too fat,' Mr Raftiche laughs. Then, dismayed at the ridiculousness of what they are doing, he abruptly stops and puts one hand on her pink-sleeved arm. He feigns a breathlessness he doesn't feel.

'Every word my ex says is true.' He laughs and slaps his belly. True it may be, but, by comparison with his wife, he knows he is a virtuous man. What with the way she would get up straight after sex to make a cup of tea, every time. And those shabby old ladies' nighties with the torn lace, when the rest of the time she was stylish to a fault. Ah well, it's nothing to him anymore now. He's pleased he's been able to put it so far in the past.

He pulls his jeans up higher so that his spare tyre rises up, wobbles, then falls into place again. 'What can I do?' he asks. Yet again he laughs, and repeats the process with the jeans and the spare tyre but even now she does not respond.

'You're not fat,' she says, solemnly.

He puts his hands in his pockets and looks away. 'Ah well,' he sighs. If only she understood his little jokes, maybe even only one of them, once in a while.

In the distance, across the road that encloses the park, black smoke is rising above the trees.

'There's a fire,' he remarks, for want of anything better to say.

She too is staring at the smoke. 'It's the school,' she says. Her colourless eyes are narrowed in concentration.

'No,' he laughs. 'We couldn't be so lucky. Someone's burning their rubbish.'

'People don't burn rubbish,' she comes straight back at him. 'It's the school.'

He has to admit it's the right direction for the school.

'Of course people burn their rubbish,' he says. 'I burn my rubbish.'

But already she is moving off towards the smoke. He follows and, within a dozen steps, is struggling to keep up with her, with that funny, earnest run of hers, half bent forward, her little arms going, her little flat bottom lost in the glaring pink tracksuit.

'Hey,' he calls after her. 'Where's the fire?'

She does not slow or give any sign that she has understood. All of a sudden he is overcome with the desire for a cigarette. He stops and pats his pockets though he knows they are empty. He coughs, just thinking about it. The mucus is stuck deep down in the pits of his lungs, despite all the months of running. He knows from experience the only way to shift it is with a cigarette.

He sees she too has stopped. She is waiting by the side of the dual carriageway for a chance to cross. The traffic speeds past without a noticeable gap. He comes up beside her, breathes in the poisonous fumes and coughs deeply again. He can feel the few remaining healthy pink cells turning grey and shrivelling up.

'Not as good as a fag,' he tells her. 'But it will have to do.'

Again she does not laugh. She is frowning at something in the distance. He follows her gaze and sees that the smoke has now disappeared.

'Well,' he bends thankfully forward and leans both hands on his knees. 'I knew we couldn't be so lucky.'

But the next thing, she has darted into the road and is across in seconds. He stares in amazement. There is still no visible break in the traffic.

'Hey,' he calls to her.

She stops and turns back to find him separated from her by a wall of speeding cars. If her face was dismayed before, it is now stricken. Obeying a strength of feeling over which she seems to have no control, she steps blindly off the kerb back into the traffic. He holds up both hands in a pleading gesture.

At the same time a young woman in a sleek new car slows to allow him across. She smiles and gives him a jaunty wave, making it quite clear that it is for him she has stopped. Her elaborate earrings glint in the morning sun, giving her a kind of exaggerated glamour. It's funny, the way women take to him, women like that. He can see she's wearing a smart suit and he'll bet anything there's a smart briefcase on the seat beside her. He waves back and propels himself forward. Who knows how these things work? Ah well, there's no accounting for it.

On the other side, Ruby is waiting for him, a look of terror on her face. 'You could have been killed,' she cries.

'Me?' he answers, looking around as if there might be someone else she's talking to. It's then he sees the lorry accelerating away from them, the driver shaking his fist in anger.

Again he looks at the lorry. From the back, it appears angry. 'Sure I saw it,' he lies. How is it possible for a lorry to look angry?

'You could have been killed,' Ruby repeats. There are actual tears in her eyes.

'Nonsense.' He makes his voice sound impatient. 'There was plenty of room.' But secretly he is shaken. If a sexy smile can bring him to within an inch of death like that, what hope is there for him?

★★★

They make an odd couple, rounding the corner side by side a short while later, the tall paunchy man with his stooped shoulders and the small skinny woman dressed in lurid pink. In front of them is the empty school car park. The spread of flat-roofed, featureless buildings is likewise without sign of life. It is too early even for the caretakers.

'Oh,' Ruby says, disappointed. To get here they have skirted two vast cornfields and crossed, with difficulty, another high-speed road.

Unaccustomed to walking anywhere, she is worn out.

'Well,' Mr Raftiche scratches his head. 'So whadda ya know?' The fake gangster accent is back, unbidden. 'No smoke without fire?' he questions. 'No fire without smoke?'

Ruby looks at his large hand in amongst the thick black hair. It is the hair of a much younger man, virile and assertive.

'The walk did us good,' he sighs, willing his words back to normal. He looks off into the distance. It is a beautiful morning, briefly perfect before the dew evaporates and exhaust fumes settle over everything in a hot stale fug. Just thinking about it makes his skin itch. Ruby watches his hand absent-mindedly now scratching the side of his cheek. He has not yet shaved and each stroke produces a rich rasping sound. She cannot take her eyes off him.

'You must be exhausted,' he says without thinking.

'I walk farther than this lots of times,' she answers.

He brings his glance back to her eager little face and is overcome with sadness for her, for himself, for the day that won't stay the way it is.

'Do you?' he says kindly. Suddenly Ruby sets off through the deserted car park that leads round to the back of the school. She's walking fast as if drawn to an emergency that needs her attention. He follows and gently takes her arm, to forestall disappointment but also so that anyone who happens to be looking will not think he is embarrassed to be seen with her.

They round the corner by the art block and both smell the smoke.

'I knew it,' she says. 'I knew we'd find it.' Quickly she cuts left into a shabby tarmaced courtyard. The perimeter is ringed with a haphazard collection of loaded plastic bins, by the look of them a couple of months overdue for collection. Mr Raftiche sighs and follows. It's a dreary place, exactly where that useless son of hers hangs out with his useless friends. In fact the whole school is a dreary place that hasn't seen more than a handful of functional families for a decade. No, he doesn't mean that. It's only in bad moments that he thinks such thoughts. Most of the time he thinks the exact opposite. He sighs again and wonders how he has come to find himself, without warning, deeply depressed, sweating, breakfastless, chasing after Miss Loonytune here and her non-existent fire? He frowns, knowing he is being unfair. Who can explain these things? Who can explain anything?

Up ahead Ruby is frantically waving at him to catch up. 'Over here,' she shouts. 'I knew it.'

She is staring intently at a large grubby window half-hidden by a straggle of neglected shrubs. There are black smoke streaks around the edge and, though there is no sign of actual smoke, the smell hangs heavy in the air. As in the car park, there is no other sign of life. In fact the windows on either side are broken, vandalised no doubt in boredom or bravado by the low life her son hangs out with.

Mr Raftiche comes up beside her and peers in through the blackened window. The blinds have been burnt away but the glass is unbroken. The room is used for storage and there are stacks of discarded desks and chairs and an oddly upended table in one corner. As he looks, a boy comes out from behind the table and disappears through an open inner door. It is Ruby's son, Nicholas. Taken by surprise, Mr Raftiche does not want to believe it is the boy but of course it is so obviously the place where he would be, that there is no doubt.

He takes a step sideways to put himself between Ruby and what he has seen. 'Jesus,' he says. 'What a dump. And I thought the place couldn't get any worse.'

But Ruby has already seen. She brings both hands up to her mouth. He is afraid she is going to scream or faint and he reaches out to steady her, though she does neither.

She shakes her tiny hands up and down in frenzy. 'It wasn't him,' she says. 'It was someone else.'

Already a police car is pulling up. Already the young policewoman is getting out. Of course other people would have seen the smoke. Of course someone else would have called.

Mr Raftiche looks back at Ruby, willing her to be courageous and calm. 'It wasn't him,' Ruby says again, looking up at him.

'No, I'm sure it wasn't him,' Mr Raftiche repeats.

★★★

Shortly after this three surprising things happen. The first is that the fire turns out to have been started by an electrical fault, bare cables touching, bare cables that had been chewed by rats, or so the rumour spreads through the school. Though there was evidence of smoking and other drugs, this was quietly discounted and the building was closed and boarded up.

'Well, thank goodness,' Ruby says each time she and Robert meet in school.

'Yes, thank goodness for that,' Mr Raftiche agrees. Then, strangely, neither of them knows what else to say. 'Yes, thank goodness indeed,' Mr Raftiche repeats, rocking back on his heels away from her. You'd think there would be plenty to say after what they both know. He looks off into the distance. You'd think she would want to talk about this other thing, if only to be sure they were all right with not actually talking about it.

★★★

The second surprising thing is that, a few days later, a mother comes to visit him at the end of the day when he is alone. She comes into the classroom holding out her hand.

'Mr Raftiche.' Her gold rings flash. 'Nice to see you again.'

Their fingers close together, hers cool and lovely, his sweaty, soiled. He withdraws his hand fast. It comes to him, like a silent knife wound in the middle of his heart, that he has been thinking about her pretty much all the time since they last met.

'And you,' he says, laughing. 'Funny, I was just thinking about Saddlebags.'

She too laughs. 'I still don't know how he got that name.'

Her laugh is girlish and a little self-conscious, just the way he likes it.

He makes a deprecating gesture and presses one hand over the pain in his chest. She is prettier than he remembered and getting prettier and stranger by the day, with her new wild hair.

'It suits him,' she adds, more seriously.

Instantly he brings his look into line. She has come to discuss something serious. He places a grubby plastic chair by his desk and she sits. Today her black skirt is short and tight and she's wearing her hippie scarves like she's born to it. She crosses her legs gracefully. They are slender and girlish, exactly the kind he likes best. It's funny the way these women single him out. But whatever it is they want from him, it is almost certainly not what he wants from them.

'You don't mind my coming like this?' she asks. 'I know your time is valuable.'

He laughs and leans dangerously back in his own chair, tipping two legs way off the ground. 'My time? Valuable? You obviously don't know the first law of the staff room,' he says.

She looks back at him puzzled, prepared to be amused.

'Don't think you're somebody,' he tells her. 'If you were, you'd be out there in the real world, instead of in here.' Then he laughs, making it clear that the laughing is at his expense. But this is not what he thinks at all, in fact just the opposite. It's the little bit of long-ago Italian left in him, needing to look good and sound smart especially when he isn't either.

A tentative smile lifts the corners of her mouth. It's a beautiful mouth, sensitive, delicate, sexy. Just the kind of mouth he kisses in his dreams.

'I think you're somebody,' she tells him seriously.

He is staggered. He drops his chair forward and leans both elbows on the table. He could not be more surprised if she had ripped open her blouse and said – *Here, take me, I'm yours.*

'Ah well,' he says. 'Maybe.' He taps his hand lightly on his chest where the pain is steadily increasing.

'You know my son, Ben?' She is watching him now, waiting to judge his reaction. He keeps his face blank.

'Of course,' he answers.

'Well,' she says, 'I was wondering if I could ask you something.'

'Of course,' he repeats. 'Ask away.'

'A sort of a favour,' she says.

Again he makes the deprecating gesture with his hand.

'Well,' she repeats. 'You see he's got these friends.' Then she doesn't go on.

'Ah,' Mr Raftiche says. He knows exactly what she is asking of him. Nice boy, good home, gets in with the dossers and druggies, Ruby's son Carling, and that lot, mother worried sick. Well there's absolutely nothing he can do about it. And besides, why isn't the boy's father handling the situation? Not that he thinks there's much of a situation here that needs handling.

'I understand,' he nods understandingly. 'I'll sort it out.' These good kids, they get to a certain age, they look around for the worst pals in a 50-mile radius. Overnight they go from diligent and pleasant, to complete jerks. There's absolutely nothing he can do. Not that he thinks there's anything that needs doing. It's all perfectly normal, a temporary necessity. The boy's normal.

'It's just that he likes you,' she says.

'Leave it with me,' he continues to nod.

'He respects you,' she adds.

Again he waves his hand, embarrassed. 'I'll talk to him, tell him a few home truths.' He wonders if he's got the words quite right. They don't sound right. But she is smiling enchantingly at him.

'Me too,' she says. 'I respect you.' She pauses. 'Ben tells me things, sometimes.'

He feels himself actually blushing. It's the way she's tilting her head to the side and looking up at him. He is in danger of stopping breathing all together. The pain cranks up another notch. 'Oh,' he says. 'I'm not sure how much you can believe what these kids say.'

Abruptly she stands up. 'Of course I believe him.'

Equally abruptly he stands. He towers above her, afraid he has offended her, calling her son a liar like that. 'I didn't mean it,' he says.

'But I mean it,' she smiles. 'I know they all like you.'

She is praising him. She is perfect and she is praising him. He follows her to the door. The slope of her shoulders is more beautiful than anything he has ever seen. And the way she moves inside her tight exotic clothes, if Cleopatra had worn clothes like that, that's the way she would have moved.

At the door she turns to face him and catches him staring at her bottom.

'Well, thank you,' she says. She brings one arm up to push the pretty untamed curls back from her face. Her breasts beneath the white silk top lift with the gesture.

If Cleopatra had breasts, he is thinking, they would have lifted like that. He realises his thoughts are becoming ridiculously garbled by an accumulated sexual charge over which he again has no control.

'I can't tell you how relieved I am,' she says.

'Animals,' he tells her. 'These kids are animals. Wish I could be one of them, even for a day.' He laughs outrageously.

She gives him a quizzical smile. 'You have children?' she asks.

Embarrassed, he shakes his head. 'Sadly, no. Divorced long ago.' She gives him the same quizzical smile, then turns to leave. Her pretty city shoes tap down the corridor.

He watches her until she is out of sight. The tight black skirt both hides and reveals the shape of her, exactly as she intends. He continues to stand in the doorway until there is no longer any sound of her. Then he goes and sits in her chair. He gets up. He groans. He sits in his own chair. He sweeps the exercise books off the desk into the open drawer and slams it shut. He walks to the window and looks out as moody, gloomy, brooding, downcast and outcast as any of those he teaches. But when he closes his eyes, just for a second, it is Ruby who jumps into view, funny skinny little hair-brain in her outsized pink tracksuit.

★★★

Within a quarter of an hour, the third surprising thing happens. Without deciding to do it, Mr Raftiche walks around to the empty buildings at the back of the school. It is not on his way to where he parks his car and he has not been there since the fire. Call it curiosity, he tells himself. As soon as he rounds the corner, he sees Ruby. She has her back to him and is staring at the boarded-up window. She turns at the sound of his footstep. Her expression is suddenly frantic.

'Well hello.' Mr Raftiche grins. Deliberately he keeps his voice jovial. 'Great minds think alike, yea?'

Again he wonders if he's got the words quite right. She is cowering away from him, clearly frightened. He covers the remaining distance between them in two powerful strides. Then, without knowing he is going to do it, he bends low and kisses Ruby on the cheek. Her skin is unexpectedly soft, truly amazingly soft.

'What are you doing here?' He laughs, looking at the place he has just touched with his lips.

But her frantic expression remains. He rests one large hand on her shoulder. He can feel the thinness of her through the fabric of her summer cardigan. She is trembling.

'What am I doing here?' he says, beaming at her, willing that expression to soften. He looks up at the cheap hardboard nailed over the window and at the ugly smoke streaks. The whole place is a shit-heap. No one has even bothered to clear up the broken glass.

'What's anyone doing anywhere?' he asks.

But she treats the question seriously, staring up at him with those wide injured eyes. Gently he removes his hand from her shoulder.

'He's back,' Ruby tells him. But she sees he has no idea what she's talking about. 'Nicholas,' she explains. 'He ran away.' Her voice trails off. 'For a while.'

Of course, he ran away, Mr Raftiche thinks. What else could he do? 'You didn't tell me that,' he says.

She gives him a little sideways look like she's being told off. She doesn't have to look like that on his account. He's not telling her off.

'I don't know what to do,' she whispers. It is as close as she has ever come to admitting that her son is a lout and a loser who takes drugs and shoplifts for his elective sport. Of course she's here looking for him, to see if he's gone back to his old ways.

'I can't stop thinking about it,' she adds. 'At night.'

'At night?' he repeats. At night she should do what he does, a half bottle of whiskey, jerk off, go to sleep. 'Want me to talk to him?' he asks, again placing his hand gently on her shoulder. 'Tell him a few home truths? These kids, they're animals, running in packs. It's probably not his fault.'

Ruby gives him a hurt look, hurt and at the same time grateful. Funny little lame-brain, getting hurt on her son's behalf, but then that's what mothers do. It's something he likes unconditionally, that loyalty of mothers, even if the son is a mass murderer. As if it isn't enough to get hurt on your own behalf. 'Well why not?' He tries to make his voice sound confident and approving of himself, of her, of her son. 'Why not indeed.' But his voice trails off, thinking what can he possibly say to a boy like that? There is nothing anyone can say. Listening is not one of his communication skills, much less taking advice. And the other ways of communicating are unthinkable.

'That's nice,' Ruby adds. It hangs in the air, an expectation of the impossible.

Suddenly it starts to rain, no warning drizzle, but instant hard, cold rain. Ruby draws her cardigan tightly together but she does not move away. Instead she hunches her shoulders forward in that funny, spinsterish way of hers like she's a hundred years old and about to keel over. 'It wasn't much of a fire,' she says. 'It put itself out you know.'

'I know,' he says, moving away, suddenly tired of her, her needs, her life, everything about her. 'Let me give you a lift.'

'Everything's gone wrong for him,' Ruby adds, still looking up at the smoke streaked window. 'He didn't mean to do it.'

Mr Raftiche takes a second step towards the road, hoping she'll follow. 'You'll get soaked,' he says. 'Let me take you home.'

'He needs a father,' Ruby does not move.

'Don't we all,' he says, realising too late how bitter he sounds. As if anyone could disapprove of anything about her, poor little hurt innocent.

But she looks up at him. 'It's all right,' she says. 'I live near.'

'You do?' he questions, surprised. But what has really surprised him is that all the while they have been talking, he has been feeling the softness of her skin under his lips. He resists the urge to watch her walk away, knowing he does not want to see what he will see. Instead he plunges both hands in his pockets. But then he does look and in the distance he sees her scuttling away, already bedraggled in the wet, her skirt clinging awkwardly to her skinny legs, her lank hair outlining the tiny pinball head.

★★★

The next day Mr Raftiche calls the boy Ben in to see him.

'So,' he says carelessly. 'Settled in OK?'

The boy shrugs his shoulders and maintains a sullen silence.

'Oh please,' Mr Raftiche says. 'Call me Ratface. Feel free.'

The boy does not laugh. Mr Raftiche sees that, like his friends, he has mastered the art of being bored. But this one, at least he can read. At least he feels a little shame. You can see it there in his look sometimes, when he doesn't know you're looking.

'Everything all right at home?' Mr Raftiche asks.

Again the boy shrugs his shoulders. He makes no effort to hide his disdain for the question. Secretly, Mr Raftiche agrees with him. There's a lot to be said for lack of dialogue. A whole lot of problems you can't talk about simply go away after a while. Take his own marriage for instance, pretty much all of it. Ah well, that's another chapter unread, another book best left unopened. Besides, it doesn't matter to him anymore. He's forgotten it completely.

'Your parents getting divorced?' he asks, following a hunch. Or is it a wish?

At last the boy gives him a quick look. 'Probably,' he says scornfully.

'Ah well,' Mr Raftiche says. He has not expected an answer and doesn't know what to do with it now he's got it. 'Ah well,' he repeats.

The boy shuffles uncomfortably from one foot to the other. Mr Raftiche sees and is sorry. It was not his intention to make the boy uncomfortable.

'Your mother,' he says and then he stops abruptly not knowing what to add. He thinks for a minute, watching the boy. Good-looking kid, lots of advantages, of course he's only temporarily throwing them away. He'll find the right friends, the nice kids, and sooner rather than later. But the mother doesn't know that.

'These friends of yours,' Mr Raftiche changes direction. The boy's look of scorn deepens. 'You know the pub isn't the epicentre of life,' he tells him. There, he's done what he promised, advised the boy, like she wanted. 'OK, OK,' he raises both hands. 'Beat it,' he slips into his fake American gangster accent. Still the boy does not laugh. Ah well, at least he's kept his part of the bargain, done what he promised her. But the way the boy is, he guesses the parents fight all the time. He's never met the father, but her, the way she looks, the way she looks at him, that's a look that's got some explaining to do. Still, the kid will be all right. So his happiness contains a nugget of sorrow, so what's wrong with that? The sand in the oyster, the little bit of shit in the cream that makes the best yoghurt. So whose happiness doesn't contain a nugget of something or other? No one's, that's whose.

★★★

Shortly after, he deliberately seeks Ruby out in her little crowded office. 'We could go out,' he says, drawing her aside, 'if you want to.'

Ruby is flustered and drops the papers she is carrying. 'Out?' she repeats.

He bends to help her and their knees touch. 'You know, a date,' he answers, swivelling slightly so that his thigh presses against hers. Then he is instantly ashamed. He has made her quiver increase to the point of dysfunction. Yet he moves away more slowly than necessary.

'A date,' she repeats.

'Yes,' he says, 'if you want to.'

'Where?' Ruby asks.

'What do you mean, where?' He has to check the impulse to mock her. Instead, he withdraws his thigh and gets up. She remains squatting at his feet, clutching the loose papers which seem to have taken on a restive life of their own. He looks down at her little rounded shoulders and the top of her funny little head where the parting in her hair is too white and not quite even.

'Just asking,' he says more gently.

Still she does not get up. Finally he reaches down and slips one hand under her bony arm to help her. But at his touch she starts to again tremble violently. He tightens his grip and lifts her up. She weighs nothing, nothing at all. For some reason he suddenly remembers the card making the rounds of the staffroom last term, in sympathy at the death of her mother. He signed it of course, but it meant nothing to him at the time. Now, however, it is something tangible about her person, like another one of those pink cardigans of hers, but this one made out of loss and short measure. He sees the other two secretaries are embarrassed.

He releases her arm. 'I thought maybe it would help,' he says kindly.

'Help?' she repeats, her voice too shaking. And he sees it is impossible, everything with her is as impossible as this attempt at getting something said. 'Ah well,' he sighs. 'It's just a thought.'

★★★

At the end of another afternoon Mr Raftiche keeps the boy, Ben, back after class. 'Your mother,' he says. 'I thought I might get her in here for a little talk.'

The boy slides towards the door. 'What for?' he asks.

'I don't know,' Mr Raftiche answers. 'This and that. Rock and roll.' He sees the boy is not amused. 'You,' he adds.

'Me?' The boy turns back to face him, sullen.

'You're right,' Mr Raftiche says. 'Boring subject. You're dead right. But you know you gotta learn this stuff we teach you here so you can denounce it intelligently in later life.'

The boy does not laugh and slides away. Mr Raftiche calls after him. 'You can go mad you know, from not doing your homework.'

For some reason this little exchange has left him elated. He is laughing to himself as he tosses exercise books into his briefcase. She would have laughed, the mother, looking at him sideways out of those lovely eyes of hers, appreciating him. *You're so funny, Robert, the things you come out with.*

★★★

A short while later, he walks the long walk through the school corridors to the far car park, where lately he has been leaving his car, if only to put off the time of getting back to his own empty house. Besides, it's funny but walking the corridors he can think better. *You're so passionate Robert*, she, the mother, is saying, *the things you come out with.*

Suddenly Ruby is there beside him, half running to keep pace. He looks around, startled. There's no one else in sight and no reason for her to be in this remote part of the school. She must have been following him.

'Well, well, well,' he laughs. She is staring at his face in dismay. What is it she has seen in his expression, taking him by surprise like that? Anguish? Rage? 'I was just thinking about you,' he lies.

He stops and bends to kiss her cheek as he did before. His lips are an inch from her skin when he draws back. He can't do it.

Unaccountably, the pain in his chest has returned and he straightens up, tapping the breast pocket of his jacket with one hand.

'Ah Ruby,' he says, looking into the distance. Her wide frightened eyes follow the direction of his gaze where there is nothing at all. 'I was thinking about our date,' he adds.

Her lips move soundlessly, as if trying to form words in a strange new language. Well perhaps that's exactly what all this is to her, an incomprehensible, strange language. 'We don't have to,' he says. 'You don't have to say anything now. Maybe think about it.'

He looks down at her. She doesn't understand his jokes. She doesn't understand when he is being serious. Everything is hopeless, unthinkable. They walk on in silence, awkwardly, side by side, out of step. When they reach the car, Mr Raftiche turns away. 'Such a small fire,' he says. 'So much trouble.'

Ruby nods her head in agreement and, when he opens the car door for her, she gets in without hesitating.

She directs him down a small street through a maze of decaying nineteenth-century terraces. Quickly the streets get narrower and the houses meaner. Finally she speaks. 'There was a lot of clearing up after Mother. I haven't finished.'

Mr Raftiche is not sure he understands what she is trying to tell him. Is it that she's afraid he's going to come in with her, follow her up to the bedroom? 'There was a lot of clearing up after the divorce,' he tells her. 'I haven't done half of it either.' He laughs but she doesn't join in. Funny creature, the things she thinks of. But what's even funnier is the things he comes out with. Clearing up, who is he kidding? The house is as his ex left it, all those years ago. He has touched nothing.

They drive in silence for a few more minutes until Ruby tells him to stop.

He looks out at a tiny dismal place, one window downstairs, two upstairs. He guesses the mother had the front bedroom, the daughter the back, the son downstairs on the settee and nothing will have changed, except the mother now sleeps in the cemetery. He can't bring himself to go in.

She opens the car door and waits for him. When she sees that he is still gripping the steering wheel with both hands she looks up at the unlit windows and says, 'No one ever stopped me in the street and asked me to be in a film.'

Mr Raftiche snaps his head around in surprise. 'What did you say?' he asks. Funny little unpredictable stick insect, the things she comes out with.

She leans in before closing the door. 'Mother told me someone once stopped her in the street and asked her to be in a film.'

'They did?' he questions, not believing her.

But she knows he has heard and she closes the car door carefully, obeying a surprising, instinctive understanding of the value of the last word.

Through the rain on the windscreen, he watches her walk the two paces up to her door and put the key in. The things she comes out with, funny little half-baked potato.

'Well, who would have thought it?' he calls after her through the open window, meaning to be kind about the dead mother. But then he isn't sure if he's got the words right or if it's what he meant to say in the first place. She's giving him a hurt look. 'Me, who'd stop me in the street for anything?' he calls again, meaning to encourage her, but guessing he's chosen the wrong words as usual. 'I've talked to him, you know, Nicholas. Told him the whole truth and nothing but the truth like we said.' She is staring at him, open-mouthed. Now why did he do that, lie like that? She'll find out. 'Of course he won't tell you,' he adds lamely.

★★★

At his own house, the light bulb is out in the sitting room. He takes off his shoes, finds the open bottle and a clean glass, intending to sit in the dark and drink whiskey until he is nineteen again. But the trouble is, he can't get her out of his mind. Not her, the goddess, he doesn't want to get her out of anything, but her, Ruby, funny little drowned rat, always hovering on the edge of life asking permission to appear briefly. If only she weren't so skinny. If only she could maybe wear something a little bit nicer. Ah well, who is he to criticise? He pats his growing paunch, loosens his belt and drinks down another inch. If only she went to a better hairdresser, maybe had one of those makeovers, like in the magazines he reads in the dentist's waiting room. Then again, he's already swallowed his pride over so many things it's given him permanent indigestion. He brings his hand up to the pain in his chest. Funny little creature. Yet, those kind of small, still ones tend to fit snugly around no one but you. There's something to be said for that. Then, after drinking another two inches, he suddenly comes up with the word desperation, hers not his. Funny language, English, with all these words for shades of misery and only a few for the reverse. Not like his own language. He empties the bottle and vaguely senses there is a lack of honesty somewhere here. Words, like the law, do what they're supposed to do. You can't blame them for your own failures. But he's asleep before he finishes the thought, snoring drunkenly.

★★★

Two days later, without ceremony, Mr Raftiche pulls Ruby out of the office so they can talk, this time alone in the corridor.

'Perhaps we can go somewhere?' He sees no reason not to come straight to the point.

'All right,' she agrees at once.

He thinks she has not understood. 'I mean away,' he explains.

'All right,' she repeats, looking trustingly up at him.

He is stunned into silence. The jokes die in his throat. There will be no need to pass this off as a clownish aberration. 'I'll fix it then,' he says.

She nods her head in agreement, and lowers her eyes shyly. He sees from her earnest expression that she has understood everything, perhaps better than he has. And he guesses that she sees perfectly, in the gravity of his expression, that he intends what she thinks he intends. He sighs. It's all so complicated.

Two days after that he tells her about the caravan.

'It's all right,' she says. 'I like caravans.'

Funny creature. He wasn't apologising for it. He didn't think it was an insult to her. 'It's very remote,' he tells her. 'In a field.' His voice is wary.

'That's nice,' she answers compliantly.

'It's bound to rain,' he adds.

'It always does in Wales,' she agrees.

★★★

Early Saturday, a few weeks later, he collects her. She is waiting for him on the doorstep, wearing a new tracksuit he guesses she has bought for the occasion. She picks up her suitcase as soon as she sees his car. The tracksuit is black with a silver stripe down each sleeve and leg. The intense blackness of it sucks all the life out of her pale features. On the way here in the car, he realises he has been hoping she will not be wearing the pink tracksuit. Now he is not so sure. He sees that she has an absolute inability to get it right coupled with an absolute determination to try. The result is incredible and sadder than he has expected.

He leans over and opens the door for her. 'So,' he beams happily, 'you want to be in a film?' He pitches his voice high with self-mockery. 'I got the camera. You got the looks. Whadda you say?' He uses his fake American gangster accent. But, instead of laughing, she is disconcerted.

'I wondered,' he lowers his voice back to normal and doesn't look at her shapeless stick ankles as she manoeuvres herself into the car, 'what happened with that?'

Now she looks distressed, the beginnings of panic in her inability to understand him. And they have only been together for about three seconds.

'The film,' he explains. 'Your mother.'

'Oh,' Ruby answers. 'Oh that. She did it.'

He lets out a laugh. It is not the answer he has expected. 'Your mother was in a film?' he says, shaking his head with wonder. It is so unbelievable that he believes it entirely. 'What sort of a film?' he asks, meaningfully. 'One of those adult only?'

Ruby rounds on him. 'Of course not,' she is almost crying.

At once he is contrite. 'I didn't mean that. I was only joking.' He wants to touch her, to draw her to him, but guesses it would be the wrong thing to do. 'Absolutely not,' he adds.

112

★★★

The caravan is worse than he expected and he expected bad. He has found out about it from a card in the newsagent's window. Spartan he looked forward to, the joys of Calor Gas fumes, candles, and yellow powdered soup dissolved in water. But this cheerless, forgotten heap, and then he can't think of the right word to finish the sentence.Home, it isn't, holiday accommodation, never. Nor is it the sanctuary he hoped for, cut off from everything familiar so that they could shed their inhibitions, well hers mostly, and wander freely over the empty green hills, the two of them, freshened by the freshness of their surroundings, maybe holding hands. No, the word he comes up with is shit-hole. It is what his form would say. And they would be right.

The aluminium exterior is rusting. He didn't know aluminium could rust but it seems here it can. There's a corrugated barn to one side, fallen in, overgrown with nettles, and infested with rabbits judging from the droppings on the doorstep and everywhere else. The grass is close cropped and churned up, exhausted and fouled by the needs of large grazing animals, probably cattle, though he is none too sure about these things. The whole place is careworn and impoverished, sunk in years of gloomy neglect, just like himself, just what he was trying to leave behind.

He does not have the courage to look at Ruby's face. All the horror and dismay will be right there for everyone to see. Funny little thing, the way she lacks those female wiles. The way his ex could hide everything that was going on, she was a professional, a genius. Ah well, that's a finished chapter now, no concern of his anymore.

He sees the flimsy aluminium door has been left open for them and finally he dares to look over at her. To his amazement, she is grinning.

'What a dump,' she laughs. Her grin lights up her funny little face.

She goes ahead of him and pushes the door open the rest of the way. He watches her, waiting for the start of dismay, or to become what they call 'crestfallen', a word he has only recently come across and has taken a shine to. But instead she is giggling. She looks back at him with an abandoned smile.

'It's appalling,' she cries for joy. 'Seriously terrible.'

113

What he does not know is that in an expensive hotel with silent carpets and gilded bathroom fittings, she would have shrivelled in on herself. Room service would have terrified her. Climbing between the crisp sheets of the king-sized bed, she would have died. What he also does not know is that in her suitcase she has packed liquid detergent, bleach, Ajax powder, toilet rolls. In his box of provisions he has packed whiskey, port for her, and the cheap instant foods of his return to bachelorhood.

'Speaking of films,' he says, reaching back into the car for the cine camera. It is a new toy, bought to cheer himself up. He holds it out for her to admire and winks suggestively. 'Thought we might capture those little unforgettable moments.' He brings it up to his eye and pretends to film her. 'Nice,' he says. 'Very nice.' But, through the lens, he sees her face staring back at him at last rigid with shock and horror. At first he does not understand but then all at once it comes to him and he can't straightaway find the words to explain to her that what she thinks is not what he has intended. He sees that she is thinking, mirrors on the ceiling, the two of them copulating, and him wanting it all on film for some sleazy purpose. What he has thought is picnics in the sun, fluffy white sheep on the hillside. But of course how can she have known that? How can she ever have known anything about men and their intentions?

Quickly he puts the camera back in the car. 'Anyway,' he says. She is trembling all over, making no attempt to hide the stricken expression on her face. 'I haven't got the hang of it yet.' He takes a step towards her but at once she disappears into the caravan.

He goes back to the car and slowly unloads the things they have brought, giving her time. After a few minutes he follows her in, talking as he enters. 'So, what do you think?' He laughs his 'this is no laughing matter' laugh. He sees that the place is every bit as bad inside as out. The plastic windows are crawling with flies. The bare mattress is stained and torn. He never thought to bring sheets. The tiny kitchen is greasy and fugged. There are no doors to the rat-hole cupboards. The Calor Gas is there all right. At least that's something. He looks over at her face, hoping to see her party humour restored by the awfulness of it, or at the very least her English Dunkirk spirit. She has her back to him. Her shoulders droop, her skinny bottom sags in the black joggers. Suddenly he longs for his ex to be there to turn on him with the insults hurled like grenades, before storming out the door. She had her favourite words in these situations, pathetic, useless, loser.

'Well,' he tries again, making his voice as cheerful as he can. 'Home sweet home.'

She keeps her back to him. Her shoulders droop lower.

'Guess I'm dog meat,' he adds. He finds he is starting to lose heart for all of this. When she still doesn't answer, he goes back out and brings in the box of groceries, dropping it heavily in the middle of the table. The whole structure shakes with his coming and going.

'We can do something here,' he exclaims again trying for cheer. What he'd really like is to make a start on the new bottle, the two of them sitting outside on their coats under that big tree over there. Things would soon look a whole lot better, with only the effort of bringing the glass up to their lips.

Instead he goes over and connects the gas. The farmer has left them two large plastic bottles of water. He fills the ugly, pocked kettle and puts it on to boil. 'Lets get to it then,' he says. It seems they will have to unpack and put things to rights before he can suggest the bottle, the coats, the tree.

Suddenly Ruby raises her head and sniffs the air. 'What's that smell?' she asks.

He too sniffs the air and shrugs his shoulders. 'Animals,' he suggests.

'It's not animals,' she contradicts him. 'We have animals.' She lifts a corner of the mattress and finds nothing. 'We have a dog,' she adds.

'Not pets, farm animals.' Mr Raftiche keeps his voice kind. He doesn't like this new bossiness of hers but he is prepared to put up with it to see her interest rekindled and the camera hopefully forgotten.

Ruby screws up her face with disgust. 'It's disgusting.'

Now that she's mentioned it, he realises she's right and he's surprised that he hadn't noticed sooner. The smell is everywhere, foetid and putrid. Then again, it's so much in keeping with the place, maybe it's only natural he didn't notice. He goes over and pushes at one of the plastic windows. Instead of opening on its hinges, the whole thing comes away and falls to the ground outside. But the air coming in is worse than ever. 'There,' he says. 'You see? Farm animals.'

'It's not farm animals,' she insists. She turns full circle looking critically at the caravan. Everything is moulding, disintegrating, decaying. It's no wonder there's a smell. 'It's filthy,' she announces.

Mr Raftiche sighs. 'Maybe we should forget the whole thing. Give up a bad job.' He's sure he hasn't got the words right on that one but she understands what he means because she comes straight back at him.

'Oh no,' she says. 'I can clean it.'

Now she is starting to sound better, more like her old self.

'But I don't want you to.' He tries to make his voice sincere. He is thinking about the bottle, the tree, the coats spread out. Actually, on second thoughts he wouldn't mind waiting for her. Maybe just a little cleaning.

He judges that, out of just plain common decency, he should offer to help, push the broom around a bit, if there is such a thing as a broom around here. But already she is moving aside the things they've brought in, ready to begin.

'Call me if you need me,' he tells her, quickly collecting the bottle and a glass. He points to the tree. 'If you need any help.' She's suddenly such a funny, bossy, little thing. Who can tell what she wants?

★★★

An hour later, or three glasses depending on how you measure time, he looks in through the open door to find her on her hands and knees washing the floor with a new pink-striped dishcloth. There is a bottle of cheap disinfectant beside her. She doesn't notice him though he stands there for some time. She is totally absorbed in what she is doing, totally oblivious to him. Ah well, he thinks, perhaps it's just as well, the way things are going. At least she seems to have forgotten about the filming business, not that there was anything that needed forgetting about.

What he does not know is that she has seen exactly what he has been doing for every second of the last hour. She has seen the level of the whiskey in the bottle dropping steadily. Her eyes have been drawn to his long legs stretched out in front of him and the way he likes to rest one arm behind his head, the other across the mound of his stomach with the glass balanced on his crotch. She has seen how regularly he has lifted the glass to his mouth and how regularly he has leaned over to refill it. First the camera and now this. And they are miles from anywhere, just the two of them. And it will soon be night-time. Frantically, she pushes the cloth into the corner and drags out bits of hair and toe nail clippings. And now he is standing there staring at her.

After another hour Mr Raftiche again comes to the door and leans heavily to one side. Ruby is sitting crammed into the window seat behind the fold-out table. In the hot afternoon sun she has taken off her tracksuit top and is wearing a plain white T-shirt. She has no breasts.

'My,' he exclaims, looking at her chest. 'My, my, my.' He is lost for words. The place certainly looks a whole lot better and he sees that she has thought to bring sheets, though she has not made up the bed. They are neatly folded in a plastic bag. 'Well, well, well,' he adds. 'My goodness.' The place is transformed. They can be cosy here after all, the two of them, light the candles, a bite to eat. 'My word,' he says.

'It's still there.' Ruby's voice breaks into his reverie.

He looks back at her breastless chest, unsure he has heard her. 'What?' he asks. 'What's still there?' She has taken him by surprise.

'The smell,' she says. 'It's still there.'

He brings his eyes to her face and sees she is still distraught. Nothing has changed. 'What smell?' he asks, finding he needs to hold on to the table to keep his balance.

She cowers away from him. He has forgotten all about the smell. But sure enough, rising up through the layers of bleach and disinfectant, there is the same unmistakeable odour of putrefaction.

'Well,' he says, searching for the words to tell her it doesn't matter. They are here, the two of them, the place looks wonderful, a bite to eat, wait for darkness, light the candles. What does a little smell matter? 'Well then,' he says. 'Well then.'

'I think we should complain,' Ruby says.

'Complain?' he repeats.

She looks up at him like she looks at the first years who deliberately go to her office to fart. He knows they do it on purpose so she'll look like that, shocked and dismayed. He makes a huge effort to stop himself laughing.

'You should do something about it,' she says. 'You paid.'

But it's all too much for him, getting in the car, finding the farmer, making him understand, even if he were still capable of driving, which is doubtful.

Then out of nowhere he has an inspired idea. 'It's under the caravan,' he tells her. 'That's where it's coming from.'

She looks up at him, surprised. And when she sees the way he is staring at her chest, her expression turns to fear.

He tries to look away from her but can't. There is no need for her to look at him like that. He would never do anything she didn't want him to. He might have had a couple of drinks, sure. But isn't that the point? The two of them? Up here? Together? Just waiting to see what's what even if it's maybe nothing. If that isn't the point, what is?

Concentrating on exactly where he places each foot, Mr Raftiche goes out and bends down to look under the caravan. The wheels have been removed and replaced with piled breeze blocks. Someone, a long time ago, has wedged a length of decorative wooden lattice around the base in an effort to pretty the place up. He peers in through the gaps in the jagged wood and finds it immediately. His stomach heaves, but then that's the drink. After all, he's seen worse things than this. Maybe not recently, but he has seen things in life. Who hasn't?

Suddenly she is standing behind him, screaming into his right ear. He reels back, grabbing at her to steady himself. He didn't know she was there, creeping up like that, funny creepy little thing. She screams again and he instinctively brings his hands up to cover her eyes. She is staring at the straw and rags. There are eight dead puppies in a languid heap, only a few weeks old by the look of them. In the heat they are decaying fast, bloated and covered with swarming black flies.

★★★

118

At the same time the farmer stops his jeep at the gate and looks up at the big man behind the caravan with his hands strangling the tiny woman who is bent over in front of him screaming away for all she's worth. He's seen some goings-on up here. They have a good laugh at the goings-on what with the hippies taking their clothes off all over the place and the kids who come up here to do it all day and all night. It's no wonder the place is falling apart. But this, there's never been anything like this, never anything violent.

He approaches warily, sizing up the big man, strong, but slow, by the look of him. Still, he doesn't want to have to take him on. Suddenly the little lady stops screaming and looks over at him. He sees she is not so young as he thought. She's plenty old enough to know what she wants. Maybe he should just leave them to it, whatever they're up to. After all, it's none of his business.

He stops ten feet from them. He sees she is crying. On second thoughts, he can't leave her like this. Not with the big fellow twice her size. He could break her in half with one hand by the look of him. And enjoy it. The farmer takes another step closer and again stops. On the other hand, he's a mean looking fellow, unpredictable. These ones who beat up on women, he's got no time for them. If it was the fellow's wife, well maybe. But it's not the wives that get brought up here. Thirty-eight years, he's never seen a wife up here.

'Oh the poor things,' Ruby sobs, directing her gaze under the caravan. 'Poor little babies.' The big man too is staring at something under there.

At last the farmer comes up behind them and looks where they're looking. He sees the pups immediately.

'Well, what do you know?' He pokes his head and one shoulder through the gap in the lattice, then withdraws quickly, brushing at the flies that have followed him. 'Well what do you know about that?' he repeats. 'So that's where she had them.'

The big man gives him a questioning look. The little lady is crying away. He sees he'd better explain it to them, not that there's all that much to explain.

'The bitch was hit on the road,' he tells them. 'We knew she'd had them.' What he doesn't tell them is that it was him that hit her, coming back from the pub, maybe driving a little bit fast on the homestretch, and she'd only run out to welcome him home. He shakes his head and tries to look saddened. In fact, he is saddened. Each of those pups was worth near enough twenty pounds, good pedigree stock. 'My God we looked,' he says. 'We never thought of up here.'

He stares sadly off into the distance in the direction of the farmhouse. 'Who would have thought it?' He turns back to them. The little lady has stopped crying now but she's shaking like it's the middle of winter. 'There's no accounting for bitches when it's their time,' he says, watching her. She's upset all right. 'Come down to the house,' he tells them. 'I've got some nice fresh eggs for you.' He casts an eye over their newish car. He always gives the ones with any money a half dozen eggs and then they buy the honey and his wife's strawberry pies. 'Come with me,' he adds, kindly.

He takes Ruby by the arm as if leading her away from a tragedy and is shocked at her thinness. He guides her over the rutted ground to where he has left the jeep. Poor thing, there must be something wrong here, some wasting disease. His own missus is 17 stone and still counting, something you can grab a hold of when the spirit moves. Carefully he lifts Ruby into the jeep, putting both hands on her waist and then letting them slide over her buttocks as she steps up. She's just about as skinny as he's ever known. And she keeps shaking and looking over her shoulder for the big guy, kind of frightened, but he's gone behind the tree to take a leak.

★★★

A short time later, walking back to the caravan, Mr Raftiche tries out a joke. 'Did you see that guy?' His American gangster accent twangs in the still evening air. 'You know his special skill was opening his eyes. That was more or less it.' He looks over at her. She is carrying the eggs, the honey, and the strawberry pie for safekeeping. She has been silent for the last half hour. And now she acts as if she hasn't even heard him. It wasn't that bad a joke. Ah well, he sighs, at that moment deciding to return her untouched. She is not to be the next woman in his life. Changing women, after all, is like changing deck chairs on the *Titanic*.

He laughs out loud at his own joke. After all, there's no one else to laugh at them.

For a few more minutes he concentrates on placing each foot just so in the pitch-black darkness that has gradually overtaken them. He is sober enough to want to be careful but not sober enough to make this happen. But then he can't resist looking over at her. He can barely see her in that ridiculous black tracksuit. It seems his whole life is turning black. His flat is black with no carpets and burnt-out light bulbs all over the place, His teeth are black around the fillings. His black hair is black and the black hair on his body is even blacker because his skin is getting so pale. Pale for an Italian, his ex used to say, running her hands up and down the length of him. But that's a closed book all right, closed and long forgotten.

It takes them no more than a few minutes to return their provisions to the car. Mr Raftiche drives carefully and tries not to think about what a fiasco all this has turned out to be. Ruby is still silent, now cradling the eggs, the honey and the pie in her lap. When he can stand the quiet no longer, he sighs and tries out another joke. 'Ah well. You know what they say. If the play's a flop, bring on the dog.' He looks over at her. She's still acting like she hasn't heard him. 'If the play's a disaster, bring on a dog with a bandaged paw.' He laughs heartily and glances at her again. 'Guess that's the wrong thing to say.' He waits for her to agree. She doesn't. 'Under the circumstances,' he adds, bitterness creeping into his voice.

They drive a while longer in silence until he again has to speak. It is not in his nature to leave things unsaid. No gags, no chance, he has always believed. 'Listen,' he says more kindly. 'Sure it was a miserable weekend. A happy weekend is hardly worth your while, right?' He tries another brief laugh. Again she ignores him. Why does she have to make everything so complicated? What he wants is a woman who's just going to walk in and ask — *Where's the bed?* Now that would be a great weekend all right, though he has enough self-restraint not to tell her this, under the circumstances. But that would be near enough his idea of perfect. Beautiful boredom in bedrooms, like in arty films. Ah well, he should have known better than to expect things to turn out the way you expect.

★★★

A few hours later, approaching Ruby's house, they are both still sunk in miserable silence. Mr Raftiche skirts the edge of the estate, driving slowly. He is searching for the right street and does not want to admit to a lingering alcoholic stupor. More than once on the drive he has had to force himself awake. She will disapprove. Finally he pulls up in front of what looks like the right place.

There is a light on in the downstairs front room. Mr Raftiche peers in but there is no one in sight. 'He at home?' he asks. 'Your son?'

Ruby doesn't answer.

He waits but nothing happens. Again he peers towards the lighted window. 'He's a good kid,' he lies. 'He'll do OK once he settles down.' In fact the boy is lazy, stupid, easily led. 'You'll see,' he adds. 'I did talk to him you know.' He waits for her to thank him. 'Twice in fact.'

'You said,' she tells him. And he remembers that he did. She steps out of the car and looks back at him. 'You're disappointed,' she says.

But he has exhausted his store of goodwill towards her and can't find it in himself to disagree. He gets out and carries her suitcase to the doorstep.

'I know you're disappointed,' she says again. 'I couldn't stay, not after that.' her voice trails off miserably.

He looks at her anguished little face and wonders just exactly how seriously it is possible for anyone to take life. Then he feels ashamed. 'Look,' he tells her more kindly. 'If you like me, I like you. There you go. That's how it is.' He intends it as a criticism of himself but she ducks her head away from him and grimaces. Her look cuts right through him. He brings his hand up to the increasingly familiar pain in his chest. Then he bends forward and rests his forehead lightly on her shoulder.

'Listen, Ruby.' He lifts his head and looks down at her. 'What you have to know about men, they lie as they breathe. It doesn't mean anything at all. The real stuff is underneath, out of sight.'

She is looking back at him with incomprehension. He has to admit, these things he's coming out with sound like nonsense. It's because he's sobering up too fast. Quickly he laughs and hands her suitcase in through the open door.

'We'll do it again, shall we? Push the boat out?' He does not wait for her to answer, but turns to leave.

'He doesn't understand Shakespeare,' Ruby calls to him, out of the blue. 'Why do they have to do it?'

Mr Raftiche turns back. 'What did you say?' She's always doing this to him, coming out with these things, just as he's walking away and wanting to forget all about her.

Then it comes to him, it's the boy she's talking about, her son. Now she's home she's thinking about him. Well why not?

'He doesn't?' Mr Raftiche says. 'Well neither do I.' He looks at her in amazement. Funny little fur brain. And here he thought it was himself that was the centre of her fears and worries. That'll teach him. He gets into the car, closes the door and rolls down the window. 'All those highfalutin words,' he laughs and looks at her worried face. 'That's the purpose. It's to make you feel stupid.'

He sees at long last one of his jokes has made her smile. 'Don't worry about it,' he says. Funny little soft soap. She cares so much about that half-arsed loser of a son that instantly he forgives her for everything, the ruined weekend, the misunderstanding about the cine camera, the tracksuit, everything.

'He'll be fine. You'll see,' he says. 'And as for us, we'll be fine too.' He gives her a jaunty wave, then cringes in dismay. Now what made him say that? Fine is the last thing they will ever be. Hopeless, forlorn, wretched maybe, but never fine.

★★★

Later, in bed, Ruby is writing in her notebook. She is adding something to her list of Robert's jokes and finishes with the words 'lie as they breathe'. She smiles as she writes, knowing he doesn't mean it, the things he comes out with. She's not sure exactly what he does mean but a lot of the time she can see it's funny. Plenty of people don't understand that about him. They think he's odd. But she knows he doesn't mean half of what he says, or does. Like with the cine camera. He didn't mean anything by that, funny great bear. And it seems he isn't going to hold it against her, everything going wrong the way it did and her getting upset about the pups. And, as if that weren't enough, he's taken the trouble to talk to Nicholas. If anyone can sort him out, Robert can. She could just hug him and hug him for that. She closes the little pink notebook and tucks it under her pillow. She draws her little girl's legs up to her spinster's chest and curls around herself contentedly in her little girl's bed. If he were here now she would just hug him and hug him, silly great bear.

8. MARRIED WITH CHILDREN

This morning before Amy left with her father and brother to get the things for the party, she put two lipsticks, an eyeliner, a mascara and a foundation in the pillowcase on her bed, expensive brands, interesting colours. Now they are not there. She guesses Vanessa has been snooping and found them. It is not what she has expected to happen because Vanessa does not like dirty sheets and never touches their beds. It would go something like this. *Am I expected to do everything around here? Am I? You have food on the table. You have only to ask and I'm out the door driving you around. Do I ever say no? Can you remember a time I ever said no to anything?*

At home her mother changes the beds when she thinks of it. In the old house it was pretty often, in the new house hardly ever. No one minds.

'Shit,' Amy says under her breath. This is what Ben would say if it were his things Vanessa had been snooping in. She tries it out again. 'Oh shit.'

The lipstick, eyeliner, mascara and foundation are not hers. She has taken them from Vanessa's dressing table, from the little left-hand drawer where Vanessa has hundreds of these things. They are both interesting and somehow boastful, what her mother would call trashy. She is instantly drawn to them.

Now, in the distance, the phone is ringing. She counts nine rings and on the tenth Vanessa picks it up, exactly as Amy knew she would.

'Oh,' Vanessa says breathlessly. 'You just caught me going out the door.' Vanessa is in her dressing gown, rollers in her hair, smoking a cigarette.

This afternoon, soon, there is to be a party for your birthday, for two hours from four until six. You have wanted an evening party, a film and then food and maybe dancing. When you asked your father, it was

Vanessa who answered. *No, James the evenings are your time,* meaning her time. *I'm not having a house full of screaming children.*

I'm eleven, you interrupt. *I don't scream.*

I beg your pardon? She looks at you and waits. *Eleven? You are ten. Until your actual birthday, you are ten.* Again she waits.

And you have wanted the boys from your old class because you don't have any friends in your new school and are probably never going to have any friends there. But Vanessa has said you are too young for boys. Your father shrugs his shoulders when Vanessa makes these kinds of pronouncements, as if to say *I'm on your side but let's just let Vanessa think she's right. You know how it is.* But the trouble is, you don't know how it is. And however it is, it changes all the time.

While Vanessa is on the phone, Amy goes into the big bedroom where the bed is neatly made and clothes are out of sight in wardrobes and drawers, unlike her mother's bedroom where things spill out onto the floor, the chairs, the bed. At home, scarves hang from doorknobs and necklaces are draped around lamps. And there is never any problem with trying things on. In fact, it makes your mother look straight at you and laugh when you try her things on. Here, the trying on is furtive, worrying.

Amy picks out two bracelets, one gold set with multicoloured stones, the other an intricately carved red wood. Of the two, she prefers the gold, but the other is so odd and strange she is drawn to it. When she slips it over her wrist, it is of course much too big. Carefully she avoids looking at her father's trousers and white shirt, newly ironed and folded neatly on the dresser. His blue tie is there as well, the one you and Ben bought him for his birthday. But these things are reflected in the big wall mirror and it is impossible to avoid seeing them. Amy does not understand why his clothes are here when he has his own flat and, when she asks Ben, he says grow up, shit-head.

Vanessa puts down the phone and sighs. She goes into the kitchen where James is sitting at the table reading papers in a yellow folder. She wishes he wouldn't work at the weekends and leave the responsibility for the children to her. He looks up. 'This party,' she says, annoyed. 'I'm beginning to wish I hadn't agreed.'

He waits to see if she will go on. The party was her idea, not his.

And, when she doesn't, he says, 'The party's a good idea.' Again he waits, then adds, 'A nice idea.' He is hoping this will please her enough for him to be able to get back to work.

'Hah,' she says, not believing him.

James reaches over and pulls one of her hands into his own. The work has to be done today. 'They're children,' he says. 'It's a party.' And he shrugs his shoulders. His eyes dart to the wall clock above the window. It's far too early for a drink, even a small lunchtime drink.

Vanessa knows that he is right. They are only children after all. And she did keep it down to twelve when Amy wanted twice that number and half boys. Girls are bad enough but boys, that would have been a real disaster. Her thoughts trail off to Ben and how he disappears every Saturday the minute he arrives, no matter what she has planned, as if he can't stand the sight of her. And she knows what it is his father's worried about. Well, thank God he's fifteen. Not much longer and he'll be gone for good, off to uni, a job in the long holidays. And with Amy eleven, there's maybe five years there. Then it will be just the two of them, enjoying life, doing what they want. She smiles to herself, satisfied with her cleverness and with her luck. What's a party, after all? Nothing, that's what. She is satisfied too that the long years in no man's land are over, the place where you could either be married with children or not yet. Well, she can forget about all that now. She is pleased to have arranged these things so that much less effort will be required of her than is usually required of women in these situations. Yes, life is sweet. She gives his hand a squeeze.

'It's time,' James is saying looking again at the clock. Well, it is Saturday after all and there are different rules at the weekend. He takes the gin bottle from the cupboard and waves it in her direction. She shakes her head and gives him a disapproving look, but knows better than to say anything. He has told her often enough what Sarah says at times like these.

James sees the look and doubles the measure as he pours. A look like that is guaranteed to drive a man to drink. He adds another measure just to be on the safe side. But she is good with the children. She is keeping Amy well away from those things, boys, make-up, things that her mother was letting her get away with. No discipline, that about sums up Sarah. And as for Ben, he pours in the tonic and takes a long sustaining drink. As for Ben, he looks at the glass and, finding it half empty, tops it up with more gin. As for Ben, he needs discipline and Vanessa is good at that. That's what kids need, discipline and healthy sports, things which Sarah doesn't know the meaning of. When he and Vanessa are married, when all this fuss is over, he'll slow down on the drink. Things will even out and he can relax off a bit. He takes a third long sustaining drink. And it's not just the children, she is good for him as well, putting him first, believing in him, things Sarah forgot fast enough, as soon as it suited her to forget.

★★★

Later, Vanessa finds the two bracelets in the pocket of Amy's jeans. Of course she has missed them straightaway, not that she was wanting to wear them. But they are two of the most obvious pieces of jewellery she owns. Now if the silly girl had taken a simple gold chain or a pair of pearl studs, it might have been weeks before she noticed. She smiles with satisfaction.

'It's our secret,' she is now saying. 'I won't tell your father.' She looks at the sullen child. 'I won't tell your father if you promise not to do it again.' She waits. 'Do you promise? Amy?'

Amy is staring at the floor. Her throat constricts. The words won't come. It is not what the doctor said is supposed to happen. He has told her mother that children talk happily at home with people they trust and are unable to speak to strangers, at school for example. But, for her, it is the opposite. She likes strangers and often strikes up conversations on buses and in shops. She is worried that she might forget how to speak altogether if she does not keep practising.

'Amy?' Vanessa says again. 'Our secret, do you promise?' She rests one hand on Amy's shoulder and pushes down hard. The child resists. Vanessa increases the pressure and finally Amy nods her agreement. Withdrawing her hand at once, Vanessa smiles. 'Now say you're sorry and the whole thing is forgotten.'

Vanessa bends forward and lifts Amy's hair off her shoulders, holding it lightly in her hand. The gesture is surprising and Amy flinches away from her. Vanessa tightens her grip and arranges the hair behind Amy's ear, pulling a little too hard for comfort. 'Just say you're sorry and that's that, finished and done with.' She pulls a second time.

Still Amy is silent.

Without warning, Vanessa drops the hair and pushes Amy hard, two sharp jabs in the centre of her chest. 'You might get away with that with your mother,' she sneers, 'but not with me.' She pushes a second time and Amy is forced to step backwards. 'You think I don't know what you're doing?' She pushes again, the same short vicious jabs with two fingers. 'I know exactly what you're doing.' She draws the words out. 'I can see straight through you.' She leans forward into the child's face. Then, catching a glimpse of herself in the hall mirror, she suddenly steps backwards. She does not like what she has seen. 'Even if your mother can't,' she adds.

At the door she turns back. 'It's because you're adopted, you know. That's always a mistake if you ask me.'

Amy smiles behind Vanessa's retreating back. Adoption, that old thing, she's known about that forever. Is there no end to Vanessa's stupidity? Apparently not.

★★★

Later, the presents are piled on the little table in the hall. They are all prettily wrapped in colourful paper. In the other room Vanessa and James are arguing. Amy stands and listens. She guesses it is about her and what she has done. She is thinking that arguing is a large part of what you do when you're grown up. They all do it. She is thinking about the builder in the new house and the hippie when he broke Ben's window. She is thinking about the parents of her other friends. It's what they all do, all the time. She picks up one of the presents, a small yellow box, and puts it in her jacket pocket.

'Don't,' Ben says. 'Don't do that.' He closes the door behind him allowing a whiff of the night-time city to enter with him. He knows his sister is in enough trouble already, not going to Vanessa's party, and taking the presents will make it worse. He doesn't see why she shouldn't open them, they're for her. But he knows it will make it worse. 'Put it back,' he says. 'Vanessa's probably counted them.'

In the other room Vanessa is saying, 'You have to talk to her. She's your daughter, not mine.'

'I will,' their father answers.

'How could she do this to me? Why?'

'I don't know,' their father answers.

'And it's not just her, you have to talk to Ben too. He probably put her up to it.'

'I don't think so,' their father says. 'He wouldn't do that.'

'You're probably right,' Vanessa snaps back. 'Amy is perfectly capable of thinking this one up on her own.'

Amy has noticed that sometimes the noise of the traffic on the North Circular makes it hard to hear what's being said, especially in the rain, which she particularly likes.

'They hate me,' Vanessa says. This is a new idea to Amy. She doesn't think she hates Vanessa. Mostly she just wishes Vanessa didn't exist.

'She's with him now. I saw them,' Vanessa is saying. 'You could talk to them both.'

'Oh,' their father says. 'Good.'

'Good,' Vanessa repeats. 'What do you mean, good? You mean "Oh good, now's a good time to talk to them"? Is that what you mean?'

The next thing, their father is standing in front of them. Ben sees he is a little unsteady on his feet, not much, just a little.

'You're back,' he says, stepping forward to put his arm around Amy. He pulls her close. 'Ben,' he says, his eyes lingering on his son's unhappy face. He waits. 'So,' he says, and stops, seeming to have nothing more to add.

'What did she tell them?' Ben asks.

'She told them Amy had an asthma attack,' their father answers.

'That was quick thinking,' Ben laughs. 'Good old Vanessa.'

Again their father falls silent. Together they listen to Vanessa clearing up in the other room, and to the sound of the traffic that is oddly comforting because it is nothing to do with any of them, and to the rain that falls like a gentle benediction, regardless of everything that's been going on in here.

Then Vanessa is standing in the doorway. 'Go to your room,' she says to Amy. 'Do as I tell you.'

At once Amy turns and runs up the stairs. She sees Ben slip out the front door and she hears her father say, 'Hang on a minute.' Amy doesn't stop. She hopes he is saying this to Vanessa and not to her but it doesn't seem likely. She knows she has done a really bad thing, not going to the birthday party. She is always doing bad things though she never means to be bad and has no idea where the ideas come from. It probably means that she is crazy.

As she passes by the big bedroom, she sees two of Vanessa's scarves lying on the bed. Quickly she gathers them up and takes them to her room. She sits at her little dressing table, which Vanessa has bought and which is too small for her to fit her legs under. She picks up her scissors, intending to cut up the scarves but, when it comes to it, she can't do it. The scarves are too beautiful, shiny and intricate, silky to the touch. She slips one, then the other around her neck. Instantly her own face is brighter and more interesting. She tries tying the scarves in various ways but nothing seems to work. Vanessa knows lots of ways to do it. Her mother usually just throws them over her shoulders. But whatever Amy tries looks somehow wrong. Eventually she takes the scarves off. Knowing Vanessa will find them anywhere in the room, she slips them into her school bag, buried deep under the exercise books and bad-smelling food wrappers. And all the while she is thinking that today she has passed some unwritten point of no return so that there is something forever fixed inside her, a black spot of badness that will never go away, even if she lives to be a hundred. The scarves are nothing, the make-up, the bracelets, all unimportant now that the line has been crossed.

★★★

After James has left with the children, Vanessa looks at the pretty presents piled on the little hall table. She has told Amy that she intends to return them, all of them. She has made a point of explaining that this is the right thing to do, under the circumstances. The circumstances being that what Amy has done in not turning up for the party can never be put right but at least returning the presents is better than nothing.

The house is blissfully quiet. Vanessa picks up the same little yellow box that Amy chose earlier. She opens it. Inside there is a delicate gold charm bracelet. If she takes off the charms, it's quite a useful little chain. Vanessa puts it aside. Quickly she works her way through the other packages. Most are girlish toys which she drops to the floor with the wrapping paper, but there is a nice little notebook, pink of course with flowers and bears, but really quite good quality. And there is some stationary that will be perfectly useable, again really quite good quality. These Vanessa slips into the table drawer. Then, as often happens at the oddest of times, she finds herself thinking about him, the fiancé who jilted her all those years ago, and how she had trusted him with her girlish heart. He treated her monstrously. She will never forgive him. She will never be shaken from this view, though everyone else saw it as a blessing in disguise for both of them. Without quite knowing when it happened, this has become her story. And James, the children, are a small chapter added on along the way.

Later still, in bed, in the depths of the night, Vanessa indexes his faults, the fiancé. The index is never in any particular order, neither alphabetical nor chronological. And it is never finished. Tonight it starts — *Say you're sorry.* This is something he never did.

★★★

As he lifts his sleepy daughter from the car, before she wakes, James says to Ben, 'So what's going on with Vanessa and Amy?'

Ben shrugs his shoulders. 'She hates us.'

Sarah is there, taking Amy from him, helping her into the farmhouse.

'She doesn't hate you,' James says to his son. 'Don't be ridiculous.'

Ben walks away, not looking back. 'That shows what you know,' he says.

'What kind of a stupid thing is that to say?' James watches his son walk off into the darkness. He doesn't follow. 'No one hates anyone,' he says. 'She cares a lot.' Then he goes into the farmhouse and shuts the door behind him, leaving his son outside.

For Ben this is a depressingly familiar situation, pointless and hopeless in equal measure. He tries to listen to his breathing, as the hippie has told him to do, to let time pass, find its own pace. But all that happens is the onset of boredom. He'd rather forget about anything finding its own pace and instead face the full glare of what is on offer. Already they are arguing in the kitchen. He sees, through the uncurtained windows, that Amy has taken herself up to bed and is buried under the covers.

'So you're saying that I neglect them?' Sarah is asking. 'You think I neglect Amy and Ben? That's what I'm doing?'

'You do,' James agrees. 'You don't take responsibility for them, not really.'

Sarah stares at him. 'I can't believe I'm hearing this, even from you.' She lets go a little laugh of derision. 'It's funny. It really is. Hilarious.'

They fall silent, both dispirited by the predictability of what they are each saying.

'And I suppose Vanessa is perfect. She never neglects anything. The perfect Vanessa.'

'Don't be stupid,' he runs his hand across the pain in his stomach, pushing in gently, feeling for the outline of the tumour. 'There's no talking to you when you're like this.'

'Stupid,' Sarah repeats. 'I'm stupid? I'm not the one living with Vanessa.'

'Now you're just being ridiculous. All I wanted to do was talk about the children. I'm worried about them. And you turned it into a thing about Vanessa like you always do.' He turns away from her.

'A thing about Vanessa,' she calls after him. She attempts another laugh of derision but it comes out bitter and spiteful. 'I don't believe you.'

But in fact she believes him entirely. He has a way of ending all their arguments with a remark that works its way in through her ear and down her throat where it sticks, leaving her choked up for hours. And he walks away feeling wronged, nursing that stupid imaginary pain in his stomach, as if she feels any concern for him.

Now, she watches the tail lights of his car disappearing down the drive and sees that Ben is still outside, doing something to his bicycle in the light of the open sitting room window. She calls to him but he ignores her. She leaves the door open and goes up to her daughter. Finding her asleep, she returns to stand at the front door and wait.

What she does not know is that Amy, wide awake, is listening to the crumbling wall of childhood, which, as it crumbles, leaves her terrified in an agony of incomprehension and with a glimpse of a future so impossible that she can find no reasonable place for herself in it.

And Ben, older, clearer, is starting to see who makes the rules, who makes the mistakes, who's backed into a corner, who makes the running. It seems this is just the way it is with everyone beyond a certain age. It seems they are always arguing and always have been, though another part of him thinks this probably isn't so. It might be only once in a while but the force of the arguing has spread across all the other days, like a sticky urban fog, blocking out other things that his reason tells him must be there, the good things.

And as for Sarah, how can it be that the more she practises her road to new freedom, the less free she feels? An insidious numbing effect is slowly taking hold. The experiences of the last few months have invested her with fresh new emotions, as she hoped they would. But the emotions are resentment, fear and sorrow. She props the door open with a chair and turns on as many lights as she can find that still work, so that the derelict farmhouse will look warm and welcoming for the boy outside in the middle of the night with his bicycle. Beyond this, she has no idea what to do, only that she must do something.

9. BOOZE AND FLOOSIES

In the dark, defaced house, James, Sarah and Ben are unexpectedly having breakfast together when a small package is delivered for Tord Willibroard.

Ben looks at it and at once guesses. If he's lucky, he'll get a couple of hits off the hippie later on.

James holds it up and reads the strange name. 'Who's this?' he asks. 'What's going on?'

Sarah too looks at the package and shrugs her shoulders.

'It's the hippie,' Ben says.

'The hippie?' his father repeats. 'That's his name?'

'Yea,' Ben answers. 'Turd.'

'Ha!' James laughs. It's true he's heard the builder, Clive, call him that. 'That Clive,' he says. 'He's a moron.'

Sarah again looks at the name and address. She has never heard Clive call the hippie anything, though it's true they don't seem to get on. 'How can you say that?' she asks. 'You have no reason to say that.'

James gives her a withering look. Quickly she turns away.

He flips the packet angrily towards Ben. 'He's not having his supplies delivered here.' He draws out the word supplies as if it's some sort of perfidy. 'You tell him.'

But already Ben is disappearing through the back door.

'Why did you do that?' Sarah asks. 'You know what we agreed.' She too jumps up, but by the time she gets outside, Ben is nowhere in sight. She sees the hippie, Tord, has removed most of the porch roof and left it scattered about like so much detritus. Here's another thing that has got worse, not better. How can this be happening when they are spending money in such quantities and so fast that it makes her feel ill? Can spending money make you sick? It seems unlikely, but then again, nothing much these days is turning out the way she expected. She again looks down the drive for Ben and instead sees Clive in the distance where the long drive joins the lane and where the lorries have repeatedly laid waste the pretty greenery. There is a dog running beside the van. With Clive now working for them full time, the inside of the house looks more than ever like a bombsite. There are still packing cases in the front hall and half-unwrapped dishes scattered over the floor. A stack of unglazed window frames props up the dismantled banister. There are piles of broken plaster in every room, no hot water, no shower, one cracked, dirty toilet used by all of them. Is this then what the new life is meant to be, this wreckage? It's so unimaginative, she is disappointed. If it has to happen, she would rather it took the form of something electrifying and uncontrollable so that she would be quickly overwhelmed and all decisions removed from her.

James passes her on his way to the car. He is carrying his suit jacket over one shoulder, as if he had something to feel jaunty about. 'I'm going to be late,' he says. 'I can't keep doing this.'

'How late?' she asks him.

'Late,' he answers.

'Good,' she says then regrets it. She sounds like a petulant child. Again this morning in bed they have argued about Ben, and about moving here. She knows these continuing arguments are her fault, the way she is always turning the conversation around to the same thing. She has no other conversation with him except the children and it has no other shape except argument. She knows it has been this way for many years.

James too sees Clive's van turn into the lane at a speed that ought to land him in the ditch but never does. He watches the other man's approach. 'What a wanker,' he says.

He sees Sarah is also watching the speeding van.

'You know the other day?' he turns back to ask her. There isn't much time the way the van is closing in on them.

'What?' she says, her voice still sullen.

But then he doesn't go on. She looks at his face and chooses from the many things she has done wrong. 'If you're going to have the last word, you might as well make it count,' she says. He likes having the last word.

But James is frowning, not paying attention to her. He is examining the pain in his gut, outlining its parameters with his fingertips. The sore area has increased in size but the intensity has decreased. In his heart he is convinced it is a malignant tumour. In his heart he also knows that illness stalks us all. You need your wits about you to stay one step ahead of it. You can't get distracted.

In the big city car James accelerates fast away from the house and towards the approaching van. He knows the builder, Clive, lies and cheats to get what he wants and enjoys doing both. Well, why not? He enjoys those things as well. In fact, the only difference between himself and other men is that he admits it. He gives himself a generous amount of credit for this honesty. The big, expensive car and the builder's van come together, then pass each other with only inches to spare. The open car windows visibly shake and the van sways dangerously sideways as the impacted air currents collide. James laughs out loud. Yes, you need to have your wits about you twenty-four hours a day, one way or another.

Watching from the roofless back porch, Sarah has brought both hands up to cover her mouth. It seems they must hit. Ben comes up beside her, with his schoolbag over his shoulder. Together they watch the car and van approach then separate.

After a long moment's silence, his mother says, scornfully. 'It's so predictable. There's nothing a man won't do to impress another man.'

Ben winces. He knows they are angry with each other because of him. He has again heard every word of their early morning argument. And now, waiting for his father to leave, he has crept around the back of the house and deliberately thrown the new fork and shovel into the watery moat to join the wheelbarrow, the rolls of wire, the hippie's junk. He deserves it. They both do.

His mother turns suddenly to face him. 'Did Mr Raftiche talk to you?' she asks.

He shrugs his shoulders.

'Well, did he?' she asks again.

'Sort of,' he answers, sliding away.

'What do you mean, sort of?' Her voice rises. She doesn't mean to be angry at him yet these days everything always ends in an argument.

'What did he say exactly?' She steadies her voice. But then she sees he is not really listening to her. He is watching the van coming up the long drive, the farm dog now some distance behind.

'I have to do more homework,' he answers.

'Homework?' she repeats. 'He told you to do more homework?'

She finds herself looking at her son, unexpectedly alert to him. Here's something else that's going on. Daily Ben's clothes have been getting skimpier, tighter, blacker. All that lolling insolence, that's not for nothing. And it's not for the usual rebellious things either. She guesses he's moved on to the next step of unhappiness and confusion in life as boys his age usually do, as her brothers did with, often as not, dire consequences.

And now it's obvious that Mr Raftiche has not kept his promise. 'You know,' she says, 'if you spend a lot of time driving around in fast cars, you end up dying in fast cars.' Watching the car and the van has unnerved her. Ben is out all hours with those friends of his, out in their souped-up death traps on wheels.

He turns away, giving her a look of disdain. Everything he does is wrong. She hates his new friends. She hated his old friends even more. 'Everyone drives faster than you,' he tells her.

'And maybe everyone is stupid,' she snaps back. He looks so like his father, the bag slung over his shoulder, hooked by one finger. But she sees that he's already taller than his father and quite nicely filled out. How did this happen? When did this happen?

At the same time Clive pulls into the yard and the hippie's girlfriend gets out of the passenger side. She flashes Ben a smile as if she knows him. 'Neat car,' she says, 'your dad's.'

'It's a tank,' Ben answers. He can see the outline of her through the long, transparent, gypsy skirt. She's also wearing one of those tops that leaves her middle bare and she's got a tattoo on her stomach that wasn't there a few days ago. 'I want something fast,' he adds. He is not at all surprised to find her here. Everything about her is so strange and wonderful that nothing she does could surprise him.

She sees him looking at the tattoo and comes over to show him. 'Like it?' she asks. Ben finds he is unable to answer. The tattoo is a flower with a butterfly perched on one petal about to take flight.

'It's the resurrection,' she explains.

He lets go a sharp little laugh. Standing here, right up next to her, he is lost for words.

'It is,' she insists, tossing her hair over one of her shoulders. 'You know, hope, stuff like that.'

Clive is unloading lengths of wood from the van. 'Tossie,' he says. 'Where's that boyfriend of yours? Why is he never around when there's work to be done?'

Tossie ignores the question.

'Did it hurt?' Ben asks.

'You bet,' she answers, lightly brushing at the injured skin with the tips of her fingers. 'I thought I was going to die.'

He can't take his eyes off her and now he's thinking about her stretched out on a table with some hairy weirdo bending over her, his hands on her flesh.

'Still, you got to suffer to be beautiful,' she adds, at last giving Sarah a quick grin.

Ben stares at her. The way she used the words suffer and beautiful in the same sentence, it's too much. He can hardly breathe.

Watching the two of them, it comes to Sarah that this girl uses her body as her office. She buys and sells from it. And you can be sure Clive has been buying, possibly James as well. But what can Ben offer? What can he yet know about all of that? 'Listen Ben,' she says.

At once Ben turns and walks fast down the lane, looking briefly back at his mother. There's no way he's waiting around here for a telling-off, in front of Tossie. Nothing is worth that.

'Jesus, Toss,' Clive says, approaching the two women now standing together under the broken-down porch. 'What did you say to him?' But he is not interested in the boy. He is taking in the tight jeans, the long flimsy skirt, the pretty scarves, the one dark and unhappy, the other young and bright. Instantly the boy is gone from his mind.

He takes his time walking up to them. Might as well give them a chance to appreciate what's on offer.

'Me? Nothing,' Tossie answers.

'You drive too fast,' Sarah interrupts. She is frowning into the distance where Ben is still visible. 'You're going to kill somebody.'

To Clive it appears she has other things on her mind, things other than him. 'What did you do to him?' he asks, also looking after the angry boy. But, before she can answer, he turns to Tossie. 'That boyfriend of yours is a piece of worthless shit.'

Tossie laughs and her beads rattle prettily. He sees that she at least doesn't have anything else on her mind. His eyes wander over the tattoo, the long legs under the revealing skirt. Without warning, he finds himself thinking of Di, the state she's in, slouching around, milk leaking everywhere, screaming at him one minute, weeping the next. Who can blame him for looking elsewhere? No one, that's who.

Sarah takes out the packet, which she hands to Tossie. 'Speaking of Tord,' she says, 'this came for him.'

Both Clive and Tossie stare at it. She turns it over in her hands, knowing exactly what's inside. She glances at Sarah. 'He's moving,' she explains.

'Moving,' Sarah repeats. None of this makes any sense to her, not the conversation, not the girl's knowing Ben, nothing. It's as if they live by different rules, rules that are much more interesting than the ones she understands. She feels suddenly old.

'Yea, well.' Tossie pushes the packet casually out of sight under her scarf. 'We only just decided.' She turns to Clive. 'It's for his motorbike,' she lies.

'Where are you moving?' Sarah questions. 'I mean, not away?' She is surprised at her sudden concern that the girl should be leaving. She does nothing useful in the house. And she is obviously dangerous in other ways.

'We found a place,' Tossie answers. Again her beads rattle prettily. In fact they have not found a place and it's a big worry. She doesn't know why they couldn't have Mum's old room but when she asked, Ruby flew at her like a mad woman. And they've lost track of the rent arrears on the council place where they have been living. But who cares anyway? It's out in the middle of nowhere. The rooms are dark and pokey. The whole place is ugly. Unlike here, here it's beautiful.

'Where's that then?' Clive asks, giving her a look. This is the first he's heard of it.

Tossie holds his gaze. 'You'll see,' she says, 'when the time's right.'

Quickly Sarah turns into the house. She does not want to see the looks that are being exchanged in front of her, as if she doesn't know what's going on.

'Listen,' Clive moves up closer. He leans forward to whisper into Tossie's hair. 'You know I don't give a fuck.' As he speaks, he lifts one tiny beaded plait and fingers the curious texture of it. She might be only a kid but she sure knows what's what. He picks up another strand of plaited hair and rolls it between his fingers. He can see that Tossie's a little bit excited, a little bit scared. He likes that in a woman. He likes that a whole lot.

Half-heartedly she pushes him away. Then she steps up close again. She likes it when he stands right up next to her so she can feel his breath on her cheek. She likes the way he's twisting her hair in his hand. She likes the way he's tucked his cigarettes into the sleeve of his tight black T-shirt, casual like an afterthought.

'Me neither,' she says, turning the packet over in her hands. 'What's there to give a fuck about?'

Clive doesn't answer. It isn't as if Di hasn't asked for it, the way she's let herself go this time. And the house is a shit-heap. There's nothing but baby clothes and baby food, baby smells, babies crying. Who can blame him for taking up another offer? No one, that's who.

As he is about to let his hand slip down to her breast, he sees someone move across the window inside the kitchen. A flash of something has caught his eye. It's the kid, the other one, the mute girl.

'Listen,' he says to Tossie. 'I'll catch you later.' He gives her one of his amused, good-natured looks. 'Whatever that boyfriend of yours is up to,' he adds, 'I don't know about it. Whatever you're up to,' he goes on and then finishes the sentence with a caress, his right hand dropping at last to her left breast.

★★★

In the big, dark room, Amy, in her pyjamas, is standing with her mother looking at the stone floor. The stuff Clive has put on is blistered and peeling. Already the new gas cooker is growing a skin of grey mould from the bottom up and the untouched boxes of towels and sheets smell of damp. Amy kicks at one of the stones. She has been trying to arrange things neatly in the kitchen the way they were at home. She has cleared the table and pushed the chairs into place. She has attempted to wash the dishes in the sink, but with only cold water, they aren't looking quite right. The stone floor, however, is so far beyond anything in her experience that she does not know what to do to make it normal again like a floor should be. She sees that her mother feels the same and a cold dismay lodges in her throat. She turns away before her mother can say anything encouraging and over-enthusiastic the way she always does, but her escape is blocked by the builder standing in the doorway.

Out of habit, Clive is letting his eyes wander over the two of them. The kid's cute, little stick legs but already an arse that you want to look at. And the mother, the way she rolls her jeans up at the bottom, those beads and chains. He looks more closely, not sure when it happened but she's become someone different, someone more available to him. How did he miss that? He's seen it before after all, plenty of times. Once the long skirts and all those beads appear, they become suddenly available, not just to him but to all men. Whatever it is they're trying to prove, he's all for it.

He sees she is frowning at the messed-up floor. 'Looking good,' he says. Casually he comes up close behind her, not as close as with Tossie. You got to judge these things right. You get too close, it scares them off. You don't get close enough, they're not sure what's going on. And he wants her to be absolutely sure this time around. He bends down and runs his hand approvingly over the nearest stone. It's a mess, some stuff he got cheap left over from another job.

'Believe me,' he says. 'It's the best thing for it, stones like that. It'll last for years.'

She takes a step sideways and says disapprovingly, but not like she really means it, 'That's what I'm afraid of.'

He wants to reach out and touch her but with the mute kid standing right there staring up at them, never saying a word. 'Don't look so worried,' he says, bringing himself back up close again. The feel of Tossie has whet his appetite.

She too kicks at the sticky stones. 'Worried,' she repeats with a little laugh. 'What have I got to be worried about?' In fact she couldn't care less about the stones. She is thinking about their earlier embrace, how they both carried it off as a friendly gesture, something friends do everyday. If only he didn't flirt with every female in sight. If only his conversation took off in other directions, at least once in a while. She finds herself remembering Mr Raftiche, laughing down at her and telling her how it's easier to be miserable in a small place. The memory of it makes her smile. It's as if she has no defence against remembering the things he says. In her experience these kind of sharply unbidden memories are usually about pain and shame, the things she's done that turn out to be worse than anything else around, the things she would give anything to be able to forget. But not this, this is a memory of pleasure.

'That's my job,' he tells her, 'worrying.' He has seen her smile but, when she doesn't go on, he is disconcerted. She's taking her time to make up her mind. Well, that's OK. If it's worth having, it's worth waiting for. That's some smile she's got.

Behind him, he hears Tossie come into the room. Now the three of them are watching him. With his bare hands he heaves up one of the biggest stones. 'A couple of patches of damp,' he says, 'nothing to worry about.' He lifts the stone and rests it on his knee. The muscles in his sun bronzed arms flex. He presents the two women and the silent girl child with the handsome curve of his back, then turns to face them with the giant stone cradled in his arms like some grotesque baby.

'Here, try it out,' he says grinning, taking a step forward towards them. 'Let me see how you look with it.'

Sarah laughs and steps back. He is showing off of course. But then again, he has those shoulders to show off and those thighs.

Tossie holds her ground and reaches out for the stone. What a wanker, showing off like that.

He laughs and drops the stone aside. Funny kid, never misses a chance. 'Never miss a chance, do you?' he says to Tossie.

'Dead right,' she answers, holding his eyes. 'Never.'

***

Later that afternoon Dianne comes in through the front door, which has been taken off altogether and is now propped haphazardly against the far wall. She is pushing the twins in an old-fashioned double pram. She calls out but no one answers. In the distance, somewhere upstairs, she hears voices and laughter. She stops and listens for several moments. It is his voice, her voice. She knew it. She knew it for sure when she couldn't get him on the phone the day the babies were born. He's never out of touch, day or night, might miss a job. She stands for a long time and listens to the voices. They are too far away for her to hear more than a murmur, but it's quite clearly his voice and hers.

Finally, she takes a tentative step towards the stairs but the way is blocked by a ladder and a pile of new wood. Here's something else she doesn't want to know about. Clive has been working here for months, taking their money. He doesn't know it but she watches his bank account. And the place looks worse than ever. There's old newspapers and packing boxes everywhere, rolled-up carpets, plaster falling off the walls and left lying. No one deserves to live like this. She could have liked Sarah, given half a chance. They could have been friends. She understands Clive has to lie and cheat. It's a matter of pride with him. But this, he's gone too far.

Dianne leaves the pram by the door and puts one foot on the bottom step. Then she does not know what to do next. She doesn't want to confront them. If it weren't for the babies and Davey, she might just up and disappear. But where could they all go? A woman with three kids? Nowhere, that's where. There's a burst of laughter from upstairs. She guesses they are in bed, Sarah on her back, Clive on his side, looking down at her, playing with those gold chains she likes to wear around her neck, picking them up, rolling them between his fingers to feel the texture.

Suddenly someone comes in behind her.

'Well, hi there,' Sarah says, as if finding Dianne here is something that happens every day. She walks straight over to the pram and looks down at the beautiful sleeping babies. She rests one hand gently on each of the little shapes under their white blankets. 'Oh,' she says. It's the first time she's seen them since the hospital and she doesn't trust herself to say more. The feel of them has taken her by surprise.

Dianne stares at her in disbelief. Everything is there to be read on her face but Sarah does not see. Absent-mindedly she is rearranging the tiny blankets, pulling them up and tucking them in.

'I did shout,' Dianne finally says. She goes on fast. 'I came to see Clive. I need the van.'

At last Sarah looks up at her. 'Oh,' she repeats. 'He's upstairs, I think.'

'Upstairs,' Di repeats. Involuntarily her eyes scan the ceiling. It is quiet now but, in her mind, she can hear them talking and laughing. Laughter like that you only get in one situation.

For a long time the two women stand on either side of the pram looking down at the babies. The house is now absolutely silent. After a while Dianne says, 'Listen, tell Clive I'll catch him later.' Quickly she turns the pram to leave, as if needing to get away from something dangerous.

'But you can go up,' Sarah offers.

Di shakes her head. 'It's nothing. I'll catch him later.'

She pushes a length of board out of her way and manoeuvres the pram through the missing front door. 'You know,' she says turning to smile at Sarah. 'Who wants to live in a house where there's fitted carpets and matching furniture anyway? I never trust people who live like that.' Thinking they could have been friends, who was she kidding? Not herself that's for sure.

Sarah walks with her to the drive, single-file along the rough path they have trod through the nettles and grass. Her eyes are drawn repeatedly to the babies in the pram. 'You come out with some funny things,' she says.

Di lets out a harsh little laugh. She has never found herself funny, though she wishes now she could think of something funny about what's going on upstairs. Well let's just say what Clive's doing up there is so doubtful, there can be absolutely no doubt about it. But she does not tell Sarah this, even for a laugh, especially not for a laugh.

'We've got to be quite good friends, haven't we?' Sarah says.

Dianne looks off into the distance, down the long potholed drive. She is embarrassed at what Sarah has said about being friends with her. Those designer jeans, those gold rings and chains that Sarah wears, she has an idea what they cost. People who buy stuff like that don't get to be friends with people like her, not friends like she means friends.

When Dianne doesn't answer, Sarah looks at her unhappy face. She likes Dianne, her steadiness with the children and her waspish, throwaway humour. 'You've lost weight,' she says.

Again Dianne laughs sourly. What she says is true. In the mirror, her clothes sag, her flesh droops. She appears to be dissolving downwards like a melting candle. Then she looks back through the broken door into the too-quiet house. 'I'm smoking again,' she answers. 'Whenever I want to stuff my face, I have a ciggie instead.'

Sarah laughs. 'That works.' She also stares absent-mindedly back towards the house where Clive is working somewhere. 'But I find love is better,' she adds, 'better than smoking.' She knows it's not love that she is really talking about but something a whole lot simpler.

Dianne gives her another quick look, shrewder this time. Suddenly she sees a troubled woman who, like herself, has had her eyes on the main chance for a long time or, if not that, any chance that might come along, maybe even a chance like Clive. 'Me, I'd rather get cancer,' she answers. The funny thing is, she means it too. If it weren't for the babies and Davey, she'd just smoke and die as fast as possible. Especially Davey, he's such a funny little sad sack. She couldn't leave him without her to fight his corner.

'Tell Clive I'll catch him later,' Dianne repeats. But she doesn't trust her voice to add anything further.

'Sure,' Sarah answers. She sees again how unhappy Dianne looks and guesses she doesn't know the half of it, married to a man like Clive. If only Dianne knew how to protect herself a bit better. But then she stops, realising it is herself Dianne needs protecting from. She closes her eyes in shame, a few seconds worth, and misses the brief sight of her son slipping in through the kitchen door, his schoolbag slung over his shoulder.

★★★

On his way up the stairs, Ben is aware of voices above him, but he is thinking about his mother and the fat woman with the babies. He likes the fat woman when she stops to talk to him. She tells him disgusting things about the babies and she has never once asked him how he is getting on at school. Surprisingly, he likes finding out things about the babies.

He pushes open the door into his attic bedroom and stops dead. Tossie, Clive, and the hippie are sitting on the floor in front of him. Tossie is between the two men and her flimsy top has fallen off both shoulders. She is giggling and leaning into Clive. Tord is slumped against the wall with his eyes closed. He looks long gone. Clive is rolling a joint with neat, precise gestures. There's a pile already rolled beside him.

'Hey there,' he says, grinning up at Ben.

'Hey there yourself,' Ben answers. It comes out sullen which is not what he intended. It's just finding them all here in his room like this. And, judging from the smoke, they've been at it for some time. He drops his school bag on the bed and sees that it is messed up in a way it wasn't when he left this morning. There are tools and wood scattered around the room but the window has still not been put back in place.

Clive finishes and lights up. He passes first to Tossie. She leans forward and rests one hand on his knee while she takes her hit, then she motions Ben over. Ben squats slightly behind the little group, keeping his distance, but Tossie reaches out and pulls him towards her.

'Come on big boy,' she says.

Caught off balance, Ben falls forward into her lap. The feel of her is both pliant and strong. Again it takes his breath away.

She laughs. 'Did I just say that? I can't believe I said that.'

Ben has no idea what she has just said. He pulls back, feeling her arms resist his retreat. 'Tell me I didn't say that,' she laughs.

But when he looks at her face, what he sees is a smile so sexy, so inviting, he can't believe his luck. She puts both her arms around the back of his neck and pulls him in until he rests up against her. Over her bare shoulder, he can see the hippie with his eyes closed, his mouth open, and Clive laughing to himself as he rolls up yet another joint and drops it in the pile at his feet.

To Ben this is just about the best situation he has ever found himself in, in his entire life. This is just about as close to perfect as it's possible to get, Tossie, unlimited weed, Tord asleep. He moves a little closer into her embrace.

Suddenly Clive laughs and Ben looks up, startled. Clive is staring at the door, with a big stupid grin on his face. He shakes his head in mock dismay and looks at the joint in his hand. 'Guess we're busted,' he says.

Ben twists sharply around and sees his mother standing in the doorway watching them. He has no idea how long she's been there. He has no idea how long anything has been anywhere. At that moment, Tord takes in a great snoring breath that causes his shoulders to rise and fall with the effort. The sound is at the same time grotesque and repellent.

Sarah looks at the hippie, at the line of dribble down his chin and the way his head is toppling backwards. His flies are open. She looks at the others looking up at her. She can see at once that she should not have come and turns to leave.

Clive calls after her, 'Hey.' But he doesn't trust himself to find the right words. That was some serious expression on her face. Of course he understands it is because of the boy. He listens to her descending the uncarpeted stairs. Then he turns to Ben. 'Your mother,' he asks, 'she's cool?'

Ben answers immediately. 'No way.'

Clive gathers up the pile of smokes and stuffs them in his shirt pocket. 'Guess we're fucked,' he says. He takes a cigarette from the other pocket and lights up. He thinks for a long minute then turns back to Ben. 'You sure about that? She seems kind of cool.'

'Jesus Clive,' Tossie says, finally pushing Ben away. 'Of course she's not cool. What do you expect?'

Clive tosses the unfinished cigarette out through the missing window. This is not a good situation. 'She's pissed off?' he asks Ben. 'You really think so?'

Ben shrugs his shoulders.

'She'll come round, right?' Clive looks at the boy for reassurance. He does not want to lose this job that pays out regular, no questions asked, a situation that does not come his way every day. 'Maybe just give her a little time, yea?'

★★★

On the stairs, Sarah is dismayed. They didn't have to look like that on her account, like she was some sort of enemy or something. In fact, she would like to be in there with them if it wasn't for Ben. It's only for him that she disapproves, her failure with him bringing her inch-by-inch closer to a collapse she hasn't named yet, but one she thinks will be total and irrevocable. And maybe she's a little annoyed at Tossie, the way she's always throwing herself at Ben. She knows exactly who it is that's going to get hurt if there's any hurt going around. And when isn't there hurt going around? But she's not angry at anything else, except maybe the way Clive throws himself at her too. As if Di doesn't have enough on her plate. That Clive, it didn't look like he was saying no to much of anything. Still, there's no reason for them to look at her like she's some sort of enemy or something.

Halfway down the stairs she remembers why it is she came up in the first place and turns back. In the room they are all still sitting on the floor exactly as she left them. No one is speaking. The only sound is the hippie snoring.

'I forgot.' Sarah addresses this to Clive, ignoring the others. 'Dianne was looking for you.'

'Me?' Clive says, clearly surprised. Through the window he has seen Dianne pushing the pram along the lane. But it seems that was hours ago and he has long forgotten.

'I think she needs you to take her somewhere,' she adds.

Clive watches Sarah again turn to leave the room, with those tight jeans rolled up at the bottom, pretty ankles. He is looking at her with that look older men keep for the young girls they are doing something wrong with because those girls are engaged to their best friends, or girls whose sisters are their wives. But the thought trails off, unfinished and confused, leaving him with a sense of unease.

Ben gets up and moves across to his table on the other side of the room.

'Listen,' Tossie says, again looking sideways at the boy but speaking to Clive. 'I owe you.' Her voice is desirous, acquisitive. But as soon as she has said it, she has forgotten what it is she owes him.

It is not, after all, in her nature to owe anybody anything.

'Forget it,' Clive says. He is well used to her self-seeking little games and he is both gratified and uneasy. He decides she can do anything she wants and he'll go along with it. He looks at the boy sitting at the table. If only she didn't throw herself at every man and boy in sight. If only she didn't throw herself at him. How can he be expected to say no? It's more than is reasonable to ask of any man.

He turns to Ben. 'Your mother,' he says. 'Got to keep her sweet, right?' He winks at the boy and when Ben doesn't respond, he goes on. 'She's cool you know. I think you're wrong about that.'

★★★

In the kitchen Sarah is searching through the packing cases that are lined up along the far wall, now stuck fast to the stone floor by whatever new thing the builder has put on it. Her movements are angry. Her gold rings flash. Her gold sandals catch the late afternoon light. She looks expensively cultivated for just such a moment. Clive cannot take his eyes off her. The girl upstairs, a few seconds ago, she could be a million miles away, a million years ago.

'Listen,' he says to Sarah, indicating some vague area behind him with a manly shrug. 'You don't want to take too much notice of all that.' He is watching her pretty mouth as she smiles cynically. 'Kids these days,' he adds, hoping to distance himself from whatever blame is going around. 'It's what they all do. It's no big deal.' He sees that her smile is hard-boiled beyond his expectation. Well, she's not the only one who has learned to live life in cold blood. He's about to tell her exactly how it is that he knows it's no big deal, but he's having trouble making his thoughts cross over some sort of invisible barrier into words. He is not used to finding himself short of a smart thing to say.

'Do you want a drink?' she interrupts.

He takes a couple of steps into the room, as if given permission in some sort of code only they understand. 'Sure,' he answers. 'Why not?' He guesses he has underestimated her. She is unhappier than she looks.

Sarah pours whiskey into two cut-glass tumblers. It is to find these that she has taken the trouble to search through the packing cases. Her own mother used these glasses to subdue her guests in years past, these and the heavy ornate silver that is somewhere in one of the other boxes. 'So, Clive,' she says, studying her outsized glass. All the sadness of every failed marriage in the universe seems concentrated in this illicit, calculated, brown drink. 'It's what they all do,' she repeats his words.

He raises his eyebrows quizzically. In the mirror, he knows it is a gesture that makes him look boyish and innocent. And at this moment he judges he needs all the help he can get.

'So?' he questions. 'We drinking to that then? What they all do?'

She shrugs her shoulders and then salutes him with the heavy ceremonial glass. Her gold bracelets slip prettily down each wrist.

He takes another couple of steps towards her. He has no idea what's going on and is only relieved that she isn't angry at him. He accepts the ornate glass, sips the expensive whiskey and allows himself a quick look at her breasts.

'No,' her voice is dry, bitter. She is smiling mockingly. 'We're drinking to nothing. Just drinking.'

It comes to him with a jolt that he amuses her. It is the last thing he expected, to have caused her amusement. 'Yea?' he questions. 'I'll drink to that.' But in truth her smile has left him unnerved.

She sips her own drink, not liking it. Watching him, she sees he has, as she expected, a charlatan's approach to relationships, everything on the outside, easy to see, easy to lie, easy to get rid of. He doesn't deserve Dianne, no way. She understands he is no different from any other man. His pastimes are all based on cruelty to women, to each other, to passing weaklings. Unlike her sex whose pastimes are based on exclusion, assessing, worry. 'You're a bastard,' she tells him with the same dry self-reproaching smile.

'You bet I am,' he answers, taking another step towards her and grinning with relief. He lifts his glass and tosses the drink down in one great pleasurable swallow. 'You fucking bet I am.'

★★★

Upstairs, in the high attic, the room is now quiet and still. Tord is slumped against the wall still deeply asleep. To Tossie, it looks like he might never move again. She glances sideways at Ben, sitting at his table staring at a pile of magazines. 'That Clive,' she says. She is studying the manly width of the boy's back, though his neck is skinny like a child's. 'Guess he's done his three minutes work for the day.' She laughs. 'He's always got more important stuff to do.'

Ben gives no sign that he has heard. He is thinking about the builder downstairs with his mother. They'll be talking about him, his mother explaining the problem, the builder agreeing with every word.

Tossie sighs and comes over to stand behind him. She sees the magazines he is staring at are boy's action comics, dog-eared and worn through years of use. She guesses he is going over familiar territory. 'So,' she says. 'You doing your homework?' She presses herself against the back of his chair, not touching him. She lets her scarf trail across his right arm and hand.

'No way,' he snaps back. 'I never do homework.'

She laughs. 'Me neither.' She moves over to the boy's narrow bed and stretches herself out. 'I hated it,' she adds. She puts one arm behind her head and closes her eyes. 'Homework, don't remind me.'

After a few minutes she says, 'Got any stuff left?' Briefly she opens her eyes. Tord is still so far gone he'll be lucky to get back before next week. The boy is getting up and coming towards her. Quickly she closes her eyes again.

For a long time Ben stands by the bed looking down at Tossie, with the freshly lit cigarette smoking in his hand. It is all he has to offer. He does not know what to do. The shape of her is perfectly visible through the thin clothes. She is beautiful beyond anything he has ever seen. Yet he remains curiously unastonished, as if he expected no less. It is ugliness that would have stunned him. About Tossie there is nothing ill proportioned or misshapen, no wrinkle, sag or blemish. She is perfect.

Suddenly she reaches out and grabs hold of his wrist with one hand. With the other hand she removes the cigarette. Keeping her eyes closed and keeping hold of him, she inhales deeply. 'Ah,' she sighs. Then slowly she pulls him down onto the bed beside her. Her grip on his arm allows him no choice, yet he could have twisted free with the slightest of gestures. She eases sideways to make room and, when he is stretched out beside her, she moves again but this time to nestle up against him. 'Ah,' she sighs a second time, like an affectionate child. She stubs the cigarette out on the wall behind them.

Ben finds that somehow his hand has come to rest on her bare midriff. His fingers are burning yet clammy with sweat. Her skin beneath his touch is sweetly cool.

After a few minutes she lifts his hand and moves it to her breast. This is beyond his wildest dreams, that he should find himself on his own bed with the sexiest, most beautiful girl he has ever seen and she has just lifted his hand and put it where she has. He looks down and sees that the ink from her tattoo is smeared across her white top and her bare skin. But, before he has time to figure this out, she has moved one leg on top of his thigh. He feels her muscles tense full-length ready to roll herself over on top of him. He finds he is holding his breath. He is dazzled, spellbound, half-dead with desire. 'Ah,' she sighs for the third time.

Suddenly there is a great drawn-out wail from the other side of the room, desolate and blood curdling. Tossie stops with a judder. Ben freezes. The cry comes again, like a half-starved wolf across the frozen tundra. Lucid in shock, Ben knows he is about to be killed. He wills his breath to stop, his heart to fail, so that it will make the rest of the coming agony quicker. He looks over Tossie's shoulder at Tord and she twists to do the same. Together they brace themselves for what is about to happen.

But Tord is not looking at them. He is standing at the missing window looking down at the ground below. He brings both hands up to his hair and tears at it. 'Fuck!' he wails, drawing the word out in anguish. Still without looking at Ben and Tossie in each other's arms on the bed, he rushes out of the room and down the two flights of stairs. They can hear him crying as he goes, 'Fuck!' elongating the word in the throes of some mad desperation. They can hear him outside, wailing. 'Fucking fuck!'

Tossie twists herself off the bed and is at the window in two strides, with Ben immediately behind her. Below them Tord is pacing back and forth by the side of the moat where his motorbike is lying on its side, three-quarters submerged. The handlebars are twisted awkwardly backwards. There is a strong smell of petrol in the air.

153

'Fuck,' he is chanting. 'Fuck the fuckers.'

Tossie gives a little scream and she too rushes from the room. In a few seconds she is at Tord's side, staring at the motorbike. She reaches out to touch his arm but he yanks himself away. She tries several more times until, without warning, he stops and rounds on her.

'You fucker!' he cries.

Tossie steps backwards, not sure of what she is being accused. There is, after all, some considerable choice.

'You fucking fucker!' he repeats, raising his fist as if to hit her. 'You did this.'

'Me?' Tossie flinches but stands her ground. Sure, she's always mad at him for something but she would never do anything like this. Other things of course, other guys to make him jealous, but never anything like this. 'I never!' she shouts back at him. 'I wouldn't.'

But he is now wading into the thigh-deep water. Contorted with the effort, he tries to lift the bike. It is stuck fast in the muddy clay. He turns full circle and stares back at Tossie. His long tunic drips water. His wild hair swings. His arms lash out. In his rage, he is lost to reason or sense and Tossie does not try to speak.

Upstairs in the high attic, Ben is watching. He can see that it took real courage for Tossie to stand her ground with Tord, behaving like a mad man, the way he is. She is more wonderful than he imagined. There is no one else in the world like her. Down there beside the moat, she is a slender goddess, bold-spirited and far out of his reach. It is a realisation that dismays him into instant misery, that and his part in exposing her to this peril.

★★★

At the open kitchen door Sarah and Clive are also watching the strange scene. She has no idea what is going on. But Clive knows exactly. He alone has seen the boy creeping around the side of the house like he was up to no good, which for once is the truth. He's seen the boy roll the motorbike down the slope into the moat. He has also seen Di pushing the pram and talking to Sarah. They walked right past and didn't notice a thing.

'Jesus,' he says, easing himself further away from her. He is hoping he can slip out without getting involved. 'What the fuck?' he says to Sarah.

She shakes her head. On an empty stomach the whiskey has already clouded her thinking. She knows she has decided she and James are totally finished but she has decided this so many times over the years it is beginning to lose credibility, even inside her head where anything can be decided without consequence. And now she sees only that whatever is going on with the wrecked motorbike suddenly appearing in their garden moat, it is again some evidence of her failure to hold things together, to keep normal life going.

'Jesus,' Clive repeats, looking at the bike and then at the mad hippie and then at Tossie, trying again to step closer to him. It seems he ought to say something, try to explain, maybe claim it was an accident. But, before he can think of what, the big city car rounds the corner and pulls in next to his van. He watches James get out. Here is the last person he wants to see right now, the husband, wanting explanations.

James looks at Tossie standing half in the water next to the hippie. He looks at the twisted motorbike in the middle of his moat. He looks at Sarah leaning in the kitchen doorway with a glass in her hand, obviously pissed. He turns to Clive. 'What the hell?' he asks.

Clive shrugs his shoulders and scratches the back of his head good-naturedly. 'Don't ask me,' he grins. He peers purposefully into the distance. 'Guess it's every man for himself.' He laughs.

'What?' James looks at him in disbelief. The builder's a wanker, sure, but he's not an idiot. What is he talking about? Again he looks at Tossie and the wrecked motorbike, and at Sarah in the doorway.

'What are you saying?' he asks Clive. 'What the hell is going on?'

Again Clive shrugs his shoulders. It seems it's all for the best, what with the ciggie he tossed out the window and the petrol leak in the bike. It could have been a whole lot worse. There could have been an explosion, people killed. The kid did everyone a favour in the end.

'Did Tossie do this?' James asks, watching the girl in the water.

'Could be,' Clive answers.

'What the hell?' James repeats, looking back at Tord who is again trying to pull the bike from the moat. He doesn't believe the builder, not for a moment. And what is Sarah's part in all this?

'He's a whole hog of a man,' Clive grins in the direction of the distraught hippie, as if by extension claiming some sort of credit for himself, for all this, for the two agitated women, the drama. After all, credit is one thing, blame another.

'Jesus,' James says. 'I don't believe any of this.'

Two and a half hours on the motorway, stuck in traffic, his guts aching worse than ever, this is the last thing he needs. He looks up at the windowless window and sees Ben suddenly twist away, guilt written in every gesture. Here's another problem he doesn't need at the end of the day. He looks at the roofless porch, the broken back door, the builder's debris scattered around the yard. And inside it will be worse. He looks at Sarah. 'Jesus,' he repeats, pushing past her. 'I don't want to know.' He has spotted the open whiskey bottle in the middle of the kitchen table. 'Just don't fucking tell me,' he says, willing the pain in his gut to recede just long enough to allow the first shot to slip past, unnoticed, so that the second will be a workmanlike pleasure and the third can be savoured slowly, maybe with a little accompanying conversation. Already the moat, the builder, the hippie, his unhappy son and lost wife, all forgotten.

10. NEW LOVE DELIGHTS

Predictably, Ben is obsessed. Even asleep, he never stops thinking about Tossie. He knows this because when his eyes snap open at three in the morning, or seven, he is in her arms, with an erection and a conviction he has been there all night. They are making love but haven't finished yet. Her hands wander up and down his torso. His hands cup her breasts and, when they're not doing that, they're following a natural pathway to down there. His eyes snap open.

Now, in his restlessness, Ben is walking from the car to the school gates. He has not responded to his mother's pleading look.

'You'll be OK?' she has just asked.

But he is thinking about the feel of Tossie's skin and the little appreciative noises she makes.

'Why isn't there any petrol in this car?' she asks. He's taking it, she thinks. And she hasn't been paying attention. Here's another disaster waiting to happen. She feels the chill wind of failure blowing through the open car windows. With her son she is, as ever, thwarted, outplayed.

A few seconds later, Carling runs straight past Ben and stops with his back against the plinth that supports the concrete statue of the school's founder. Placed dead centre in the entrance, it is hoped the statue will give the school a higher status. In fact what it does is to provide a venue for the most obvious lavatorial jokes, some funny, all obscene. Today, at quarter to nine in the morning, the statue is wearing a plastic apron in the shape of a nude female. Hardly anyone even bothers to look.

In passing, Carling makes a grab for Ben and misses. 'Hey, shit face,' he shouts and throws a set of keys, underhand like a girl. In the next second he is down with four boys, his friends, on top of him. They are beating him up good-naturedly, taking turns and not hurting him too much. Ben catches the keys and immediately thrusts them out of sight in his jacket pocket. The others do not seem to have noticed, though one of them turns to him.

'Saddlebags,' he calls, equally good-natured. 'What'cha?'

Ben shrugs his shoulders and watches them casually kick Carling's legs. A few seconds later, by unspoken agreement, they have finished and move away in a tight, satisfied group, pleased to have a head start on the main business of the day which is inflicting casual violence, on each other and on any available objects.

At the same time Mr Raftiche comes up to stand beside Ben. He is watching Carling get up and dust himself off. 'You know,' he says to Ben, 'one of these days you guys are going to learn to communicate without either beating each other up or shagging each other stupid.'

Ben looks at him astonished. It is not what he expected to hear from a teacher, and in that ridiculous American accent.

Mr Raftiche turns to Carling, who is limping towards them. 'Good thing those were your least worst friends,' he says. 'Good thing I arrived in time,' though he has no illusions that his arrival had anything to do with the break-up of the fight.

His thoughts are interrupted by Ruby who runs up to them out of breath and sobbing. 'Why didn't you stop them?' she accuses him. 'You could have stopped them.' Frantically she grabs at her son. Carling pushes her away.

'Me?' Mr Raftiche laughs. 'But there were ten of them.' In fact there were four.

Out of the blue, it comes to Ben that the only person here who is really upset is Ruby. Now she is trying to lead Carling in towards her office and he is resisting. At last he breaks free. 'Jesus,' he says. 'Mum.' Nervously he looks over his shoulder.

Mr Raftiche takes Ruby's arm. 'He's right,' he says. 'It was nothing, a boyish scrap.'

'But they were kicking him.' Ruby's face is stricken. 'They could have killed him.'

'Nonsense,' Mr Raftiche reassures her. 'That wasn't real kicking.' He turns to Ben. 'Was it?'

Ben looks from one to the other and nervously fingers the keys in his pocket.

'You see.' Mr Raftiche gives her little huddled shoulders a fatherly squeeze.

Seeing his opportunity, Ben slips away after Carling. He is drawn to whatever trouble is on offer and, judging from Carling's face, there's something going on here. Bored witless in the classroom, Carling comes alive when he is up to something. You could say it's his one gift. And this morning his face is energetic, enthusiastic, creative.

Mr Raftiche leads Ruby inside where, though neither of them knows it yet, more trouble is waiting. A small crowd has gathered outside the main office, the other two secretaries, a couple of staff, a handful of students. The office door is shut. The lights are off. Clearly they are locked out.

The small group mills aimlessly around. No one seems too bothered, finding it quite pleasant not to have to get on with the work of the day, just yet. But Ruby brings her hands to her mouth and gasps in horror. Instinctively she knows that whatever is going on, it's her fault. She reaches into the bottom of her plastic handbag where she keeps the extra set of office keys, though it is not her responsibility to lock or unlock anything. Surprisingly, they are not there. Again she gasps in horror. She has never needed these keys before, and now the one day when she does, she has left them at home. They are in her other bag, the straw bag with the pink raffia flowers. She knows absolutely that is where they are.

Several others have noticed her stricken face. 'Oh dear,' one of them says. 'We hoped you'd have a set.'

'I do,' Ruby says. But then, overcome by her limitless failure, she can't go on.

'The caretaker has lost his,' someone else explains, adding wryly, 'what a surprise.'

Overhearing this exchange, a few people drift off.

'Don't worry about it.' Mr Raftiche leans down to speak to her alone. 'Treat it as an unexpected holiday.' He gives her his best grin.

But her frightened little face is screwed up in an agony of self-blame. He sees that she is hopeless, an emotional cripple. And, in his experience, emotional cripples always end up abused and victimised. He sighs and turns away, knowing he is not above such things.

★★★

Many times during the day, Ben fingers the keys in his pocket. He has no idea what is going on and Carling has disappeared altogether. He tells no one. Rumour drifts around about the office door having to be smashed in with an axe. Someone else has seen a police car. Finally, as Ben is leaving to catch the bus, his friends from the morning's beating appear from nowhere.

'Give them here,' one of them tells him.

At once Ben hands him the keys.

'You in for tonight?' another of the boys asks Ben. He is an older boy, no longer in school but often around.

But he is immediately interrupted. 'Shut up, not him.'

'Jesus, it's only school,' the first one says. 'Let him come.'

As suddenly as they appeared, the group disappears. Ben sees he is totally forgotten before the words have died in the air around him. A heavy weight of sadness rises up out of his chest and hangs in the air with the dead words, a familiar experience. The gap between what he is and what he wants to be is so huge that he can never cross it. At best, he manages a tolerable imitation. At worst, he is an obvious fake.

★★★

At home, at the end of the terrible day, Ruby goes straight to her straw bag which has remained untouched on the top shelf of her wardrobe since the summer. The office keys are not there. She searches a second time through the jumble of used tissues and sadly nostalgic shopping lists. Today is all her fault, the way they had to take off the hinges and break the lock to get in, the disruption, the expense. She is always supposed to have the spare keys. She is the official back-up. If only she weren't so useless, a useless baggage as her mother used to say, often.

Though, now that her mother is gone, Ruby has come to see how it is when you live with someone, you focus on all the bad things and fail to see what a good person they really are. Now that she's gone, Ruby sees it wasn't her mother who was bad but she herself, for not understanding. Well, she won't make that mistake with her son, no matter what he gets up to. It's her job to understand and forgive. She is preparing herself for the worst, where the keys are concerned.

At the same time Ruby is standing in her bedroom lost in lonely melancholy, Carling and the crowd he hangs around with are crossing the field at the back of the school. Ben brings up the rear, uneasily keeping some distance between himself and the others. They wait to be sure no one else is around. It is slightly more than three hours since the last bell and already the place is deserted. The staff car park is empty. The cleaners have been and gone. The lights are out.

Expertly, the boys slip in the side door of the science block. Everyone knows the doors are not alarmed, since a small explosion in the lab a few months earlier. Making no pretence at stealth, they head for the main office, Ruby's office. 'Fucking dump,' the older boy says, looking at the peeling paint and dirty scuffed walls. Because the day is hot, he is not wearing his leather jacket but a black T-shirt with the sleeves cut off. On his left arm, above the elbow, he has tied a girl's black silk scarf and, into this makeshift armband, he has tucked a pack of cigarettes. Ben has never seen anyone do this before. It is strange and wonderful, like an unexpected glimpse into someplace dark and exotic.

At the office door, they come together in a tight group, unified in the absolute conviction that money is everything. And you get money by stealing, unless you're clever in which case you get money by exploiting others. But, they are as certain as they are of life itself, that money never comes from hard work. Again Ben hangs back, disconcerted and confused, feeling ambushed. Buy why and by whom? He has gone to some trouble to be here. He wants to be here.

The first boy inserts the key in the lock but the door swings open of its own accord. Momentarily, the group is surprised into silence. They stare into the empty, darkening room. When it is clear there is no one there, someone laughs. 'Fucking hell.'

'Fucking shitting hell,' Carling adds.

Already the others are circling the room. Already they have found the cash box which is locked. It is immediately obvious they have no key small enough to fit, so the boy with the cigarettes tucks it under his arm. 'It's fucking empty,' he says. 'Fuck it.' He gathers up two football trophies from the display shelf. Judging from the weight, they might be valuable. Someone else picks up an electric typewriter, scattering papers as he does so. Phones are being severed from their connections with swift surgical precision.

There is a shout of glee from the other side of the room. 'Holy shit,' Ben says, holding up a state-of-the-art cine camera.

'Fuck,' Carling adds approvingly.

The others are pocketing anything that looks like it might be worth anything, a radio, a silver framed photograph, two unopened multi-packs of chocolate, even biros and coloured notepaper.

'Come on.' The boy with the armband heads for the door. 'It's crap.' The others follow at once, leaving behind a devastation of messed-up paper, knocked-about books, overturned chairs. In the stillness of the late summer evening, the small shabby office looks like it has been visited by a mysterious and self-contained natural disaster while everyone else was at home watching TV and calmly eating their evening food.

Within an hour the radio, the phones, the two football trophies and the cine camera have changed hands for a bit of dope, a few pills, whatever happened to be available to them at that moment.

Within a second hour, the pills and powder have been smoked, swallowed and inhaled.

Within the third hour, Ben, at least, is home in his own bed, leaving the others scattered off into the night, to get lucky.

'He'll kill me,' Ben has said to the others, meaning his father. 'He has guns.'

'Yea?' one of the group sneers. 'Your old man uses guns? On the job?'

'Arsehole,' Ben answers. 'He just has them.' Then he gets out of there fast. He hears them laughing.

For Ben there is only one person he wants to get lucky with, now more than ever. The feel of her breasts, the imagined taste of her down there, rises up in his heightened thoughts until he can barely breathe.

She fills his head, his body, the room, the fields around the house, then the whole world.

★★★

When Ruby arrives at school the following morning, ten minutes early, she finds the office door open and the caretaker standing bewildered in the glare of the over-sized fluorescent lights. The room is wrecked.

'It's not my fault,' he tells Ruby. He kicks at a scatter of phone books, knowing yesterday he left his keys unattended and some little sod has nicked them.

Ruby stares at his angry face, then at the mess around her, knowing that her keys are missing and there is only one person who could have taken them.

'It's not my fault,' the caretaker repeats, registering her stricken face. Funny creature, taking it to heart like that. It's only a crappy office when all is said and done. The insurance will pay for whatever is nicked.

Ruby can see at once that what is missing is everything that's worth anything. She looks at the bottom shelf for Robert's cine camera. It is not there. If yesterday was bad, today is going to be unendurable.

'The little sods.' The caretaker again kicks at the debris. 'They won't get away with it.' Then, looking at her face, it suddenly comes to him. That son of hers, what's his name, Carling, where there's trouble he's got his stupid arse in it. He casts a furtive glance at Ruby. You don't have to be a genius to put two and two together.

'So,' he says casually. 'You found your keys then?'

Ruby looks away and shakes her head. 'Not yet. I think they're in my other bag,' she lies and is immediately horrified. Busily she uprights her chair and clears a space for it amongst the clutter on the floor. All the while she is looking for the camera. He has left it with her for safekeeping and, with his hand on hers, lovingly shown her how it works.

'Oh yea?' the caretaker laughs knowingly. 'My missus has one of those, other bags.' Again he glances at her stricken face. It's so obvious he doesn't know why he didn't think of it before. Why should he take the blame for anything? He'll say he's just remembered that he left the keys in the wife's car and she went off with them, accidental like. 'Listen,' he tells her magnanimously, 'I'll send someone to give you a hand.' Ruby looks up and attempts a grateful smile. She knows he won't.

As he turns to leave, Mr Raftiche comes into the room. He sees there are tears in her eyes. 'Oh Robert,' she sobs. 'It's all my fault.'

Quickly he puts his arm around her skinny, slumped shoulders. Briefly it looks like she might actually collapse. He too stares at the messed-up room. 'Hey.' He gives her shoulders what he hopes is a jolly squeeze. He waits for her to stop shaking, but she doesn't. 'Hey there,' he repeats. If only she didn't blame herself for everything that's going on. His ex, now she would have looked around for the nearest available sucker and pointed the finger so fast that her own innocence would have been a foregone conclusion. But then, he's well past thinking about his ex. All that is history, over and done with. What does he care about any of that anyway?

For a long moment he keeps his arm around her and holds her close in the way, he hopes, a brother would. Then he starts to speak. 'You know,' he tells her, 'psychiatric hospitals are full of women saying it's all my fault. And prisons are full of men saying I didn't do it.'

He gives a sharp little laugh. But Ruby is shaking her head and wringing her hands in a torment of self-reproach. She has no idea what he is talking about.

'It's all my fault,' she says.

Mr Raftiche sighs. It's hopeless, as he thought. Yet he keeps his arm around her quivering shoulders for longer than any brother would and longer than is strictly necessary.

★★★

The same morning, knowing there will be trouble, Ben has watched his mother's car disappear after dropping him off at the founder's statue. Today the statue is wearing an outsized sanitary towel. Then he has slipped around the back of the playing fields and caught the bus home again. It is a familiar manoeuvre. Now he is waiting in the corrugated shed, hoping Tossie will arrive with Tord. Her arrival is unpredictable and many days it is a fruitless wait. He passes the time digging holes in the ground with a stick and brooding. It occurs to him that the only place he feels at home is in a shed. It occurs to him that this is not a good thing. But mostly he thinks about Tossie. In his thoughts, she is in his arms, writhing gently, letting him take the lead.

★★★

Today he is lucky. He has hardly been ten minutes in the shed when Tord pulls up in an old shit-heap of a car he's acquired from somewhere, since the motorbike was a write-off. Immediately Tossie throws open the door and turns back to shout something at him. Her beautiful face is rigid with anger. Her shoulders rise up, her hips twist, she slams the door hard. The next thing she is striding towards the house. Her fabulous breasts swing first to the left, then to the right. Ben cannot take his eyes off her. Already Tord is speeding down the lane in a haze of riled dust, his own anger seeming to fuel the car to high-octane speeds it would not otherwise be capable of.

A few minutes later his mother appears, casually throwing her pretty gold-chained bag over her shoulder. Some days she likes to get out of the way and leave Tossie to do the cleaning, if you could call it that. Some days she doesn't. In a few more seconds she too is speeding down the dusty lane. Ben decides to give it ten minutes so as not to appear too obvious.

A few seconds later he comes in through the broken kitchen door. Tossie, standing in front of the open fridge with her back to him, is startled and cries out. But when she sees it is only him, she laughs.

'You scared me,' she says. She grins happily. Again she sees that he is going to be some great looking guy, one of these days. She comes over and puts a hand gently on his arm. 'What are you doing here?' she asks. She feels him sway. Poor kid, he must be sick, to have come home like this in the middle of the morning. 'You OK?' she asks. She steps closer, pressing herself against him and lifts her hand to feel his forehead. He really is filling out nicely. If only he were just a bit older. Though she seems to remember there was a birthday celebration recently. If only her friends wouldn't accuse her of cradle snatching. She pushes his hair back. He feels cool enough. 'Want me to make you a cup of tea?' she asks, shifting her weight to the other foot so that her breasts move against him. 'Want me to bring it up to your room?' He really is going to be a looker. And the nice thing is he doesn't know it yet. Most guys, Tord included, once they figure it out, there's no stopping them. Little bastards turn into huge bastards overnight.

In his room, Ben quickly throws off the school uniform and kicks it out of sight under his bed. He pulls on the black jeans. They fit tight, which is a new experience for him and one he quite likes. Next he pulls the black T-shirt with the cut-off sleeves on over his head. This too is satisfyingly tight. He flexes his biceps and inhales deeply, causing his chest to expand. Lastly, he puts the two silver earrings in each ear and slips a silver band on each wrist. What with the silver belt buckle and the silver studs on his boots, he has taken on an interesting metallic appearance. This too is a new feeling and one he finds exciting. Yet again he is surprised at these changes in himself though he has deliberately caused them to happen.

He sits down on the edge of the bed to wait. Five minutes pass, ten. How long can it take to make a cup of tea? He squirms restlessly, then jumps up and paces twice back and forth across the tiny attic room. He can wait no longer.

At the bottom of the stairs, he hears Tossie talking to someone, and there is a baby crying. Warily, he comes into the kitchen. Dianne is sitting at the table, one hand rocking the pram. Davey is on the floor at her feet, pushing a red toy car with no wheels. Tossie is holding the other baby, the one that is crying. When she notices him, a look of surprise crosses her face. It is obvious she has forgotten all about him. She gives him an outrageous wink, as if to say *You think I could forget about you? Never.* Then she brings her attention back to the child. 'Oh baby,' she says, as the little girl nuzzles her breast. 'What are you doing?' She looks at Ben and laughs. 'Oh baby, baby,' Tossie says, lifting the child up over her head.

'Stop that,' Dianne tells her. Her voice is flat, almost disinterested. 'Give her here.'

Tossie laughs and hands the child over. At once Dianne opens her man's denim shirt and removes a huge blue-veined breast from inside her bra. Instantly, the crying stops. The baby moves her head from side to side across the monstrous nipple. Then, in the next instant, she has clamped herself on and is sucking vigorously.

Astonished, Ben is not sure he has seen what he thinks he has. It all happened so fast. Of course they have had films in school about babies feeding, contraception, birth, all that. But everyone knows those kind of films have got nothing to do with what really happens. And now Dianne is lighting a cigarette with her free hand. Bored, she drops the match into an empty saucer.

'Want me to take this one?' Tossie asks, already manoeuvring the pram towards the door. Dianne lowers her eyelids wearily.

'You too Davey,' Tossie adds. She holds out her hand for the silent little boy.

Then she turns to Ben, who is still staring at the feeding baby, and flashes him a smile that promises him everything he ever dreamed of, which is after all easy enough since there is only ever one thing in his dreams. He follows her like a lost lamb. She can do anything she wants with him. She is his fantasy and love, his greatest desire, his reason for existing in this life.

'Yea, thanks,' Dianne says, giving Ben the same weary look.

Tossie and Ben, with Davey following, walk to the edge of the derelict orchard and stop in the place where the ground slopes gently out of sight from the house. In the three or four minutes it has taken them to get here, Ben has worked his way through a range of emotions that would have drained the life out of a more experienced lover. He has been sick with fear, in an agony of desire, overcome by self-doubt. Now he is terrified, desperate and overwhelmed.

'Hey Ben,' Tossie says, looking at the mutilated T-shirt. 'Those guys you hang around with, you don't have to do everything they do, you know.'

Ben stares at her pretty face. He has not heard more than three words of what she has said. The blood is pounding in his ears. She is moving closer.

'They're a bunch of losers,' she adds. Grinning, she puts both her arms around the back of his neck and fiddles with the silver earrings that gimlet his delicate ear lobes. 'All this,' she says. She is again thinking, if only he were older. If only her friends wouldn't laugh at her. She moves closer still and again presses her breasts up against him. How unbelievably good-looking he's going to be in another year or two, with those shoulders, that face. If she's the first, he'll remember her forever. When he's old and grey, and trying to jerk off, he'll still be thinking of her.

Unnoticed, the little boy Davey wanders off and is confronted by an expanse of empty fields. He turns and heads forlornly back towards the house.

'You'll forget me,' Tossie says, letting her hand linger on the back of his neck. She can feel him tremble. Tough and cynical by the age of thirteen, she herself has not trembled this way for many years. Briefly, she is overcome with sadness for the little girl she once was and couldn't wait to leave behind. As for Tord, serves him right. It was not her fault about the motorbike. He has no right to blame her for that.

'Black is not your colour,' she says, pulling him down to the ground beside her. She has decided to let him do it, but not here. Besides, in her experience, which is lately her experience with Tord, the fun stops once you've let them do it. Tord wouldn't be kissing her all over with his eyes closed and shaking from head to foot, no way, the bastard. She told him a thousand times the motorbike wasn't her fault, the stupid shit.

★★★

In the kitchen Dianne is still feeding the other baby and talking on the phone. Unseen, Davey creeps in and slides into his now familiar place under the table. The stone floor is less cold than it used to be, but more sticky. Every time he moves, something sticks to his shorts. Gently he cleans the stuff off the bottom of the little red car. Then he hugs the car tightly and lies down beside it. He hears his mother say, 'Who is this?' a second time before she puts down the phone with a bang.

On the note pad Dianne is writing – Clive rang, no message. She knows that the baby has finished feeding and has fallen asleep on the nipple. This one does. The other one doesn't. Tenderly, she removes the infant and stares down at the beautiful still face and at the grotesque veined lump that is a part of her that used to be familiar but now has been taken over by something else. She too is overcome with sadness. Exhausted, hormones all over the place, stones heavier than she's ever been before, still she knows that the sadness has to do with a lot more than these things, as if they weren't enough to be getting on with. She kisses the baby and lays her in the cloth bouncing-cradle. She can't keep coming here every day. And, when she's not here and he is, if it isn't Sarah then it's Tossie. She knows him so well, the bastard. And she puts nothing past him, her own sister, most men would draw the line. And, if it hasn't happened already, then it's only a matter of time.

Accidentally, her foot strikes the little boy's arm. 'Davey,' she cries out. 'What are you doing under there?' She reaches down and lifts him up. She nuzzles him in the way that always used to make him laugh. Silently he clings to her. In her arms he is thin beyond belief. How did this happen and she didn't notice? He used to be such a plump rosy little thing, always a biscuit in his mouth, enthusiastic about food. Now, whatever she fixes for him, he leaves it. She hugs him tightly and after a long moment, she whispers into his hair. 'So, Inga, we got a problem here?' But the child does not respond.

★★★

A week later Sarah is talking to Mr Raftiche. 'You know,' he is explaining. 'They all do it.'

'I've heard that before,' she retorts. She has been told about the break-in and guesses the rest. It is for this she has sought him out.

Mr Raftiche chooses his words carefully, out of respect for her anguish over the boy. They have had this conversation before, or a version of it and he wishes he could think of something new to add, something that would make her flash those beautiful blue eyes at him with interest and excitement. Today she is wearing a long white dress, one of those loose clingy things, with gold chains at her neck and wrists, and gold sandals. He sees her toenails are painted gold, a nice touch. She sure knows how to put it together. In his experience, the women who can do that are the ones he desperately wants but can't have. If interest and excitement aren't on offer, then respect will have to do. Suddenly he is ashamed. She trusts him. She has come to him trusting him about something important. The pain in his chest appears out of nowhere, exactly where it always is, coiled and waiting.

Sarah looks trustingly at him. 'His father and I both think it's a good idea to get him away from those friends of his,' she says.

'Ah,' Mr Raftiche answers. He knows exactly who she's talking about, in that tone of voice, Carling and that lot. Poor Ruby, it's not her fault. The boy needs a father.

'Can you talk to him?' she adds. 'He listens to you.'

At that moment Ben enters the room.

'Ah,' Mr Raftiche repeats. 'Here you are.' He does not want to have to confront the boy, especially not with her here. He's a good boy and, in his experience, the good ones don't need to be told. They grow out of it just fine. And the bad ones, there's no point in telling them anything anyway.

Ben does not reply.

'So,' Mr Raftiche rocks back in his chair. He is finding it hard to think of anything to say, trustworthy, wise, even funny, anything would do. Absent-mindedly he massages the pain.

Still Ben is silent. He has positioned himself halfway between them and the door, knowing that they are expecting him to explain himself, knowing that blame for the break-in has finally worked its way round to include him.

'Well then,' his mother says. 'Go on, explain yourself.'

'Listen,' Mr Raftiche interrupts her. 'I don't want any explanations here.' He has seen the boy's sidelong glance into the middle distance before he swivels back with a lie. For twenty years he has been watching them do it. 'Just don't lie, cheat or steal unnecessarily,' he tells Ben.

Sarah stares at him. Her pretty mouth opens prettily in surprise. 'What kind of advice is that?' she asks. But she is smiling. The smile grows into a grin.

Mr Raftiche grins back at her.

'You're his teacher,' she laughs. 'You can't say that.'

She is so beautiful grinning at him, with the gold earrings flashing like that and the gold chains disappearing down the cleavage revealed by her white dress.

Unnoticed, Ben slips away. He knows when his mother starts to flirt, his presence is no longer required. He has heard that laugh before, seen that smile. Relieved, he slips through the door and is instantly out of sight.

'They don't take me seriously,' Mr Raftiche says seriously, noting the boy's disappearance. He can't take his eyes off her. The tiny, constricting pain has now spread all the way around the circumference of his heart. Lately beautiful women have had this effect on him, even strangers in the street. Come to think of it, lately all women have had this effect on him. The pain works its way inward until it comes out the other side, like a Cupid's arrow, gathering strength all the while. It's a stupid image. He'd laugh if it didn't hurt him so much.

'Yes they do,' she tells him, also watching the boy disappear. She is thinking, what a nice man. What he says is so funny and true. If only he knew how to dress better. If only he didn't stoop like that. Being tall is a good thing, but not if you stoop. Yet, what he says is so funny and surprising that it has left her with the conviction that Ben will be just fine. Now how can you explain that? She watches him grinning and massaging his chest oddly and realises that she is suddenly happy. All her troubles have mysteriously disappeared. 'I do too,' she adds.

★★★

When she gets back to the car, Ben is there before her. He has removed his school uniform shirt and underneath all along he has been wearing the black T-shirt with the cut-off sleeves. Already he has put back the silver earrings and strapped onto each wrist what looks like a spiked dog collar.

She looks at him and sighs. She is glad James is not here. She will not tell him about this new trouble. He will blame her. No, for her part, the sigh is not for all the junk he is wearing, or for what he's got himself into, but because, sitting beside her, he suddenly seems so much older, more manly. She sees her time with him is almost over.

Then, something else comes to her, out of the blue. The way he looks, it's the way Clive looks. The way he keeps getting into trouble all the time, this business with the school office, what goes on up in his bedroom, you can be sure those are the things Clive did when he was Ben's age. You can be sure those were not the things Roberto Raftiche did in his boyhood, nor were they the things James did.

Dismayed into silence, Sarah puts the key in the ignition and turns the engine over without clutching. The car lurches forward.

'Shit,' Ben says. 'What are you doing?' He gives her a quick hostile look.

'Sorry,' she says meekly. The thoughts that have come to her in the last few seconds have caught her off guard. She tries again, this time with the car properly in gear. 'There,' she says, treating him to a self-deprecating grin, 'knew I could do it.'

He looks at her with disdain.

She flinches. Lately her emotional spectrum has been narrowing alarmingly, despair, dismay, disappointment. But how can she convince him these are judgements about herself and not about him? He is looking out the side window, deliberately ignoring her. 'You know,' she says to his hostile back, 'to you it's just growing up. But to me it's the best of life.' She doesn't know why she's said this. It's not something she's thought before. In fact it sounds like something Mr Raftiche would say.

Still he ignores her. She can see the tendons tighten in his slender boy's neck as he twists further away from her.

'It's true,' she tells him, knowing that it is.

Then, after a few moments, when he still does not respond, she adds, 'Guess maybe I shouldn't have said that.' The vision of herself as having failed at something that can never be put right, has returned stronger than ever. Well no, not stronger than after the lost baby, but near enough as strong. Near enough as makes no difference.

11. THE SAINTS BAVRO, JAMES AND WILLIBROARD

On his way to the AA meeting, James stops for directions at The Nag's Head. He has one Stella. Well, you have to, don't you? Taking up the man's time like that. He is told to go past The Red Lion, left at The Morgan, left again at The Talbot Arms and it's under the church, the place where the meetings are held, opposite The Pierced Piers.

It turns out The Red Lion is at least 2 miles out, so that by the time he gets there he has forgotten the rest of the directions. He has another Stella and a JD chaser. Well, why not? After all, it's the last time. Overcome by the significance of the occasion, he has another Stella.

Back in the car, he is very careful. Your luck can run out just like that, with no warning. The number of men he knows, the wife driving them everywhere with that look on their faces. He unscrews the half of Jameson's he has on the seat beside him. Well, it is the absolute last time, for ever and ever. There's no way he could put up with that look on Vanessa's face when they're married. And she'd know how to do it all right. She wouldn't even need to practise. He has another small quaff and is astonished to find the bottle empty. He knew at the time it was a mistake, buying a half. Only kids and dossers buy halves. It's only because it's the total and absolute last time, one for the ditch so to speak. He forgives himself the mistake.

With fortitude, he drives right past The Morgan. Surprisingly, it feels good, very good. A pub's a pub, when all's said and done. And a drink's a drink. He can take it or leave it. Going to the meeting is not his idea. It's to satisfy his doctor, the car insurance, Vanessa. The pain in his stomach cranks up another notch. Despite what the doctor says, he knows it is caused by a cancerous tumour which at this very

173

moment is spreading throughout his body. He puts the empty bottle to his lips and sucks at it like a baby. God knows life is hard enough. Any little pleasure you can find along the way, someone is going to want to take it away from you. Sure, he'll go to the meetings but where's the harm in the occasional drop of the old wallop? Nowhere, that's where.

He turns left at The Talbot Arms and spots the church, across the road from the pub with the strange name. He presses one hand into his abdomen, feeling for the tumour, and with the other he turns the car into the paved area in front of The Pierced Piers. Pain like he's got, there's only one thing for it.

At The Pierced Piers, the builder and the hippie are sitting at a table in the corner. James goes straight over to them. 'Fancy meeting you here,' he says.

They stare at him in astonishment.

'So what are you having?' he goes on fast.

Clive looks past James at the closed door, until it is obvious that she, the beautiful Sarah, is not with him. 'You alone?' he asks.

'What are you drinking?' James asks again.

The hippie pushes his empty pint glass forward.

Clive too pushes his empty glass in James' direction. 'Haven't seen you in here before,' he adds, glancing again at the street door.

James shrugs his shoulders. 'You know how it is.'

While he's at the bar, Clive turns to Tord. 'Jesus,' he says.

'Yea,' Tord repeats. 'Jesus.'

They both watch James from behind, noting how unsteady he is on his feet. Yet the way he whips round with those drinks balanced in both hands, that's the whip of an expert.

James drops into the vacant chair, already drinking from the pint as he sits. His concentration is intense. Then he laughs, picks up the whiskey glass and holds it at shoulder height. 'A talentless nobody in a miserable marriage dreading old age.' He seems to have forgotten the presence of the other two men. He knocks back the whiskey.

Clive and Tord exchange looks. It is some weird toast. They too pick up the small glasses and drink.

'Only kidding,' James tells them, 'only kidding.' He has passed the point of good spirits and is now doggedly morose. The other two are some way behind him.

'Women,' James sighs.

'Yea,' Tord agrees. 'Women.'

James looks over at him, taken by surprise at the disgust in the other man's voice. 'Hey,' he says. 'It's only conversation.'

Suddenly Tord slumps forward and rests both elbows on the table, cradling his head in his hands. His waist-length hair, which he is wearing loose as a concession to the night out with his boss, spreads across his shoulders and arms. James stares at it fascinated. It is the longest and dirtiest hair he has ever seen on a man.

'She trashed my bike,' Tord moans. 'The fucking bitch.'

The two men greet this information with silence.

'Man, how could she do that?' Tord pleads, looking from one to the other.

'You like it like that?' James asks, still staring at the hair. He looks over at Clive. Clive shrugs his shoulders but the shrug is complicit. James is being invited into something.

'Tossie?' James asks, picturing Tord's girlfriend in her long flimsy skirt, standing half in the moat. 'Tossie did that?' He is surprised, but not all that surprised. Nothing in the man/woman thing surprises him any more. 'Why would she do a thing like that?' he asks.

Tord shakes his head. 'Oh man.' He is clearly distraught.

James takes a long serious drink from the pint glass. 'She's mad at you?' he asks.

'Oh man,' Tord again moans.

Clive too drinks deeply. 'She did it to get even,' he lies. Then, after a few moments, he adds, 'She's mad at him.'

The three men drink on in silence. 'Women,' Clive says in his turn. It is clear they are, for the moment, in complete agreement about this at least.

After a few more minutes, James speaks. 'That's low,' he says, 'trashing your bike. A man can go mad.'

'Fuck her,' Tord adds.

Clive watches them carefully. He alone knows what really happened to the bike. Lying is so sweet, he sometimes wonders if, apart from feeding and clothing his family, he has any other reason for living.

James finishes the last of the beer and studies the dregs. 'How low can you get?' He is thinking about Tossie and Ben and what Sarah has said about finding the two of them together up in the kid's bedroom. 'The bitch,' he adds.

Again, silence falls on the little group. An indeterminate amount of time passes.

'She did that?' James turns to Clive. 'She trashed his motorbike?'

Clive inclines his head and again looks past James at the door, which has remained firmly closed. 'Seems that way,' he answers.

'The bitch,' James repeats.

'Fuck her,' Tord again moans.

James decides he dislikes all of them, the builder, the hippie, Tossie. He is also thinking about the feel of her flesh under his own hands the other day. She was willing all right, at least for those few minutes until she changed her mind. It's been a while since he felt breasts like that, young, with nothing to spare. Not since his own days of hanging around in pubs with his mates, all of them dressed in tight synthetic black. He was as mean and self-interested as any of them, where women were concerned. Now of course he understands these things better. 'Fucking little tart,' he adds.

Clive leans back in his chair, giving James a sharp look. Funny the way you never know about people. Him with his flash car and that city job of his, who would have expected him to turn up here in the middle of nowhere, pissed out of his skull?

'Still,' Clive adds. 'What do you expect?'

'Fuck her,' James adds.

'Man,' Tord moans.

Just then a woman calls out to Clive from across the room. The three men turn at once to look. She has stopped in the doorway, obviously on her way out, and is now frowning in their direction.

'Clive Bavro,' she calls out, turning back to bear down on them. She is a big, buxom woman with over-permed, metallic hair. Her scent arrives before she does. She plants a large enamelled hand on Clive's shoulder and squeezes hard. 'Clive Bavro, you bastard,' she laughs. She keeps her hand in position, her fingers digging into his shoulder as if in the next gesture she might wrench his arm around full circle and hit him in the face with it. She looks powerful enough for almost anything.

'You bastard,' she repeats not altogether good-naturedly.

Then she looks over at her companion, a smaller, vaguely younger woman dressed in the skimpy bright clothes of an off-duty schoolgirl. 'Look what the cat dragged in,' she says to her friend. She laughs loudly and a number of people turn to look. 'The biggest bastard I know,' she adds, finally removing her hand, 'married my daughter.'

Unobserved, James eases himself off his chair and heads sideways towards the bar. This calls for another drink. A reunion always calls for another drink.

Tord flicks his eyes over the skinny woman then brings them back to the huge breasts of Clive's mother-in-law. He imagines them as twin boulders tightly restrained in a giant black lace bra. Her cherry-red jacket hangs open like curtains on the window of the world. Restlessly, he changes position in his seat.

'Well, what do you know?' Clive says carefully. He is trying to remember what he's done recently to offend her. There is a lot to choose from. 'How are you?' he asks.

'Fine, fine,' she answers, waiting.

What with the alcoholic fug and the surprise of being taken unawares like that, he just can't seem to get his head around remembering much of anything. He turns his attention to the skinny friend and sees the tiny red skirt reveals exactly what's on offer, which is a bit scrawny for his taste. But an offer's an offer when all's said and done. There's no way he's wrong about that and he's just about to make a move when he remembers this is his mother-in-law standing here, arms linked with her friend. Well, some things just aren't right, are they? You got to be sensitive to these things, married to Di and all. There's right and there's wrong, after all, when all's said and done.

She laughs and opens her arms wide. 'As you see,' she answers. For a moment it looks as if she is going to embrace him.

Clive unsuccessfully attempts an answering grin. 'Yea,' he says. 'You look great.' He sees she's put on some weight. It doesn't suit her, mother and daughter both.

'Listen,' she starts to say something but, noticing the others staring, she stops to pull her red jacket halfway across her front, which is as far as it will go. She returns her hand to Clive's shoulder and gives his flesh another hard squeeze. 'We gotta get going.'

Then she turns and gives her friend a shove towards the door at the same time watching Clive take in the skimpy red skirt, the flimsy top, like a placard announcing something that maybe ought to be more of a closed book.

'Right,' Clive answers feebly, unable to take his eyes off the skinny friend, flaunting everything she's got like that. He sees the people to his left are openly staring and wishes they both weren't so obvious. Maybe if they dressed a bit quieter, with a bit of class. Di's mother looks like she'd jump on you like some over-sexed dog. With his eyes half glazed over, he watches her walk away with her friend. That skirt the skinny one is wearing is so tight you can see every crack. Clive sees Tord hasn't missed any of it. The trouble is she's not a young kid to flaunt it like that. Her buttocks sag. Her thighs have no shape. His eye follows the length of her leg. Her calves are scrawny. But still, it's on offer all right, no doubt about that and an offer's an offer when all's said and done.

The two women stop at the door. Handbags are made secure. A chiffon scarf is adjusted. A watch is consulted. Their high chunky heels clump off the carpeted area onto the stone flagged entranceway.

'Jesus,' Clive says to Tord.

James returns to the table with the drinks.

'Fuck,' Tord answers.

James downs his double. At the bar he has already done the same and got the girl to refill the glass. Well, might as well, considering this time it's totally and absolutely forever the last time. Besides, the pain in his stomach is refusing to lie down and die. Casually, he again feels for the outline of his tumour.

Clive acknowledges the new round with a nod and he too shifts restlessly in his seat. He does not want them to ask about the two women. 'Mrs Sacheveral not with you?' he asks James, not sure if he dares to call her Sarah.

'You could see her clitty,' Tord says.

The two men look over at him. He is clearly too far gone to need answering.

James stares at the glass in his hand. He has a vague recollection he has been asked a question but he has no idea what it was. 'I sometimes ask myself,' he sighs deeply, 'if I have any other reason for living.' He takes a drink to help him remember what it is he wanted to say next. 'Apart from the necessity of feeding and clothing my family,' he adds.

Clive gives him a sharp look. How can two people think the same thing? He must be more pissed than he thought. Of course they're all pissed. But there's pissed and pissed. He drinks deeply and decides none of them are going to take any of this seriously tomorrow. 'That skinny one,' he tells the others. 'Talk about open all hours. Talk about giving it away for free.'

'Man,' Tord adds. 'Did you see those tremblers?' He cups his hands in front of his own flat chest.

'Shut the fuck up,' Clive tells him.

James looks from one to the other. 'Can I ask you something?' he says. 'Do you ever feel like you don't belong in your own life? Like you're a stranger in town?' He likes clichés. You know where you are with a good cliché. There's always a nugget of truth to be had in there somewhere.

'What?' Clive asks. 'What do you mean belong?' But then he sees James has no idea what he's talking about.

Again Clive looks back at the empty door through which the two women have disappeared. He leans back in his chair and stretches his legs out in front of him. 'I bet she can suck your guts out through your dick,' he tells them. Now that he's thinking about it, those skinny plain ones can deliver the goods and thank you for it afterwards. Maybe he'll call round and find out sometime. Then he remembers he has no idea who she is.

'Yea?' Tord says admiringly. He is starting to get tired of Tossie's feminist whinging. That's exactly what she is, a feminist whinger, her and her ideas. 'She a prossie?' he asks Clive.

Clive shrugs his shoulders then changes his mind and leans forward aggressively. 'You think I have to pay for it?' he asks.

Tord lurches backwards. 'No, man,' he answers. He doesn't know why he said that about being a prossie. Lately he's been thinking about it all the time, must be because he's not getting any from Tossie.

'I don't pay for it,' Clive tells him.

'She looks like a prostitute,' James interrupts.

'So she looks like a slag,' Clive tells him. 'That doesn't mean she is a slag.' How he has come to be defending her, he has no idea, that skimpy skirt that gives it all away before anyone has even asked for it.

'Yea,' James agrees. 'You don't judge a book by its cover.'

'Damn right,' Clive nods seriously.

'She's a good fuck?' Tord asks.

'A fucking good prostitute slag,' James laughs.

'You don't need to say that.' Clive is suddenly outraged. Deep in an alcoholic daze, he has forgotten that it is Di's mother they are talking about. He glares at James. 'You're talking about my wife's mother. You didn't need to say that.'

'She's a prossie?' Tord asks. He is finding this conversation confusing.

Ignoring Tord, Clive leans into James' face. 'They all fuck.' Then he laughs. 'They're all prostitutes, every last fucking one of them.'

'You said she wasn't,' James answers, seriously. He is finding the builder's conversational changes of direction hard to follow. And he's never met the woman before. How was he supposed to know she was his wife's mother?

Clive drinks while he searches for the right word to describe her. The others wait. 'She's,' he pauses then tries again. 'She's a female.' He pronounces this with absolute conviction, again leaning back in his chair and stretching his handsome legs out before him. He is happily satisfied in the knowledge that he has not only found the right word, but he has also found someone else to take the blame for the direction this conversation has taken, someone other than himself.

'Man,' Tord adds. He is thinking how right Clive is. That's exactly what's wrong with Tossie. 'A female,' he repeats with disgust.

'That friend of hers,' James asks. 'Is she a prostitute?'

Clive gives him a long, suspicious look and, in the process, forgets to answer the question. In any case, he has no idea who the other woman is, only that he intends to call round sometime.

'I saw her clitty,' Tord says again. The other two turn to stare at him. It is just possible he knows the skinny one and she's put out for him. It's also possible he's talking through his arse.

'You're talking through your arse,' Clive tells him.

At the mention of the word arse, the three men fall into a silent reverie. Clive is thinking about Sarah in those tight jeans she wears. James is thinking about Tossie and how she deliberately teases him, giving an inch, taking it back the next time. And Tord is thinking about the big woman with the tremblers and her skinny friend with the clit. He'd like to have them both at the same time, one on top, one at the side. Man, that would really blow you away. And to hell with Tossie and her feminist whinging.

Their reverie is interrupted by the sound of breaking glass and a girl's cry. Across the room a man jumps to his feet, dragging his companion with him. He is holding her by the hair so that her neck is bent painfully backwards. It is at once both shocking and hideously compelling. The big room falls instantly silent.

'Jesus,' Clive says quietly.

'Man,' Tord echoes.

James shuffles restlessly in his seat but does not get up.

The girl cries out again. She has both her hands wrapped round the man's wrist in an attempt to prize him loose. Her efforts are clearly doing little more than annoying him. He jerks her head backwards, then lets her go. She cries out a third time.

Both Clive and James jump to their feet. Both glance across to the bar, but it is only kids working there and it is obvious there is little they can do. The man with the girl is stocky and powerful. She, by contrast, is delicate and helpless. Now he is gripping her by the upper arm and she has gone all limp, leaning awkwardly away from him in an attempt to avoid further pain.

Together Clive and James approach warily.

'Man, oh fuck,' Tord says, watching them go.

He, the attacker, sees the two men coming and grabs the girl tighter. A fourth time, she whimpers in pain. He has that bulldog obstreperous look that develops in someone small who has all his life been bullied by someone big. It is clear he is in the habit of doing exactly nothing to avoid quarrels.

'Yea?' he says to the approaching pair. 'You want something?'

'Listen,' Clive says reasonably, stopping some way short of the man's reach. 'Let her go.'

'Yea?' the small man says. 'Fuck you.'

'Come on,' James repeats, even more reasonably. 'Let her go.'

He, the bulldog, further tightens his grip and twists her arm for good measure. Calmly he picks up his cigarettes and lighter and puts them in his pocket. 'Fuck you,' he repeats. Then he starts pulling the girl towards the door. She makes a feeble effort to resist, but it is obvious to everyone in the room that her chances of changing what is going on are exactly nil.

'Man, oh Jesus,' Tord says, mesmerised.

Both Clive and James keep pace with him, step for step, just out of reach. 'You don't want to do that,' Clive says. 'She's just a kid.'

'Let her go,' James adds, reaching the door first.

The small man pauses and looks from one to the other. It's obvious they're both pissed. The idea of them stopping him is laughable. He laughs.

At the same time James is wondering if the man is going to laugh before or after he hits them. He guesses it's probably both, and during as well.

Suddenly he, the bulldog, drops her arm. 'Fucking cunt,' he says to no one in particular. Calmly he turns and walks out the door. It is all over in a matter of seconds.

'What?' Tord says. At some point he has come up and is now standing beside them. 'What the fuck?'

Both Clive and James turn to look at him. Both are thinking, it's funny the way they never noticed exactly how tall Tord is, or how broad those shoulders of his are. And he's young, in his prime.

'What the fuck's going on?' Tord asks a third time.

Ignoring him, they turn to the girl. She is crying, making no attempt to hide her face in her hands the way most women do.

'The bastard,' Clive says, looking nervously at the door, then back at the girl. Now that he looks properly, it is clear that she is a cut above the usual. Take the crying for instance. A woman crying is all right in theory, but a bugger with real snot and tears. Yet she is carrying it off just fine. Again he looks at the empty doorway, then quickly back at her. He does not want to take his eyes off her even for a few seconds, even to be sure the guy is really gone.

'No one should do that,' James says, also watching her. He has registered how young she is and how well-dressed, almost formal in her black outfit where everything matches and nothing screams out at you like the things most of the girls wear these days, like the ones that hang around after Ben.

'The bastard,' Clive repeats. He has registered how pretty she is, the sweet mouth, the fine clear skin, so lightly and perfectly blonde. Even after her ordeal, not a hair is out of place. 'Want me to go after him?' he adds.

At last she looks up at the three men and shakes her head. Clive finds himself gazing straight into her eyes. They are the most beautiful eyes he has ever seen, innocent and devouring at the same time. Involuntarily, he takes a step forward. Yes, devour me.

But she shakes her head again and looks down at the floor. 'Don't do that,' she whispers.

James too has looked straight into her eyes. He is finding it hard to decide if they are her best feature or not because all of her is pretty much perfect. The little mouth, the way she holds her shoulders, she is what his own mother would have called a peach, a word not used by anyone else to describe a girl in decades. But those are some eyes she's got. He doesn't blame Clive for showing off. Want me to go after him? Who is he kidding?

'Listen,' James touches her arm gently. 'Would you like us to go after him? He shouldn't have done that.'

'Too right,' Clive agrees. 'He's a nutcase. He needs teaching a lesson.'

But again she shakes her head and keeps her beautiful eyes focused on the floor. Her little girl's shoulders are shaking.

'The three of us,' Clive adds. 'We can get the bastard.'

'What the fuck?' Tord asks. He never had any intention of doing anything and only came over to get a closer look at the girl's tits before the guy pulled her out the door. 'What the fuck?' he repeats.

The girl continues to shake silently.

'A drink?' Clive asks. 'Let me get you a drink.'

She doesn't answer.

'Maybe we should take you home,' James offers.

Again she shakes her head.

'No, of course not,' James says. 'Bad idea.' He looks across at the bar and sees there's a phone. 'I'll call you a cab,' he says.

At last she nods her head in agreement.

The three men hover closely around her in a protective huddle. Clive is leading her towards the nearest chair while James picks up the phone by the bar and Tord keeps an eye on the door, just in case.

★★★

Across the road, the AA meeting has ended and Roberto Raftiche is leaving with the others. Through the lighted windows in The Pierced Piers, he sees the three men crowded around the pretty girl in black. Straightaway he recognises James, the husband. At once he brings his hand up to the pain in his chest.

'Ah, Sarah,' he says sadly. Mr Raftiche watches James detach himself from the others and move across to the bar, obviously to get another round in, the bastard. If he had a wife like Sarah, he wouldn't be leering over young girls in pubs and knocking back the booze. Yet in his own youth he was not above such things. It is from those years, hanging around in bars, that he dates his most aggressive appetites. He was then as mean and self-interested as anyone else. His throat constricts. He hasn't had a drink in a month. Yet every day he can taste it there in the back of his throat, tantalising him. If he had a woman like Sarah to come home to, he wouldn't need to be here at these meetings. Again he presses his hand to the pain in his chest. He knows he is going to die from a massive coronary. It is only a question of when. Please God, don't let it be tonight, he begs. Just let me have one more conversation with her, a few minutes will do, a few seconds, or even if it isn't a conversation, just to look at her. The pain eases. He keeps his hand pressed to his chest and waits until it has receded enough for him to step out into the street.

Some time later James arrives at the farmhouse. Sarah is in bed, reading. Without asking where he's been, she turns the light off and closes her eyes to sleep. Straightaway he climbs on top of her but she pushes him roughly aside.

'Stop it,' she says. 'Where do you think you are, Vanessa's?'

'I'm a saint,' he answers, then falls at once into a deep, silent, saintly sleep. In his sleep he presses one hand to his stomach, as if in the grip of some strange torment.

For a long while she lies awake watching him but remembering Roberto Raftiche, his hand pressed to his heart and telling her he has swallowed his pride so many times it has given him permanent indigestion. How she laughed.

Then, out of the blue, she is pierced with a strange, unexpected longing. It is a longing for the sound of traffic in the street outside the windows, especially for the sound of cars speeding through the rain. She listens for a bus pulling away, or a train in the distance, even church bells would do. There is nothing, not a sound. They are after all surrounded by empty fields. Holding her breath with the effort to listen, she is overcome with a second pang, not as powerful as the first, but powerful enough to draw her face into a grimace. It is the longing for the background hum of a well-run house. She listens for the freezer cycling on and off, for the dishwasher draining, or the sound of the heating boiler pumping hot water through the radiators. It has been so long, all these months. But there is nothing, only silence inside and out. A stranger, floating by the uncurtained bedroom window and looking in to see the handsome man lying fully clothed beside the pretty woman, he with his arm across his stomach and she with the desperate grimace on her face, would think – for shame, what have you done to each other? And why? Whatever it is, you shouldn't have done it.

★★★

Arriving home to a totally dark house, Tord goes straight up to the bedroom. Tossie is not there. 'Fuck,' he says and falls at once into a deep sleep. Straightaway, in his dreams, he is doing it with the fat one, while the skinny one impatiently waits her turn. She is so desperate that she is jumping up and down in anticipation. James has already gone off with the classy one but he is not at all disappointed. In fact, the only hitch is Clive. Clive is nowhere around and this is making him feel uneasy. Exactly like Tossie, who is nowhere around. A thought, something important, slips into his mind and out again before he can grab it. It has something to do with Tossie and Clive and it makes him moan restlessly in his sleep as if in the grip of some distressing sexual torment. Then he remembers he's mad at her, Tossie, the bitch. In fact, he's mad at all of them, Clive, the bastard, the social where his welfare cheques were stopped last week, bunch of wankers, the council for the pile of threatening letters lying unopened on the hall floor downstairs, fuckers, the Inland Revenue, fucking fuckers. Gradually he drifts into the soothing depths of deepest sleep but the grimace on his face does not ease.

★★★

In fact, at this moment, Tossie is throwing the last of her scarves into the back seat of the borrowed car parked by the side of the deserted road. She and Ben are lying together across the front seats. The gear stick is digging into her back and they are both stoned and drunk.

'Hey Ben,' she sighs then forgets what it is she was going to say to him.

Ben is silent. He is terrified. He started to be terrified when she started to take off her scarves. It's not her that he's terrified of, but himself. He is afraid that when the time comes, and this time it is obviously coming, he will not know how to do it. Twice before she has unbuttoned her shirt and allowed him to put his hand on her breast but now she has taken her shirt all the way off. He has a vague idea that she has thrown it out the car window but this is so improbable that it might only be his imagination. He lifts his head high enough to look outside but can see nothing in the pitch darkness. She pulls him back down and presses him against her. She moans and arches her back. He freezes, locked tightly into a petrified spasm and his terror cranks up another notch.

Then, without warning, the car is suddenly full of light. Another car has come up behind them with its headlights on bright and a man is already getting out. Tossie gasps. She has at once recognised Clive. She sits up and pushes Ben away. Frantically she searches for her shirt and, when she can't find it, she reaches over and grabs a handful of scarves from the back seat. She does not want him to find her here with the boy. Anyone else, she couldn't care less, but not him. Her loosened breasts brush across Ben's face. The sweet smell of her sweat lingers tantalisingly in the air.

Clive peers in at the two of them. On his way home, he has spotted the car parked out here in the middle of nowhere where no one has any business to be at this hour of the night. He is looking at one of Tossie's breasts poking through the hastily bunched scarves. She is looking at her shirt lying on the ground an inch from his right boot.

In the next instant she has dropped the scarves and opened the car door. Clive is forced to take a step backwards and he is now looking at both her uncovered breasts. He is thinking, why is it that the ones with great tits always have that look on their faces as if they know something other women don't know? Tossie is looking like that now. But this is as far as the thought progresses and not because Tossie is standing in front of him twisting first one shoulder backwards, then the other, as she eases her arms into the sleeves, but because it is as much as his alcohol-sodden imagination can come up with. He sees she is in no hurry to do up the buttons.

He glances into the front seat and is surprised to find Ben hunched forwards in pain. Now that Tossie's breasts are out of sight, he is ready to have a go at the boy but something stops him. Instead, he finds himself overcome by an unexpected disappointment. Lately he's been thinking a lot about Tossie, maybe about starting up something with her. Not that he'd leave Di and the babies, that would never do. But he and Tossie could have had some fun, discreetly, even expensively. She would have liked that. After all, it's not like he's getting any from Di. It's not like it's his fault or anything. But to be out here with a kid like that. And despite the long hair, the earrings, the leathers, he's only a baby. If only she'd grow up a bit more herself. If only she had some restraint, maybe some judgment.

187

'So,' Tossie says calmly. 'What are you doing here?'

Clive points his handsome chin in the direction of the black fields stretching beyond the pool of light surrounding the two cars. 'I could ask you the same question,' he answers. 'I thought you were sheep stealing.'

Tossie looks lingeringly into his eyes then off into the distance. Sure enough a few sheep are straggled across the slope of the field. They seem to be grazing, even at this hour of the night.

'Me?' she laughs.

He brings his eyes back into line with hers. Her pretty bright laugh twinkles out into the still night as she again looks lingeringly up at him.

'Me?' she repeats, positioning herself so he can't see the boy. She hopes he hasn't noticed who it is.

Ben leans further forward and throws up in the narrow space between the door and the seat. He has had too much to drink and too much to smoke, both of them too fast. Like Davey, he attempts to push it out of sight with his hand. All the while he keeps his eyes on Tossie as she presents herself to Clive, one shoulder, one hip, in that self-possessed, self-doubting, slightly panicky way he recognises as his own. He looks at the pile of sick. She will be furious. It's not her car. He thinks perhaps he should scoop it up and put it in his pocket, but decides in the end it is not a good idea.

★★★

A short time later, muttering to himself, Clive arrives home. He parks the van and leaves the keys in the ignition. 'The little tart,' he is saying. 'The bitch.'

Inside, the house is dark and Dianne is in bed asleep. He climbs on top of her. At once she awakes and pushes him off. 'Get off,' she says. 'You stink of booze.'

'I did it,' he says and falls asleep before he can finish the sentence. She guesses whatever he did, he did it with some woman.

Later, in his sleep, he moans repeatedly as if in some kind of sexual torment. Dianne throws the duvet off onto the floor and leaves it there as she gets up to feed the babies who are now both crying in the next room. She looks at him lying with his hand on his crotch. He is frowning deeply, with a serious pleasure. She can guess what that's all about. If only he had something else on his mind other than that. If only he didn't chase after every female within reach. She could put up with it if only there was some other side to him, something for her to wait for other than that.

★★★

Some miles away in the ugly housing estate, Ruby lies dreaming of her Roberto. A stranger floating by her window and looking in might well be surprised at the look of happiness on the tiny plain woman's face. The bedroom is shabby and too girlish for someone her age. Her mother is dead. That useless great son of hers is, at this moment, throwing up on the doorstep below this very window. The stranger, if kindly, would not want to be the one to tell her that no one beyond the age of six is happy. Adulthood begins when you first realise you are not leading a charmed life.

A few miles away, on the other side of town, Roberto Raftiche is lying in bed wide-awake, staring at the ceiling. He is longing for a drink. Of course there is nothing in the house. He wouldn't be so stupid, but the late off-licence might still be open. Or he could ring up someone, Ruby for example, she wouldn't mind. And she'd be sure to have a dusty bottle of Christmas sherry in the back of some cupboard somewhere. Not perfect, but it would do. He knows she'd do anything he asked of her, at any time of the day or night, without dreaming of questioning that which he asked. He looks at the travel clock by the side of the bed. It's two-thirty in the morning. Two-thirty wouldn't bother Ruby, funny little crestfallen creature, if that's the right word. He'll have to look it up tomorrow, funny little droopy, downhearted, downcast, hopeless, hopeful little caged bird.

12. THE BIGGEST TASK IS TO SET ASIDE DESIRE AND REFOCUS EMOTION

In the waiting room at the surgery, James Sacheveral and Roberto Raftiche are eyeing each other. This has been going on for some time.

Mr Raftiche finally leans forward and says in his fake gangster accent, 'Diets.' He pats his stomach accommodatingly and grins. 'Up to here.'

James looks at the fat man's rolls of flesh. 'Sure,' he agrees, though he himself has never needed a diet and therefore has no real idea about any of this.

'We've met,' Mr Raftiche pronounces.

James gives him a blank look, a shade away from hostile. He has no recollection of ever having seen this man before.

'My daily diet,' Mr Raftiche goes on, 'a little ridicule, a little shame.' He spreads his arms and displays his paunch. 'As you see,' he laughs loudly. They are alone in the waiting room.

James grimaces. For some reason the man's gesture has awakened the pain in his own gut and he presses the underside of his forearm across his slim front. He knows it's cancer and he hasn't long to live. He's sure he's losing weight, though with Sarah's scales packed away somewhere and Vanessa hiding hers in the bathroom cupboard like they're some sort of shameful secret, he hasn't weighed himself since before the move.

Seeing the other man's obvious discomfort, Mr Raftiche puts his right hand on the pain in the centre of his own chest. For some reason the other man's gesture has quickened the familiar burning ache. 'Ah,' he says, understandingly.

Again the two men eye each other but their conversation does not continue. James is thinking, a crackpot, a weirdo, the worst kind, the ones who insist on talking to strangers.

And Robert, sensing the arousal of certain animal passions, repositions his glasses with one finger. If she, Sarah, were mine, he is thinking, I would laugh in the face of this pain. There is nothing, certainly not anything so trivial as an early death, that could keep me from worshipping her. Surreptitiously he glances at the boyish middle-aged husband across from him. Yet in his heart he knows, when you live with someone day in, day out, year by year, you forget what a marvellous person they are and focus instead on the disgusting way… but the thought stops. He can think of nothing disgusting that she, Sarah, might do.

James is called in to see the doctor first. Almost immediately, it seems, he is back again, crossing the room with his slender man's lightness of step.

'Hey, how long you got?' Mr Raftiche calls out, laughing.

James stops, momentarily at a loss. Once out of the waiting room, he has completely forgotten the existence of this fat man who claims to know him. Now the man is grinning away like he's just said something clever. He scowls in the man's direction, a weirdo all right, definitely the kind who make a nuisance of themselves with complete strangers.

'Ben,' Mr Raftiche adds, his voice rising questioningly as if James might not remember his own son.

James gives him a hard look. What has this man to do with Ben?

But, before he can ask, the man is off again in that stupid fake gangster accent. 'So, what did the old sawbones say?' he asks.

'How do you know my son?' James answers.

Mr Raftiche ignores the question. 'Bet it's an ulcer,' he says. 'Bet anything.'

It is exactly what the doctor has said. 'He said it might be cancer,' James tells him.

A look of horror falls unbidden across the big man's face. 'Cancer,' he whispers, shocked into silence. He feels the pain in his own chest rapidly enlarging, launching forth a dozen jets of liquid fire through his clogged and collapsing arteries. One such jet streams down his right arm and only stops when it reaches the tip of his smallest finger.

'But it could be an ulcer,' James adds quickly.

Mr Raftiche looks at the handsome man on the other side of

the room then down at his own burning hand in surprise. Suddenly it comes to him. He is jealous, jealous that this man should have only an ulcer when he himself is faced with an imminent massive coronary. Not now, he begs yet again. Not like this, not without seeing her once more. Through a fog, he hears the other man saying something.

'Tests,' he is saying. 'I'm not bothering with those. An ulcer, you just drink a lot of milk, right?'

Mr Raftiche nods his head in agreement. He is so jealous and in so much pain, he can no longer speak.

James Sacheveral looks mistrustfully at the fat man wringing his hands oddly. 'You know my son?' he asks again.

The fat man nods his head. Then he holds out his throbbing hand. 'Roberto Raftiche,' he introduces himself.

At last a look of understanding spreads across the other man's face. 'Mr Raftiche,' James repeats. The two men shake hands. So this is Mr Raftiche, the Italian teacher. It comes to him that this man has been in their conversation practically every day since they moved here. Sarah talks about him all the time, at breakfast, in bed, you name it. Mr Raftiche said this. Mr Raftiche did that. And hey, guess who I saw in the park this afternoon, Mr Raftiche.

'My wife thinks a lot of you,' he says, 'a whole lot.'

Suddenly Mr Raftiche lets out a strange strangled gasp and starts staring at his hands like they belong to someone else. He's holding them up, turning them around every which way. What does she see in him, James is thinking, this fake, fat, weirdo?

'She thinks you're really something,' he adds, with uncharacteristic generosity.

Without warning Mr Raftiche jumps up. He towers above the smaller, lighter man. Now he is laughing, still staring at his hands. The pain has suddenly and mysteriously vanished, just like that, gone. Seeing the look of dismay on the other man's face, quickly he stuffs both hands in his pockets. 'I'm getting married,' he says equally without warning. Then he laughs nervously. It's true, he has been thinking about marrying Sarah, all the time, but intending to ask Ruby. It's just that he's been so busy lately, what with one thing and another, he hasn't got round to it yet.

'Getting married?' James says. 'I'm getting married.' He too has spoken out of the blue. It has only just come to him, this very moment that this is what is going to happen. He and Vanessa, it's like a steamroller he hasn't the strength to stop. It's laughable, trying to stop a monstrous moving machine with your bare hands. He laughs. As for Sarah, with the divorce nearly final and with the children growing daily away from them, it seems they have reached an end of something. It is just that neither of them has got around to making the final move yet, what with one thing and another.

'Married?' Mr Raftiche repeats. His face is delirious. The gangster accent is back, unbidden. 'You and Mrs Sacheveral splittin' up then?' he asks.

'What can you do?' James shrugs off the other man's strange outburst. He is thinking about the builder, Clive. He knows that's what's going on, him and his black shirts, and the way he's always looking at her crotch and her breasts. He hasn't missed any of that, the bastard. It's the builder and it's been going on for a long time. And when it isn't the builder, it will be someone else, someone more suitable. He at least is willing to give her some credit in that department.

'Yup,' he answers casually, 'divorced then married.' And for the second time, the conversation dies.

Mr Raftiche takes his hands out of his pockets and sighs.

Deep in thought, James too sighs. He is thinking, that Clive, what does she see in him? What does she see in any man except himself?

'When?' Mr Raftiche asks casually.

'When?' James repeats. In his annoyance about the builder, he has forgotten what they have been talking about. For some reason the fat man is looking anxious. He must mean the tests, the operation for the ulcer.

'Right away,' James answers. 'It's urgent.' He is thinking maybe he will have those tests after all. A lot of the time he feels rotten and his shit is a funny colour. Besides, he has to admit, the pain has been getting steadily worse.

Mr Raftiche nods his head sympathetically. This guy means business. Sarah will be a free woman, lonely, needing him. 'It's a shame,' he says, continuing to nod. 'A real shame.' Who will she turn to in the middle of the night when she is overcome with sadness? Who will help her with all those things that she is too beautiful to bother about? Slowly a grin of pure bliss spreads across his face. He has no idea that he is smiling.

Seeing it, James edges sideways towards the door. Here's another thing. Why is she always talking about this fat, grinning weirdo? He eyes the man's rolls of flesh suspiciously. What is going on here? Is there no man too obvious or too unhinged for her attentions? He gives Mr Raftiche a last reproving look. The man is certifiable.

★★★

At the same time Clive is showing Sarah the attic bedroom he has been working on. When it is finished, it will be some great room. His only worry is that it won't be him lying in that bed over there on a slow afternoon, looking out over the fields, bottle of wine.

'Is there a problem?' Sarah asks. At once she is uneasy, here with him, a bed on the other side of the room. All these months, she's sure she's hardly been in this room, hardly noticed the bed.

'Problem?' he exclaims, looking at her breasts. He shakes his head in disbelief. 'Can't say that's something I have a lot of. You? You got a problem?' He takes a step closer to her. 'Something I can help you with?' He takes another step closer. 'I'd like that.'

But when she doesn't answer, he sees that she is as usual messing him about. Well, if that's the way she wants it, he's still prepared to string along. Some women are like that. They can't get the words out straightaway. Others, words are just a waste of good fucking time. Personally he prefers the latter, but then again, he prides himself on being a man of wide-ranging tastes.

He looks around at the scattered debris and the plasterboard stacked in the middle of the floor. When he's finished it will be nice and light, big windows overlooking the fields. There will be room for a nice new king size bed. He could come and go with no one the wiser. This he doesn't tell her but she might be figuring it out for herself, the way she's gone all quiet.

Sarah gazes forlornly around. She is thinking if only he wasn't so predictable. If only he had something to say instead of always ogling her the way he does. If only his jeans weren't quite so tight, or maybe if he wore something else once in a while, something – and here she stops to search for what she means – something with intelligence.

He catches her expression. 'Listen,' he says. 'You got to use your imagination. Strip the floors, bit of paint, nice new furniture.' He sees she is looking at the saggy double bed the hippies left behind. It is what he has been waiting for, a man and a woman alone together in a room with a double bed, anything can happen. Come to think of it, he has waited long enough.

He comes up behind her and stares at the curves of her buttocks in the tight jeans. She is so close he could reach out and help himself. And why shouldn't he? Hasn't he put himself out, gone along with her and her ideas even when they cost him? He can smell her shampoo and the fragrant cleanness of her skin and clothes. Unlike Di, who these days stinks of cigarette smoke and baby sick. He eases his hand forward but she steps sideways out of his reach.

In fact she has not noticed his move. She is staring at something under the bed, what looks like the remains of a tiny animal. The neat little pile is crawling with maggots. How can this have been here all these months and she never noticed? Is it some wild animal that has come in to die in the night? Why she should be surprised she doesn't know. The whole place is disgusting. This new piece of unworthiness is nothing out of the ordinary.

He also looks briefly at the carcass then back at her. Those rings she wears are old gold, probably handed down through her family. The skimpy tops that reveal the outline of her beautiful breasts look like pure silk. The jeans have an expensive designer label. She shouldn't be troubled with all this trouble. She should be having some fun, and with him. He wants to reach out and pull her close to him so that he can feel the full length of her and make her happy. Instead he thrusts his hands deep into his pockets and fingers the reassuring outline of his own genitals. Come to think of it, he is getting seriously tired of waiting.

She sees his angry scowl. She guesses he is thinking, as she is, that the whole place is impossible. The whole thing is impossible. In fact everything is impossible and, when faced with insurmountable impossibilities, maybe it's better to cut your losses.

He sees her frown and takes another step towards her. Yes, he is thinking, she is unhappy and the unhappy ones are the easiest of all. Misery has always been his front door to the physical side of things. Except funnily enough with Di. Her misery is something else altogether.

'No,' he says when he sees she is about to say something. A good shag is what she needs, not more useless talk. 'Don't say it. There's no need.' Again he reaches out to pull her towards him and put an end to conversation with something a whole lot simpler. After all, you don't talk about rope to a man whose father has just been hanged. 'What we do need here,' he says again, laying an arm gently across her shoulders. 'Is a plan. You and me.' Yes, he sighs, he has waited fucking long enough. And the way she's looking at that bed, there's no doubt about what she really wants. She's hardly taken her eyes off that bed, hardly since they got here.

'A plan?' she says. 'You and me?'

'Oh baby,' He pulls her tightly to him and buries his face in her hair. He breathes deeply as if having been deprived of something essential for his being for a long time.

She twists awkwardly away.

'Oh baby,' she hears him say again as he brings his face in towards hers. He matches her twisting movements with little excited writhings of his own, all the while tightening his grip on her. The strength of his embrace takes her breath away. Feeling light headed, she closes her eyes and at once sees Mr Raftiche standing beside them, peering down with clinical interest. *Ah well.* He smiles, positioning himself so that he can get a better look. He laughs that sweetly bitter laugh of his, still watching them intently. *You know,* he is telling her, *that man is conceived in selfishness, born in pain, and it's downhill from then on, stopping now and then on the way to do something really mean and ugly.* Again he laughs. *Me included,* he adds, before fading away into nothing.

'You know what?' Sarah says.

Taken by surprise at the sudden sound of her voice, Clive lets go his grip and she slips easily from his embrace.

She looks over at the maggots. 'I once knew a boy who used to put maggots in his mouth.'

He drops his hands and lets her go. 'What?' he says.

Quickly she walks over and peers down at the little carcass. 'To warm them up in the winter when he went fishing,' she explains.

'You're kidding,' he says, at a loss. No woman has ever said anything like that to him before, and at a time like this. He scowls at her. 'Why'd you tell me that?' he asks.

She looks at his handsome bare arms. 'So that if they wriggled on the hook faster the fish would be more attracted,' she patiently explains.

'No one would do a thing like that,' he says.

'It's true,' she tells him. 'It's someone I knew.' She is watching him with the same clinical interest Mr Raftiche showed towards the two of them a moment ago.

Clive shakes his head in bewilderment. He runs his hands through his tightly-growing hair. 'Why'd you tell me that?' he repeats, knowing exactly what it is that she is doing. 'It's a fucking stupid thing to say.' His eyes are involuntarily drawn to the maggots. 'You'd have to be a real fucker to do that.'

'It's true,' she insists.

'So fucking what?' he says. 'I don't want to know stuff like that.' As he talks, he finds he is having to stop himself from telling her to fuck off. He crosses to the other side of the big empty room, away from her, again running his hands through his hair.

All the while she watches him with the same detached interest. He hits the window frame with the side of his hand, hurting himself.

She shrugs her shoulders.

'I'm off,' he says heading towards the stairs, knowing he does not want to lose this job that pays so well, knowing he has already said too much, behaved badly, but knowing also that the way back is easy. He'll pretend it never happened.

★★★

Feeling worse, James decides work can wait. Vanessa, the drive to the city, it can all wait. Instead, he returns to the wrecked farmhouse. The builder's van is not in the drive. That makes a change, he thinks sourly, the builder not here, not working, what a surprise.

In the house, he finds only Ben and the twin babies. They are on the floor in the stone kitchen, the babies strapped into bouncers, Ben stretched out on the blankets he has taken from the pram. He has one hand protectively resting on one tiny foot and in the other hand he holds a gently smoking joint, one of many by the look of the place. There are beer cans scattered around, dismembered cigarette packs and overflowing ashtrays.

'What's going on?' James asks. He is disappointed not to find Sarah. He has wanted to tell her about the cancer and the divorce and to see the look on her face. He knows in a few hours it will not be so easy to say.

Ben looks at his father through the heavy smoke. What's going on is not his fault. Carling and the others have only just this minute left and he is about to explain this when his father interrupts.

'Why aren't you at school?' he demands.

Ben gives him a pitying look. 'It's summer,' he tells him. 'Remember?'

In fact the new term started some weeks ago but his mother no longer insists that he go to school in the car with Amy and his father wouldn't have noticed anyway.

'You look like shit,' James says, looking at his son. There's grease and some sort of metallic black colour in his hair. His clothes are greasy too and full of holes. There are no laces in his boots. Where they flap open, his skin is filthy. 'And what are you doing with those babies?' he asks.

'Nothing,' Ben answers, sullenly.

At the sound of the man's angry voice, the little boy Davey slides his skinny legs further in behind the curtain in the doorway where he is hiding. No one has noticed him all morning and he's hungry. Carefully he draws the fabric around him, like a shroud.

'Where's your mother?' James asks.

'Dunno,' Ben answers.

'What are you doing with these babies?' James repeats, bending down in front of the twins but keeping his distance. He does not want to have to do anything about the situation here. Fortunately, the babies look perfectly fine.

Ben rouses himself to think of a proper answer, one that his father will accept. 'I'm looking after them,' he explains.

'I can see that,' his father snaps. He scans the room. He can see also that the others have been here, Ben's friends. There is definitely a situation going on here all right.

'I like looking after them,' Ben answers. But it is the wrong thing to have said because now his father is looking worried and pacing up and down.

'God,' he moans. 'Why do you always have to find the biggest louts around? Why can't you have nice friends?' He clutches at the pain in his stomach. 'Don't answer that,' he tells his son. 'Don't even try.'

As the angry man's feet approach dangerously close to the curtains, the little boy flinches further back. Every day he has found a smaller and smaller place to hide and now the space he is taking up is so small, it seems he must surely be invisible at last. He peers through a tiny tear in the fabric and sees that suddenly the big man is no longer in the room. His friend, Ben, is making some more smoke come out of his mouth and it looks like one of the babies is about to cry. Sure enough, the next thing is that first one baby and then the other lets out a wail. Davey presses both hands over his ears and starts straightaway to think of something else. This is what he always does when the babies cry and he has learned to do it by himself, without help. He is very pleased with this small, independent achievement.

Quickly James walks away from the noise that is starting up in the kitchen. Though there is clearly a situation that needs dealing with, he does not want to be the one that does the dealing. With luck, the women will turn up before he has to think about what to do.

In the front hall, he sees that the morning room door has finally fallen off its rotten hinges and is now wedged at an oblique angle against the wall. Someone has hung an old curtain in its place. He also sees that the floorboards have been taken up so that it is impossible to reach the stairs without having to jump. He decides this is too much of an effort and turns instead into the big cluttered sitting room. Instantly he can see that something has changed. There are still packing cases stacked against the walls. The rolled carpets are floured delicately with plaster dust like giant confectionery. The bay window is still broken and water-stained wallpaper still hangs in mouldy strips down both sides. Then he sees what it is that has surprised him. The rest of Sarah's clothes, her tight black suits, her winter coats and bags of paired shoes, have been unpacked and are lying across a pile of newly-stacked timber. They are carefully arranged and look like they are waiting to be collected.

Relieved that the big man is nowhere in sight, the little boy, Davey, shuffles along behind the ragged curtain until he can slip behind the broken door. He is pleased to have found another new and interesting hiding place that wasn't here yesterday, though he is getting cold from standing in bare feet and he is very hungry.

His movements, tiny and quiet though they are, have attracted James' notice. He returns, peers in at the boy and asks, 'You don't know where Sarah is I suppose?'

Davey stares back at this stranger wide-eyed with terror. He is too frightened to answer even if he did know what was expected of him.

'Ah well,' the man finally says and goes away, leaving him where he is.

James leaps across the gaping floorboards and climbs the stairs. He passes what would have been their bedroom had things been different. He passes the dank recess they use as a bathroom, allowing himself the briefest of glances. Everything is as it has been for the past months. Her shampoos and cosmetics are ranged along the window ledge. Laundry is piled in the corner. The saucer of bright blue rat poison has this morning been refilled. Yet he is uneasy, spooked even.

He climbs the second flight of stairs to the boy's room in the high attic. Here too the room is cluttered with Ben's things in the usual way. The place where the window should be is now covered with plastic, criss-crossed carelessly with packing tape. Water has stained this wall too and part of the ceiling has come down in the corner. That's new, but nothing else. Yet the feeling of unease is growing stronger. He looks into the other attic bedroom, the one with the mouldy bed that no one uses. All is as it was. He understands that he is looking for her and he cannot stop himself.

Suddenly James leans forward and clutches at his stomach. He cries out in pain. Here's something else that he has not bargained for and does not deserve. Self-pity rises up in his throat and he grinds his teeth in an attempt to contain it. He laughs bitterly. The whole thing is too funny for words, beyond a joke.

He crosses over to the boy's bed and lies down, stretching himself out full-length. Immediately, the pain eases and, relieved, he closes his eyes. Of course he is uneasy, being told about the ulcer, being told he has to go for tests. Anyone would be spooked. Of course he had to have a drink on the way home, anyone would under the circumstances. And of course the doctor is wrong. Doctors get it wrong all the time. You're always hearing about how they said it was only stress and the next thing the poor bugger is dead from a massive tumour. He keeps his eyes closed and thinks about what to do about this situation. But there doesn't seem to be any worthwhile answer.

★★★

Several hours later, Tossie stops mid-gesture and listens. 'What's that?' she asks.

'What's what?' Ben answers. Finding her suddenly here, he has forgotten that anyone or anything else exists. Time has elongated beyond recognition and certainly his father must have left hours ago. They have just smoked the last of the weed and she is lighting a cigarette.

'Someone shouted,' Tossie says.

'No they didn't,' Ben answers. He looks over at the babies. He has only just got them settled and wishes she would now make a move but she seems uninterested, unlike other times. He has no idea why this should be and even less of an idea what to do about it.

'Yes they did,' she insists. She listens but the big house is silent. These old places, they have weird noises. She ought to know. She draws the smoke into her lungs and, finding it displeasing, drops the cigarette into an empty beer can and looks over at the boy. She could swear he's filled out in just the last couple of weeks. He's still thin but now he looks strong. She likes that in a guy, not too obvious, something in reserve, not too up front, but just enough. Come to think of it, this is the way she likes most things life has to offer. She lowers herself to

201

the floor beside Ben and rests her head sweetly on his shoulder which seems somehow more substantial now. She sighs and nestles in closer, caressing his boyish chest with one hand.

Suddenly Tord is standing in the doorway. 'Well fuck me,' he says grinning.

Tossie twists around to look at him. 'Jesus. You frightened me,' she says. 'What are you doing here?' Just when she was thinking it's true, he has definitely filled out nicely in the past couple of weeks. 'Are you following me?'

One of the babies starts to cry.

Tord gives a snort of derision. 'Following you,' he repeats. In fact, he has been searching for her all afternoon. He has wanted to show her his new girlfriend and now he finds her just when his new girlfriend has had to get off to work. 'You,' he repeats with even more derision. He would like to tell her about this girl's white coat and her full-time job in the lab, a professional job, and she's his girlfriend. But all he can say is, 'Fuck you.' She, his girlfriend, works in the new toxicology analysis room at the chicken factory. That'll knock the shit out of Toss all right.

'Jesus, Howard,' Tossie jeers. 'Piss off out of my life, will you?'

Ben stares at the hippie. It is the first time he has heard his proper name, Howard. But he does not dare to laugh.

'Wanker.' Tossie turns away from him and back to Ben.

'You owe me,' Tord says, his voice rising menacingly.

The second baby starts to cry.

Again she twists around to face him. 'You? I owe you? Just how do you figure that?'

Ben reaches out to calm the babies but, at this touch, their crying increases. He rocks them in their separate bouncers and looks from Tossie to Tord. Obviously they are picking up where they left off. Then, without warning, it comes to Ben that he does not want to get hurt because of Tossie. He has thought that he would die for her and now here he is hoping Tord will just finish and quietly go away. Again he looks at the hippie, at his height, at the strength in his arms, at his face clenched in fury.

'Lying, fucking bitch,' Tord snarls.

'I never touched your bike,' she shouts to be heard. 'I wouldn't bother. And anyway you could have got it out if you wanted to.'

'It's fucked,' he says stepping up close to her. 'The bike is fucked.'

There is a brief moment when it seems he is going to hit her but then he looks over at Ben. 'School kids,' he sneers, 'best you can do?'

Tossie holds her ground. 'Do,' she answers. 'It's none of your fucking business what I do.'

'Fuck the fucking lot of you,' Tord says. 'But you're gonna pay me.'

Through the window, they watch him stomping off towards his old car. On the way he picks up the second of the new wheelbarrows and hurls it into the overcrowded moat which, daily, is becoming more like an aquatic scrapyard.

Both the babies are now screaming and Ben removes them from their cloth bouncers with an easy dexterity. Quickly, Tossie steps forward to help but then stops. She is not sure she would know which strap to unbuckle or which bit to fold back. And where did that tenderness of touch come from? He does not need her help.

'Ben?' Tossie touches his shoulder lightly. But the boy is engrossed in soothing the tiny crying babies and he doesn't answer. 'You know I don't think of you as a school kid,' she says. 'You're not a school kid. Not really.'

Ben holds the babies to him awkwardly and whispers into their hot, wet faces, first one and then the other. 'Here,' Tossie moves angrily to take one of them from him. 'I came to get them anyway.' She gathers the blankets from the floor in a heap and throws them into the pram.

'Wait,' Ben stops her. Carefully he hands the second baby to her. Carefully he stretches the sheet tight over the mattress. Carefully he tucks the blankets in at the bottom and folds them back ready.

Tossie drops the two babies side by side in the oversized, old-fashioned pram. Their screaming cranks up another notch. She looks down at them with absolute loathing. 'Jesus,' she says, glancing back at the boy. 'I got to get out of here.'

But Ben is already stepping over the wedged door and does not answer. He jumps across the gaping hole in the floor and takes the steps two at a time. His cheeks are burning. He has no idea what is going on with Tossie, with the hippie. He knows only that his part in her life is less than irrelevant. It is so far past irrelevant that it is non-existent, nothing, a blank.

In the high attic bedroom he finds his father asleep in his bed. He stops in the doorway, unable to enter. He cannot remember the last time he saw his father lying flat out in bed, probably not since he was little and used to rush in to be with them in the mornings. He is surprisingly unnerved by the sight. While he watches, his father lets out a great sighing snore that seems to come up out of nowhere and go on forever. Quickly Ben backs from the room. The whole thing is freakish, disconcerting. In fact the whole afternoon has been so odd, he feels slightly deranged. It comes to him that this is why his sister pretends not to be able to speak. He used to think it was stupid, what she did, but now he sees that faced with all that's been happening to them, it might be better to get by with small crazinesses. The bigger ones are too complicated and difficult.

★★★

Meanwhile, Ruby is sitting on the bottom step outside Mr Raftiche's front door. The tiny garden is obscured by huge, brutish conifers that cast a funeral gloom over the already dismal end-of-terrace house. He is late. She looks up at the peeling paint on the shabby front door and at the two dark grimy windows, imagining how she will put all of this right. There is no bathroom too stained, no cooker too greasy, no woodwork too chipped that she can't scrub, polish or bully it into order. When they are married, she will work so hard and with so much pleasure that he will take her little face in his two hands and look laughingly down at her. *Ah, Ruby*, he will say. *What would I do without you?* He will shake her playfully. He will beam.

Lost in reverie, she has not noticed time pass, several hours of time in fact. Nor has she noticed the rain, which has slowly progressed from a few drops to a steady drizzle. And one more thing she hasn't noticed, Robert's face appearing for a brief moment around the overgrown hedge and then disappearing so quickly that even the most attentive person might easily have thought they were mistaken.

But they would not have been mistaken. He has forgotten that he has asked Ruby to meet him here after work. He has forgotten because, feeling unwell, he has called in sick and taken himself off to the doctor. Then, in euphoria after his meeting with James and finding out about the divorce, he has spent the day wandering in and out of shops looking for Sarah, guessing this is where he might find her. In his progress he has bought two outrageously stylish suits, much more stylish than anything that soon-to-be-ex-husband of hers would ever wear. Coming out of every double glass door, behind him in every please-pay-here queue, around every corner, he has looked for Sarah and not found her. Then to come home and instead find Ruby sitting on his front step, her skinny shoulders hunched forward in that transparent nylon raincoat of hers, it's more than he can bear. In the briefest of glances he has seen how the rain has thinned and matted her already meagre hair. He has seen her expression, far away and tenderly patient. He has forgotten that he has told her he has something important to ask her. It is no wonder that she is staring off at nothing with that look of a child who still believes in heroes and simple truths. And now, now that Sarah will soon be free, he does not know how to face this other woman so inadvertently in the middle of his life.

Mr Raftiche retraces his steps, silently, quickly. There is an expression of anguish on his own face. 'For shame,' he is saying to himself. He clutches both hands to the pain in the centre of his chest. 'For shame, for shame,' he repeats again. Yet he walks resolutely away, leaving her sitting in the rain, the stylish suits and bright new shirts flapping about his knees in their garish plastic carrier bags.

★★★

On the boy's bed in the high attic, James is dreaming about women – Sarah, his sister, his mother, his first girlfriend Gwen, his second girlfriend Barbara and others who drift in and out as he himself drifts in and out of deep unconsciousness. Strangely, he has thought he heard Tossie's voice, but only for a second, so that now he is dreaming about her. He knows she has made herself available to him. Yet when he tries to think past this, to take up what is on offer, he draws a blank. She is young and what his American grandmother would have called 'sassy' with a mixture of reproval and respect. There will be plenty of other men to take up what he hasn't. Now there's another woman in his life, Vanessa. Women, they have many beautiful things. They have soft voices and fragrant hair. They adore you or else they mean business. Vanessa, she means business all right. He lets go a deeply drawn-out sigh at the impossibility of it all.

His thoughts are garbled, yet he feels only a little pain, more like a touch of indigestion. He wishes he had a glass of cold milk but the effort of getting up and going down to the kitchen and the likelihood of finding any there, is more than he can manage at the moment. He thinks about dying and how at the very end, when it comes to begging, no man begs for just one more day at work, not ever. He thinks about how Vanessa will enjoy his death. She will be very good at being a widow. Overwhelmed by self-pity, he forces himself back to consciousness and hears a car pull up under the window and Sarah's voice as she pays the driver. The sound of her voice is comforting, soothing even. So much so, that he drifts back into deepest sleep.

★★★

Finding no one in the kitchen, though it is obvious what has been going on, Sarah is now unpacking more of the boxes in the big sitting room. She understands that her secret self makes certain choices, rejects others. This is not a matter for blame but for curiosity. Working at high speed, she has emptied and piled their books haphazardly around the room. Now she is pulling out the boy's roller skates and battered tractors, which should have been thrown away before the move. In her hands these abandoned toys feel small, familiar, accusing. She places them on top of the books. The next box is filled with lampshades and light fittings. These too she stacks in any unfilled space she can find. The room now looks like a badly managed warehouse. When there are no more boxes near at hand to empty, she goes out into the hall and drags in a black plastic bin bag filled with blankets and small cushions. She has no intention of allowing herself to give up. Her little family, it is after all the only thing she has done that she is proud of. She piles the cushions and blankets on top of the rolled carpets from the old house.

Now she needs Ben and Amy to help her drag in the remaining boxes so she can empty them. Where is everyone anyway? She guesses James has walked with them to the pub, sensibly leaving his car behind. Well, that makes a change. She knows exactly what they will say when they see what she has done. They will not see all this mess as a step forward. She looks around the wrecked room and has to agree they will be right. Who is she kidding anyway, a step forward? Her life could not get any worse. There is nothing else that could happen, no further mistake or disaster. She decides the next thing is to buy some food. About that, at least, no one could be scathing or dispirited. Yes, she will cook a proper family meal, the first one in the new house. Quickly she gathers up the car keys and within minutes she is speeding down the long potholed drive, unaware of the stricken boy in the shed, missing the sight of the silent girl moving from one upstairs window to the next to see what is happening, and oblivious to the man sleeping in torment in the high attic bedroom.

★★★

A short while later Tossie wheels the babies into her sister's house. Already Dianne is bending over them, peeling back the soaking blankets.

'For God's sake, Toss,' she says angrily.

'Me?' Tossie answers astonished. 'What have I done?'

'It's raining,' Di tells her. She drops the wet blankets onto the floor and holds the babies awkwardly to her. Underneath the layers they are actually quite dry. 'Didn't you notice?' she asks.

'Of course I noticed,' Tossie snaps back. 'So what?' Lately, with Di, everything she does is wrong. She's always angry. 'Don't take it out on me just because you started smoking again. And you didn't tell me,' she adds.

Dianne gives her a withering look. She has no intention of telling Tossie anything. Sisters on TV soaps are always doing that, having serious, confrontational conversations and then making up. What a joke. And not the funny kind either.

The two fall silent while Dianne prepares to feed the babies and Tossie removes her own wet scarves. Underneath, her T-shirt clings to her slender breasts, outlining them prettily. She lifts the wet fabric away from her skin then pulls it tightly back into place, looking admiringly down at herself. She is not wearing a bra. She turns to Di and catches her looking.

'You shouldn't leave them with him,' Tossie says. 'You know he's at it all the time, don't you? He's out of his skull.'

'I know that,' Dianne says, lighting up a cigarette. In fact, she does not know it. She has thought Ben a nice boy, despite the clothes. And, when he offered, she seized the chance. Not many come along these days. No, she knows he is a nice boy and she trusts him absolutely with the babies. It's hard to explain but she just knows she can trust him. 'He's a good kid,' she tells Tossie. 'They all do it at that age. You ought to know.'

Now it's Tossie's turn to give her sister a look. She watches her feeding both babies, propped on pillows, one at the breast, one with a bottle. Dianne drags deeply and exhales over their tiny heads.

'Besides,' Dianne tells her. 'He really likes them.'

Tossie's look deepens to disgust, as if anyone could like the twin babies. She watches her sister suck the life out of her cigarette then stub it out in an overflowing saucer. Immediately she pulls a fresh cigarette from the pack and lights up.

'Why do you do that?' Tossie asks. 'You could wait. How about a few seconds?'

'Smokers have that thin, ruined look,' Dianne tells her sister, wearily.

'Yea sure,' Tossie comes straight back at her. 'That's before they die, maybe a couple of months before. The rest of the time they're a mess, like you.'

Dianne knows that what she says is true. She smokes resolutely on. It is her only hope. Lately she has started to put on weight again. All the miserable weeks of breastfeeding, waiting for the pounds to fall away like the magazines say, and they're falling on instead. Well at least she's putting a stop to that and getting them both on bottles. She closes her eyes, just for a second, and drops instantly into semi-consciousness. In her reverie, she is coveting all the impossible things — good teeth, implausibly sun-lit rooms, unearned money, permanent thinness.

She snaps her eyes open. 'Where's Davey?' she suddenly asks. 'He was with you, right?' Tossie shakes her head.

The two sisters hold each other's gaze for a long, hostile moment and then Dianne drops the babies into the pram and rushes out the door. Through the window, Tossie sees her looking frantically for the van. It isn't there. In the next instant Dianne is running down the road towards the old farmhouse, her heavy breasts lurching from side to side, her baggy maternity dress flapping over her swollen, blue-veined legs. In her heart Tossie knows that he will not be there and it is somehow her fault. She is only hoping that he is not lost to all of them forever, though she deserves this new tragedy. She deserves it, but Di doesn't.

★★★

At the farmhouse Dianne is relieved to see lights in the upstairs windows but there are no cars in the drive or sheds. Inside, the place is deserted. 'Davey?' she calls out and, when there is no answer, she steps into the dark kitchen. 'Sarah?' she calls. But the house is silent. She hurries through the kitchen into the hall and stops in confusion. The place has deteriorated worse than ever. Now there are no floorboards and a plank has been laid across the joists to get to the stairs. The cold smell of mould and rot rises up from the cavity below. 'Davey?' she calls again. When there is still no answer, she draws in her breath, closes her eyes and scurries across the plank into the big sitting room. Here there is more fresh devastation. It looks as if someone has deliberately trashed the place. Books and clothes are strewn around the room. The windows are ripped out and part of one wall has been knocked down so that she can see through into the next room. Both are empty. Maybe Tossie is right about the boy being out of it. You'd have to be out of it to put up with living like this. 'Where are you Davey?' she calls, frantically.

In the silence, as her voice fades and before she shouts again, she catches the faintest reply, not an answer but a scuffle, a deliberate delicate scratching. She turns full circle. 'Davey,' she calls yet again. 'I'm here. Where are you?'

Without hesitation, she runs back to the kitchen and sees the door wedged at a crazy angle. Behind the door she also sees one tiny bare foot. In the next instant she is lifting the door away from the wall. It slips from her grasp and crashes down behind her. The little boy looks up, wide-eyed, at his mother. He is holding his red toy car in one hand and the other is thrust deep into his mouth, all the fingers at once. She bends and gently picks him up. He is cold to the touch, much too cold. She wraps her arms tightly around him and wills her own warmth to pass at once into his tiny frame. Slowly she carries him over to the one sturdy-looking kitchen chair and sits heavily with him in her lap.

For a long time she presses the little boy to her and rocks silently back and forth. Carefully, so as he won't know she's doing it, she examines his limbs. He seems fine. After a while, his shivering stops, though he still feels much too cold. He has not cried or spoken. Tenderly she caresses his matchstick arms and legs. How did she come to let him out this morning in shorts and no shirt? It is not a warm day. How did she let him get so thin? There isn't enough flesh on him to cover his bones. She runs her hands again over his knees and elbows. Bits stick out everywhere. How has this happened? She's his mother. It's her job to keep the world of pissy alleyways and shitty behaviour at bay.

For a long time she rocks the little boy in her lap until she feels able to get up and take him home. She does not see Amy crouched on the stairs, silently watching. She does not look back at the derelict farmhouse with the missing windows, broken doors, and stench of rot. Frighteningly, it is too much like what is happening in her own life.

13. WE SING, WE DANCE

Vanessa pulls in and parks the big city car behind her own little Mini. She helps James to get out. He is leaning heavily on her and can barely keep himself upright. Amy and Ben follow, not looking at each other, or at much of anything.

'Shit,' James says. 'If a man can't get drunk at his own wedding, when can he?'

No one answers him. Vanessa has pushed open her front door and is now half-dragging, half-shoving James in towards the couch. Once there, James drops down and closes his eyes. He moans twice, seemingly in pain. But Vanessa has already left the room. Amy sits in one chair, Ben in the other. They wait in silence still not looking at each other and only occasionally at their father when he moans again. After a while, Ben goes over and looks down. He sees that his father has wet himself. Secretly he does not blame Vanessa for being angry, though he thinks she has no right. She is, after all, married to him now. But the thought gets no further. Again he waits. Then he turns and leaves the room, picking up his father's keys from the hall table as he goes by.

Amy watches her brother through the window. She sees him start up the big car and pull slowly, carefully away from the kerb. Then he is gone. The house is silent and Amy waits. After a while she too gets up and looks down at her father. She sees he has wet himself. Fascinated, she stares at the dark stain that has spread across the crotch of his pale grey wedding trousers and onto Vanessa's silk couch. Secretly she is pleased about the couch. Vanessa will be angry. Then she remembers Vanessa is already angry. But the thought gets no further.

Some time later Vanessa comes back. She has changed from her delicate mauve wedding suit into black trousers and an old sweater. Her handbag is across her shoulder and she is carrying a black coat.

Though it is spring, a pretty spring wedding with tulips and lilies-of-the-valley, it is still winter cold. She looks down at James, ignoring the silent girl. 'Bastard,' she says under her breath. She is thinking she will never forgive him for this. The party should be going on right now. They should be dancing, eating, laughing. It is, after all, her wedding day. And, God knows, it cost enough. No, she will never forgive him for this, never. 'Fuck you,' she adds as if trying out the words out for the first time. Then she too turns and leaves the room.

Amy has never heard Vanessa swear before. It is something she seriously disapproves of and has told them often enough, and now twice in a row. Again she watches through the window as, this time, Vanessa gets into her little car and drives off, pulling away fast. She waits, shivering in the cold. The little pink jacket bought for today is useless against the arctic cold of Vanessa's house.

Some minutes pass before Amy again gets up, this time to go upstairs. She returns with a small quilt from Vanessa's bed, what's now Vanessa and James' bed, and arranges it carefully over her father so as to hide everything that is going on as completely as possible. Her father is now snoring deeply. It is the sound of being warmly, vigorously alive. But the house is freezing.

In the kitchen Amy turns on the oven as high as it will go. It is the only thing she can think to do to make the house warmer. Then, since the oven is on anyway, she takes out Vanessa's largest mixing bowl. From the cupboards she pulls out things at random, vinegar, flour, dried fruit, gravy mix. These she empties into the bowl, closing and returning the packets to their proper place on Vanessa's shelves. From the fridge she takes milk, margarine, ketchup, eggs. These she adds to the mix, adjusting the liquids to create a satisfying thickness. She adds soya sauce and wine. The mixture bubbles as if suddenly brought to life in a mysterious alchemy. Amy searches for other things to add and finds chocolate and cocktail cherries in another cupboard. But the bowl is getting full and she knows it will be too heavy to carry to the oven. Vanessa will be furious if she spills any on the kitchen floor which is strangely carpeted and impossible to clean up, unlike her mother's stone floor where debris settles happily unnoticed. Amy places the bowl on the centre oven shelf, carefully sliding it into place.

Leaving the oven door open, she returns to the sitting room and pulls the big armchair over to sit beside her father. She wishes there was a television but it is something else Vanessa disapproves of and will not allow in the house. At home the television, when it works, is on whether anyone is in the room or not. It is a sort of comfort and they have been known to get through three televisions in one year. Here the house is silent and perfect, except for her father's life-affirming snoring. She lies down on the floor beside the couch and wraps her arms around herself to wait. A not unpleasant smell is already drifting in from the kitchen, a smell of some strange, terrible tasting medicine disguised as food, something that will fool absolutely no one.

★★★

Some hours later, Ben pulls slowly, carefully, into a double parking place. He is starving and has found some money in his father's glove compartment, a small amount but enough for a burger and chips. There was food at the wedding, lots of it, but it didn't look like it was meant to be eaten so he hung back, taking one tiny sandwich, then an even smaller pastry. He has already spotted the two girls sitting at one of the flimsy plastic tables by the door. Their gypsy hair trails over their shoulders. Their bizarre Friday night hooker's clothes flash in the passing car headlights. They look bored, exotic and beautiful. He knows them from school, Shona and Stacey. Everyone at school knows them.

Ben slides sideways through the open door, ignoring the girls. They glance at him briefly, marginally less bored. He understands that what they are approving in him is all that his mother finds most disturbing. Briefly, longingly, he wishes they were all still children, energetic, enthusiastic, creative. But the thought is gone as fast as it came. Who would be like that again? No one, that's who.

'Hey Ben,' one of the girls calls over to him. 'Is that your car?'

Ben holds up his father's keys and indifferently shrugs his shoulders, turning away from them to give his order at the counter.

The two girls look at each other then burst into derisive laughter. 'Yea?' Shona says. 'Right.'

'Yea,' Ben answers. He is a little scared, a lot excited.

'Take us for a ride then,' Stacey says.

Ben shrugs his shoulders. All this has happened much faster than he anticipated. And now the two girls are getting to their feet, deliberately not looking at him.

'Maybe,' Ben answers. 'It depends.'

Again Shona and Stacey exchange looks. 'Told you so,' Shona says.

Ben collects his food, already eating as he turns to face the girls. Shona reaches out and helps herself to a chip.

'We going or what?' Stacey says, sounding as if she could care less.

Shona lifts her arms and tosses back her rat's tail tresses. 'Told you so,' she says.

Ben starts to walk away. The two girls follow listlessly a few paces behind, unimpressed and choosy. He is now wild with excitement, but containing it better than Vanessa her anger. What Tossie had, they have double and better. Already he can see that it will be Stacey, for the sweetness there is about her. Casually he drops back until he is walking beside her.

★★★

At his father's car, Ben turns the engine over and it starts perfectly first time. He puts the car in gear and shoots into traffic much too fast. He has only driven this car once before today, though he has taken his mother's new small car many times without her noticing.

The two girls laugh. 'Hey Ben,' Stacey says. 'When did you get your licence then?'

He turns and gives them a knowing look.

'It stinks in here.' Shona screws up her sharp little face. 'Like drinking.'

'Yea?' Ben says. 'So where do you want to go then?' He picks up speed casually, dangerously. He is looking for somewhere to impress them. Any place slightly off will do, a biker's pub, a graveyard, maybe someplace where there's been a multiple pile-up, with lots of people killed. In the mirror he looks at the girls in the back seat. The car swerves dangerously onto the verge, then back onto the road.

Shona is looking out one side window, Stacey out the other. They are indifferently waiting to be disappointed. Frantically he picks up speed still further. He knows nowhere around here. At the old city house he could have taken them loads of places. But here, there's nothing. Fields and sheep. It's a shit-hole.

Without planning it, he finds he has turned down the road to the farmhouse. After all, he hardly knows any other roads. Shona is on to it at once.

'Hey Ben, you used to live out here, yea?'

He doesn't answer.

Stacey gives her a look.

'What?' she says, peevishly. 'What did I say?'

But Ben is already turning into the lane that leads to the long potholed drive. He slows the car and negotiates the S-bends, like his father when he's pissed, with commendable care. For a long time they are all three silent. Then Ben speaks. 'I'm going to see if anyone remembered the guns. You can wait in the car.'

Shona shrieks with laughter. 'Guns? You have guns?'

Stacey gives her the same look as if to say, smart sure that's OK. But cruel not OK.

'What, your dad used guns?' Shona asks. 'On the job?'

Ben puts his foot down hard on the accelerator and the big powerful car picks up speed along the straight approach. He pulls up in front of the corrugated shed, braking too hard and locking the wheels. The two girls are jolted forward and both of them scream out. As soon as the car stops, they push open the doors and jump clear.

'Remind me not to take any lessons from you,' Stacey says, slamming the door behind her. She does not want the others to see that she was scared. More importantly, she does not want to die.

In the house Ben can see that someone has been nosing around in the few days since they moved out. Things they left behind have been scattered around the place. He hurries through the downstairs rooms and the girls follow. He does not want them to see that he is upset. Sure, the farmhouse was a shit-hole but now they have nowhere, a tiny flat and weekends at Vanessa's. Everything is gone. Everything is lost. More importantly, he does not want to cry in front of them.

'Slow down, will you?' Shona calls after him. She is struggling on high stacked heels and in a long tight skirt that is slit up one side revealing the full length of one perfect bare thigh. She is shockingly erotic.

Ben takes the steps two at a time, increasing the distance between himself and them. He stops in the doorway of his high attic bedroom but does not go in. The plastic window covering has come loose and is flapping in the late evening breeze. More plaster has dropped from the ceiling. The bed is still there.

Shona comes up behind him and pushes past. 'This your room?' she says, stepping into the bare room. Stacey too comes up behind him but she stops in the doorway.

'Is this it?' Shona asks, looking disappointed. 'Where's the guns?'

Ben doesn't answer. It looks to him as if Shona is going to step up behind him, push him effortlessly through the missing window and then laugh as he plummets to his death. He stares at her, stunned. He knows he is a flincher, a deserter. He has never had what it takes, unlike this girl who is bold and reckless. About her there is the determined flash of stardom.

'Come on Shon,' Stacey interrupts. 'Let's go.'

Shona looks at her friend with contempt. She moves around to the other side of the bed to look out the window. In the dying light the fields are smoothly green and beautiful. 'What a shit-hole,' she says. 'Who would want to live way out here?'

Stacey has seen the boy's unhappy face. 'Come on,' she says. 'Let's just go, OK?'

In the car, the engine turns over but refuses to start. Ben holds the clutch down and pumps the accelerator. He can see it was a mistake to bring them here. His misery cranks up another notch.

'What's wrong?' Stacey asks. She is sitting in front beside him, Shona in the back.

Ben does not answer. He has watched the petrol level drop as he drove out of the city and now it registers below empty. 'The car's been in a couple of smash-ups,' he tells the girls.

'You do it?' Stacey asks, looking at the scratched and dented bonnet. She is flirting with him.

'You're out of petrol,' Shona says. 'Shit for brains.' She hunches down in her seat and stares out the window, more bored than ever. 'I'm not walking,' she announces.

'No it's not,' Stacey says. 'It's not his fault it won't start.' In her experience, flirting makes guys feel good and she doesn't mind doing it. After all, everyone at school knows he's in trouble all the time but it's got nothing to do with those guys he hangs around with, Carling and that lot, unlike what they all think. There's something else going on, something much more interesting and probably sadder. She'd like to let him know that she thinks this but can't think of a way, except by maybe putting her hand on his thigh but she's not going to do this in front of Shona, no way.

Ben tries the engine again but already the battery is starting to fail.

'Stop doing that,' Shona tells him. 'Don't you know anything about cars?' Her voice is scathing.

'Shut up, will you,' Stacey turns to her friend. She has watched the unhappiness on the boy's face steadily increase all afternoon, despite her best efforts.

Ben gets out of the car and opens the bonnet. He looks at the dirty complicated engine and understands that with girls, all triumphs are fleeting followed immediately by heartache and despair.

'It's the plugs,' he lies. 'There's enough fucking petrol.'

★★★

It is the afternoon of the wedding. Sarah has been invited, for the sake of the children, now that things between them are all adult and civilised. It was Vanessa's idea. She dresses carefully in the tight black suit, discarding the beads and scarves of the last few months. About the whole thing with Vanessa, she has few thoughts anymore, except to see that it has made the distance between herself and James open alarmingly fast, when in fact this distance might only have been tactical on her part after all, and really just an expression of profound remorse for her failings, not that she would ever have told him that. She does not head for the city but instead drives to Roberto Raftiche's house where she finds him outside on the pavement, peering through the hedge. He is visibly startled to see her.

'I don't know why I'm here,' she tells him miserably. 'I'm supposed to be at the wedding. Vanessa needs her audience.'

He stares at her for a long lingering moment. 'It doesn't matter why you're here,' he answers seriously. 'Come with me.' Again he peers through the hedge. He'll just have to take a chance that Ruby is gone. He didn't see her a moment ago but that doesn't mean she isn't round the back digging up the stinging nettles or pulling greasy leaves out of his drains. He shakes his head sadly and moans.

At the sound, Sarah stops. He's such a strange, serious man. She shouldn't have come. 'I shouldn't have come,' she says, but he continues to stand and stare at something in the garden. When he doesn't contradict her, she is unnerved and searches for something else to say. She would like to tell him about the marriage and her regrets and the way it's taken her by surprise. But he is behaving so oddly, peering around like a stalker. If only he didn't do these things all the time. If only he just behaved normally, at least once in a while.

She looks at his sadly worried face. 'Do you ever look out at the world and wonder how it works?' she asks him.

Caught off guard, he swivels round and stares intently at her. He guesses she is talking about that ex-husband of hers. 'Of course not,' he blusters. 'Men never wonder how the world works. We make it work. Of course we don't wonder.' He laughs and, without thinking, takes hold of her upper arm. Touching her, he is acutely aware of his deep unhappiness that has, without warning, sprung into relief when happiness is unexpectedly beside him, available. Having her here, he could sing, he could dance. After all, she's free, isn't she? In fact, he's heard that this is the day that husband of hers is remarrying.

'You have sexy purchase,' he tells her.

She looks up at him, bewildered, and then down at his huge hand gripping her upper arm.

At once he lets go and again laughs. 'It means. . . ' But then he stops. In fact, he doesn't want to put into words what it means, knowing only that it arouses in him a physical hopelessness.

'I know what it means,' Sarah says. If only he weren't such an odd man. And he's getting odder every time she meets him. Yet, what he says is always funny and true, about men never wondering how the world works. James never wondered. Clive certainly never wonders.

'Listen,' she says again. 'I shouldn't have come.' But she makes no move to leave.

Mr Raftiche presses both hands over his heart and gives her a look of such profound longing, that the rest of what she is about to say shrivels and dies in her throat.

'Please,' he says. He gazes solemnly at her beautiful, miserable face. Then he laughs and turns to lead the way up the narrow path, saying loudly over his shoulder, 'Don't want the tears. No histrionics. Who cares? No one cares, that's who.' He can see she is upset about the wedding.

Sarah looks at him, startled.

'On the ice,' he explains. 'Ice skating, that's what my ex used to say when I fell.'

It's such a funny thing to have told her, out of the blue, she smiles unwillingly.

Mr Raftiche allows his arm to rest, for the briefest of moments, across her shoulders as he steers her towards the sitting room. He is experiencing a shock of pure ecstasy. This is the moment he has dreamed of every night for a year, since he first saw her. Or at least he would have dreamed of it if he had dared to allow himself the rapture of dreaming about her. She is a goddess. He is ranting.

'You are a goddess,' he tells her.

She looks up at him, the smile quickly fading. 'Ice skating,' she says. 'It doesn't seem like something you'd do.'

He doesn't answer. His ex was a great skater. They went often. But he sees that now she has stopped in the doorway and is looking around the room. It is the first time she has been here. The way she has stopped, it seems she is not prepared to move a step further.

Sarah looks at the bottles and understands that here at last is the explanation for his strangeness and for the funny curious things he comes out with. There are empty bottles on every surface – Jack Daniel's, Jameson's, Seagram's, every variety of single malt. There are boxes of bottles on the floor by the sagging settee, bottles lined up on the mantelpiece – Smirnoff, Gordon's, Fleshman's. A Stewards Cream of the Barley is propping up the aerial on the television. So that explains everything, his charm especially. She should have guessed. It is, after all, a familiar enough situation in her own life. She is struck through by a despairing sense of loss. Her James is gone forever, him and his drinking, him and his working, his strength that she depended on.

Roberto Raftiche hesitates for no more than a second, then crosses the room in three powerful strides and throws open the curtains. 'These haven't been opened since 1963,' he laughs. Next he switches on the overhead light, then moves quickly around the room turning on the two table lamps and the floor lamp. Last, he bends and ignites the fake coal gas fire. The extravagant light glints off all the glass surfaces. It is a splendid sight.

Finally he turns to her. 'I'm lonely without them,' he says. And again he presses both hands to his heart. 'Them,' he says, looking at the empties. 'Not the contents, I'm long finished with all that.'

She looks from bottle to bottle and not at him, thinking. He sees that she is thinking and remains quiet. A whole minute passes. They are into the second when she speaks.

'I can understand that,' she says.

He lets out a great sigh of enchantment. Not only is she a goddess, but she understands and forgives him. She is perfect beyond his wildest expectation. He is in seventh heaven, on cloud nine, in this strange numerically crunched-up language that he will never be sure of.

'Let me kneel down,' he says, dropping to his knees in front of her with an alarming suddenness.

Startled, she steps back.

'You are wonderful,' he says. 'More than I ever dreamed.' Then he sees he has said too much, revealed more than he intended, and he laughs his sweet self-deprecating laugh. 'Something else my ex said, just don't try for it on the first date.'

Now Sarah too laughs, but she is not quite sure what it is she is laughing at. Again he is making her uneasy. 'Your ex,' she says. 'I guess she was really something.'

'Gone,' he answers, waving his arms in a gesture of extravagant finality. 'Gone and long forgotten.'

Mr Raftiche retraces his steps, turning off the lights. It is, after all, only mid-afternoon and he has made his point. 'Listen,' he says, indicating the bottles with a sweeping gesture. 'Truly, all this finished years ago. I go to the meetings.' And, because he is not being entirely truthful about his struggle, he looks out the window instead of at her. There is a large pile of wilting stinging nettles in the middle of the garden. It was not there this morning.

'There's something else,' he goes on quickly before she has a chance to speak. 'If you leave aside my post-adolescent, anti-social personality disorder, I'm available to look after you forever, you know.'

Again Sarah steps back startled. It has been many years since she has had a proposal, if that's what it is. She has heard other women say this is what happens, though. As soon as you're available, they come out of the woodwork.

'But it's too soon,' she says and then feels bad. Out of the woodwork is such an unkind thing to think about him. 'I mean, nothing's done. I mean we've moved, it's done but it doesn't feel that way. I mean I still have to sell the house.' She is jabbering.

'Oh that,' he brushes her objection aside with another wave of the hand. 'A couple of solicitors, that's mine, this is yours, nothing to it.' He is making it sound as if he speaks from bitter experience.

'You speak from experience,' she says, not wanting to hurt him. She is surprised at herself, at her confusion.

He shrugs his shoulders. 'Marriage,' he goes on. 'I know it's hardly necessary these days. But I'm an old fashioned kinda guy.' The gangster accent is back unbidden. 'So whadda you say, kid?'

She laughs, uneasily, not sure if perhaps he is joking. She studies his grinning face and decides he is joking, maybe to cheer her up in his strange unpredictable way, and she answers jokingly. 'I thought you'd never ask.'

'You thought I'd never ask?' he goes on quickly. 'I thought I'd never ask. What did I ask?' He takes her perfect, pretty hand in his big, graceless paw.

'So?' he questions, leaning forward, pressing her hand to his chest.

Alarmed, she pulls free. He was not joking. She takes a step backwards. He takes a step forwards. She sees it is all hopeless and looks up at him with a deeply pained expression.

There is a sudden light tapping at the window and both turn at once to look. In truth, they are both relieved to look away. He gives a little gasp and lurches across the room. In one swift gesture he yanks the curtains closed without acknowledging the odd, bedraggled, little woman outside. He moans and rests his forehead against the faded fabric.

Sarah stares at him, astonished. 'Who was that?' she asks.

He moans again by way of an answer. Sarah eases sideways towards the door. That's not the moan you use when the person you paid to clear up the garden has come to tell you they've finished for the day, or if maybe your next-door neighbour, who is a bit of a nuisance, has popped round uninvited. No, that moan is something else all together. It really is, as she thought, totally and absolutely hopeless. At the door she glances briefly over her shoulder and finds he is looking at her with an expression so stricken with horror, that she at once comes back to him, reaching both arms up behind his neck and drawing him to her. She brushes her lips chastely across his. If only whatever it is that is going on wasn't going on. If only she were in happier circumstances. If only the whole thing wasn't – she pauses to think – so completely absolutely beyond hope, to the bitter end, hopeless.His expression of horror changes instantly to one of anguish. He is speechless, staring at her. Where are his jokes when he needs them? He clutches at the pain in the centre of his chest, pressing it tightly in place as if it might escape and fly around the room, upending furniture and smashing bottles in a frenzy of despair. Again he moans, unable to stop himself.

★★★

When he hears her car is gone, Mr Raftiche pulls open the curtains and finds Ruby still standing outside the big, dirty window, looking forlorn. At once he pushes the window open. 'Ruby,' he says, trying to sound surprised and pleased but managing neither. Today she is wearing another new tracksuit, this one with huge, horizontal, red and white stripes across the jacket. It makes her look round and unsinkable like a life belt.

'I saw you had visitors,' she says. 'So I stayed out of the way.'

He looks at her hands. They are caked with grey, greasy dirt and covered with scratches.

She sees him looking. 'I was cleaning out your drains,' she explains. 'But then I got cold.'

'Oh Ruby,' he says sadly. Then he hurries on, trying to make her smile. 'It's a beautiful spring day and you're a pretty lady.' He lays one outsized hand on her fleshless shoulder and looks at her seriously. 'You should be out shopping for clothes you want but don't need and then wearing them, all at once.' It is what he should have said to Sarah. Where were his jokes when he needed them more than ever before?

She looks at him, bewildered. 'It's no trouble,' she tells him.

And again he sees that emotional cripples are for abusing, always. 'Oh Ruby,' he again says, sadly. It's all so hopeless. He takes one of her tiny, dirty, scratched hands in his own and looks at it. It is nothing like Sarah's. 'With your bare hands,' he says and feels her quiver. He opens the window wider and pulls her into his arms. 'Ruby, Ruby,' he says. 'You need someone to take care of you, not the other way around. You should be worshipped and adored.' He keeps his arms wrapped tightly around her. 'Worshipped and adored,' he repeats, unable to think of anything further to add.

★★★

Later that evening he writes to Sarah withdrawing his offer. In the letter he tries for parody but expects he achieves only bombast. After due consideration, he tells her...

When he reads the letter through, he knows he is making an even bigger fool of himself but he hasn't the heart to try again. He finishes – isn't this too funny for words? He does not expect an answer. Yet, curiously, his deep desolation is already moving towards resignation from which, he knows, it will further advance through humility to maybe a modest kind of optimism. After all, there is no choice really. She was embarrassed.

Upstairs Ruby is finishing putting the bathroom to rights. He hears the toilet flush. If only she weren't so eagerly servile. Ah well, fashionable ladies in beige with bright scarves, all shoulder pads and painted nails, what does he want with them? But if only he could teach her the meaning of the word friendship, with it's lovely implied equality. He brings one hand up and presses it over the pain in the centre of his chest, now receding and taking its place in the background like an old familiar companion. The pain these days rarely leaves him. It is a daily weight pressing down on him. Then again, he has always known he has suffered from the heavy weight of superfluous emotions, compared with other men that is. And, lifting the glass, he has also known that alcohol and a sound heart don't mix. If you like a drink, you really shouldn't bother too much about the other.

Ruby comes in and finds him draining the glass. She cries out. At the sound, he opens his eyes and signals her over with one large hand. The other remains clenched tightly around the drink.

'Come here,' he calls her. 'Come, come.'

She obeys and he draws her into a chaste embrace. Somewhere along the way, she has exchanged her tracksuit top for a fluffy pink cardigan. It clings gently to her arms and slowly he strokes the fabric, as if she were a cherished child. 'Ah well,' he sighs, again looking at the glass. 'I want to be happy and I want you to be happy. So happy your jaws will seize up from smiling and you'll scream for mercy.'

Ruby looks up at him, lost and adoring. She has no idea what he is talking about. She knows only that he shouldn't be drinking. The doctor has said. He needs looking after, that's the problem. He's let things get into a terrible state. Of course, he's unhappy. Who wouldn't be, all alone with no one to look after him? She is waiting for him to ask whatever it is he has told her he wants to ask. She has already made up her mind that she will do it, whatever it is. After all, marriage, these days no one even thinks about that any more. She will be perfectly happy with whatever he suggests.

★★★

Thankfully, the twin babies are both asleep at the same time and Dianne is at last arguing with Clive. It is an argument that has been waiting to happen for a long time. 'I don't believe you,' she is saying. 'I don't believe anything you say anymore.'

'Trust me,' he answers.

She stops rocking the oversized pram and looks at him. 'Trust you,' she repeats derisively. 'What would I want to do that for?'

They fall silent. In the brief calm, the little boy Davey eases himself around the edge of the room on his bottom. When he reaches the door, he twists over onto his hands and knees and disappears soundlessly into his place behind the settee. The room is dark. The television is on, and neither of his parents has noticed his move. For a while he pushes the little red wheelless car back and forth, until he sees a scattering of black, wizened berries under the settee. Suddenly he is desperately hungry. He knows his plate of sausages is still on the table in the kitchen but lately he has not been able to eat the food his mother prepares for him. One forkful and he brings it all up again. He picks up a berry and puts it in his mouth. It tastes terrible so he spits it out again quickly. Yet he is so hungry he tries the same thing with a second berry. It too is bitter beyond anything he has ever tasted and he dribbles it out of his mouth onto the floor.

In the kitchen Di is now facing Clive, with both hands on her huge hips. Clive is looking at her, momentarily silenced. She sees his expression change to something she can't straightaway get a fix on. She knows, despite the months of feeding the babies, the smoking, the yellow fruit diet, front on she is bigger than ever.

'You look like shit,' he tells her.

'So what do you expect?' she snaps back at him. She knows she is out of control and gaining weight yet again. Her stomach, the great empty sack that once held the two babies, now hangs down in front in flaccid folds that overlap obscenely. It shows no sign of shrinking away as seems to happen with other women. And her breasts, gross blue-veined blobs that ache and burn constantly, so much for the bliss of breastfeeding that everyone is always going on about. She has not let Clive see her fully undressed since the birth. She does not want to let him anywhere near her real humiliations.

'Why don't you just piss off out of my life?' she tells him.

'It's what you want?' he asks.

But, before she can answer, Ruby comes into the room. Her face is glowing and she has obviously been hurrying.

225

Both Clive and Dianne stare at her in surprise. They are well used to Ruby's painful little dramas but this happy excitement is not like her. Her skin is curiously mottled, colourless underneath but flushed on top as if she has in fact been through something amazing. Her hair is flying about her face, girlish, almost pretty. It is not like Ruby at all.

'Jesus,' Clive says, staring at her.

Ruby stands in the doorway. 'I'm getting married,' she tells them, looking from one to the other. She has to tell someone.

They are both silent. 'You're kidding,' Dianne finally says. Her voice is calm. It is how she speaks when a child is injured or maybe seriously ill and everyone is too upset to make sense of what's going on. 'Who?' she asks.

Ruby looks from one to the other. 'It's Robert,' she says.

'Robert,' Clive repeats. 'Who's he?'

Dianne shrugs her shoulders, a gesture of disbelief.

At this Ruby begins to cry, making no effort to hide her distress. It is so unexpected. She has been bursting with happiness and now it is obvious they don't believe her.

Dianne leans forward and puts her arm around her sister.

'What the fuck?' Clive says, looking at the two half-sisters, polar opposites but the same in ways he can see but not explain.

'Ruby,' Dianne says, 'why are you crying? What's going on?'

But Ruby is shaking too much to answer. She has no idea why she's crying and can't seem to get the words out. Even if she could, she has no idea how to answer her sister's question. 'I'm getting married,' she repeats hopelessly.

'Are you sure about this?' Dianne asks. She does not entirely believe her.

Ruby sobs, 'Of course I'm sure.'

'Jesus,' Clive repeats. 'Probably some weirdo.'

'Shut up Clive.' Dianne's voice is icy, but all the while she is looking worriedly at her sister. 'When did all this happen?' she asks.

'I don't know,' Ruby lies. For some reason she does not want to tell them it was only this afternoon. For some reason the whole thing seems suddenly impossible. And she's not sure she actually heard him ask her, not in so many words. She gives her sister a pained look.

'How can you not know?' Dianne asks.

'Jesus, fuck,' Clive says, 'another fuck up.'

'Shut up Clive,' Dianne repeats. She tightens her arm around her sister and draws her close as if she were a child in need of comforting. It is obvious that something has happened to Ruby, but what? With Ruby, things are rarely what she thinks they are. Take that useless, lying son of hers, to listen to Ruby you'd think he was a saint, whereas the truth's a whole lot more obvious.

'I'm going to make you a cup of tea,' Dianne says. Her sister's sudden appearance has destroyed her flimsy composure. One minute she and Clive are having a little talk about their own problems, the next minute the whole place is filled with someone else's disasters.

When Dianne has left the room, Clive leans forward and says to Ruby, 'What are you doing here?' He does not want to have to pick up the pieces yet again. He is tired of Ruby and her cock-ups. Yet secretly he is glad not to hear Di's answer to his last question. Why go there? Life is tough enough.

'I didn't come to see you.' Ruby snaps back. It is obvious they dislike each other and have done so for many years.

'Well that's a relief then,' Clive answers.

Dianne puts the tea on the table in front of her sister.

'It's true,' Ruby repeats. 'I am getting married. Why shouldn't I?'

'No reason,' Dianne says, lowering herself wearily into her chair. 'Have you told Toss? What did she say?'

At the second mention of the word marriage, Clive understands for certain that it is, as he thought, a cock-up and it's going to involve him, probably going to cost him, paying for some wedding. 'Jesus fucking Christ,' he repeats.

And in the next instant Ruby jumps up. 'You hate me. I know you do.'

'That's not true,' Dianne says. 'He didn't mean anything.' She gives Clive a look. 'Of course he doesn't hate you.'

'I'm going,' Ruby announces. She has no idea where she's going, only that she does not want them ruining what she has with Robert. She looks over her shoulder and sees Dianne pushing past Clive into the doorway.

'Ruby wait, please wait. We think it's wonderful.'

'No you don't.' Ruby looks back at them. The last thing she wants is them all standing around feeling sorry for her. They don't believe what she says. They don't believe anyone would want to marry her. 'I am getting married,' she says. 'You can't stop me. Robert asked me this afternoon and we're doing it right away.'

Dianne and Clive watch her hurrying down the drive with her funny little clockwork run, and turning unexpectedly left into the middle of nowhere. They exchange weary glances. 'I'll go then, shall I?' Clive says.

A few minutes later Clive's van pulls up alongside Ruby. 'Get in,' he orders.

Ruby ignores him. She trusted them.

'Get the fuck in,' Clive repeats, holding the door for her.

In the car they are both silent for a long time. After a while Ruby speaks. 'Go on, say it. I know it's what you're thinking.'

Clive gives her an odd look. 'I'm not thinking anything,' he answers. 'I'm taking you home.'

'You're thinking who'd want to marry her? That's what you're thinking. Everyone wants to marry Tossie. You want to marry Tossie.'

'I'm not thinking anything,' Clive repeats, surprised at her outburst. 'Marry whoever you want.'

Ruby gives him an icy look. 'All you and Di ever do is fight,' she says. 'You said yourself all you ever do is fight.'

'Sure we fight,' Clive agrees. 'What's that got to do with anything?' What he doesn't know is that Di has explained to her sister that the central preoccupation of Clive's life is himself and absent-mindedly along the way he's acquired a wife and three children. There's not a lot of room left for anyone else whose central preoccupation is anything other than him. Unaccountably, Ruby has understood this. She also knows that it will not happen to her and Robert when they are married.

'What you don't know,' Clive says. 'What you can't begin to know...' And then he stops. He's been through enough with the women in this family, all of them. He doesn't need this.

'What's that supposed to mean?' Ruby snaps.

'It means,' Clive tells her, 'I'm taking you home. What you do is

228

your own business. Di's got enough on her plate. Leave her out of it.'

For a brief moment Ruby hesitates, surprised. But it has always been this way with Clive. What her sister sees in him, she has no idea. It will not be this way with her and Robert. They will never argue, never for a moment.

★★★

Di watches Ruby finally get in the car. Then, shaking her head, she drags herself slowly back inside where both twins are now crying. She picks them up, putting one on each shoulder. Back and forth she walks, between the oddly-blackened cooker and the stained sink until the babies quieten. She hears a funny little scurrying noise from behind the settee and she stops some distance away. 'Davey,' she says quietly. 'Can I ask you something?'

But the little boy doesn't answer. She waits, rocking the babies. Mercifully, they seem to be falling asleep.

'What I want to ask you,' she goes on, 'is if maybe you'd like to come sit in my lap? What do you think?' Deliberately she looks out the window and not at the place under the settee where she knows he's hiding. 'I'm just putting the babies down,' she says and, mercifully, both babies allow themselves to be put down, one in the old-fashioned pram and one in the bassinet which is already too small. Mercifully they are both perfectly content, a new and small step forwards.

Davey hears his mother's deeply drawn-out sigh. It is a familiar sound and not one he particularly likes. Lying flat on his stomach, he slowly eases himself all the way under the settee. Here is a surprising thing. Before, he was too big to fit under and now he has grown smaller. In his experience, this is not what usually happens. He has been growing bigger, when his mother measures him on the wall. Yet it is quite nice to be able to fit under the settee. In fact, it is something he has always wanted to be able to do. The berries are still there, sticking to his shirt and hands but he doesn't try again to eat them, though he is hungrier than he has ever been before, and cold. He shivers and pushes the little red car with no wheels back and forth.

Dianne listens to the same little scratching noise, like a tiny mouse rummaging for food in an upturned cereal box, and then Davey's head and shoulders appear from under the settee. She sits in the old armchair by the window and waits, not watching him approach. When she feels an almost weightless shoulder pressing against her, a delicate hand on her knee, she bends and lifts the little boy into her lap. He weighs nothing, nothing at all, less it seems than either of the babies who are both dense and solid. She pulls him tightly to her, wrapping the shabby outsized cardigan around the two of them.

Of course she has seen the crushed berries on his T-shirt and the stains around his mouth. She knows there is no fruit in the kitchen. It has been a long time since she's bought and served fresh fruit to anyone. 'Did you find some berries?' she asks. 'Were they on the floor?'

Solemnly he shakes his head. Of course she remembers the basket of berries almost a year ago. She remembers every second of that day as if it were happening right now. She remembers the tightening pain, the fear. She remembers the basket in her lap and how she thought at the time there were deadly nightshade mixed in with the currants. But, curiously, she has no memory of Davey on that day. Her mother and phoning Clive and not getting him, these are all as clear as right now. But where was Davey? She hugs him to her.

'Did they taste nice?' she asks him.

Solemnly he looks up at her, making no answer.

'Bet you were hungry,' she goes on, running her hands up and down his little matchstick arms. 'You want something to eat now?' She closes her eyes just for a second. She is so tired and the house is so quiet. She thinks about maybe taking Davey to the hospital and what they would put him through. They'd have to pump out his stomach if there were any doubt. It would be terrifying and painful for him.

'Did they taste bad?' she asks. 'Bitter? Did you spit them out?'

But the little boy has closed his eyes and is breathing peacefully, half asleep against his mother's chest. She listens for a long time to his little heart beating and to her own pounding away deep inside her. She is so tired and Davey is falling softly, wonderfully asleep in her arms in a way he has not done for a long time. Mostly he is tense in her arms, or stoical. But now this is as it should be, a sort of bliss that has come to the two of them, unexpected and out of nowhere. She closes her eyes again, overcome with tiredness. Poor Ruby, what terrible mistake has she made this time? What is it that's going to stab her in the heart yet again?

She presses her lips to Davey's forehead. He is warm and sweet smelling, perfect. She nuzzles his cheek and sighs. Lately her life, like that of the babies, has resolved itself into the simple question of need and relief of need. And, in so doing, she has forgotten things that have no business to be forgotten. No, she decides, pain and terror are not going to happen to her little boy. None of that is going to happen while he has her to protect him and look after him. Again she nuzzles his cheek and breathes his sweet exhaling breath into her own lungs, testing it for life. And, finding it true, she closes her own eyes and is instantly, deeply asleep.

★★★

Some days later, Tossie knocks gently on the back door of the now empty farmhouse. There is a dim light on inside and she is a little scared. The big, scratched-up city car is parked in its usual place by the corrugated shed. It looks abandoned. The front windows have been left open and there's another messed-up dent in the side. Tossie moves around to the front of the house and sees someone has propped up the front door and nailed it in place with three horizontal planks. The old For Sale sign has been put back by the broken gate. When no one comes in answer to her knock, she again goes around to the back, pushes the door carefully open and goes in. The stone kitchen is dark and empty. The light is coming from somewhere deeper in the house. She shivers. It's always cold in here and it always smells of rot. She could have told them not to bother with this room. The farm dog, Megan, growls and Tossie jerks sharply at her lead. She does not want anyone to hear, just in case. She is glad she has thought to bring the dog with her. They are both wary and tensed for trouble.

Slowly Tossie eases her way towards the light, which she now sees is coming from the far end of the big sitting room. Twice she has to stop to move things out of her way, first the door from the kitchen to the morning room, half-twisted off its hinges and then a rough saw horse blocking the stairs. But when she finally peers into the room, she sees only that someone has hung a bed sheet across the far alcove to curtain it off. The light behind this makeshift partition is not bright enough to reveal much of anything, though she can see a sort of shape.

Again she resumes her slow progress, keeping the dog close at her heels. She knows that animals are useful in these situations. They take violence without it mattering too much, whereas she herself could be broken with one blow. Slowly she pulls back one edge of the sheet and finds Tord sitting on the floor with his eyes closed, a rollie dangling in one hand.

'Jesus Tord,' she says, relieved.

His eyes snap open in alarm and he gives her a look that instantly denies everything no matter what the evidence. But when he sees it is only her, his look changes. 'Fuck,' he says.

Tossie looks back at him with defiance. He doesn't fool her. He's not a guy who can look at you like that and mean it.

'Hello Howard,' she says, tauntingly. 'What are you doing here?'

He turns his back on her. 'What does it look like?'

Tossie comes closer and peers over his shoulder. What it looks like is that he is melting candles in a tin over another candle. What it is for, she does not want to know. It will be another one of his stupid schemes to make money. It will not make money.

'Don't tell me,' she says, looking around her. It seems Tord has made the alcove his own. His sleeping bag is spread out in one corner and his rucksack is propped beside a broken chair. His clothes are draped across a motorcycle frame and there are a couple of baked bean tins and a mess of chip wrappers on the floor.

'Got anything to eat?' she asks.

He does not bother to answer. After a while, Tossie sighs. She slips her own rucksack off her shoulders and lowers it to the floor. This is not what she expected when she came up here. She's not sure exactly what she did expect, maybe to find Clive, working late, all alone. After all it's been his job for more than a year and God knows he's never at his own house. Or maybe to find Ben, but this is a thought she does not want to pursue.

After a few more minutes, she tosses her scarves back and their beaded fringe tinkles delicately. 'They leave any stuff?' she asks Tord.

He gives a contemptuous snort and indicates his feet. Tossie looks. He is wearing a pair of women's sandals with tiny gold straps that don't fit across the width of his feet. They look ridiculous.

Tossie sneers. 'You look ridiculous.'

Again he doesn't bother to answer her. Again she sighs.

'I'm going to poke around,' she tells him. She does not believe him, about there being nothing here. Tord's fine if it falls in his lap. Otherwise, he can't be arsed. But for once he is telling the truth. The old house is empty of anything useful. She guesses, from the look of his little space, that Tord has been here long enough to have sold anything worth anything. She guesses also he has been kicked out of their other place. Neither of them after all had paid any rent for a long time. Twice more the dog growls deep in her throat and Tossie stops to listen to the scurrying noises under the floorboards. 'Rats,' she says to the dog. She is not in the least frightened. Nothing with four legs frightens her. It's the kind with two legs you have to watch out for.

On her progress she collects an old curtain that has been taken down from the tall landing window and abandoned. She can see that tomorrow she'll have to bring a few things up here. Back in the alcove, Tord is eating a sandwich from a paper bag. 'Bastard,' she says to him good-naturedly.

He picks up another sandwich from the bag at his feet and tosses it to her. She arranges the curtain on the floor opposite him and sits to eat, picking off bits of crust to share with the dog. The homemade candlelight glints off her wild beaded hair and her beautiful skin. It highlights the blondness of his hair and emphasises the width of his manly shoulders. The grime on his jeans fades into nothing. The flickering of the little yellow flame obscures the collapsing ceiling and the water-stained walls. She can see that he is lonely, really, just a bit tricky and peevish with the small things like someone who doesn't really understand about stuff. She gives him a sideways assessing look. It's nothing she can't handle, after all. In fact, she likes handling things.

'So,' she says. 'Mind if I hang out here?'

He shrugs his shoulders and gives her a what's-it-to-me look. It doesn't fool her.

'Why am I asking?' she asks. 'What's it to you?' But there is no anger in her voice, nor any in his ignoring her. Secretly, he is glad to see her. Secretly, she is glad to find him here.

★★★

At the end of the week Clive comes out to the farmhouse and finds the two of them digging in the old corrugated shed.

He looks at Tossie's beautiful body, bent forward so that her breasts hang loosely in the flimsy top. 'Looking for something?' he asks.

Tord looks up at him, surprised. 'Shit,' he answers. 'What the fuck are you doing here?' Now that he no longer works for Clive, he can say what he wants. The trouble is he can't think of anything to say.

Clive too bends forward to look into the cluster of holes. 'Found anything?' he asks Tossie.

'Fucking plenty,' Tord answers. In fact, since they first noticed the holes, they have searched several times and found only a cluster of Coke cans and the wrappings from half a dozen take-away burgers. But they are not yet convinced there is nothing here. After all the kid must have hid his stash somewhere. He was a real airhead. And he had money, what with that dad of his going off to work in the City and keeping another woman. That doesn't come cheap.

Clive turns back to Tossie. He couldn't care less what they're doing up here, her and that useless hippie. Why he ever gave him a job he can't figure out. They're probably surviving by selling each other pictures made out of leaves, him and the others that live up in the hills, that and their dole cheques. In his experience that's what hippies do. 'I was worried about you,' he tells Tossie. 'Di was worried.'

She snorts. 'Yea sure.' She knows he is lying. And she knows too that whatever happens, nothing is going to stick to Clive. Di's the one who's going to get the blame. If there's any blame lying around unclaimed, Di'll find it. 'Fuck off Clive,' she tells him.

Tord hurls the spade to the ground and walks angrily off towards the house. He can see what Clive is up to, the bastard. Just when he and Toss were getting it back together again. The man's a fucking shit-face. A couple of hits and then he'll have the courage to tell him what he thinks. Especially about the way he's making a move on Toss.

Clive comes a step closer to Tossie. She is warm from the digging and her female smell surrounds her. He breathes in deeply but not so she'll notice him doing it. 'You and him?' he asks. 'Something happening?'

Tossie watches Tord disappear into the house. 'Fancy your chances then?' she says, turning to face Clive. He's so obvious.

'What chance is that then?' he answers, pleased. Again he moves a step closer. This is more like it, the little tart.

'Don't be stupid,' Tossie answers. 'You missed that long ago.'

Clive looks at her in surprise. She has wrong-footed him. 'Who says I want a chance?' It is of course exactly what he does want.

'Not with me,' Tossie repeats. 'With her, Sarah. That's why you're here, right?' She has heard about James's wedding in London and about what happened after so that now Sarah will need all the help she can get.

'No way,' he answers. 'What would I want with her when I could have you?'

'Jesus Clive,' Tossie gives him a look.

Of course he has tried in the past weeks to make it happen, offering himself to Sarah, help with the move, anything she wants. If she'd let him, he would have made her forget all right. But she wasn't having it, no longer even bothering to mess him about. And now, with the husband gone like that, all of a sudden, no warning, it's changed things, made them tricky. He's not so sure there's anything he wants there after all.

'You know what she said?' he now tells Tossie.

Tossie looks off into empty space, a bored-to-distraction look.

'She said "Talk to me",' Clive tells her. 'What the fuck does that mean? What do I want to talk to her about? The fucking weather?'

Tossie turns away from him. 'Clive,' she says. 'You're a bastard.'

'Yea,' he says, grinning hugely. 'Of course I am.' He comes up behind her and presses up close.

'Want me to talk to you?' he asks, bending to kiss her neck.

'Don't bother,' she answers.

'You and I,' he says, turning her around to face him. 'We understand each other. That's what I like about you.'

He leans forward to bring his lips to hers and fails to see her troubled look. She is thinking, he is right. The two of them are scruffy in character, devious, selfish, and they have an instant understanding that comes from this.

'Bastard,' she says again, pushing him gently away.

'Too right,' he agrees with her, pulling her back. 'A nice guy is hardly worth your while, yea?'

'Yea,' she says. 'You get bored.' She allows him to fondle one breast. 'And then you're on the slippery slope to pointless conversation,' she adds.

'That's exactly what I mean.' Clive again grins hugely. 'Exactly what I mean, pointless conversation, who needs that?' She really is kind of funny, the little tart. If only she didn't put it about the way she does all the time. If only she kept some of it for him. Even if she only pretended to keep some of it for him. He laughs out loud.

Tossie pulls back. 'What are you laughing at?'

He looks at her fondly. 'Useless words,' he says. 'Talk.'

She thinks for a minute. 'You mean like – it's all my fault.'

Again he laughs. 'That's a good one.' Funny thing, the way she always knows what to say. She's never short of a smart remark. He gives her an affectionate kiss. He'll have to watch himself with this one. If only Di would get her act together. If only the babies didn't cry all the time. If only things were just fine at home, then he could forget about all that, let them get on with it, while he gets on with this, which is how it should be. And Di never lets him near her these days. Who can blame him for looking elsewhere? No one, that's who.

He kisses Tossie again, replacing some of the affection with an equal amount of lust, just the way he likes it. 'You don't want to stay way out here,' he tells her. 'I hear there's some bullocks have escaped and gone feral in the woods. It's not safe. You want to come down and live with us.'

Tossie leans back and gives him a shrewd look. 'Yea?' she says. 'What a good idea. Let me get this straight, live with you and Di? And Di's OK about this, is she?'

Clive shrugs his shoulders, unwilling to answer in a way that's going to cause problems for himself. 'You and me,' he finally says. 'You and me.' And he draws her into another embrace.

'Yea right,' Tossie answers. 'You and me and Di.'

★★★

At the funeral, the crematorium is full of women. It is Mr Raftiche who notices.

'What's this?' he says to Ruby. 'Am I the only one?'

She looks at him, unhappy and bewildered. What she sees is that she is the only one wearing a black outfit and it's far too big, though it was the smallest size in the shop. She, Sarah, the widow, is wearing a long grey skirt and a skimpy silver top. That's not right, surely. And the others, there's red, blue, cream, a couple of young ones in jeans and beads and things. That's not right either. But no one's wearing black. She looks up at Robert, on the verge of tears.

He sees and takes her hand as she hoped he would. Lately she has even dared, once or twice, to take his hand first but not here, not in public. Never mind about the dress anyway. He won't have noticed. He never notices what she's wearing and she can take it back to the shop tomorrow. She has kept the tags, undamaged. Tomorrow she'll put them back in and return the dress. With the money she intends to buy a pink and white calico duvet cover and curtains for what is going to be their bedroom. He has told her to do what she wants with the room, like an old married couple. He has told her he wants her to fill it with black velvet and murdered animal cosmetics. She is getting used to his little jokes by now. He's so funny.

The boy, Ben, is sitting between his mother and another woman. The two women are talking over his head and he is hunched forward miserably. He is not listening to his mother and Vanessa. In his imagination he is again hearing his father's last breath. He hears it all the time, the long drawn-out exhalation of a lifetime's disappointments, or at least that's what it sounds like to him. The disappointment he knows is mostly his fault, because of the way he is. And he's still told no one, except Carling, that he wasn't there. Amy was on her own. He should have been there, not Vanessa finding Amy alone with him.

237

And she's the one who wouldn't let Amy come today, because she's upset enough already. He sees that it is Vanessa's game. She's the one people believe. Well, not him. You'd have to be a complete idiot to believe Vanessa. And another thing, he has promised himself he will never leave Amy alone with Vanessa again. His shoulders droop. His breathing is shallow. Already he knows it's a promise he can never keep.

Mr Raftiche comes up to the boy and, releasing Ruby, shakes his hand, formally, seriously. He holds it in his own for a long moment. Then he smiles. 'The trouble with these events,' he says, 'they make you so miserable you're afraid you're going to join right in and die yourself.' He looks up at the raised podium or whatever it's called in these places these days. 'Then when the vicar's got going, you're afraid you're not going to die.' He laughs.

The boy grimaces, but Mr Raftiche doesn't notice. An extremely attractive woman in a tight, shape-hugging blue dress is climbing up to the pulpit. Her dress is one of those long sleek things that Chinese women wear. It hides everything she's got except for the fact that's she's slender and graceful beyond belief. She opens a book, ready to begin. Mr Raftiche stares at her, openly enthralled. He exhales, a long drawn-out breath of desire, disappointment, and the impossibility of everything, which seems to come up out of nowhere and go on forever. Ben visibly winces.

Briefly Mr Raftiche glances down at the boy and sees he is hunching even further forward in the depths of his misery. It is entirely understandable. To lose a father, so young, it's a terrible thing. He places one large, fatherly hand on the boy's shoulder. The beauty on the raised podium starts to speak and he drops into the nearest seat, taking Ruby with him.

'My dear, dear, friend James,' she begins, then pauses for effect. Her bright hair is piled into what he thinks is called a chignon.

'Your father,' Mr Raftiche leans forward and whispers to the boy. 'He was everything I ever wanted to be and never managed.' Staring at the stunner, he is thinking how the man, James, from what he knew of him, seemed to have access to an endless supply of long-limbed blonde beauties. And here's another one just to prove the point. How did he do that? God, he could do with a drink.

But the boy looks embarrassed and Mr Raftiche is again not sure he's got the words right. 'Hey kid,' he nudges him sideways with his elbow and lets the gangster lingo take hold. 'Jeeze what a guy.'

He sees Sarah watching him and, worse, listening. He wills himself to be quiet and returns his attention to the speaker but she has finished and is already stepping down. He leans across to Sarah and asks, 'No one here from work?' Though he isn't sure what the father did at work. He always assumed it was something in business that made good money with little effort. Maybe he was wrong. The man is dead after all, out of the blue and in his prime. He presses his hand to the pain in his own chest, suddenly uneasy.

'She's from work,' Sarah answers, indicating the blonde vision he has been ogling. 'And so are they.' She indicates another group of six or seven women sitting to her left. She frowns. His strangeness never ceases to surprise her, the things he comes out with, the things he wears. She allows herself a quick glance at his suit. The lapels appear to be sewn on the wrong way so that they flap across his front like folded bat's wings. The fabric has an iridescent stripe that glows of its own accord. It is strange and wonderfully stylish. She is embarrassed for him.

Again Mr Raftiche nudges the boy. 'Looka those beauties wouldja.' He is unable to stop himself. 'Jeez, they're sumpin. Wouldja believe that guy, your dad?'

Now he sees that Sarah looks stricken. What is he saying? When all he wants to do is tell her she is the one who is beautiful, a beautiful life-enhancing object in a life-destroying world. He strokes his hand across the pain in his chest, seeking out the central source and not finding it. Panicking, he jumps out of his seat and Ruby jumps with him. A new speaker is climbing to the podium, carrying a guitar.

'This is Vanessa,' Sarah whispers, indicating the woman she has been talking to. 'I guess we're both widows.'

Mr Raftiche nods and starts to back away. He sees that Vanessa too is beautiful and he no longer trusts himself to speak. And as for her, the most beautiful of all, Sarah, widowed, divorced, it is as if arrangements have been made by God himself about which there can be no doubt. Here she is for you, God has said, widowed, divorced and lonely, what more can you ask?

He backs away faster. What is happening here? He clutches his chest with both hands. Is this pain then going to be the final one? In his haste, he collides with Ruby behind him and grabs her arm to steady them both. His hand closes on empty fabric. The sleeve of her black jacket is so huge and her arms are so spindly that there's nothing there. His thoughts get no further as he is overcome by a sudden, obliterating desire for a drink.

He passes Clive going towards the front. The two men nod but do not speak. They are both pressing at the centre of their chests. The guitar player launches into something fast and gay, probably difficult to play.

Ruby gives Clive a huge grin. Here at last is someone in proper black. He is wearing a black shirt, black tie, black trousers, black shoes. She widens her grin improbably.

Clive gives her a puzzled look. She's sure giving him the eye all right and at a funeral too. Is there no end to Ruby's strangeness? And what is that black thing she's wearing? It looks like it's about to fall off her and die in the aisle. Ruby, he never thought about it like that. But it's been his experience that the funny looking ones are really something, once you show them what to do. And best of all they never give you any trouble afterwards.

He rests one hand on Sarah's shoulder, a manly, consoling gesture, then slips into the seat Mr Raftiche has just vacated. He is close enough to smell her familiar shampoo. She glances back at him with the briefest look of acknowledgement. A single gold chain flashes as she turns. He is so close he could reach out and caress that beautiful neck. He decides he is, under the circumstances, prepared to forgive and forget. He is prepared to give her a second chance. Normally he wouldn't but sometimes you got to swallow your pride. Speaking of swallow, God he could do with a drink, just to settle this strange left-handed pain that's been coming on lately. And him, the husband, pegging out like that with no warning. Jesus, you never know. He strokes his chest absent-mindedly with small, delicate, circular movements while the guitar player changes over his music.

At the opening chords of 'In The Bleak Midwinter', everyone gets to their feet. Unseen by those at the front, Tossie slips into the back row. She is not sure she is welcome, but seeing Clive sniffing around Sarah makes her feel more at ease. She sees Ben looking miserable, poor kid. She has heard how he ran away and left his father dead drunk after the wedding, with the other kid, the little mute girl, there all alone. That's a bugger all right. When she told Tord about it, he laughed. That's the trouble with him, he laughs when he shouldn't and doesn't laugh when he should. If only she didn't need a place to live. If only she had some money. She's going to show them all one day, she just hasn't figured out how to do it yet, but she will. One thing's for sure, there's not going to be some man involved. She doesn't know why she didn't figure this one out sooner. Right from the start, right from when she was tiny, for example, she loved her older brother to distraction and in return he tormented her. And her dad, she loved him too, the ten minutes a week he was around. She was always perfect with him, they all were, never out of line. And they were complete shits with Mum. Then when Dad came home and Mum started in with her whinging about all the things the kids had done wrong, it only confirmed his belief that all women were stupid and incapable, and he'd slap her about to shut her up. Men, who needs them? You got to be an idiot to give them the time of day.

The music finishes and at the front Clive laughs, a full-throated, look at me laugh. The disapproving glances of the women seek him out. He grins his modest grin, a modest man with nothing to be modest about, and hopes they'll notice.

★★★

Di shifts one baby to the other shoulder and puts the phone back. He's not at any of the places she usually finds him. Not remembering this is the morning of the funeral, she hopes she has interrupted something going on. Lately, she has taken to ringing him ten or fifteen times a day, especially when she thinks he might be with her, Sarah. About Tossie, living up in the old farmhouse with the other hippies, she prefers not to think at all. Tossie who always says you can't make an omelette without cracking eggs, then goes through life a professional omelettier. Well, she's not going to be one of those smashed-up, thrown-away eggs. Shame, if it weren't for the way she looks at Clive, she could have forgiven Tossie her many faults. That's what sisters do after all. She picks the other baby out of the bouncer and with one on each shoulder, she resumes her pacing between kitchen and sitting room. And as for Clive, he's a total shit. If it weren't for the babies she'd be out of here. You wouldn't see her for dust.

Her route takes her around behind the settee and she sees one of Davey's legs sticking out. He is under there again, playing with his cars. Here's another thing that's wrong, the way she still can't get him to eat, the way he never says anything. She wishes she could go back to the time when he was chattering away non-stop from the moment he tumbled out of bed, always something to say, always a clever question, always a chockie in his mouth. And now, nothing, silence.

She leans down and, with a sudden sharp pain in her kidneys, remembers the way her own childhood was lived at ground level. That was a long time ago, another life where there was some small happiness. It's a good thing she's forgotten all about it. 'Hey,' she says. 'Davey.' But there is only silence. Adjusting the baby with difficulty, she stretches herself flat on the floor and peers under the settee. He is asleep, a frown on his face. At night he always sleeps with a frown until something twists inside him and jolts him out of sleep into a confusion that is inseparable from pain. Then he cries out and she goes to him, every night, exactly the same. She knows about this confusion and pain because the same thing happens to her in her own sleep, every night regular as clockwork. She straightens up and reaches for the last quarter slab of cherry cheesecake and the phone. It's too soon, he won't be back at the yard yet from wherever he's been. She dials the number anyway.

★★★

The service has finished and people are starting to make their move. Mr Raftiche is explaining to Ruby that you don't have to have a vicar these days. It's what the family wants that matters. She clings to his arm and looks at him with confusion and dismay.

He laughs. 'You're looking at me like I'm something from outer space.' The fake American accent is there at the ready. He laughs again but she continues to frown in consternation.

'Ah well.' He helps her on with her black jacket which she has unfortunately removed. Two of the buttons of her black dress are undone revealing the hollow emptiness that is her chest. He hopes, for her sake, no one else has noticed. These days he feels like something from outer space, an alien, lost in a place he only imperfectly understands, if at all.

He passes the builder, Clive, talking to the pretty hippie. 'Everything's a joke with you,' he overhears the man say. Then, without warning, the builder looks up and gives Ruby the eye. There's absolutely no doubt about that look. Even Ruby can't have failed to understand what's going on.

'Nothing's a joke with me,' the pretty hippie answers. It seems they could cheerfully kill each other.

And now Ruby is staring at the builder with that look of terror that means she has no idea what's going on. Again he takes her tiny hand in his big paw. 'Ruby, Ruby,' he says. 'I know it's not the time or place but I have to tell you.' He stops. She is looking up at him with total trust. Only a complete bastard would ever do anything to hurt her. 'Ruby, Ruby,' he repeats. 'It isn't me. I'm not the one.' He sees she has no idea what he's talking about. 'Treat it like a dress rehearsal,' he goes on, desperately gathering pace. 'The real one will come along soon enough.' He pulls her hand to the pain in his chest and entwines his fingers with hers. 'You are so wonderful,' he adds but sees by her look of bliss that this is not what he should have said. He removes her hand from his and turns deliberately away. Ah well, next time he'll just have to make a better job of it, when he's maybe had a tiny drink to steady himself.

Outside he finds the boy, Ben, standing by himself, a little way apart from the others, looking bored and scared in equal measure. A look like that, the kid must now be thinking about girls.

In fact, Ben is calmly thinking about Shona and Stacey and how nothing much matters anymore. Dead fathers, lost houses, making a fool of himself, what does he care? Fuck all is what he cares. Poised between the horror of what has happened and the terror of what is about to happen, he knows only one thing for sure and that is worse things are going to happen to him, and after them, worse still.

Mr Raftiche comes up to him. He knows what he is going to say, the one about learning not to be afraid of girls the way as a child you have to learn not to be afraid of bugs, in the fake American accent.

But he stops before he gets there. It comes to him that it is his function in life to tell all the town's jokes, apparently all at the same time. Some function. Instead he puts his arms out and gives the boy a quick hug. He guesses it is all right for him to have done that. It is, after all, a funeral.

He sees her, Sarah, watching, and opens his mouth to speak. She is staring at him, waiting, but he has no words ready. He tries hard to think of something, maybe about the insanity that mysteriously comes over him whenever he sits down to write a letter, but she'll think he really is mad. He realises his thoughts are hopelessly garbled.

Seeing both of them so forlorn, Sarah detaches herself from the group she is with and comes over to stand beside them.

Mr Raftiche now takes her pretty hand in his big ugly paw. He guesses this too is acceptable. The rules are, after all, different at funerals, and at weddings. It is obvious that she misses that husband of hers and it is right that she should. He notices that the builder, Clive, is watching her every move and Ruby is watching his every look and gesture. 'You know,' he says, 'we should introduce Vanessa to that builder of yours.'

She looks at him surprised, puzzled. Then she laughs, lifting her chin and looking straight into his eyes. 'You are so right,' she says. 'You are absolutely right.'

'Ah well,' he says, taking both her hands. 'But it seems to me that when you try to figure out people, you get them wrong. In fact, you get them wrong before you even meet them. You get them wrong all the while you're with them and then you go home and tell somebody else about them and get them wrong again. And the same goes for them with you. That's just the way it is.'

She smiles up at him. 'Yes,' she agrees. 'That's true.'

He lets out a sharp, mordant laugh and gives her hand a little squeeze. 'I know this isn't the time or place,' he goes on, 'but I have to tell you. I meant what I said before. I'm yours totally and forever.'

Sarah raises one hand briefly to caress his face. 'I know,' she says. 'You are a piece of good luck I don't deserve. Believe me, you don't know how much I don't deserve you.' They move apart and he goes to stand by Ruby's side and she by her son's as is right and proper, for the moment.

At the sound of his strange laugh, several others turn to look at him as well, Clive and the pretty hippie, Vanessa, the looker who made the opening speech. They have seen the beautiful widow caress the cheek of the tall stooped man. He shrugs his shoulders in their direction and finds he is grinning hugely. He presses his palm to the centre of his chest in the old familiar gesture but it seems the pain too has deserted him. He's not worried. It will be back. All around him, Sarah, Ruby, the unhappy boy, the builder already half-drunk before they even get the wake started, it seems that silence has come like a poultice to heal the blows.

'Ah well,' he says a third time, unwilling to disturb such a fragile pleasure more than that.